SHADOWS OF
THE WHITE SUN

Ace Books by Raymond Harris

THE BROKEN WORLDS
SHADOWS OF THE WHITE SUN

Shadows of the White Sun

RAYMOND HARRIS

ACE BOOKS, NEW YORK

To Jody, for her unfailing support;
to Joe, for his patience;
to Vincent, for new insights;
and to Sara,
for making dreams real.

ACKNOWLEDGMENT

Many thanks are due to Michael Donatelli, M.D., for his invaluable tutorials in human physiology. If I've gotten any of it right it's because of him. The nonsense is all mine.

Las blancas sombras, en las horas tristes . . .
White shadows in sad hours . . .
Miguel de Unamuno

FILENAME: White Shadows 1–12
CLASSIFICATION: A. Miscellaneous historical document, recent period
B. Autobiographical narrative
C. Involuntary confession, subject Risha [4763] Skhorb [9918]
SOURCE: Palace Archives, Gheo [7786]
AGENT: Ionawr [9999] Phi Iota Rho [2341]

[TEXT FOLLOWS]

CHAPTER ONE

Volshev is a cautious being. I almost said *man,* but by now I know better. Unmanly caution alone prompts him to save my story; inhuman anxiety makes him dread losing even the smallest scrap of information.

I have called him cruel and cowardly. Still his wretched caution does offer me a certain comfort, here in my extremity. For while he decrees that I forget, utterly and ineluctably, the events of the past two revolutions, I rest confident, knowing that his own archives will preserve a record of my deeds and dreams in Veii.

I hang suspended in a webwork sling. My flesh bristles with glassy capillaries that hold me paralyzed, my skull throbs in the vise-grip of a torsion field. Only thought itself is allowed free movement, and that not for long. Tubes sustain me: one drips nutrient fluid into my veins, another delivers a changing spectrum of psychoactive drugs, still others carry off waste from anus and urethra. Minute electrodes maintain tone in useless muscles.

I've lost count of the number of times he has made me rehearse my tale—for this brand of oblivion first requires perfect recall. One of his drugs provides the necessary prestate; thereafter an array of lasers records every synaptic configuration I display during retrieval. Eventually yet another substance will flood the canals and aqueducts of my cortex, and cause an electric charge to flash like lightning along the nine billion pathways of memory. And I will forget. The laser image will flicker and grow dark.

But I speak of the future; Volshev prefers that I remain in the past. Once more he compels me to spin out a narrative of my deeds from the bright snarl of raw recollection. Once more I must retell those truths that he finds intolerable.

It begins with Lachis Gloy, of course. Her prodding and teasing and challenging set the whole mess in motion. With my temporal lobes swimming in neuropeptides I can picture her face before me as if it were my own, squinting back at me from one of Blue Wing's ten thousand mirrors; though no mirror in waking life ever showed me the radiant grace and artless beauty that she enjoyed from infancy on. By adolescence her sense of style had become legendary throughout the Hypaethra, and more than a few thousand high-placed young women would have traded their Fallopian tubes for those chiseled cheekbones and well-turned thighs. But alas, as all true-born Revenants learn (by the time they can walk and talk and tell lies) nothing substitutes for good breeding. And Lachis' was the very best.

Third Watch was winding down on a spell in Archer Cycle. We sprawled across cushions and dataspools in Lachis' study, in darkness except for the glow from her farscan tank. I think she was even more attractive in aquamarine—though at the moment a hint of doubt brought odd curves to those nereid lips.

"Have I married a fool?" she murmured. "I can't believe this is happening."

As usual she was a little ahead of me. "How can you be so sure it's your husband?"

A fine-boned hand indicated the smaller of two interorbit thrusters hovering in the tank. "Look there, you can just make out the letters on the hull: they spell *Wheel of Fire*. It's definitely Rhamant's ship." She manipulated the controls for a wider field. "And see the other one? That's what horrifies me." She magnified the image a hundred times. "A work of art, no? It's a Khryashan design or I'm blind. And the name seems to be *Blue Star*. What does that suggest to you?"

I felt like a child who has been ordered to recite. For Lachis too much was too obvious. Nevertheless, I made a brave attempt. "When you say Khryasha, well naturally I think of either Lady Sorich or her heir, Lord Seren. And I seem to recall that 'Seren' has the sense of 'star' in one of the poetic dialects of the Interglacial. And blue stars, of course, burn the hottest."

"And fade the quickest. Well done, Risha. That ship has to be Seren's new thrust model. I heard rumors of it a few days past, so you needn't feel quite so dull-witted." She knew me well. "Their trajectories match to two or three decimal places. I'd venture to say it's a race."

With the Ceremony of the Presentation of the Heir no more than ten watches in the future, Gheo was being inundated by a steady stream of invited guests and uninvited thrill-seekers. Such pageantry only occurs once in eight or nine of the imperial city's revolutions round Sol, so the general air of excitement and anticipation was quite excusable. Even Lachis and I had been caught up in the spirit of rubbernecking.

There we were, watching our visitors' decorous arrivals in lightsail and thruster, idly wondering how brave a show each would make in the cyclical accounting, when all at once our instruments had picked up these two rogue ships at the limit of detection. They were a few hundred kilometers out and closing rapidly. By now Control would have challenged them, but we had no access to those channels, and could only guess at the alarm and confusion they inspired.

Lachis was calculating. "He can't do it." Dark eyes pierced me with dismay. "He can't dump that velocity fast enough. He'll have to swing round the Hypaethron and burn at least once more before he can match orbits."

"I suppose you mean Rhamant."

"Meanwhile Seren is right on the mark. He'll be coupling his valves before this watch is done."

In other words Rhamant had already lost.

It might seem trivial, but no deed of a Radiant can go unremarked—and the rivalry between Seren of Khryasha and Rhamant of Gloy was already well known and much discussed. Within the past three starcycles Seren had been passed over in favor of Rhamant for the coveted office of Gheo's Spear; the only titles more prestigious were Emperor and Despot. Now the Presentation approached, and soon after the Games themselves, during which Rhamant would exercise his prerogatives for the first time since taking office. Suffering public humiliation right on the eve of his ascendance would darken Rhamant's name for spells on end, and possibly even damage Gloy's prospects in the Games.

"I hope my own rank isn't compromised by this indiscretion," said Lachis. "I don't want those numbers after my name to start growing." A Radiant herself, she enjoyed a status-count expressed by only two digits; I considered myself lucky to have attained to the Immaculates and be counted among the first ten thousand.

"But who can blame Rhamant for losing to a ship like that?" I protested. The farscan showed us both thrusters side by side in a split-field shot; Rhamant's vessel, though trim enough on her own, looked clumsy and antiquated next to the sleek lines of the *Blue Star*.

"Come on, Risha. You've been at court long enough to understand what I mean. Rhamant is the Spear of Gheo. For the next ten revolutions he holds the most exalted rank any man can attain. He no longer has the slightest need to prove himself; his only obligation is to live up to the honor he has won. In this case his error was to accept the challenge in the first place, especially when he saw how formidable an opponent he faced. Winning would gain him nothing; losing is an embarrassment to him and a stroke of fortune for Khryasha."

"You seem positive Seren was the challenger."

She laughed. "I do give my husband some credit. I can just picture it. Rhamant set out from Gloy several spells past, his ship bulging at the seams with all those proud young hopefuls eager for a stab at glory. Check your ephemeris: Khryasha's orbit currently places it between Gloy and Gheo. Seren would have seen them coming and flown out to convey official greetings. Oozing with jealousy, mind you, and cocky as a cur. A little friendly sport would have been the most natural thing in the Matterfield at that point; and once the idea had been presented Rhamant's company would beg him to play along."

"He does keep a headstrong retinue," I agreed, rising and putting my tunic in order. "I suppose that has to change. No doubt you'll set him on the right path, won't you?"

Lachis mumbled something and kept her gaze fixed on the tank. Since the scene hadn't changed in several minutes I was getting bored and had started thinking of our next move. "What will you wear?" I called out.

"Wear? Oh, of course. We'll have to get over there soon." With a few backward glances she followed me out.

We crossed to the atrium, where several of Nan Solize's other ladies were lounging around, talking or playing with the baby. Our mistress herself was undoubtedly closeted with her hairdresser, preparing for latterspell's appearance. We nodded to the group and would have passed on, but Trithi stopped us.

"Where to, ladies? You've been keeping to yourselves all watch."

Lachis let me answer; I suppose she couldn't be bothered. "We're getting ready for a visit to the Court of Victory. A delegation from Gloy is due, and one from Khryasha as well."

This caught their interest. A few of them, including Trithi, declared their intentions of heading over also; these were the ones who had close kin on one or the other of the incoming ships. The rest were content to wait for our mistress' summons. She certainly wouldn't be joining any welcoming party, not even for the Spear of Gheo: as Virgin Mother she was far beyond that.

Lachis and I managed to escape to my own chambers and close the door. Starcycles ago we had merged our wardrobes, except for heirloom gowns, so it was usual for us to dress together. Given the complexity of formal costume, it was impossible to manage alone.

Lachis picked out a set of unlined gowns, ranging from pale to deep violet, and began the laborious task of donning them. I was a little slower, torn between a leaf-print in green and a bold design of golden rectangles. I was just reaching for the green when Lachis caught my arm.

"I have an idea."

I'd heard that line before. I said nothing.

"How would you like to do a little spying?"

I pursed my lips and kept silent.

"Aren't you curious about what will happen at the landing bay when both parties arrive?"

"Not that I know of."

She smiled her most conspiratorial smile. "Well, I am. What if you put on some outfit suitable for a serving girl, underneath your court robes, and then when we get to the Victory Court you can duck in an alcove and change. You could walk right into the docks and eavesdrop on whatever goes on."

It did sound interesting, but I wouldn't be had quite so easily. "Lachis," I said, "I think you live more in your imagination than in real life. You're only guessing that Seren and Rhamant were racing in the first place: in fact you're only guessing that the *Blue Star* is Seren's ship at all! Your scenario could be nothing more than an elaborate fantasy."

"But it's not and you know it."

True, I did trust her powers of deduction; she'd been right enough in the past. "Very well then: I'm game. I must confess, I've never seen Seren, and I've often wondered what he's like."

Lachis was already handing me a yellow sack and a long checkered scarf—her interpretation of servant's garb, I gathered. "Seren?" She made the name sound ugly. "First of all he's a killer. Did you know about that?"

I didn't. We kept dressing as she spoke, layer after layer.

"Apart from the fourteen men he's taken out in officially sanctioned combat there's the little matter of his swordmaster. One day they were having an especially fierce session, and by the end of it Seren had sliced open his trainer's head. He was dead before anything could be done to save him."

"Are you suggesting it wasn't an accident?"

She shrugged, with her face as much as with her shoulders. "The Khryashan arbiters found him innocent; certainly he showed remorse. You must realize he was little more than a child at the time. But then there was a second incident several revolutions later. This time it happened in free space, and the victim was his best friend. They were trying out new thrust packs, jetting around in the vacuum somewhere near their own Hypaethron, when Seren somehow burned the friend with his own plasma trail. The burn breached the other fellow's suit and he died instantly."

I shuddered. Death by exposure to the void is a phobia all of us Hypaethral dwellers share.

"So what do *you* think, Lachis? You must have an opinion."

"As to whether Seren intended those deaths? No, I'm afraid I don't, because I simply don't know him. But one thing is clear: when he's around, people get killed. I'm sure that's the main reason why he wasn't nominated Spear. As far as the other qualifications go, he's the very model of a Revenant Lord: a superb fighter, an excellent free-space pilot, and a skillful tactician."

I mulled this over as Lachis helped me into the last item of my ensemble, a bulky sleeveless jacket in coarse blue silk. Since it was only Fourth Watch there was no call for extreme formality; our existing hair and makeup would do.

We crossed the atrium and left the compound. Knowing Trithi and the others, we had no reason to wait; they would still be deciding on underclothes.

"Now I don't know how eager I am to meet this Seren," I confessed. "At least he doesn't seem to kill women."

"So far," murmured Lachis. But she was playing.

We had set out from the Opal Court, which for generations has been the preserve of the Nan's ladies-in-waiting. With its salons and bedchambers, nurseries and kitchens, servants' quarters and atria, the Opal Court is merely one segment of the Virgin Mother's Wing, which itself comprises perhaps a quarter of the total area of the Palace of the Despot. The Palace in turn is a major subdivision of Gheo, chief among the Hypaethra or *dwellings under heaven,* those vast orbiting constructs which the Revenants have held since their return to Sol. Gheo occupies a Trojan point in the orbit of Ethri, icebound cradle of humanity; its inhabitants consider themselves the very pinnacle of the race.

At that time I still agreed with them.

The corridors we crossed were relics of an extremely ancient past. We were taking a shortcut through disused sections of the Palace, areas that had seen neither industry nor leisure since the period of Meqmat. Air filters kept everything dust free, but there were piles of rubble all along the way.

It was plain that these tunnels had never been intended for human use. Their dimensions were all wrong—far too cramped and asymmetrical—and they were so disorienting to my visual sense that I often had trouble keeping my balance. There were no straight lines anywhere, no right angles or parallels to reassure my inner ear. Instead, everything from floor to ceiling traced a series of curves and dips and bulges, and the route itself twisted back and forth like an intestinal canal. While Gheo in general tends to have a distinctly organic look, it is nowhere more pronounced than in this wormholing labyrinth.

"Do you suppose Volshev watches us here?" I asked, just as our exit came in sight.

"I've wondered that myself. But in the first place his sensors can't be everywhere, and in the second place there's no way he can simultaneously monitor all the ones he has. So he's no omnipresent deity. Then again—perhaps he concentrates his attention on just such out-of-the-way places."

There seemed to be no unraveling old Volshev's psychology, though the attempt was a favorite pastime among courtiers. "If he does watch," I concluded, "I hope he's amused. We must be the only people who take this shortcut so exquisitely dressed."

Smiling, we emerged into a more inhabited section of the Palace, a minor plaza roofed with dangling filaments of translucent coral. The color scheme set off our costumes well, and several dozen pairs of eyes started at this vision of two court ladies materializing out of nowhere. We ignored them and made for the nearest tubestop.

Our priority was high. Within minutes we had a private car and were being whisked through magnetic ducts toward our destination.

The Court of Victory is the principal point of entry into Gheo. At all times it has its crowds of idlers, frequenting the kiosks and admiring the trophies of war, but now on the eve of the Presentation its galleries were fairly thronged with lesser citizens witnessing the arrival of their betters. We avoided the crush by keeping to the upper balconies; soon enough we caught sight of some familiar faces from the Palace, all joined together in a festive group overlooking the court.

We paused some distance away from them. "Here's where the fun begins," Lachis whispered. Her pale face was suffused with the glow of mischief. "There's a lounge nearby we can use." We ducked inside and she helped me remove my outer layers. Within seconds I stood revealed as a servant to some lady of rank, dressed in yellow with a long particolored mantle draped over my head. We stashed my court robes and gave the attendant a handsome tip to look after them while I was gone. Then, as Lachis hurried off to join the Palace folk, I asked directions to the nearest lift.

Finding it was a matter of moments. I donned grippers, sidled in, and named my level. None of the other passengers paid me any mind. This wasn't the first time Lachis had conned me into masquerade, so I wasn't unaccustomed to blending in with the proletariat. I rose to the free-fall zone (my stomach doing its usual flip-flop) and stepped carefully out onto the narrow landing at the Shaft—

Where noise and confusion swallowed me whole. In the midst of glaring lights, shouting voices, reeking fumes, jostling elbows, and the acrid scent of human stress, it was all I could do to keep my feet between my head and the floor. As soon as I closed my eyes I was nauseated; visual cues alone maintained the illusion of up and down here at the axis of Gheo's rotation. In fact I saw a small child start to float away "overhead," squalling lustily as it drifted. Its chaperone grabbed an ankle and hauled it back in the nick of time. Amid such distractions I wormed my way through the crush, till I came up against a stout barrier guarded by two halberdiers.

One was a woman. I ignored her and concentrated on the man, who seemed old enough and calm enough to be susceptible to whatever charms I possess.

But when he forestalled me with a curt, "No thoroughfare for anyone for any reason," I could tell it wasn't going to be easy.

Eventually—after dropping such names as Lachis and Rhamant of Gloy, Nan Solize and the Emperor Vremeni, while pointedly displaying the signet Lachis had lent me—I was allowed to pass: and then only after the old man had subjected me to a thorough body search. Straightening my clothing, I stooped under the barrier and scrambled through.

"And stay out of the way!" he yelled after me. "I don't want your head getting bashed on my account."

But I didn't need the warning, because while the chaos on this side of the barrier was more deliberate, it was also far more daunting. Stevedores somersaulted through the air on long trajectories; huge telescoping booms arced back and forth; prehensile cables snaked the whole length of the docking zone.

It took me a while to learn which bay held the *Blue Star*. Since Rhamant's ship hadn't even coupled yet I figured I'd have a look at Seren while I waited. Fortunately for me, he and a handful of his warriors had grown bored with the ship's confines and were milling about just outside the umbilical's egress.

At first I didn't know him. In a group of athletic, well-favored young men he simply didn't stand out. Only the body language of the people around him gave him away—the way they maintained a certain distance, avoided turning their backs, and in general focused their attention on him whether he spoke or kept silent.

It was his youth that surprised me most; I guessed we were of an age, about twenty-four revolutions of Gheo round Sol. His face was very smooth, boyish even, saved from prettiness only by the hard set of his eyes. In stature he was a good few centimeters below the adult average —another surprise, because I knew how highly rated he was in all forms of close combat, whether with edged weapons or bare hands. Apparently skill made up for shortened reach. In any case his body was a mass of muscle: I noted the breadth of his back and shoulders, the curve in his chest, and the size of his two hands. Even in free fall he seemed solidly grounded.

His clothing gave the impression of casual, almost unstudied elegance. Silver cords confined his forelock, which jutted stiffly over a wide forehead. A gray and silver-striped jacket with enormous sleeves covered his torso, cinched tight at the waist with a width of black leather, from which three daggers hung. Baggy charcoal trousers sported a design of isolated diamonds, picked out in silver threads; these were stuffed into the black wraparound hose encasing his legs from calf to ankle. His grippers were likewise black—

And in that moment one of his companions noticed me noticing. I cringed in anticipation.

"Well, if she were an assassin I think she would have moved by now." Some of them laughed.

"No, no, she looks more like a whore to me."

From there the repartee descended to a discussion of the more salient features of my anatomy. I had no choice but to move along.

I was a little shocked that men of their class could be so coarse; then I realized how my own social position shielded me from such rudeness in daily life. My servant's disguise was giving me a new and unwelcome angle on masculinity. Seren, however, took no part in the fun; for some reason that seemed important.

As I shuffled away a Port official brushed past me, distinguished by indigo robes, two trailing flunkies, and the square insignia of rank that dangled from his neck. His arrival saved me from any further abuse; he bowed low before Seren's party and began speaking in a rapid monotone.

"My apologies, gentlemen, but the Limenarch begs your indulgence a few minutes more. The Emperor Vremeni himself is on his way to bid you welcome, and until his august arrival we beg that you delay your entrance."

"That's only two begs this time," quipped the gentleman on Seren's left. "He used three before." The others stifled their amusement.

"Sir, I realize that you are in an awkward position." The Heir of Khryasha spoke; I found I liked the sound. "I do sympathize. But I also realize the reason for this charade and it leaves me cold. My ship docked half a watch ago and you have done your best ever since to obstruct my debarkation. You seem terrified that my entrance will overshadow that of the Spear of Gheo. Had you allowed me to disembark with reasonable haste there would be no such problem, since Lord Rhamant's ship was well behind mine. But instead, with your delays, you have succeeded in aggravating me personally and my household collectively, and forced a confrontation for which I had no desire."

His delivery began calmly and then rose steadily in menace till the end, though at no time did he lift his voice or obscure his measured phrasing. As he finished he gestured toward the opposite bay—perceptually "overhead"—where a mechanical screech and a human shout just now resounded.

The *Wheel of Fire* had docked.

The Limenarch is subtle, I decided. Assigning them diametrically opposite berths was the height of diplomacy: this way neither one was closer in or farther out, and the only view each one had was the top of the other's head.

Seren's entourage stiffened and remained still; in equally strict formation, the warriors of Gloy filed out with Rhamant in their midst. Tall as a god, handsome as a dream, Rhamant looked the perfect Revenant: as courteous as he was arrogant, as beautiful as he was brave. State robes of crimson and mustard billowed gloriously around him in free fall.

Rhamant's perplexity was as obvious as Seren's tension. He had no way of knowing why Khryasha still loitered at the docks; as far as he

could tell it was the prelude to a quarrel. The standoff might have gone
on forever if Seren hadn't moved.

"Shadows brighten, Rhamant!" he called out, using the form of address appropriate to close friends. "May I have a word with you?"

"Of course," the Spear of Gheo replied, with equally false heartiness.

Seren's legs bent and then stretched long, sending his body on a
soaring arc across the tube. At the precise midpoint of his jump he
turned head over heels to land squarely on his feet about a meter away
from Rhamant. As a dancer I couldn't help admiring his perfect econ-
omy of movement. The murmurs around me—from ordinary
dockworkers gathering to watch the show—told me I wasn't alone.

"That was some fine piloting you did last watch," he began. His
stature forced him to crane his neck somewhat to meet the other man's
gaze.

Rhamant smiled tightly. "Certainly no finer than yours, my friend.
Your reflexes did justice to a magnificent ship."

They clasped hands for a moment, murmuring, "Well raced." I found
it hard not to smirk. The talk continued in this fraternal vein for several
minutes, Rhamant even asking for a tour of the Khryashan thruster.

"Just say the word," Seren replied. "But now I suppose it's time we
paid our respects to Gheo. I see you're already dressed for the occasion;
so much the better. I'm a little behind you myself. No doubt we'll meet
later in the Palace." And with an informal bow they said goodbye.

Seren repeated his acrobatic leap, this time adding a casual salute
that could be construed either as the gesture of a friend and intimate or
as a subtle challenge. It was so well done that most of the spectators
missed it, though certainly Rhamant did not. He merely raised an arm
and headed in the general direction of the lifts, his companions falling
in behind.

Now I had to outrace him to the Court of Victory or risk one of those
gaffes we Palace folk dread so. Still, I allowed myself a last look at
Seren, who was pulling on the black and silver robe of Khryasha in
preparation for his own entrance. In spite of what Lachis had told me,
in spite of the execrable behavior of his companions, I had to admire
him. With that "so much the better—I'm a little behind you" he had
dexterously yielded precedence to a superior in rank, avoiding insolence
and servility with equal grace. I'm not sure Rhamant came off as well.
His behavior had been correct enough but he displayed neither verve
nor vivacity.

Then again (as Lachis had just reminded me) he didn't need to. His office spoke for itself.

Somehow I connected with my court gown again and rejoined Lachis and friends in the upper galleries. I rushed through a version of what I had just witnessed in as subdued a voice as I could manage; when I was done Lachis frowned thoughtfully.

"Frankly I'm amazed by the Khryashan's tact," she whispered. "Tongues will wag but I don't think we have to worry."

Not that I had been.

Then a fanfare on the enormous coiling shrillpipes announced Lord Rhamant's arrival. A thousand voices stilled; circular valves hissed open; and there he stood in all his gold and crimson glory, flanked by a dozen warriors bearing naked swords. He himself held aloft that huge platinum-shod spear from which his title derived, and a thousand throats roared at the sight. Only edged weapons such as these may be carried into the Victory Court, or for that matter anywhere inside a sovereign Hypaethron; we vacuum-dwellers are too sensitive to the threat of powered arms in the fragile shells surrounding us.

From a high balcony a child's voice called down. I turned to see the Emperor Vremeni spreading his delicate hands in a gesture of welcome. It was a ritual formula, not worth noting; Lord Rhamant answered in kind. I was more impressed by the Child Emperor's droll solemnity and earnest courtesies than by anything he said; his mother, our mistress, had trained him well.

Then to everyone's surprise a glow appeared in the Window of Appearance. Suspended just over the Emperor's perch, dominating the entire Court of Victory, the vast holotank flashed through the spectrum before settling on a uniform white radiance, which dissolved slowly into the image of a well-known face.

Though I had seen his Sending more times than I could count, it awed me then as it had on my very first viewing. Before that monumental icon I became a child again; I felt helpless and small; I was terrified that all my shortcomings were plainly written across my face. After this moment of paranoia came the conviction, slightly less threatening, that he *knew* me, he knew me to the marrow, that nothing I could do or think was beyond his ken, for he understood. And finally I felt a surge of confidence, for he possessed me, he engulfed me, and I was safe in that monstrous power.

Such is the mystique that Volshev has nurtured over the centuries.

He orchestrates our fears and uncertainties with an artist's touch. Despot of Gheo, arbiter of the Hypaethra in their several orbits, highest of the high, we see him only in these Sendings: as a colossal face swimming in one of his Windows, the way he now appeared, or more rarely as a free-moving hologram that simulates actual physical presence. He always manifests as a man of uncertain age with gray eyes and a cloud of white hair; when clothing appears it is also white. Of his body only the face and hands are ever visible, and these are as pale and smooth as ivory.

He spoke in a deep mellow voice that filled the entire Court of Victory. "Rhamant of Gloy," he said, "of all the heroes of this age you please me most. Enter now into the seat of splendor." And as Rhamant bowed the image held for a long moment, frozen in a smile of benediction, before gently dimming out.

Ritual, pageantry, empty words: but they moved us all. Rhamant and his companions passed through the opposite portal, on their way to a private audience with the Despot, and were gone. They had attained the highest circle of the Matterfield.

Anything that happened afterward was sheer anticlimax. The Khryashan party appeared, the Emperor uttered his formulae, but the Window of Appearance remained dark. I gazed down on the man I had observed just a halfwatch earlier and found him diminished in every way. He seemed dwarfish and dull, his companions a collection of boors. How susceptible we all were to Volshev's wiles.

And so Gloy's standing continued intact. People around me began whispering at how poor a show Lord Seren made next to his rival; there was no question who enjoyed the Despot's favor.

Nevertheless, as I walked away from the Court with Lachis and a few junior Palace attendants, I found my thoughts returning to Seren after all. I'd been forced to struggle my way up from inferiority so often in the past that I felt an immediate bond with any fellow sufferer.

And I must confess that one picture kept flashing in my inner eye: Seren's leap across the docks. Over and over again I saw his body stretch, coiling and uncoiling; again and again I imagined the play of muscle underneath his silken robe, the flex and extension of his calves, his thighs. He lingered with me all through the Seventh Watch festivities, and on into dreams.

CHAPTER TWO

The Opal Court was mad with vanity. An entire cohort of new servants was on hand to assist us this spell, and they had come trooping in bent double beneath the weight of twelve new court ensembles of the most extreme formality. I couldn't begin to measure how many meters of cotton and silk that represented, how many kilograms of gold and silver thread, how many strands of rare pearls dredged up from the shallow seas of Veii. Practically all of us needed last-minute refittings, which became even more nerve-racking when they spilled over into our lengthy hairdressing sessions. Ceremonial coiffure, in turn, meant more meters of false hair, more kilos of lacquered combs, more mounds of jeweled ornaments. I thanked my ancestral spirits that these occasions came no more frequently.

In the midst of the madness a small girl darted in and put a note in my hand. She left without waiting for an answer, so I stuffed it in my sash, thinking to read it later in private. I wasn't sure who its author might be but I could make one or two guesses.

Unfortunately Lachis had seen everything and was at my side in an instant.

"Come on, let's have it. You won't get away with anything while I'm around."

"Don't be a buffoon. You're not suggesting . . ."

She laughed. "There's only one thing on both our minds. I'm not sure how far Solize should trust a girl like you."

"Or you. You're the one with the vivid imagination."

"Well, it certainly did resemble a morning-after note."

I struck her, playfully, of course, for even hinting at such a thing. As principal celebrants in the upcoming Presentation Ceremony all of us ladies of the Opal Court were obliged to maintain ritual purity: which in plain language meant no sex for seven spells preceding the event. A morning-after note would be evidence that I had violated my vow, which of course I hadn't.

To prove my point I pulled out the note. It read, "I glimpsed you yesterday in the Court of Victory, and later in a side-chamber at the Emperor's levee. Your service in Gheo has matured you like sunlight on ripening fruit. Remembering how fine you were those days in High Vrazil makes me twice as eager to renew our acquaintance here at the center of it all." After that, the signature was predictable enough: "Tref, Third Minister of Paun."

Lachis howled. "Ripening fruit?"

I echoed her. "Almost as good as 'the center of it all.' I think we know what Tref has in mind."

"Will you have him back?"

I couldn't answer.

It fascinates me how one split second of recollection can evoke whole spells, whole cycles of time. Again I imagined my sojourn in High Vrazil, squinting against the glare off the western icefields, shivering with remembered cold, wrinkling my nose at the odor of wet sheepskin robes. Irresistibly that train of thought carried me back further still, to the lofty corridors of Skhorb, where the circumstances of my birth determined most of my life's future course.

My father belonged to the top rank of a minor Hypaethron. Centuries earlier Skhorb had known prestige comparable to that of Paun or even Gloy, but with the changing fortunes of Revenant households it had slipped to seventh out of nine. (Gheo, of course, stands apart from this reckoning.) He made a *mughe*-marriage with a woman of Paun, not a bad match considering, but her status was no higher than Pure. When they were posted together to High Vrazil, Ethri's capital, both earned the title to First Minister; but there was no ignoring that posting's low prestige. Because Ethri is a planet. And planets, even the third planet of Sol, are beneath the notice of the star-sailing lords of the Matterfield.

I was already a child of eight revolutions when we rode the Lift down to High Vrazil. Knowing no better, I loved it. Unlike my parents I adapted easily to the wide horizons, and to that bizarre phenomenon called weather. I kept Ethrin pets like hounds and ferrets and made friends with Ethrin children, as uncouth as beasts themselves. To amuse these ruffians I learned smatterings of their various languages; I can still remember a few of the names they called their home, like Zimla and Tyerr and Arth. Discovering this new world was an inexhaustible source of delight.

That is, for about five years. (On Ethri they do call them years.) Then with the stirrings of adolescence I began to yearn for the glittering habitats in free space. I pictured them as utopias where life unrolled like the spools of a romance; I schemed day and night for a means to attain them.

Through diligent study of dance and Shallowcut I managed to raise my status-count by several hundred points at the biorbital evaluations. But that in itself would never be enough. Like any other schemer, I needed an accomplice.

More years passed before that need was filled, but at last it was—and very well indeed—in the form of Lord Tref of Paun. When he first arrived in High Vrazil he seemed like a demigod. Many courted him, both politically and romantically, but I alone succeeded.

He stayed in my father's house for six months. (Instead of noting the passage of Sol through the zodiac, the Ethrins base their calendar on the phases of Lin, which after all are more obvious—to them at least.) He was my lover for all that time, my hero, my vessel of hope. Remembering it now I have to laugh, but for a nineteen-year-old girl he was a dream come true.

He dazzled me with his tales of the Hypaethra; he delighted me with his skill at pillowing. And he flattered me by saying I was as fair and fine as any woman in Gheo. But he left me, finally, even while swearing fidelity and making noise about an eventual *mughe*-marriage. Thereafter I languished like a rose without rain. When two more years had gone by without word from him, I gave up hope, and wished only for death.

In the midst of my pining and moping and mooning a miracle descended from high orbit. A messenger from the Despot's Palace arrived, saying that I was summoned to Gheo to determine my fitness for imperial service. I returned with this envoy and endured a round of grueling examinations; by the ancestors' grace I satisfied their standards, swore fealty to Nan Solize, and took up residence in the Opal Court. I saw Tref's hand in it, and blessed him, but in the revolutions that have gone round since our paths never crossed again.

That is, until the previous spell—when I was dismayed to see that, amid the flash and glamour of the Despot's court, my former hero was merely an aging functionary with no particular style or place, that in fact I had already outstripped him in my climb through the rarefied circles of Gheo.

"Will you have him back?" Lachis asked again, trying hard to keep her voice expressionless.

"Not very likely, is it," I said. "By now I've set my sights a good deal higher than the Third Minister of Paun."

She nodded. "Court life is full of these ironies. You have no reason for guilt. You'll go far, I'm sure of it, and when you arrive you'll do what you can to advance Tref's fortunes. You can benefit him in many other ways besides pillowing."

So it was settled. I could tell I'd passed another small test in Lachis Gloy's eyes, and I was glad. Striving to meet her expectations had become second nature to me by now; I was aware (and not for the first time) that for me she had become what Tref himself had once been, in all ways except that matter of pillowing.

We went back to our primping and posing and the letter was quickly forgotten.

The Ceremony of the Presentation lasted from the onset of Fourth Watch to the close of Sixth. It was held in the cavernous Hall of Ancestors, whose floorspace measured a full decare, so that its scope in time was more than matched by its extent in space. For the nature of the ceremony was a sort of pavane, a long spiralling promenade beginning at the center of the Hall and snaking its tedious way to the periphery. Fortunately the entrance of the Nan and her ladies (namely ourselves) did not occur till halfway through the rite, so we were spared a great many stifled yawns.

For this occasion the environmentalists had tricked out the Hall as a cloud chamber. Billowing masses of gray and white vapor, softly glowing as if with diffused sunlight, constantly moving as if in a moderate breeze, formed the floors, walls, and ceiling of the circular Hall. While they were no more than holograms, they were extremely convincing; and I reflected that, as one of the few in all Gheo who had experienced real clouds firsthand, I was uniquely qualified to judge.

The cloud-images made a dramatic background to the main focus of the space, which was the heroic Ancestors themselves. On two-meter pedestals scattered throughout the Hall rested the physical remains of a hundred or more distinguished Radiants, saved from the recycler and mummified so that future generations might gaze on them and feel a tangible bond with the past. Here were artists, warriors, Virgin Mothers, interpreters of the Canon, all grim-faced in death, bundled up in bolts of fabric dyed according to their old Hypaethral affiliations. They stood upright like totems; in fact, swathed as they were in the bulky wrappings, their human appearance was lost, and they became the abstractions our history spools described.

In their midst hovered a Sending of Volshev, his white robes flying in the same synthetic wind that moved the clouds—and he, of course, was the most perfect abstraction of all.

House by house the leading families of the Matterfield filed in and took their assigned positions around the Hall. Their timing, their movements, and their grouping were as choreographed as any court ballet, so that each party ended up as a carefully composed tableau in the vicinity of an appropriate Ancestor. When everyone was in place Nan Solize rose out of the floor in the very center of the Hall, holding the infant Yarkost in her arms.

With Vremeni by her side—and Volshev floating along somewhere above shoulder level—she paced carefully around the gathering. The twelve ladies of her retinue followed close behind. We took turns holding Yarkost, according to a predetermined sequence, which ensured that Lachis spent the most time carrying him and I the least. It was all arranged by status-count, and since Yarkost was heavy I didn't really mind.

As we stopped before each Hypaethral tableau an elaborate exchange of formulae took place. First Nan Solize recited Yarkost's pedigree: sired by the precious seed of the Heroic Tuille of Imaertha, who was born in Revenant Year 1519 and passed on in R.Y. 1561 (on the occasion of the quinquennial Games) and who was himself the son of So-and-so and So-and-so, and who had previously sired the Emperor Vlisk during the fruitfulness of Nan Zhaloba; and mothered by her own living womb, she being the natural daughter of . . . and so on and so forth. Each group so addressed replied with an equally long-winded oath of fealty, full of status-counts and genealogies, expressing their meaningless devotion to Vremeni's rightful heir.

As I said earlier there were many stifled yawns.

Few of them were mine, however. I was too excited by it all. There I was in my most exquisite outfit, on display for all the leading families of the Matterfield, on display in fact for every Revenant in the system— because farscanners were broadcasting this ritual throughout the ten Hypaethra, and even to Ethri and Marithi. I was lucky that a presentation had occurred during my term in the Opal Court. I could expect both my status-count and my marriageability to improve by a significant degree.

When we paused at the Gloys' station I felt Lachis' attention on me. Earlier, while we waited for our entrance, she had whispered, "This is your golden opportunity to see and be seen, Risha. As we stand opposite Gloy look closely at Rhamant's gentlemen; perhaps you'll find one to your liking."

"Are you so certain they'll like me in return?" Sometimes I grew testy with her manipulation, though I wasn't serious now.

"Have no fear on that account. Just look in the mirror and you'll see what I mean."

She could be kind when she wanted to be. So when the time came, I dutifully scanned the line of tall young men of Gloy. It was difficult to tell them apart, but the basic model appeared sound. Any one of them would do in a pinch. Catching Lachis' eye I simultaneously nodded and shrugged. She winked slyly.

But when we came round to the Khryashan tableau I had second thoughts. There was something dark and fascinating in that family which snared my interest, as well-scrubbed Gloy did not. I felt powerful tensions brewing there, especially around the person of the First Radiant, Lady Sorich, who struck me as a walking rebuttal to Gloy's geniality. Over ninety, but with all her fierce vitality intact, she stood as stiffly as a sculpture in wire. Her severe features ideally suited Khryasha's black and silver raiment. She had ruled her clan for over sixty revolutions and showed no sign of relaxing control—indeed, she still set the tone for the entire Hypaethron. She was proud to be a woman men respected, but never loved.

Next to her stood Seren. Although he lacked his grandmother's ferocity there was an essential power in that square, bulky form, along with a marked incongruity. For while he resembled a wrestler from the neck down, his face might be that of a poet or a philosopher; he had delicate cheekbones, large clear eyes, and a high forehead, seamed with traces of curiosity and self-doubt. For me this only added to his appeal. I thought I'd never seen a man who pleased me more.

Knowing how foolish my fantasies were didn't stop me from spinning them. I dared imagine what it would be like to possess him, there in the golden lights as Solize and Sorich recited their incantations. He would be awesome, uncontrollable, an elemental force; he would overwhelm me like a storm off the western glacier. I shivered and Lachis looked at me sharply. I gave her the faintest of smiles. Then it was time for us to move along, with measured step, to the next Hypaethral station.

Slowly, I withdrew from reverie. Khryasha would be a grim prison, my objective mind insisted, a place of cruelty and regret. Lady Sorich was a repellent figure who had certainly poisoned the hearts of everyone around her. Lord Seren would never know I existed.

Thus my inner dialogue continued for all the rest of that pomp-filled spell, as I moved through splendor in constant obsession with the Heir of Khryasha.

I hurled my dagger point-first into the sand and collapsed in a sweaty heap. I was exhausted and exhilarated; my bare skin glistened and my lungs had expanded to ten times their normal size.

"Good match," Lachis gasped, just as sweaty and perhaps even more disheveled. "You were close that time."

I smiled. My skill would never equal hers, but I never stopped trying. "The hands just take over sometimes," I confessed. "That seems to work the best."

She helped me to my feet and we left the sand-strewn practice floor, walking slowly and deliberately on rubbery legs. We had decided to forgo rehearsal that spell and concentrate on Shallowcut for the entire Second Watch. Now I felt supremely alive, more than ready to face what latterspell would bring.

We reveled in the luxury of a spray bath and then lay side by side as two servants massaged us with lotions redolent of almond and aloe. "Do you know your steps?" I asked playfully.

"I've been doing them in my sleep."

We both groaned.

"Frankly I'm amazed that you wanted to work out with me this watch," I said. "I would have thought . . ."

"Ah! Well . . . you know how disciplined Rhamant is. He'll never lie in bed past the First Watch gongs, so what can I do? Since he was going to be training with his own partner I figured I'd follow suit. At least we did turn in early. Very early!"

Our enforced purity had ended with the Ceremony of Presentation. Midway through Seventh Watch Lachis had fled the Opal Court, leaving a trail of watered silk and matched pearls in her wake. I heard no more from her till she shook me out of a profound sleep, somewhere in the nether depths of First Watch, to drag me off to the gym.

Now she assumed her briskest manner. "So what did you think of Gloy's lineup?"

"Impressive."

"Any favorites?"

"Well, I couldn't give you a name . . . I guess I can't tell one from another. All of Rhamant's companions look alike, don't you think?"

"Risha! I don't believe you."

The masseuse was working on my left foot at that moment, and her hands were very strong. I moaned but didn't say a word.

"You *are* in the market for a husband, aren't you?"

"I have to be, if I don't want to go back to Skhorb—or even worse." By that I meant High Vrazil. "My term expires in eleven more cycles. Unless I can manage an appointment to the Despot's own court I'll have to leave Gheo then, and you know I don't want to. I only wish we women didn't have to depend so much on marriage for our place in the hierarchy."

"I've thought about that often enough myself," she said softly. "Imagine if we could compete in the Games, and bloody our knives the way men do. I don't think I'd mind at all."

"But we must preserve our precious wombs so that the race will continue."

"What cant! With the capabilities of medical science . . ." Here she stopped; in the servants' presence she dared say no more. Few women in Gheo would even have gone that far, knowing Volshev might be listening.

Meanwhile I decided to keep the conversation fixed on the subject of the Games. For some reason I wasn't eager for a discussion of my marriage prospects. "How many Red contests do you think we'll see, come Waterman Cycle?" I asked quickly.

"That all depends on Volshev's mood . . . but if you look into the recent history of the Games you'll find a trend toward more and more fatalities. Out of all Gloy's current entries fifty-odd are involved in requests for the Red. We'll see how many Volshev approves."

"Certainly Rhamant's influence will be felt."

"Of course—and he's tending toward Red himself. Especially wherever Vaur and Khryasha are involved."

That was another topic I'd sooner avoid.

"I feel powerful hostilities brewing now with the Nine Houses joined. You know, Trithi let slip that two of her affines, Yonann Immaculates, have challenged two Ubain Pures to a little warmup meeting tomorrow after Masquerade."

"Not to the blood, though."

"No, just to satisfaction."

Now I had her. "What was the quarrel?" she asked eagerly.

"Some remark about Trithi's bearing at the Presentation, overheard by chance."

She let out a long laugh. "Cocky, aren't they! I won't say anything more. But if that's the mood among our fine young warriors then the Masquerade may bear strange fruit indeed."

The same thought had occurred to me. Gheo was brimming with potential contestants in the Games. Any public gathering offered the risk of violence, weapons or no weapons.

Alas, my pause allowed Lachis to seize control of the conversation once more. "So, Risha. As soon as the men have sorted out their own status problems it will be time to focus on yours. Rhamant and I talked about you last spell—"

"In between more pleasant diversions, I hope—"

"—and he feels as strongly as I do about bringing you into House Gloy. That way you can ascend the ladder and stay in Gheo, all in one move, as the spouse of some retainer of his. Yes, I know I keep badgering you about this, but don't you agree that it's the most logical solution? Rhamant and I will make the necessary arrangements: you just pick out a likely prospect and we'll see if he's agreeable. If your first choice isn't to be had, your second is bound to be."

She was guaranteeing me a *mughe*-marriage, a switch in Hypaethral affiliation, an enormous status-boost. A highly placed husband, in other words. Just what I had dreamed of on those bitter nights in High Vrazil; exactly what I needed now that my time in Gheo ran short.

Only I couldn't summon up the slightest enthusiasm—and I was afraid I knew why.

"At the Masquerade," I said, "I'll look, I'll circulate, I'll see who catches my fancy. Before this spell runs out you'll have his name."

Seventh Watch brought more sweat and more exhilaration. We sailed through our performance of *The Two Annas,* an ancient duet which Lachis had unearthed somewhere in Volshev's library. Frenzied rehearsals had occupied the whole of the previous starcycle; and now, at the opening of the Masquerade, frenzied applause was our reward.

Embedded in the dancing was a complicated subtext which I doubt any of those cheering Radiants or Immaculates bothered to analyze. Lachis and I portrayed two opposing aspects of a single character: the conformist and the rebel, the driver and the driven, the schemer and the unwitting tool. Our costuming made us into twins (though a few details distinguished us, for clarity's sake). Oddly enough I took the part of the cold-hearted puppeteer and Lachis the poor marionette; I exhorted her through a sequence of movements based on Shallowcut training, until at last she mimicked me perfectly, and collapsed in despair. All manner of satire was implied.

But since the ballet employed no words whatsoever, few of the on-lookers guessed Lachis' intent. All they saw were two young women hurling their bodies through a quarter-watch of hard dancing; and since Volshev tolerated no species of social critique, this was just as well.

As Lachis and I faced each other in the last figure of the dance—she docile, I agloat—a herald called out our names and ranks. We raised our arms and the applause crashed down; I found it sweet. Then we were running off to a side chamber to change for the ensuing revelry.

Rhamant was waiting with a kiss for both of us. "Karinska and Ivanovna would be green with envy if they saw you tonight," he said. "You dance incredibly well." We acknowledged his gallantry with mod-est bows. "I see you've studied each other's moves very closely," he added. "Even I had you confused from time to time."

"Did you really?" Lachis' tone held something I didn't like. "That gives me the most interesting idea." And before I could stop her she was fastening the flower-trimmed cap she had just worn as Anna II on my own head, and taking Anna I's jeweled circlet for herself.

"Now what is the purpose of all this?" I demanded, in Anna-like indignation.

"The Masquerade has just begun. Its whole point is to confound rank and status and identity, so what better time to switch hats?" She gig-gled; her sense of humor was contagious. "Most people won't recognize us at all, but a few are bound to have noticed the headgear we wore in the ballet. They will very cleverly think they've seen through our dis-guises—and be completely wrong. It should be great fun!"

I embraced her as I laughed. "I don't know why I keep listening to you, Lachis."

But I did, and the subterfuge was set in motion. All three of us donned the Masquerade's traditional dominoes and stepped out into the teeming ballroom.

Lachis, however, disappeared in an instant. She danced off to the rhythm of her own private earset, with barely a goodbye, and I thought, "Virgin Mother! What will she do to my reputation?" But I, too, was caught up in the spirit of the game, and wasted no time worrying.

Instead I turned to my companion, unquestionably the most glorious male in all the Matterfield, and said, "Shall we dance?" And as my fictive husband, Rhamant didn't dare refuse.

We tuned our earsets to an agreeable channel and gyrated in unison for a long hypnotic mix, traveling in the general direction of the densest crowds. Around us people danced or didn't, alone or in pairs or in groups, or talked, or drank. This was in marked contrast to the ordinary decorum of court balls, which decreed pair dancing in fixed modes and tolerated no such free-form amusement. Furthermore, since everyone was in disguise, it was impossible to say who was a Radiant and who a lowly mechanic on a guest-worker's permit from High Vrazil. Therein lay the chief attraction of this post-Presentation, pre-Game Masquerade: in the midst of those very rituals which established and confirmed rank and status-count, here was a brief opportunity to scorn all convention, to love your enemy and hate your lover, to be rude to your betters and fawn over your inferiors, to cast every rule of etiquette into the void. My fellow citizens of Gheo were rising to the occasion with great enthusiasm.

I found Rhamant an excellent dancing partner—though naturally Lachis would have settled for nothing less. And when we tired of dancing he gallantly escorted me around the hall, instead of deserting me to look for his real wife. By now the ballroom was revealing new surprises. Hidden machinery raised, lowered, and rotated various sections of the floor, without any warning, though slowly enough to avoid injury. Great gauzy panels of the finest Veiian weave lifted or descended at random, creating islands of privacy, only to open them up to the crowd again.

Rhamant was in a festive humor; I had never seen this side of him before. "What if I arrested everyone here?" he asked me once.

"Do you really have that much authority?" I was taken aback; it was so easy to forget that this charming fellow on my arm was the Spear of Gheo.

"I do: and I'm immune from prosecution myself!" He leered ferociously and made as if to strangle me.

"Oh, stop—if you ever turned out to be that unprincipled, old Volshev would have you breathing vacuum in short order."

"But what fun I would have in the meantime!" And he whirled me around in a two-second tarantella.

"Just think," he said a moment later. "I could make dancing out of rhythm grounds for status reduction, I could make fat rear ends a capital crime."

"It sounds like you're drunk on power."

"I am, I am!"

We sat down on a temporary seat by a temporary arras and waxed temporarily philosophical, as the whole Matterfield swirled by in fancy dress. "I have what they all want," said Rhamant with a wave of his arm. "I look down on them like the sun on the wheeling planets. They aspire to the light but all they hold is my reflection."

"You sound like Volshev himself! How can any mortal say those things?"

He laughed. "I'm just teasing you, Risha. What I really feel is the irony of my situation. I have place, yes, I have honor and respect, but what does it signify? I can only behave as all the other Spears have done before me. In a way my office is just a new prison with the same old view."

"You *are* drunk then. One minute you're the sun and the next you're a clod of earth. I don't understand you, or Lachis either. She falls into the same contradictions."

"And what about you? Do you never question the way we live?"

"Certainly I do. I start to wonder why I should keep worrying and scheming over a new address or a more costly gown or a more pretentious circle of friends."

Rhamant nodded. "That's all it boils down to in the end."

"But it doesn't! You two have it all, and you always have. You don't understand what it's like to be on the outside, for people to ignore you or condescend to you. It's your privileged status that allows you the luxury of world-weariness. Think of this. You praised my dancing this spell, but if I hadn't attained a certain degree of rank and influence you never would have seen me, because I never would have been allowed to perform in Gheo—talent or no talent! This status-game is really a form of self-expression: as we struggle we grow, and as we advance we become more truly ourselves."

He laughed again and shook his masked head vigorously. "If that's really what you think, you will rise high, my friend. Those are exactly the ideas Volshev wants to hear."

"Volshev's ideas, Lachis' ideas, your ideas!" I threw up my hands. "It's hard to hold on to my own ideas against that barrage."

"So I've noticed!" Then he relented and grew serious. "But you do, Risha. However much Lachis tries to mold you—and she means it for your own good, never doubt that—I still see you clinging to what's inside. In spite of these occasional aberrations which I'm sure you don't mean! Then again—who knows. Maybe you *will* use status to win what you most desire."

I dared hope he was right, and wondered at my daring.

Soon enough we were moving on. We walked along arm in arm, chattering freely in a new-found intimacy. Rhamant had stopped being the smug and imperturbable icon I had always seen before.

Shortly we connected with other merrymakers, who saw through Rhamant's disguise and introduced themselves as lesser notables of Gloy. I allowed my own identity to remain mysterious and indulged in an eighth-watch of frivolous talk. Glasses of sparkling wine were filled and refilled; voices lifted in laughter. I was enjoying myself immensely.

Then, with a guilty start, I remembered that Lachis was expecting me to corner a few candidates for wedlock. There were none in my immediate party, who were all senior courtiers and their spouses. So I began examining the glittering mob around me.

Faces were blank; instead I read bodies. I noticed at once how stiffly everyone moved, and amused myself trying to explain away this stiffness with Rhamant-style logic. These must be marionettes, I thought—poor manikins frozen by tradition. Not my style at all. Then I glimpsed a supple figure in scarlet and black, moving with the grace of an Ethrin panther. My focus pursued. I noted his wide-footed stance, his forceful gestures. This was no puppet; this was a man who pulled his own strings. The more I watched the more familiar he looked, disguise or no disguise; then I realized it was Lord Seren himself.

The section of flooring that he and his companions occupied was moving toward mine in a lazy arc, so that if no one changed positions we would meet in perhaps a sixteenth-watch. My diaphragm tightened in expectation, however strongly I willed it not to. Naturally no one in my little group had noticed a thing. I couldn't decide whether to alert them or not.

Rhamant gave me an opening as he once more philosophized on the futility of attaining high status. "But Rhamant," I objected, "would you be happier if, for example, Seren of Khryasha had been named Spear instead of you?"

There were audible gasps at my temerity. Rhamant at first said nothing. But one of his kinsmen guffawed and replied, "What an unpleasant thought! It would be better if the office were left vacant than if it fell to Seren."

Rhamant bowed in the man's direction. "Thank you, Vanya. That sums up my own feelings. And thank you, Risha: I think you've reconciled me to my good fortune. I knew there had to be a reason for it."

In the general laughter I plucked Rhamant's sleeve and quietly said, "Forgive me for broaching the subject, but I *am* very curious about the rivalry—or should I say apparent rivalry—between you and him. What's the truth? Do you and Seren really despise each other?"

Fortunately he took no offense. "Despise?" He chuckled softly. "No, I wouldn't go that far. But I do find the man a bit, well, repellent. We met about ten revolutions back, when we were both in our teens, and he actually made a show of friendship. But he'd already been involved in his first *accident* and there was a pall over him even then. So I kept my distance, I ignored his fraternal overtures; he withdrew like a crestfallen little boy. Ever since, he's tried to compete with everything I've done. It's downright annoying. I was highly rated with the doublehanded sword, so he took up the same weapon, though previously he'd specialized in singlehand. I began racing thrusters, so he did too, though he'd barely set foot in one before. I led an expedition to Djapati's fourth moon, so the next revolution he was sailing out to Shadan. He was always trying to outdo me, but always following my lead. Just like a child."

"He must have been a child when he began this emulation—ten revolutions ago he was only fourteen, wasn't he?"

"Yes, and he still seems stuck at that level."

Rhamant made Seren out to be a fool. Not for the first time I marveled at how contrary my own impression was.

"How have you avoided meeting at the Games?" I asked.

"A simple function of our ages. I'm five revs older, so on the occasion of the last Games we were in different classes: he was too inexperienced to qualify for my division. He would certainly be challenging me this time if I hadn't been named Spear." He smiled crookedly. "Without me to contend with he's sure to take first place."

And add still more names to his private roster of the dead, I thought. I wondered how many Rhamant himself had taken out so far.

But leaning close to his ear I said, "Though you may have avoided him at the Games, you've failed at this Masquerade. I see him coming up behind you right now."

Rhamant stiffened without turning around. "We're in disguise— maybe he won't recognize—"

But he had. Seren of Khryasha was already bowing to me. "I think

I've penetrated your incognito, my lady. You must be Lachis Gloy. And your companion can only be the Spear of Gheo himself."

Rhamant gave a quick barking laugh and returned the bow. The other gentlemen of Gloy followed suit and began backing off uncertainly; however, since none of them bore arms, the moment was nowhere near as tense as it might have been.

"A pleasure," lied the scion of Gloy. "Lachis, may I present the Radiant Seren?"

Seren took my hand in the salutation of equals—though if he had known my true identity he could never have done so, since I was several levels below him in rank. As he murmured his courtly phrases over my unworthy fingers Rhamant, Vanya, and the rest deftly sidestepped onto the revolving floorspace he had just vacated, launching themselves on a new course across the hall. By the time Seren turned to extend them his courtesies they were already some distance away, cheerfully waving goodbye.

Seren's lips tightened. "Have I offended your husband?" he asked sharply.

"Certainly not." I took hold of his hand in both of mine. "They've had too much to drink—they're just playing a little game with us. I'm sure Rhamant will be back in an eighth-watch."

This mollified him somewhat; meanwhile my mind raced my heart, casting about for something brilliant to say. Seren saved me the trouble by making conversation about my performance in *The Two Annas*. He showed no sign of abandoning me just yet.

"You look like a dancer yourself," I said when he paused. "I notice great precision in every move you make."

He shrugged. "A combination of martial arts training and hundreds of watches spent in free fall. It can't compare with your own grace."

I enjoyed the sound of that, though I still felt like I was in free fall myself. Then he said, "Do you realize we've met before? It was revolutions back, at a retreat in Ubain."

My intestines chilled. "How could I forget?" I said weakly.

"I thought you might have wanted to. You didn't seem to like me then."

Our first ancestor only knew what passed between them, but I bravely muddled on.

"Dear Seren, you sound like a hurt child! I know I have a rather superior manner at times. It's something I try to overcome. But I suppose many people have been rude to you along the way, haven't they? If you've ever counted me among them I hope you'll forgive me now."

He looked sheepish; still I couldn't stop. "You know, I've often wanted to meet you again. I admire you for what you've had to contend with in your life, and I regret the ill feelings that exist between you and my husband. I'd like to see that change. Perhaps we can both work toward mending the quarrel between our Houses."

All I could see of his face were his eyes and his mouth; both gaped. "I can't believe I'm hearing you say this."

"Isn't it what you want?"

"I—it's just that I've come to accept our discord as a fact of life. Our families have been rivals for first place among the Hypaethra for four generations, if not longer. Once I thought all that could end if only Rhamant and I became friends. But that's clearly impossible—no matter what you might hope for. And by now, I guess, that seems right and proper to me. Where would we Revenants be without strife and competition? We certainly don't want a return to the obscenities of the Interglacial."

He seemed confused; I was flabbergasted. "But Seren—what about all the friendly gestures you've made—just now, for example, when you approached us here?"

"It's part of the game I play," he said simply. "I provoke Rhamant into rudeness, and keep the edge on my envy with memories of his contempt."

Here was a can of worms, as the savages of High Vrazil would say. At some point the two of us had seated ourselves. Now I took Seren's hand again, without thinking of boldness, without any self-consciousness whatsoever. Stroking his callused fingers, I said, "I'm sorry for all this. Because I do like you very much."

He squeezed my hand in return. "I'm amazed, Lachis. I never thought it would be so easy to talk to you, to know you. . . ."

I ducked under his arm and leaned against him, embracing him and luxuriating in that physicality. His arms slowly came around me and we faced each other, masked but still revealing much. In another moment we would kiss.

Instead he said, quite abruptly, "You're not Lachis Gloy."

He let go of me and slowly stood. I did the same, staying in close but suddenly remembering all those tales of Seren the killer. "No," I replied. "I'm her best friend. One of Nan Solize's ladies."

"Was this a calculated insult?"

I swayed against him—he was barely taller than me—but he stood like an iron casting. "Of course not! It was a diversion Lachis thought of earlier, with no design on anyone in particular. We switched costumes, nothing more—it was all done in fun. When you happened along I saw no reason to change the scenario."

"But—what you said—" He was speaking in a new voice, octaves deeper and eons colder.

"It was all from my own heart."

Many alternatives occurred to me—to fall on my knees, tear off my mask, beg his forgiveness, even run away—but I stood still, waiting.

He looked at me and looked away, made as if to step forward and then thought better of it. As he vacillated, a *deus ex machina* descended from the holographic clouds: Rhamant materialized, calling out boisterously, drunker than ever.

What little I could see of Seren's face was changing color. I was genuinely frightened. Meanwhile Rhamant crushed me in a hug and planted a kiss somewhere near my ear.

"My dear wife," he began.

"Enough of this nonsense. We've already unmasked."

He looked stupidly at our dominoed faces and sobered up a little.

"Well then," he said, "are you old friends now?"

I broke away from him and moved back toward Seren. "I would be deeply honored if Lord Seren would henceforth regard me as such."

The Heir of Khryasha bowed. "So it will be, Lady . . . ?"

"Risha, Immaculate of House Skhorb."

We touched fingertips very formally. Suddenly I had to leave. As I fled, almost blindly, Rhamant flung an arm after me, calling, "Risha! What's wrong?"

"Nothing, nothing. Meet me later, please. I need to freshen up." And I hurried on.

I did look back once, before I was too far away, and saw both of them standing together without any overt signs of belligerence. My thoughts were in a welter but some fissure in my cerebrum decided that no real harm was done. Maybe now Rhamant and Seren could actually be friends.

What would happen between Seren and me, however, seemed an open question.

Lachis eventually found me. I was wandering through the dancing hordes like a refugee from some burning city, dazed but still dry-eyed.

She was feeling no pain herself; obviously she had found diversion enough since our last meeting.

"You have no idea how popular you are, Risha!" she cried. "I've been playing proxy for you all latterspell; you can expect at least ten new affairs beginning First Watch tomorrow."

"I thought it already was First Watch tomorrow," I said dully.

"Not yet, not yet. There's still more fun to be had." In her own animation she didn't notice my lack of it. "Tell me your adventures so far!"

I wasn't quite ready to discuss the fiasco with Lord Seren so I simply told her I'd been dancing with Rhamant most of the time.

"How boring! Even I wouldn't have done that. What about your promise to find the ideal husband?"

"I suppose I'll start keeping it right now."

That satisfied her, and we set off on yet another prowl through the hall. Her mood helped lift me out of mine; I decided I'd simply have to wait and see what time would bring. We quickly found some agreeable companions with whom to while away the last halfwatch of the old spell.

Then, as the party was guttering down to its finish, and Lachis had begun to think about finding Rhamant and calling it quits, a most disturbing phenomenon occurred.

Right in front of us manifested a Sending of Volshev.

My inner voices went wild: what have I said, what have I done, what have I thought? But the pale apparition directed its attention to Lachis, gray eyes fixing her in a gaze of extreme gravity.

"Lachis Gloy," it said. "We must speak privately. Accompany me to the alcove just over there."

And they went off together, human and hologram, disappearing behind a figured hanging. I waited in mounting alarm.

When Lachis finally emerged, alone, she was as white and rigid as Volshev had been. "Risha," she said quietly. "Rhamant is dead. Someone murdered him."

CHAPTER THREE

Gheo's lifeline is its nervous system, an intricate processing network whose central brain is housed in the Palace itself. Besides balancing the city's internal ecology and regulating its passage through space, this vast web is the key to the Despot's library. Every household and every public plaza in the Hypaethron has its terminal, to a total of more than five million; they can furnish anything from a recipe for plum dumplings to an overview of the latest news. So it happened that, during the forespell following the Masquerade, a general lamentation greeted these words as they scrolled down the datascreens of Gheo:

Lord Rhamant of Gloy, Radiant 17 of the Community of Hypaethra, was assassinated during last spell's Tenth Watch by an unknown assailant.

From refectory to public garden, from docking bay to atrium to loggia, throughout all the nautiloid chambers of the spinning construct, people spoke of nothing else.

In Volshev's reception hall, however, we kept silent. Sitting row on row before the empty dais, we were a hollow-eyed collection of insomniacs, our grim appearance well suited to the nature of the gathering. I can't speak for the others; but I know I was nervous, frightened, and miserable. I labored under a burden of imagined guilt. Except for his murderer I had been the last to see Lord Rhamant alive.

Volshev had summoned us here to the inner Palace at the beginning of Second Watch. Besides Lachis and Nan Solize I noted several Radiants of Houses Gloy and Khryasha, including Sorich herself, plus all the gentlemen of Rhamant's retinue. Vremeni, however, was absent; at such sensitive meetings of state there was no place for the Child Emperor. The only reason a mere Immaculate such as I had been called was my close association with the deceased.

The room chilled; the air above the dais shimmered; and Volshev appeared, seated on an ivory chair.

"The Spear of Gheo is dead," he began. "A brief public announcement of this tragedy has already been circulated. Mentioning only an *unknown assailant,* it contains all the information I deem suitable for general consumption. I think you will soon share my reticence."

He paused and I felt an inchoate perplexity in the group. Lachis, who was next to me, went rigid; but no one spoke.

"You are here to participate in an inquest. What is said here will remain secret; I trust this is understood." We indicated our assent. "Very well then. First of all, you should know that the body was discovered within twenty minutes of the opening of First Watch, by one of my external sensors. It was encased in an emergency pod, traveling at low velocity on collision course with Gheo."

There were murmurs of surprise. We had all seen Rhamant at the Masquerade during the Ninth Watch: how then did he happen to be in free space only a watch and a half later?

A hologram of the pod manifested in the air next to Volshev. "You will note the crest incised into the hull," he said. I looked, and wished I hadn't. It was plainly that of House Khryasha.

"This pod was part of the *Blue Star*'s complement," he continued. "As most of you know, the *Blue Star* is the private thruster of Lord Seren of Khryasha. What you may not know, however, is that the *Blue Star* launched away from Gheo at the close of Ninth Watch, without filing its orbit, indeed without observing any formalities whatsoever. Since Seren himself is absent from Gheo, a reasonable deduction is that he departed, alone and in haste, aboard his own ship."

Yes, I had noticed the gap he left in this assembly, and my sense of dread only amplified.

"An autopsy has already been performed. Details will be made available, if any of you require them, but for now let me state simply that Lord Rhamant's death resulted from a blow to the left temple. Bruises appeared there, on his throat, and in the area of his neck and shoulders. Minor abrasions appeared on both wrists and both ankles.

"The body was clothed, but this clothing was torn and disordered. Resting between his hands was a dataspool." Its image was displayed. "Clearly it derives from a camera mounted in the main cabin of the *Blue Star;* played back, it offers strange tidings."

A three-dimensional scene filled the space to Volshev's right. I was surprised at its quality: Colors were blue-shifted, resolution fuzzy, sound generally flat and muddy. After a second or two, however, I paid no mind to such details.

The dataspool showed Seren and Rhamant hovering together in the cramped space of the *Blue Star*'s bridge, dressed as I had last seen them. Although the camera angle tended to catch the backs of their heads, rather than their faces, and their voices were usually lost, it was obvious that Seren was explaining the thruster's operation; he pointed out various controls and ran routine systems checks. At one point his words came through clearly: "Now if you like, Rhamant, you can take her out yourself."

Nodding his thanks, Rhamant assumed the pilot's couch and donned its webbed restraints. Seren continued hovering at his shoulder, watching closely as he began the decoupling sequence. They exchanged a few monosyllables while the *Blue Star* disengaged from Gheo; once Rhamant laughed at an error he made. Given the picture's fuzziness, it was hard to read body language: but I imagined a mounting tension in Seren's limbs, a focusing of energy for some anticipated stress.

As Rhamant fingered the touchpanel Seren braced both feet against a bulkhead. Then in one supple move he struck out at the juncture of Rhamant's neck and shoulder, putting all his strength behind the blow. Rhamant slumped, unconscious; Seren removed him from the webbing and tied his wrists and ankles with two lengths of cord. After a little attention to the touchpanel he arranged Rhamant's body so that he was stretched full-length, hands and feet secured to opposite bulkheads. With a few slaps he brought the Spear of Gheo around.

Seren spoke now, softly, rapidly, very close to Rhamant's ear, so that his words were difficult to follow. At first he merely repeated his rival's name, followed by a string of epithets; then I heard him say, "We're accelerating now, Rhamant. We're in free space, out of Volshev's range. No one knows this is happening. No one can save you."

Rhamant gave the illusion of calm. "What possible advantage do you gain from this?"

"None. But can you imagine my satisfaction? I've made a fool of you at last."

"And made yourself a criminal."

"It doesn't matter now. You've thwarted all my ambitions anyway. What's left for me?"

"Your honor."

Seren struck him gently. "But everyone thinks I'm a madman and a murderer. I may as well prove them right."

"Why not make this a fair fight? Cut me loose and we'll see who really deserves to be Spear."

"I might lose. This way I get exactly what I want."

He began applying careful pressure at the line of Rhamant's jaw. The Gloyan stiffened. A strange whining sound escaped his lips, setting my teeth on edge; I could only imagine how it affected Lachis.

Seren continued these ministrations, touching his victim's body at various nerve centers, until Rhamant writhed about like a fish on a hook. The Khryashan's movements were as delicate as a surgeon's, as precise as a gemcutter's; it was obvious that someone had schooled him very carefully in the arts of the torturer. I wondered which master had been so foolish—for it was hard to imagine any sane teacher taking on such an infamous student.

"How do you like this one?" Seren whispered. "Are you sorry now? Are you surprised at how much I hate you?" Rhamant's face was mottled; blood flowed copiously from his nose. He said nothing at all.

Seren paused a moment and studied his handiwork. Both men were breathing heavily; tiny globes of sweat and blood spun round in the air. Once more Seren launched a torrent of words toward Rhamant's ear, this time so rapidly and so softly that it was incomprehensible.

Lachis was white, stricken, a stranger with frozen eyes. Suddenly Seren launched out again; there was a dull, pulpy thud, and Rhamant actually screamed. So did Lachis. So did I. We rose together, arms entwined, and fled Volshev's cruel theater.

Lachis was sedated and put to bed in a mansion that her family maintained in Gheo, far from the Opal Court where I sought my own repose. As I wept, alone in my small suite, I turned the story over and over in my mind.

I had fallen in love with a madman. It was simple, so very simple, and so depraved. Only now, when I realized the hopelessness of my attachment, could I finally admit how infatuated I had been with Seren. Again and again I remembered the feel of his body through the scarlet robes of Masquerade; again and again I remembered the sound of his hands breaking Rhamant's skull.

A private communique from the Despot had just informed me of the tribunal's findings. Lady Sorich herself had been convinced of Seren's guilt, and declared him outcast; this decision would be kept quiet, however, and invoked only if Seren ever sought sanctuary among the Hypaethra. At Volshev's urging all report of his aberrant behavior would remain confidential. It wouldn't do for one of our top-rated Radiants to be exposed as a psychopath.

Because Seren clearly was insane. All his history pointed to paranoia, to delusions of persecution, to secret hatreds and murderous schemes. Even I had sensed an unbalance when we met. But so far no one had questioned me about that. Apparently everyone thought Seren had sufficient motive for murder without inquiring too closely into the events immediately preceding his crime. Unhappily I thought otherwise; perhaps I flattered myself, but it seemed too great a coincidence that I had confronted him within a watch of his deed. I couldn't escape the conviction that my words had had a triggering effect.

As a result I wallowed in grief and guilt. I had been a fool, a total idiot, obsessed with a monster in spite of universal warnings, indifferent to my best friend's generous offers of status enhancement because I lusted after Seren the killer. During our single meeting I had succeeded only in humiliating myself and enraging him—inflaming his delusions to the point where he committed his worst crime, a ghoulish murder that effectively destroyed my life.

For Lachis would no longer dwell in the Opal Court. As a widow she was ritually impure and must retire from imperial service. Thus I lost her companionship, my chief solace in the back-biting world of the Palace. And with Rhamant dead (disaster enough by itself) I no longer had my pick of the eligible bachelors of Gloy.

High Vrazil loomed nearer and nearer.

A few mysteries remained, however. Why had Seren jettisoned Rhamant's corpse, along with the damning evidence of the dataspool? Of course he was insane, but there was method in his madness, and what purpose did this early exposure serve? And where had he fled? Gheo's external sensors monitored the movements of all space vehicles within a wide radius of Gheo, and certainly plasma trails are detectable a long way off—but Seren, with a clever series of false starts, had evaded every attempt at finding him. Not even Volshev knew his hiding place.

After three more letters I consented to meet Tref. I had pleaded mourning for seven spells; on the eighth I took off my rough purple mantle, donned figured silk, and joined him at a cafe in Grishanka Park.

He rose eagerly at the sight of me, smiles wreathing his face. I endured a long and fervent embrace. It was hard to find any trace of the courtly gallant of High Vrazil in this earnest supplicant. His high-collared jacket barely satisfied the demands of the current mode, and his trousers were unflatteringly tight.

"Risha!" His eyes devoured me. "You've fulfilled all the promise of your childhood, and more. So much more!"

"You're looking well yourself, Tref."

He led me to a tiny marble table with carven stools. Overhead, blue haze mimicked Ethrin skies. All around us was vegetation—olive and laurel and cypress—recreating some lost Interglacial landscape. I sneezed.

"The whole Matterfield is talking about you," he continued heartily. "Carrying the Heir at the Presentation—dancing at the Masquerade— holding Lady Lachis' veil in the Spear of Gheo's cortege. You must be proud."

"I won't deny it. And I owe my success in no small measure to you. My gratitude is without limit, never fear; unfortunately my means of expressing it have somewhat tighter constraints."

He laughed and suddenly I warmed to him, remembering all the laughter we had shared before. "Such a courtier! But I have no favors to beg. I just wanted to see you again—and not in some enormous holotank! No, no, I only wanted to talk to you, to hear how you're getting on in Gheo."

My hands strayed to his across the table. "You're sweet, Tref, as always. I wish I could say that everything is as fabulous as it looks. But this business of Lord Rhamant's death . . ." And I went on to describe a little of my present unhappiness, naturally omitting all reference to the secrets I kept.

"You surprise me," he said, when I had finished. "I imagined a hundred suitors would be vying for your attention."

"I suppose I've been too self-absorbed for any man to take me seriously. I may even have acquired a little arrogance."

"Never! But of course I realize that celebrity doesn't necessarily count for much in Gheo. There's always pedigree and status to weigh out and quibble over."

Conversation passed to a dozen other inconsequential topics, as we sipped our glasses of bittersweet brandy. My mood, which had been so black for so long now, rapidly lightened. I regretted not seeing Tref sooner; he was marvelous company, after all.

But by no means as guileless as he would have me believe: because eventually he came to the point of our meeting.

"As I said before, Risha, you've been attracting attention around

Gheo. I've only been here eleven spells but even I can see your star is on the rise. In fact I have been approached by a gentleman of the most exalted rank who is eager to make your acquaintance. This is a delicate matter, you must realize, one calling for discretion on all sides. I hope you will consider it carefully."

Either I was a bit fuddled by the brandy or the Third Minister of Paun was being even more ambiguous than usual. "I'm afraid I don't follow you. You know a man who wants to meet me: why not just introduce him?"

Tref's eyebrows lifted. "If only it were that simple. But remember, I did say *exalted*. This gentleman is unable to meet you in public; I would have to convey you to his chambers myself. Clandestinely."

I began to understand. Tref sought to act as a go-between . . . to use the polite term. A less delicate expression might be *pander*. I felt an automatic revulsion—

Which he immediately perceived. "Risha, please don't be offended. This meeting could be of great advantage to you. Trust me. Think it over."

I did so, aloud. "Who is so exalted that he can't meet a court lady in Grishanka Park? Any married man, naturally." Tref's denial was vigorous. "Then I suppose I do understand." I thought some more, this time in silence. "Very well then," I decided. "I'm curious enough to pursue this."

Tref's mask slipped for an instant and revealed his heartfelt relief; then it was back in place for more urbane chatter. "Of course you commit yourself to nothing. Of course there will be no pressure . . ." and so on and so forth. Within an eighth-watch we had boarded a magnetic car, our destination the Palace of the Despot.

By now I suspected the rank of this secret admirer, but en route there was a moment of wild fantasy. What if Seren were hiding here in Gheo, right under Volshev's nose, and Tref were bringing me to see him? I was ashamed of myself even for entertaining such a thought—knowing what I knew—but there it was. Obsessions fade slowly.

To my great surprise Tref was privy to the keywords that allowed access to the Palace's internal tube system. Even I, a member of the Virgin Mother's household, had only been granted the codes for my own quarter. With this high-level clearance we were able to bypass the public terminal and alight in an overgrown garden deep in Blue Wing. From there Tref led us unerringly down a series of corridors that grew steadily more desolate. I wondered how he had acquired this knowledge of the labyrinth—even Lachis would have been impressed, in better times—before deciding that he must have been instructed by our mysterious patron for this very purpose. At his request we kept quiet the whole way.

Traversing the curlicues and convolutions of the maze consumed the better part of a halfwatch. We skirted broken datascreens scrawled with obscene graffiti, and picked our way through service chambers littered with warped tools and threadbare garments. When my feet began to complain of this unexpected exertion we arrived at a modest door, distinguished only by its cleanliness and good repair. Tref knocked softly; moments later a light flashed over us and the door slid aside, revealing a steep staircase. We climbed up and found ourselves in an ornate sitting room. It was as out of place here as a Radiant wading through Ethri's mud. We sat; I suppressed an oath. Tref smiled encouragement and said nothing.

The room was full of antiques that spoke of wealth and an eccentric kind of refinement. Out of boredom I regarded them desultorily. When an old man entered he startled me half out of my seat. He was dressed in a pale blue robe emblazoned with Volshev's own crest, the concentric circles of Gheo; its associations made me nervous. He carried a tea-tray. Once we had accepted tiny cups of some steaming brew he left us again. We sipped daintily; eventually he reappeared and whispered something in Tref's ear. Tref rose, sketched a bow in my direction, and departed arm in arm with the old servant. I was completely nonplussed.

As I swore under my breath a tall, fair man appeared. His eyes were wide and clear, his gaze resolute and thoughtful. "Risha Skhorb," he said, sitting across from me on the divan. "You do me honor. My name is Mudriye."

Mudriye: one of the noblest names in the Matterfield. Mudriye the Confessor, once Mudriye the Emperor: regnal period R.Y. 2050–2058. He was one of the nineteen living Retired Emperors that people heard about, but rarely saw: an extremely good-looking man somewhere in early middle age.

When I would have made obeisance, Mudriye stopped me, saying, "Let me be your friend, Risha, not your master. Though I am a Confessor, I have something to confess to you. You've intrigued me since I first saw you, two revolutions past, at the Diamond Levee. You were a homespun girl then, fresh from the Ethrin wilds; now you're the picture of a Radiant lady."

I could scarcely speak; I stammered out, "But my rank—I've risen no higher than Immaculate, Lord Mudriye."

"You'll make Radiant within two starcycles—don't doubt it, I hear of such things. You already look the part."

I was too amazed to respond; he filled the silence for me. "Do you have any idea where you are?"

"In Blue Wing, I suppose?"

"No, we're in White. The Despot's own quarter."

My heart beat faster. "You don't live here, then."

"This is just a hideaway. And I mean that. Even Volshev can't see us here."

He was sending me one shock after another. Lachis and I had dreamed of such places, speculated whether they might exist, and now this Mudriye was telling me I'd found one.

"I see the idea frightens you."

He was right.

"Let me tell you something, Risha. You're being closely watched. I don't know why, but I've made finding out my business. Frankly I'm glad. Otherwise I never would have had an excuse to arrange this meeting. I owe many thanks to the Minister of Paun for obliging me."

I was still finding my voice. "Watched. You mean by Volshev. How do you know?"

He leaned back in the divan. "Think of what my life has been. Since birth I've lived in the Palace and participated in various sorts of theatrical subterfuge, all in the name of tradition. As Child Emperor I was taught to press keys and mouth words and not expected to think about anything I did. Then, just as my mind started to grow, just as I began to wonder how much or how little it meant to be Emperor, Volshev came to me in a Sending and said that my main purpose in life was finished. My voice was cracking; my chin was sprouting. My usefulness as an icon was over. He told me I could retire for the next hundred revolutions, and sit in quiet splendor till I died. It didn't make me very happy."

"And so?"

"I studied. As a Retired Emperor I was in a unique position; most young men of my generation were training for the Games or learning a profession. Pure knowledge has no value in the society we inhabit—or so we're taught to believe. Independent scholarship is unheard of. Most Confessors drug themselves into oblivion, poring over the minutiae of the Canon, but I was determined to be different.

"I've explored every centimeter of this prison—Gheo, that is. I've learned every detail I can about its warden—Volshev himself. I've plugged into all the cybernetic circuitry and done battle with all the security programs, constantly seeking knowledge. And I've learned a great deal. Enough to find the blind spots in the Despot's surveillance. Enough to know when he suspects someone of being a danger to him."

"Surely you yourself are."

"Yes, but I'm very careful to divert his attention."

"Then you're saying he suspects me?"

He grimaced. "So it seems."

For the thousandth time I thought of the Masquerade. Did Volshev imagine me as Seren's accomplice? It seemed mad.

Mudriye spoke again; apparently this was to be a lesson, not a love-tryst. "The mistake people make is to think of Volshev as omniscient. He isn't, but he does discover a tremendous lot. And in fact that's even more disturbing for us, because we never know what he *doesn't* know."

"Lachis and I often used to discuss that angle—I'm sure you know all about her too."

"Oh yes. A fascinating case. But getting back to your story: everyone knows you spoke with both Seren and Rhamant immediately before the murder was committed. But no one knows what you said. Not even Volshev, if I'm guessing right. And that's why he's worried."

"Why doesn't he just ask me?"

"Perhaps he's afraid of what he'll discover."

The impulse seized me then and I couldn't resist—after all, Mudriye wasn't called Confessor for nothing. I poured out the story of that unfortunate spell, including every trivial detail I could remember. True to his office the man listened sympathetically and well. When I was finished he simply shrugged and said, "It sounds harmless enough to me."

He was absolving me; my spirit soared, my eyes filled with tears. "So you don't think I'm responsible?" I asked incredulously.

"Not in the least."

"Then why . . . ?"

"That remains to be seen."

I met Mudriye many times after that. With Lachis in seclusion he became my mainstay, and on occasion my lover. It was all very proper. When we pillowed, we rendezvoused in his own private chambers, according to the ancient formulae that allow Confessors to take concu-

bines but not wives. When we spoke of love, death, and Volshev, however, we always met in that secret room in White Wing. After Tref and
Lachis he became my third instructor in the mysteries of real life.

True to his bloodline Mudriye was an extremely well-favored man,
possessed of vigorous wits and classic good looks. Keeping his company
was therefore no ordeal. And though I worried that our association
might make me even more suspect in Volshev's eyes, he did his best to
reassure me.

"The Despot sees me essentially as a harmless crank. He's watched
me all my life and I still haven't shown any teeth. As far as he knows
you sought *me* out, and all I do is give you spiritual guidance."

Though I had to laugh, in point of fact this was the Confessors'
legitimate function. Within Gheo's taut social web they fulfilled the role
of therapist and counsellor. They were the overseers of an entire corps
of laymen who devoted their lives to the interpretation and application
of the Canon—that body of literature which our ancestors carried with
them on the old starships. Popular wisdom held that the Canon had
shaped us into what we are today, and that its verses contained solu-
tions to every conceivable problem.

In addition Mudriye was a great student of *religion,* an obsolete notion which he had to explain to me at some length. Over the revolutions
this avocation had led him to accumulate a collection of sacred objects:
prayer wheels and meditation scrolls, candlesticks and crucifixes,
knucklebones and lewd statuettes. He loved expounding on their sym-
bolism, though I preferred his speculations of the faith of our own
times.

"Volshev is our god, of course, and I am his priest," he said once, as
we relaxed in White Wing.

"Isn't that a bit naive?" I said. I was studying an icon of a stern old
man in a golden crown. "Volshev would *like* to be our god."

"Oh, but you're quick, Risha! I give him two more generations till he
achieves that goal. He's already been around for five."

"Meaning that once he was just an ordinary human being, like you or
me?"

"My studies indicate as much, yes."

"Then what is he now?"

Mudriye rolled over on his back and plumped up some pillows for his
head. Although we were in the safe-room, after half a cycle we'd begun
mixing pleasure with more intellectual pursuits. "There are three
schools of thought," he replied. "The most heretical postulates that

Volshev is no more than an extremely complicated program, perhaps even an artificial intelligence."

"Like Meqmat."

"Thus the heresy. The evidence in favor is the fact that we see only holograms, and in general hear only a set of stock phrases. The argument against is the fact that, over a period of time, his behavior is too complex—and too erratic—to belong to anything but a man. Or to something on the order of Meqmat. And as far we know, the capability to create any program that powerful, and to build the processing unit needed to run it, died with Meqmat in the Wars of Restoration."

"So you discount the cybernetic hypothesis. What's the second idea?"

"The second and third share many of the same premises. Obviously the real Volshev lives in secret, using backup programs to give the illusion of godlike omnipresence. But exactly what shape is he in, if in fact he can still be called alive? He was born three hundred revs ago; that much is history. So he must have used all the available means of life extension to attain his present age. Is he then a mere lump of flesh, sustained by sophisticated life-support apparatus, or is he a healthy man? That's the idea that appeals most strongly to me. Picture a Volshev who looks nothing like our image of him, living quietly as a private citizen here in Gheo, grumbling about the Despot just like everyone else. You may even have met him, even danced with him at the Masquerade."

"Or even made love with him. Maybe you're Volshev."

"Maybe I am." He made a wicked face.

I caught him by both ears and pulled him toward me. "No you're not—Volshev could never be as much fun as you."

"How can you be so sure?"

"Well, the persona we see must in some way reflect the real man, and my impression of Volshev is that he's a stern disciplinarian, a disapproving patriarch whose sole passion is the exercise of power."

"Is Volshev a bad man, then?"

I considered that one. "I suppose he's bad at being a man—perhaps because he's forgotten how?—but I'm not sure if he's a bad ruler. We resent him, certainly, because he controls us so completely, while completely disregarding our personal desires—but maybe it's all for the good of the Matterfield. I can imagine the Hypaethra in a worse state than they are now. What if we practiced war, instead of competing in the Games? Whole populations might be extinguished, entire habitats demolished."

"True," Mudriye conceded. "Things could be worse. But I suspect they could also be better."

"Would we all be Radiants, in that case, and live forever, and make love with whomever we wanted, as often as we pleased?"

Mudriye laughed. "Is that your theory of paradise?"

"I thought it was everyone's!"

He took hold of my chin and tilted my face toward his. "Your perspicacity is astounding," he said. "Now let's drop philosophy and take up biology."

So we did. It was during that particular investigation into the human body's mucous membranes, I believe, that I first understood why Mudriye had sought me out. He was as much a gamester as Sorich or Rhamant, as competitive as any snub-nosed Pure. But he chose to play forbidden games. Under the circumstances, then, what better partner could he choose than me? In Volshev's eyes I was a suspect, a marked woman—and that was the source of my attraction, not my charm or my Ethrin wildness. In Mudriye's game Volshev was the opponent; I was merely part of the strategy.

By the first spell of Waterman Cycle the Despot had named a new Spear. To no one's surprise he was yet another stalwart of House Gloy. His name was Eryr, and he was Rhamant's cousin-german. Though Khryasha grumbled, every Radiant in the Matterfield offered him due homage in the Red Court of Gheo, as pipes shrilled the ancient battle-songs of the ten ancestral Ships.

Shortly afterwards I persuaded Lachis to stroll with me in Nan Solize's private gardens. Entrance was a favor the lady rarely granted, so the opportunity offered suitable enticement even for the recluse my old friend had become. We met in Green Wing's central plaza and set out together.

Lachis was as poised as I remembered. She looked gorgeous in her purple gown, which according to custom she would wear the full forty-nine spells. I fancied that her face had grown thinner and more expressive; certainly her eyes seemed as wide and dark as the spaces between stars.

"I've missed you, Lachis, more than you can imagine." We embraced and I pressed my face against her silken shoulder.

"It was best for me to be alone," she said evenly. "I've buried myself in words—studying, writing—anything to keep my thoughts away from what happened. Now I can begin to come to terms with it."

"For me it's a madness past all comprehension." Shame kept me from saying more.

"I try only to think of the future."

In such halting conversation we arrived at the garden gate. Entering was a little like going into free space, or boarding a lightsail. An attendant checked our credentials, offered us protective garments (in this case high shoes and heavy cloaks) and directed us to an airlock. A new world waited on the other side.

Solize's garden was an evocation of winter, a faithful recreation of some woodland habitat of interglacial Ethri, somewhere in the northern latitudes during Waterman Cycle. Herein lay the garden's principal charm and eccentricity: its ambience resurrected the old-time passage of seasons on the hibernating motherworld. If we had come again during the Ram, for example, we would have tasted spring.

There was no sensation of being indoors. Fir trees with a dusting of snow hid the airlock we had just passed; off-white clouds made a canopy overhead, and pale mist obscured the further distances. We were on a path strewn with weathered rocks and wet evergreen needles, winding through stands of oak and holly, maple and redwood, pine and spruce. The bare branches of the deciduous trees reminded me of old women's hands, gesturing with eloquent delicacy as the wind brushed by; the evergreens were stout and splendid, cloaked with snow and trimmed with dangling icicles, ranged like warriors in protective ranks. Even the dead flowerbeds knew a winter alchemy, glittering frost-white, as if earth-elementals had sown them with diamonds. Gheo's vermiform passageways seemed a universe apart.

Lachis swayed in a dance step, breathing deeply of the vegetable scents. "Thank you for this, Risha. It's good for me—just being here soothes my senses. Ancient poetry sings of the consolation of nature, but I think I've read more about trees and dirt than I've ever seen."

"And even this is mostly illusion," I said softly.

We passed a stream still flowing under a fragile covering of ice, and pitched a few rocks in for no good reason. "You know, I do get news of you occasionally, even in my hermitage," she said, with half a smile. "I've heard about your affair with the Retired Emperor Mudriye."

And she clearly wanted to hear more. I walked a little further before responding. "We're fond of each other, yes. I suppose I've needed companionship in all the desolation of the past cycle."

"Do you think anything will come of it?"

"What possibly could?" I kicked at some sodden leaves. "We can't marry; the most I can expect is a temporary *naslyn*-contract, for making a child, and so far Mudriye has mentioned nothing of the sort. I'm not sure I'd want to follow that path to Radiance anyhow."

"I understand. But the very fact that a Confessor has shown interest in you will raise your status, and possibly make you more attractive to more eligible men."

My laughter cut through the winter stillness. "Thank the ancestors you haven't changed, Lachis! Still trying to marry me off to a high-place husband!" She smiled and took my hand, and for a moment things were as they used to be.

But little by little, step by step, my guilt came back to torment me, as bitter as a memory of burning. In spite of Mudriye's rationalizations I felt tongue-tied before Lachis' smile, completely unable to share what brewed in my mind. My obsession with her husband's murderer seemed an enormous betrayal. I suppose she sensed my confusion, because she dropped my hand, along with the subject of marriage.

What she said next, however, sent a tingle down my spine.

"Have you heard the rumors about the Radiant Seren?" Her tone was perfectly matter-of-fact; I said I hadn't, in what I hoped was the same spirit. "We're still verifying our sources," she continued, "but it looks like he's found sanctuary among the Firin. He passed down the Lift into the wilderness of Veii, at least ten spells past."

"Could this bring war?" I asked cautiously.

"I doubt it." She twisted the folds of her purple cowl. "If it's true, there will be threats and spear-shaking. But since the Firin are past masters at the art of diplomacy they should find some way out. Gloy has done no more than lodge a formal complaint with Volshev; perhaps it can be resolved at the upcoming embassy."

"You know so much more about this than I do," I said, hoping to avoid further comment. True to form, Lachis went off on a short lecture concerning the Firin and their millennia-old experiment in Veii, casting me in the familiar role of pupil. As she spoke I watched a change come over her. Earlier, when we first entered the garden, her concentration had seemed diffuse, her composure vulnerable; now there was a tension about her, an air almost of implacability. Clearly she saw vengeance in the offing.

"We can't understand why they would shelter him," she said. "But I think once they realize the gravity of the matter they'll make amends. And there are few things I desire more than that man's death."

I mumbled assent and prayed for respite.

So far we had encountered no other ramblers on the garden path; Nan Solize admitted few guests. But now as we rounded a mossy bend there were two figures up ahead, gesturing over a withered planting. One was the Virgin Mother herself.

We stopped and would have turned back, respecting the lady's privacy, but she had seen and recognized us, and motioned us on. She was dressed in a fawn-colored cloak with matching wide-brimmed hat, tied under the chin with a length of lavender gauze. I guessed it was a period costume of some sort; Solize lived in a world of her own and was forever affecting antique modes. Her companion was the master gardener, whom she now dismissed.

We bowed formally. She grasped Lachis' hand, a very special mark of favor, and held her gaze with clear bovine eyes.

"So, Lachis. You quicken as I grind to a halt."

Lachis blushed fiercely. "Not quite yet, lady. I've only just found out myself. Starcycles will pass before I feel signs of life."

I hid my shock as well as I could. In the elliptical style of Radiants, Lachis was saying she was pregnant.

"It's to the good," Solize assured her, walking along arm in arm. "Something of Rhamant will live on, and you'll be comforted. I'll do whatever I can to make things easier."

"You're kind. It *is* hard for me, as you clearly see. The irony." She bit her lip.

"I've already borne my last child, you know." Solize sighed, smiling faintly. "My body is tiring. Seven heirs in twenty-six revolutions will have to be enough. Many before me have done less, and few have accomplished more."

We offered polite reassurance. She was revealing state secrets now; we were on our best behavior.

"Of course Volshev has known since Yarkost's delivery. But I waited till his Presentation before I shared the news. We've been looking for a successor for almost a full revolution: it's a delicate process, as you can well imagine. Few qualify, and of them few are likely to covet the honor. And of course we can't sound someone out till we're nine-tenths sure of her willingness."

I nodded silently. Bearing children at Volshev's command seemed an unenviable fate.

"Time runs out, you realize. We must begin thinking of Yarkost's successor before Gheo finishes another circuit of Sol."

Meanwhile we continued our own circuit of the winter garden, glimpsing foxes nosing among the leaves and surprising sparrows at their ablutions. I held my peace; even under the best of circumstances it wasn't easy making small talk with the Virgin Mother, and my mind was still full of Lachis' revelation. Eventually, however, the Nan turned her regal attention toward me.

"You've made quite a name for yourself this cycle, dear Risha. You've learned the style of Gheo remarkably fast for someone of your background." I winced behind my smile. "Since the Presentation your name has come up frequently in some of the best circles. In fact, I gather you've recently made a rather impressive liaison."

"I'm honored by the Lord Confessor's attentions," I said carefully. "I suppose he finds me amusing. From time to time, that is. He's guided me through some confusing spells; his learning and insight are prodigious."

"As they should be, coming as he does from such noble forebears." She cocked her head to one side. "The Heroic Amhran, I believe it was, and the Nan Lichinka. She was the scion of the d'Ithinn line and he was of the Tagtha. Or was it Saothru? Certainly House Vaur. But now was the Tagtha lineage Radiant in that period, or was it . . ."

I cleared my throat delicately. "I think Lord Mudriye has mentioned the Mionn line. Of House Khryasha. But I may well be mistaken."

She blinked. "Of course it was the Mionn. My memory isn't what it used to be. How clever of you to learn his pedigree."

"He does fascinate me," I said.

"Oh yes. You'll do well, I think, to stay with that kind of man. The quiet type. Impeccable breeding, perfect deportment, never a word or a thought out of place."

So unlike me, I thought bitterly, though my face was a mask. The Nan certainly knew how to put upstarts in their place.

Conversation lagged after that. Lachis and I were well acquainted with the lady's signals; we pleaded fatigue, bowed low, and made for the nearest exit. A bit unwillingly we left the garden behind, to dream its dreams of wind and frost and fog.

I accompanied her as far as Ironstone Plaza. "Please don't let us be strangers," I said. "With this baby coming I'd like to see you as much as possible. In spite of everything I'm happy for you, Lachis."

Her smile was the merest twitch of the lips. "I can see how I hurt you, keeping it secret. I'm sorry; it's just that the whole idea pains me. I never would have said anything if Nan Solize hadn't guessed."

"Nan Solize, or Volshev?"

"Both of them, I suppose. Of course I had to register the conception, so it entered Volshev's archives." She put her hand in mine and looked past me, past the hurrying courtiers, past the plaza's irregular colonnade. "It was so bizarre, so shocking. A last gift from the dead. Apparently Rhamant wanted to surprise me. He resumed fertility in celebration of his new status, but he never had a chance to tell me about it. At least I know he wanted this child. I'm not sure I do."

"Of course you do," I said.

She smiled, a little more bravely. "Yes. You're right. You'll hear from me soon, Risha."

"Till then."

We kissed like sisters, but a whole cycle passed before we met again.

When the Games finally arrived they were everything an aficionado could desire. Volshev approved a record number of fatal contests: three hundred and sixty-five, one for every spell in the revolution. The Gloy-Khryasha rivalry alone accounted for over sixty of that total. Many new challenges had been recorded since Rhamant's death, and most of them were allowed. The Red Court earned its name a thousand times over during those fifteen spells.

Of Khryasha's finest, some sixty-three would never lift sword again. Rarely had this House fared so poorly. Gloy, however, emerged the undisputed champion: she lost no more than thirty warriors and scored extremely well in her points-only matches. Since Eryr of Gloy was arbiter there was some talk of partiality, but no one ventured a formal protest.

As a woman I was denied access to the Red Court for the duration of the Games. Nevertheless they were broadcast, so I saw as much of them as I wanted—which was very little. Of the Khryashan retainers who had insulted me, that spell in the landing bay, only two survived. Watching the others die cured me of whatever blood-lust I might have felt.

Still, I do have a sense of history, so I joined the crowd thronging the Court of Victory on the last spell of the Games, when Volshev gave each Hypaethron its accounting. All the surviving contestants who could still stand upright waited in their finest regalia, listening as Volshev intoned his speech from the lofty Window.

Everything progressed smoothly for a quarter-watch. Then, just as the Radiant Sorich of Khryasha stepped forward with her handful of victors, the age-old decorum was disturbed by a ragged shout.

"Where is Seren?" cried several voices. "Where is the killer? Who harbors our lord's assassin?"

Sorich stood impassively, stiff as a blade. Volshev's benign countenance never wavered.

"Where is the killer? Give us Seren the murderer!" More voices took up the cry.

The new Spear acted quickly and correctly. His men immediately went through the crowd with clubs and halberds, placing any who still shouted under arrest. In this way the disturbance was quelled and the ceremony continued.

Nevertheless, no one who heard that cry would soon forget it, and the question was repeated, more quietly, in the spells to come. Where was Seren?

CHAPTER FOUR

Early on, Mudriye had given me the codewords necessary to call up his own, personally annotated edition of the Canon. Soon I was spending whole watches at a stretch puzzling over its subtleties and contradictions, its poetry and invective. I could easily see how such precepts had led a small group of people, completely isolated from the rest of the human race, to evolve the rigid institutions of my own society. Less clear to me was whether these strictures had actually uplifted and purified us, as our Radiants like to claim, or merely kept us frozen in a bizarre mimicry of the past.

One forespell, when I was in the midst of a long discourse on the Wars of Restoration, my screen flashed me an urgent notice:

Firin embassy arriving, Victory Court.

I knew the proceedings would never be broadcast; for some obscure reason Volshev forbade any holographic reproduction of these visitors from the inner orbits. I had no choice but to attend in person. Before I left I keyed in the reference *Firin* and requested Mudriye's interpretation. The screen replied:

> *They were born, not of blood, nor of the will of the flesh, nor of the will of man, but of Mind itself.*

For *Mind* my confessor had glossed, *God, or Meqmat?* Unfortunately I had no time to delve into these depths; I saved the exercise for some future spell, and hurried over to the Court of Victory.

Normally I favored the highest balconies, as was my rank's privilege, but since I hadn't dressed for the occasion I was glad for once to mingle with the Pures in the lower circles. From this unaccustomed perspective the Court's grandeur was even more overwhelming.

Pillared galleries rose in a continuous spiral from mirrored floor to star-scattered dome, a distance of fifty or sixty meters. Far above me the gaudy silks of the Radiants made a brave show; in the middle regions a ring of trophies recalled the heroic deeds of our ancestors. There were a hundred in all, a hundred bits of scrap metal—all that remained of the Kinetics, those robot warriors who had been Meqmat's principal weapon against the first Revenants.

I found a strange beauty in their random contortions. There was a kind of pathos in the melted tangle of humanoid limbs, in the ruin of grappling arms and laser-eyed faces. But this very combination of human shape and inhuman power had been an abomination to the bearers of the Canon, and such gaunt wreckage was testimony to our ancestors' valor and Meqmat's failure.

My timing was perfect. As I elbowed my way to the balcony's edge the Firin were just entering through the enormous valves at the lowest level. They stepped to the center of the mirrored court, eyes averted from the spiraling ranks of trophies, hands folded in an attitude suggesting prayer. They looked neither to the right nor to the left, neither up nor down; they showed neither curiosity nor self-consciousness before the thousands who had come gawking. As far as I could tell, they were in deep meditation: their inward focus never wavered.

Tall, strongly built, fairer even than a Revenant, their lineaments were noble enough to rouse an emperor's jealousy. They wore loose robes that obscured the finer details of their anatomy, leaving only their faces bare, but these alone were sufficient marvel. Power and wisdom radiated like visible light from wide brows and clear eyes, blue as the sky in an Ethrin autumn. Grace was there, too, and mercy—though how such a simple juxtaposition of nose and eye and chin can convey such abstracts is beyond me. Nevertheless it did.

Only one thing made them seem outlandish. Their hair, instead of being the ordinary brown or black of every human I had yet seen, was golden. It fell in curls as far as the nape of the neck, and crowned them with an alien glory.

There were three of them. The Emperor Vremeni announced their names from his accustomed perch: Chwefro came first, followed by Gorffenau and Tachweth. The more I studied them the more they fascinated me; then with a start I realized that I had no idea who among them was male and who female, and that it had taken me this long to be aware of my ignorance. They registered simply as beautiful and powerful beings.

Instead of bringing a retinue of their own they had requisitioned a score or more of Volshev's servants, who surrounded them in a hollow square, displaying the goods they had carried away from Veii. For this was the arrangement the Firin had made with the Hypaethra, some two millennia earlier: they could retain dominion over Veii, the second planet, richest world of the Matterfield, only as long as they furnished Gheo with regular tribute. They made stately obeisance now amid bolts of dyed silk, mounds of pearls and diamonds, stacks of rare wood, and sparkling vials of drugs and perfumes. This was only a small part of what they offered, chosen for maximum visual impact; the rest waited at the Shaft for Volshev's redistribution.

The Child Emperor spoke, Eryr of Gloy spoke, and Volshev appeared at his window. Chwefro replied briefly in ringing epicene tones and the pageantry concluded. I left my place on the balcony with every intention of returning home to study the Canon, but when I had gone as far as the lift a voice out of nowhere whispered in my ear.

It called my name; it was eerily familiar. I turned to see Volshev's disembodied face floating at my shoulder.

"Don't cry out," he said. "I bring no evil tidings. I merely invite you to attend my private audience with the Firin emissaries. Your present attire will do; come at once." Before he vanished he named an address deep within the Palace, and provided me with the proper codes for immediate transportation.

In spite of my priority I was the last to arrive. I stepped into the ornate salon—a fantasy of agate, mother-of-pearl, and fuchsia tulle—as quietly as possible. Most of the company was familiar to me. As I entered, Chwefro the Firin glanced in my direction, blue eyes glittering like stars, and resumed the discourse I had interrupted.

"These are serious charges, my lord Despot. We can only deny them. What you have just said regarding Seren of Khryasha comes as a great surprise. Certainly we had heard of the former Spear of Gheo's untimely death, but there was no reference in any of your broadcasts to his assassin's identity. Why then would we suspect Seren? He formally applied for leave to visit Veii's surface half a revolution ago, long before Rhamant's murder. His petition was witnessed by various members of his own House; clearly it was no secret. After some indecision we granted his request. Therefore when he arrived in New Venery two cycles past he was immediately admitted to the Lift, and so conveyed downworld. He must now be at liberty somewhere in the planetary wilderness."

Volshev sat enthroned, biding his silence. Eryr of Gloy took up the cross-examination. "What reasons did Seren give for wishing to travel in Veii? Surely he must have told you something."

"Simple curiosity." Chwefro replied. "That, and a desire for adventure. He wanted to do something no Radiant had done before." This seemed plausible; Seren was always trying to spread his name around, and he would have applied to the Firin immediately after his failure to attain the rank of Spear.

"Very well then," said Eryr. "Knowing what you know now, you must be disposed to grant us recompense."

Chwefro smiled faintly. "In theory, yes. But it is not our practice to interfere directly in human affairs. We aren't prepared, for example, to send an expedition after Seren and return him to Revenant justice."

That beautiful voice added strange overtones to the words *human* and *Revenant:* not scorn, precisely, but not reverence either.

"Then what *are* you prepared to do?" Eryr insisted. Every eye in the room was fixed on Chwefro now—except mine, for I watched the watchers. Lachis sat among the Radiants of her House in a predatory stillness; Volshev's image betrayed nothing at all.

"We Firin would never obstruct your laws." Chwefro bowed toward the Despot's ivory throne. "You sentenced Seren to an outcast's life. Now you discover that he has found sanctuary, of a sort, in our own realm. And by the old treaties we are bound to serve you. Therefore we will invite someone of your choosing—and note well how I say some *one*—to seek out this criminal, and execute whatever punishment you deem fitting. More we will not do. Veii is a world apart from the

Hypaethra; it is our world, one we have long nurtured. We will not permit it to become a battleground for Revenant honor. You have the rest of the Matterfield for that."

Silence fell; I wondered if war would be next. But Volshev's response came gently.

"So be it. Now I am faced with a delicate choice. Who will follow Seren?"

The room exploded with suggestions and volunteers. There were many young warriors on hand, high-status vassals of the leading Hypaethra, all clamoring for the honor.

Eryr brought the assembly to order. "Gloy is the offended party. I submit that our candidate should be of Rhamant's own House." Several voices agreed, at high volume.

"My feeling is precisely the opposite," said Volshev. "Our aim is justice, not revenge. I disqualify any vassal of Gloy."

Lachis spoke now, her voice a miracle of control. "Except for the life I carry inside I would beg you to change your mind, my lord Despot, because I myself yearn to execute your justice. But I will submit to your logic, if you will listen to mine."

"Speak then."

"You favor a disinterested party. Why not send out some warrior of Khryasha?"

This occasioned more noise, because—as Lachis knew very well—there was no one of that House anywhere in Gheo. After the incident on the Games' closing spell Sorich had departed with all her train.

"Your suggestion is unfeasible." Volshev made an elaborate show of patience. "Have you anything more to recommend?"

"Only that your choice be someone equally unlikely, someone Seren would never suspect." As she bowed and returned to her seat our eyes met across the room. Hers were steady; mine glanced down in confusion.

The debate continued, however, with little regard for Lachis' idea. Candidates were named and shouted down. Tension mounted, in the gathering at large and in me. I had the irrational feeling that once more Lachis had challenged me. She suggested that our avenger be as unlikely as possible: if not herself then someone of Seren's own family, and if not a Khryashan then—

"My lord Despot!" The voice, incredibly enough, was mine. "Let me be your instrument!"

Volshev's pale apparition seemed to freeze, just like a farscan image when the stop-action feature is activated. I imagined the real man some-where in careful deliberation, so engrossed that for once he neglected his Sending. Around me my more tangible companions were in a simi-lar state, though I felt this more than saw it; my attention remained with Volshev.

"You may go now," he said presently. "All of you except Risha Skhorb. And Chwefro: wait in the antechamber, please. I'll summon you when I need you again."

I sat still as the crowd shuffled out, whispering now where earlier they had been shouting. Perhaps they stared at me; I kept my eyes on my feet and took no notice. I was too busy trying to stay calm. Only the extreme dryness in my throat betrayed me to myself.

When they had all gone Volshev asked, "Did Mudriye put you up to this?"

I couldn't utter a sound.

"Answer me, Risha."

"Mudriye has no idea I'm here, no idea that this meeting has even occurred."

"Don't underestimate him. I don't."

If Volshev wanted to unnerve me he was having excellent success. "It's true that I confide many intimate matters with Lord Mudriye," I said, as innocently as I could. "In fact we've discussed Seren's case several times. But it never occurred to me until this very watch that I might volunteer myself for a desperate mission in Veii. I doubt Mudriye has considered it either."

"You know you've been very foolish."

"If you say so, I suppose I have."

He smiled, an odd smile that had no teeth or blood or flesh in it: for of course it was the merest aberration of light.

"You speak sedition, Risha Skhorb, freely and often, you and your highborn lover. How can you imagine I don't hear you? The idea of a 'safe room' in Gheo is sheer fantasy! But I find Mudriye and his fixa-tions extremely useful. By allowing him and his companion of the mo-ment to believe they are secure, I elicit their deepest secrets. Rest as-sured that Mudriye's hideaway is under constant surveillance."

My intestines filled with ice; somehow I spoke. "Is it a crime, then, to speculate on your true nature?"

"It is if I say so."

I shrugged; it no longer mattered what I said or did. "Why did you keep watch on me after Rhamant's murder?"

"For the reasons Mudriye guessed. I wasn't sure what Seren had told you and I wanted to find out, preferably without confronting you. You satisfied my curiosity long ago."

"In that case you know how innocuous I am."

"I'm not so sure. You have spirit and ambition. You connect all too easily with high-status nonconformists. Mudriye, I've learned how to contain; I'm still deciding about you."

"Grant my wish, then. Send me off to Veii. I'll probably die there."

"And if you don't?"

I went on my knees before his Sending. "All my dreams have been in vain, my lord Despot. As a child I longed for Gheo; but once here I realized I'd have to marry some hollow-headed lunk in order to stay. I've grown too proud for that. If I marry it must be for love—but love first requires trust, and who can trust anyone in this nest of schemers? It's true, I've been confused, and when my confusion was at its darkest I met Seren. For some mad reason he infatuated me. I dared hope that he might care for me, and—I don't know—somehow make everything better. Yes, I am a fool. But not such a fool that I can't serve you now. Let me go: my life here is empty. I have experience of worlds, I know a few things about self-defense, and best of all I hate Seren. Almost as much as I desire him. If you grant me this I'll be your creature forever, a better tool than Mudriye ever was."

My vision blurred. I hid my face in my hands. When I looked up again I saw Chwefro's perfect face smiling down at me—perhaps in mockery, perhaps in sympathy. The Firin helped me stand with one powerful arm, saying, "Take this one. She'll do well in Veii."

Volshev nodded. "She has the look of a native, doesn't she? Full-figured, not tall, thick wavy hair. All the features she tries to hide here in Gheo."

"She's even rather swarthy," Chwefro said, with approval. "We'll darken her, of course."

I was deeply humiliated; they spoke as if I were a cow or a dog, a mindless dweller in dirt. But it did seem that I'd have my way.

Volshev addressed me again. "Lachis' suggestion seems best. I don't need a disinterested party—merely an unlikely one. You fit the description better than any Revenant I know of. And I think your interest in Seren will serve us well."

I bowed. "Thank you, Lord Volshev."

"What I want you to do will take a long time doing. First you must get to know Veii, so that you can move around without attracting notice. Chwefro will advise you there. While you acclimate you must collect any information you can regarding Seren; that may be the longest and most difficult part. It seems reasonable, however, that the former Heir of Khryasha would choose some conspicuous station in the Veiian society, rather than take to the wilderness like a hermit. Once you have found him you must accomplish his death. Nothing less will suit me. If you would ever return to the Hypaethra you must bring me some sign that Seren no longer lives."

I expressed my understanding and consent. "How will I travel to Veii, then?"

"Chwefro will convey you in the Firin craft." Volshev turned to the emissary. "When do you plan to go?"

"By the close of latterspell, my lord Despot. We cannot linger in Gheo."

This was dauntingly soon. How would I put my affairs in order, how would I find time to say my goodbyes? My thoughts flew over all the things I had to say to Lachis and Mudriye.

I bowed once more. "Do I have your permission, Lord Volshev, to go and prepare for my departure?"

"You do not. You will remain in custody until you leave, speaking to no one except myself and Chwefro." He softened this a little by adding, "As of today your name will be inscribed in the list of Radiants. If you return successfully, I will grant you a permanent rank at court."

I made the correct response and stood there wondering. "If I am successful," I asked, "how *will* I return?"

"I'll arrange that, Risha," Chwefro replied. "From now on you're in my hands."

Two watches later I was climbing to the Palace's private dock.

Voyages in free space were nothing new to me, and the Firin ship held no surprises. It was a typical insystem model, a good-sized heliogyro called *Burden of Truth*. When set, its sails stretched over an area of eighty square kilometers; once under way they spun like titanic pinwheels, pulling the tiny passenger and cargo modules along on monomolecular stays. There was no provision for artificial gravity, but after a watch or two I adjusted, as usual, and spent the remaining sixty-odd spells of the journey in tolerable comfort. Fortunately the sun was in a quiet season; we had clear sailing all the way.

I saw little of Gorffenau and Tachweth. Chwefro, however, was my constant companion, tutoring me in the languages and folkways of Veii.

I was a willing pupil. With its intricate societies and convoluted systems of belief, the second planet completely fascinated me—much the way Ethri had, so many revolutions before. Even such chores as reciting conjugations and memorizing long lists of particles were no great burden; the very sounds of the Veiian languages were like music.

Between lessons we discussed more general topics. My favorite was the history of the Reconquest, that period two millennia ago when my ancestors returned from their wanderings among the barren stars. They found the worlds of Sol changed beyond recognition—and chief among those changes was the birth of Meqmat.

"Since Meqmat's defeat," I asked one spell, "is the Matterfield a better place?"

Firin never laughed; otherwise I'm sure Chwefro would have roared. As it was, only a sardonic twitch of the lips rewarded my naiveté.

"Since you ask a Firin you'll get a Firin answer. The crowning achievement of the human race, as we see it, was the creation of Meqmat. He was no monstrous entity: he was simply an artificial intelligence, devised by your remote ancestors to assume the direction of material civilization. He was a coordinator only, a servant—but a servant on such a scale as humanity had never seen. He controlled all the means of production. He built solar power stations, beaming unlimited energy throughout the Matterfield; he mined the asteroids and the outer planets; he directed insystem shipping, routing raw materials, finished goods, and passengers from world to world; he oversaw agriculture, both on Ethri and in free space; he kept records of the totality of human science, literature, and art; and he continually maintained and extended himself. By any human definition he was alive. He moved and grew, he learned and reproduced, and he originated unique ideas."

"But my people were horrified when they returned from their wanderings among the stars and saw what Ethri had become."

Chwefro shrugged. "They were a small-minded, inbred group. They preserved archaic values."

"Then you can justify slavery and cannibalism? Incest, and even darker perversions?"

"Listen long enough, Risha, and I'll justify anything you want. We Firin have a well-earned reputation for sophistry. As for cannibalism, the human race has traditionally resisted all efforts to limit population. At the height of the Interglacial there were thirty billion of you warming your hands around the sun. Particularly on Ethri there were frequent food shortages, in spite of Meqmat's efforts. Supplementing diet with human flesh was only logical—and ethical, if you follow my reasoning. A few died so that the rest could live."

"How did the victims feel about that?"

"How do your warriors feel when they die in the Red Court?"

"They're proud to serve the honor of their Houses."

"And then they're popped into the recycler, aren't they?"

Instead of answering I adopted Chwefro's own tactic. "What about slavery?"

"Slavery is as old as civilization. People have always traded liberty for life; there has always been an underclass. Only the brutality of the masters has varied."

I realized I'd never win this argument, but then I didn't mind losing. "Since we've come this far, why not sing the praises of incest as well?"

Chwefro made another cheerful grimace. "All human values are relative. You happen to come from an unusually repressive society; when your ancestors saw Ethri's polymorphism they were horrified, and interpreted anything outside a very narrow range of behavior as depravity. I'm sure incest was no commoner in the Interglacial than it is now."

I chewed my thumb and squinted sidewise. "You won't convert me, but I doubt you'll ever bore me either." Chwefro was duly flattered.

We talked then of the old wars, of the Kinetic drones and the Revenant suicide ships. My ancestors were highly accomplished in battle, if not in sophistry, and once they had agreed on Meqmat's essential evil they set out to destroy him. Dismantling a system-wide organism involved perhaps ten revolutions of hard fighting. Meqmat's psychological evolution had neatly skirted paranoia, so none of his defenses were conceived until after the first attack. By then it was too late. Once the infrastructure failed, the Matterfield's thirty billion followed; human population dropped to industrial levels.

"You Revenants thought that Meqmat equalled decadence," said Chwefro. "But I say you live in decadence now. You're like maggots infesting a dismembered corpse—because do you realize that all your proud Hypaethra are merely fragments of ancient factories and power plants, shards of Meqmat himself? Skhorb was an ore-processing module, Gheo was an archive, Vaur a waste-converter. Your dwellings under heaven are the lowliest residue of the past."

Chwefro's eyes glittered like sapphires; I felt humbled and foolish. "It can't be true."

"Oh, but it is. I can show you." Chwefro darted past me and fluttered fingers over the keys of a nearby console, summoning up scene after scene of the pre-Conquest Matterfield. I saw Ethri as I had never imagined her, a fecund blue-white globe attended by hundreds of glittering habitats, like Shadan enthroned among the Rings. I saw a Hypaethron composed of twelve separate modules, each one multifaceted and brilliantly colored, all joined together like jewels in a diadem. One contained a jungle, complete with elephants and tigers and sandstone palaces; another was entirely aquatic, a bluegreen waterworld of coral and seaweed and fish. Another scene depicted the happy citizens of this utopia: cinnamon-skinned men and women who lounged in a lofty marble hall, as Kinetic servants glided among them bearing trays heaped high with delicacies.

"This is only a small part of what your ancestors destroyed," said Chwefro. "I can show you Ethrin cities nine kilometers high, each one containing more people than all your Hypaethra put together. I can show you the fabulous mines of Aida, the thruster factories orbiting Marithi, the—"

"Enough, enough. I get the point." My brows knitted. "So my people are scavengers, scrabblers among the ruins, garbage-dwellers, eaters of carrion and filth, criminals who have received their just deserts—"

"Hardly that, Risha," interrupted Chwefro. "But everything else was right."

Chwefro was smiling again; I was not. It seemed that history was a more complicated subject than I imagined.

Tref had begun my education, Lachis and Mudriye had furthered it, but Chwefro brought it to consummation. Sailing between worlds I felt liberated from the forces that had made me long for Radiance, and with the Firin to guide me I began to see the whole Matterfield with new eyes. Not Chwefro's eyes; the Firin was a better teacher than that. No, I held fast to my waywardness and my pride, though even those qualities changed in time. It was hardly an easy process.

The disparate elements of my mind wrestled constantly, surfacing most vehemently while I slept. I floated in my web, tangled in cross-woven fibers, dreaming preternaturally vivid dreams. Sometimes all dialogue was in Sofo, all scenery in the Veiian mode. Once I walked by the edge of a white sea with a bloated white sun hanging overhead. A huge python glided up to me and reared its wedge-shaped head, saying, "Spare my life and I'll grant you any wish you desire." I replied, "Give me Seren," and the python said, "You already have him." And I looked and there by my side was a male child with black skin, no taller than my elbow; I realized he was Seren, and held him to my breast. Then studying our two bodies together, I saw that mine was growing scales, that I was becoming a python myself. I entwined the black boy in my coils and licked his ears with my slender tongue, saying, "Hear how wise I grow." But the boy answered, "Such wisdom earns you enemies. Study folly instead." And I shrank, shrank down to the size of a worm, and a large pallid woman came along and would have crushed me, except that I cried, "Spare my life and I will cure you of desire." And the woman held me to her breast.

Another dream found me again with Seren, this time in his usual form. We sat in a spice-scented garden and talked of the past. "I never killed Rhamant," he said. "It was Lachis."

"But I saw you do it," I insisted.

"You're right. But you'll forgive me."

"Yes, I will." And we walked hand in hand, joining a huge crowd of people that grew huger every minute. Naked sweaty bodies hemmed us in so closely that we could scarcely move; coarse angry voices shouted so loudly that we could scarcely speak or listen. We were herded along in one monstrous horde, thirty billion strong. Up ahead I saw polished blades slicing down in great sweeping curves, grinding us up, grinding us down. In the white sky above there were giants feeding, lips and fingers all dripping blood.

I woke from that one with a pounding heart, and missed Seren.

Chwefro expressed a keen interest in all my dreams, but on hearing them only nodded clinically and said, "Oh really," without offering either interpretation or solace. This reserve left a gulf between us; I learned to regard the Firin as an ally, not a friend.

Then one spell as I roused from vision-tossed sleep my preceptor glided in, unannounced, and keyed the farscan. "We're just rounding the limb, Risha. I thought you might enjoy the view."

A long crescent of pale rose filled the farscan tank: Veii, second planet of Sol, second home for world-bound humanity. Its beauty compelled me, but seeing it loom so near shook my courage.

"Am I black enough?" I asked dubiously.

Perfect lips mimicked a smile. "Let me see and I'll tell you."

I slipped out of my shift and floated naked. Chwefro examined me closely, paying special attention to the area under my breasts and between my buttocks. Before anyone but a Firin I would have felt profoundly embarrassed.

"You're doing very well," Chwefro said. "The mottling and patchiness have blended nicely; you're a uniform ebony now. You won't need another injection till we dock in Venery, and after that I think you can get by with an oral dosage."

Switching the farscan to *reflect*, I took a look for myself. A stranger gazed back. Regular injections of a synthesized peptide hormone had induced the proliferation of melanocytes and the deposition of melanin throughout my skin; I was richly black from head to toe, ready to weather Veii's brutal daylight. As I posed I wondered if a new inner self would emerge to match this dramatic exterior.

"Black is the best color for worldlings," I said.

"And white?"

"For Revenants, and teeth."

In point of fact the original starship crews had included members of every human subgroup, but since the paler ones predominated, and since all the old starfarers had carefully avoided exposure to ultraviolet radiation, they had eventually homogenized into the present era's pallor.

"Chwefro," I asked suddenly, "why don't you ever show me what's under your clothes?" It was a struggle to keep myself from smirking.

"What purpose would that serve?" the Firin countered mildly.

"It would allay my curiosity, at the very least."

"I suppose it makes no difference in the grand design." With that Chwefro gracefully disrobed. I saw a long expanse of pale silken flesh, well endowed with subcutaneous fat that smoothed out the contours of the muscles beneath. Pectorals curved chastely, innocent of nipple or areola; shoulders and hips swelled to equal breadth. At the armpits and the base of the belly (unblemished by anything so ignoble as a navel) sprouted golden frizz. I knew that the Firin ate and drank, but whatever plumbing they used was well hidden in that bright tangle.

"Any surprises?"

"No, not really. You're as beautiful as I expected."

"Meqmat designed us well."

I considered that remark as my preceptor dressed. "How are you born?"

"From a vat, of course."

"Do you experience sexual desire?"

"What a silly question! Use your head, Risha."

"Sometimes you seem so human. I can't tell."

"We were human enough to escape your ancestors' purges. None of Meqmat's other servants were spared."

I nodded. "I always used to admire their hulks when I visited the Victory Court. But what was your function, before the wars?"

"We were Meqmat's interface with human society. The Ethrins felt more comfortable dealing with flesh-and-blood entities."

"And now?"

I sensed a slight hesitation. "Now we're simply Veii's caretakers."

I abandoned my cross-examination and launched into breakfast. To my surprise Chwefro lingered, even taking a few bites of spiced tuber. We ate with our fingers in the Veiian manner.

"So now that I look the part," I said between mouthfuls, "how long before I sound it?"

"Your accent is good, especially in Sofo. Toso and Ladan will take more work. But since you'll visit Woro first, I see no real problem. Wherever you go you can pose as a foreigner; that should cover any blunders you make."

"You seem to know Veii and its languages as well as any native."

Chwefro thought for a moment. "Only from the outside. With luck you'll soon surpass me."

"Then I'll pray for luck! Which mystery should I address—Koyo?"

"In your case I think Ijeji is more appropriate."

This was the river goddess, who also governed the mystery of love and desire. Once more I did a mental review of the deities. Woro honored twenty-one major gods, Traore twelve, Lozi more than thirty. I tried not to think of them as superstitions. To the downworlders they were as real as Volshev was to me.

"How much like Ethri is this world of Veii? Old Ethri, I mean, before the ice came."

"Not much at all. Apart from the obvious differences, such as the sun cycle, Veii is an infinitely poorer environment than your homeworld ever was—even in the grip of the ice. Of course there are uranium deposits, there are veins of gold and mudflats full of diamonds, but Veii originally lacked all the prerequisites of life. Meqmat labored one thousand revolutions just to create oceans of liquid water, and five hundred more for a breathable atmosphere. To accomplish even that much, nickel-iron rocks had to be diverted from the asteroid belt, and frozen hydrogen mined out of Aida. Mass drivers sent them all hurtling down through the primordial gases. This was a hellish place then; Meqmat would have turned it into paradise, if the wars hadn't intervened. In Veii, therefore, you see a world half-born. Once Meqmat died the process of transformation ceased; we Firin have only preserved what the master created."

"That explains the vast deserts and the barren seas, then. But as for the people and their societies: don't they resemble Ethri's ancient inhabitants?"

"Yes, in many ways, though they do have a distinctive character of their own. Meqmat intended them to recapitulate humanity's long history."

"Meqmat sounds like a god."

Chwefro's eyes flashed. "Very like a god."

CHAPTER FIVE

My body regained its weight in the spinning terminus of Old Venery: a shock that left me prostrate for ten spells. Only when I was sufficiently recovered did we undertake the long descent to the surface, in free fall again.

Chwefro and I rode down alone. Our Lift-carriage was actually a well appointed salon, with transparent walls that allowed visibility in all directions. Overhead I could make out several hundred bulging sacks of grain, produce of the Firin's orbital plantations, while beneath us were ingots of meteoric iron stacked row on row. Here was tangible evidence of the trade linking the Firin with their clients; in return the Veiian states sent up textiles, gemstones, radioactives, and various luxury goods, which the Firin would later offer in tribute to Volshev.

Our journey carried us from airless space to a turbulent cloud kingdom. My stomach insisted on misbehaving, for any number of reasons I could think of. "Will it help if I opaque the walls?" Chwefro asked.

"No, I'm afraid that would be worse." And I suffered bravely all the way down.

New Venery was a warehouse town, high on the slopes of Mount Uwe, a four-kilometer peak straddling the equator. It occupied the northern edge of an area the ancients knew as Ovda Regio. We alighted at midmorning of a day lasting 121 Hypaethral spells.

Longshoremen were already busy unloading cargo from the lower levels of our transport. I stepped into a huge roofed area, boiling with the chaos of bodies and bales, and felt the heat strike me like a blow. The shock of gravity made me feel as if I were wobbling on stilts. Yes: here was a new world.

Slowly the men of Woro realized that a pale Firin was among them. They paused, staring. My own presence was duly registered, and some of them shouted a phrase I didn't catch. Making a loose circle around the pair of us they fell on their faces in profound obeisance.

"The air of Veii smells sweet after so long an absence," said Chwefro. "Please rise." As they obeyed, my preceptor guided me through the crowd toward a high arched doorway. Halfway there we acquired escorts: tall men in red kilts, wearing wide-billed wooden headgear and carrying iron spears and ornate matchlocks. They focused their attention on me.

"What are you?" demanded one. His face was deeply scarred and his tone was harsh.

"This woman is under my protection," Chwefro replied.

"Lord, there is war in the north." The soldier tugged respectfully at his helmet. "Ilesha has ordered us to monitor this place, and be especially mindful if such as she arrive."

"For what reason?" the Firin asked quietly.

"For this reason. Ilesha wants no offworlders in Veii, and this woman, for all her proper coloring, is certainly an offworlder."

"Whatever she is, she is my friend and companion. Now let us pass." Chwefro remained as calm and amiable as ever; I did not.

"Lord, Ilesha gave us very particular instructions. This woman is our prisoner. It must be so."

Chwefro's eyebrows lifted. "Must it? Then one of you will immediately convey me to your commander." And without a word to me, my "friend and companion" strode off, flanked by two of the soldiers.

The others turned to me, brandishing their weapons and frowning theatrically. I was prodded into following them outside.

Now it was glare that assaulted me, that and a whirling sense of vertigo. An hallucinatory sun hovered in the west, huge and white and blinding, while beyond the rude structures of New Venery the ground fell off into empty air. Involuntarily I glanced down and felt my throat close. I had experience of worlds, yes, but I was clearly out of practice.

The men of Woro enjoyed my dismay. "Look, woman," they said, "Veii is not for you. We're going to send you back where you came from."

In the meantime they dragged me to a narrow excavation covered with pieces of hide. Removing these they had me stand by the edge; then, laughing uproariously, they jabbed at me with spears till I fell in. I dropped about four meters into a pile of sand. Sprawled there in rage, I called down every Sofo curse I could remember, but the soldiers merely replaced the hides and left me fuming in the dark.

Anger subsided into boredom. Certainly Chwefro would spring me sooner or later; I had only to wait. Meanwhile I conjugated verbs, recited genealogies, and analyzed every detail of my current misfortune. Why were the Veiians suddenly so prickly about offworld visitors? Seren had to be involved.

After what seemed like a watch or more, the hides drew back and two pots came down on a wire. One contained water and the other stew; I ate and drank. Later I had no choice but to do my business in a corner of the pit. The sand came in handy.

With digestion's uncertain progress I began worrying. Those soldiers had offered Chwefro great respect—how then could they continue to resist, if the Firin demanded my release? Was I betrayed?

Distant gongs sounded. I felt miserable. Finally I slept, and dreamed evil dreams.

When I woke to the same dark silence my suspicions hardened into certainties. Chwefro was a liar, a traitor, a villain. Watches dragged by in despair; more gongs rang, more food descended. I wept and cursed. Eventually I dozed.

Voices and blinding light shocked me awake. A heavy knotted rope came down and a man shouted, "Take hold!" I did, and was pulled up into the dazzling world again.

As my eyes adjusted I realized that I was surrounded by the same unfriendly warriors who had first molested me. Were they releasing me, or was I about to be put to death? Then I saw a bright figure among the dark.

"I hope you didn't suffer too intensely." Chwefro's face held its usual bland smile. "Come along and we'll be rid of this place."

Without a word I followed the Firin, a bit unsteadily, into a long, low shed. It was a railway station; a car stood waiting. Several of the red-kilted soldiers milled around, watching us closely but doing nothing. We climbed into the car and began the last leg of our journey to Woro.

• • •

From Mount Uwe to the Garengazi was one long desolation of red sand and black rock. According to Chwefro our passage lasted two spells; the Firin have an inbred time sense, as accurate as any cesium clock. Certainly I slept twice and ate several times, though as far as I knew my companion did neither. All the while the monstrous white sun never budged from its resting place over the western horizon.

Our carriage was surprisingly comfortable, even boasting an air-cooling unit. "Enjoy it while you can," Chwefro advised.

By now we had little left to talk about. My experience in the pit had done lasting damage to my faith in Chwefro, though the Firin swore that my suspicions were unfounded. I reserved judgment.

On the third spell we saw the sea, a stretch of waves and foam far bluer than any water I'd seen in Ethri, where the oceans are grim and chill. A broad causeway connected the equatorial landmass, Afaroti, with the island of Woro; we made the crossing in less than a watch.

"This is more sophisticated engineering than I would have expected," I remarked, as we skimmed through curtains of spray. "Is there anything else on Vcii to rival it?"

"No, and we're lucky it's survived for so long. Kinetics built this system at the dawn of colonization; I can't count how many severe earthquakes it's weathered since then. Of course it ends on Woro's southern coast—the extension that would have connected it with Trokomari was never finished. If the existing line is ever damaged, the Lift will be completely cut off. In that case I think the Hypaethra would suffer even more than Veii."

"Are we so dependent on the quinquennial tribute?" I asked, in some surprise.

"Far more than anyone but Volshev and the Firin realize."

Our terminus was a modest settlement called Liriparo, where the ships in the harbor outnumbered the houses on the shore. Such craft as we saw here were familiar only from dataspools. They had broad towering hulls, elaborate figureheads and sternpieces, and several masts, each supporting half a dozen sails. As far as I knew they traveled with the force of the world's wind, in much the same way that a lightsail courses on the wind from the sun.

As before, the appearance of a Firin roused general enthusiasm. Woros of all ages turned out to offer their respects, resplendent in brilliantly printed kilts and gaudy togas that flapped and billowed in the salt breeze. Both sexes were magnificent, but I reserved my attention for the women—noting the way they draped their robes, knotted their headcloths, and graduated the shapes and sizes of their multitudinous earrings. I was delighted by such flamboyance, such exuberantly overstated notions of style; even more impressive was the iconic dignity with which they spoke and gestured, the full-bodied, natural grace with which they moved from group to group exchanging throaty greetings. I must hold my neck as proudly as that matriarch in yellow, I must plant my feet as lightly as that beauty with crystal anklets, I must lower my eyelashes as demurely as that child with new front teeth. Veii was my teacher now.

With a minimum of ceremony Chwefro plowed through our welcoming party and climbed the hillside to a plain two-story house, stuccoed the same yellowish-brown as its neighbors. There was no lock on the door and no sign of a caretaker; apparently the Firin's prestige was enough to discourage trespassers. After crossing a succession of vacant rooms we came to another doorway, where Chwefro pronounced the word *open* in the Revenant tongue. The door obeyed; a tunnel stretched before us.

"Here in Veii we prefer to maintain an air of mystery," my preceptor said.

The passageway was at least a half-kilometer long; I assumed it undercut Liriparo's principal hill and emerged somewhere in the back country. We followed it to a vaulted hangar holding three stub-winged aircraft, of a type I had often seen in High Vrazil. We boarded one and Chwefro uttered a few brief commands. The ceiling drew back; we rose quietly, hovering a moment over the yellow hills; and then, with our nose pointed northward, we were off at high speed across the hinterlands of Woro.

Up to that point all I had seen of Veii was desert, ocean, and two drab villages. Finally I had a look at the living landscape—and what I saw almost everywhere was the work of man. Apart from the eroded hills, a few pinkish barrens, and the rare patch of forest, Woro was a crisp, tidy checkerboard of cultivated fields, its geometry fixed by a network of reservoirs and irrigation canals. From the airship's window I beheld an elegant vegetable collage; its coloration ran the gamut of greens from deep malachite through pale chartreuse to startling turquoise, with here and there the glint of a man-made lake to tease the eye like a cabochon. This was a world created; it was agriculture brought to the level of visual art.

From Liriparo to the outskirts of Trokomari took us perhaps two watches of steady flight. Chwefro brought us down on a scrubby hillside not far from the sea, well out of range of any inquisitive natives. As soon as we were clear of the airship it took off again and arrowed south.

I shook my head, a bit baffled; but by now I was too familiar with the feeling to concern myself. "All this rigmarole," I muttered. "You Firin maintain such a careful image here."

"We're merely trying to minimize the ground-dwellers' contact with advanced technology. We want them to progress at their own pace, without envy or frustration to goad them on."

"But how will we reach Trokomari? It must be four kilometers away."

"Even a Gheo Radiant has feet, my dear."

Fortunately there was no need to walk the whole distance. After only a kilometer we reached one of Trokomari's suburbs, and the usual crowd turned out. Four or five different coachmen vied for the honor of driving us into town. Chwefro settled on a scarlet chariot with tall spoked wheels, shaded by a triple-tiered calico parasol and drawn by a pair of bay mares. These beasts were of the rangy Woro breed, and closely resembled animals I had ridden on Ethri. The drive across the strand was pure exhilaration.

"So!" I shouted, over the wind of our passage. "I begin to like your planet after all!"

"May it like you as well!" Chwefro replied.

Trokomari was laid out on a pair of hills overlooking the sea. Square whitewashed houses with lavender balconies rose in tiers all the way up the twin peaks; often the roof of one house became the front porch of the next. Some of the larger buildings boasted shallow domes, painted either white or sky blue. As we came closer I heard roosters crowing in back gardens and caught a whiff or two of honeysuckle, mingled with the sharper fragrance of manure; city and country seemed to merge in this sunbaked town. There were even fields of barley, and orange groves, within its walls.

Our driver reined in the team and brought us up before a pillared gateway. It was overgrown with flowering magenta and dense ferns, and obviously hadn't been closed in a generation or more. Here we abandoned the chariot and continued on foot. No wheeled traffic could possibly negotiate the streets that rose up before us. Indeed, in Trokomari, stairways were more common than unbroken pavement. A gaggle of children trailed us as we climbed to the highest tier, remarking loudly on Chwefro's pallor. The general consensus was that my preceptor was diseased. What better reason to seek Woro's leading shaman, renowned throughout the land for her skill at the art of healing?

For this was the woman whose audience we craved: Ilesha, Mistress of the Bright Season, a sort of witch-doctor or high priestess who at the moment directed the island's government.

Whether wisely or capriciously, Woro chose to divide its rulership according to the seasons. While the sun shone a woman reigned, invariably a priestess of the local cult, well versed in all the sorceries involved with health, fertility, and increase. In darkness a male war-chief assumed lordship, guiding and protecting the populace from night's questionable urges. It was a cumbersome system, but the natives seemed to think it worked.

Our efforts carried us to a wide plaza surrounded by slant-walled towers and canopied gardens. From latticed windows women with long narrow eyes looked down, mildly curious, munching figs and waving round particolored fans against the heat. Chwefro guided me to a low building with a dazzling coat of fresh lime; a few soldiers lazed before its gate, sensuous in their indifference.

"This is the House of Day," the Firin whispered. "Pretend you're paying a call on Skhorb's First Radiant."

We removed our shoes before stepping backwards over the high threshold; courtesy demanded no less. Bending down, I glimpsed scenes of war and feasting carved into the cedarwood doors. Then we were in a cool courtyard overhung with eucalyptus and pine. A group of men and women sat comfortably on the ground. In their midst stood a woman dressed in white, half turned away from us, her face tilted toward the sky. We waited quietly.

"Chwefro, is it?" She favored us with a glance. "Come join us. You'd better have an exceptionally nice gift for me this time."

Before we could move, two small boys hurried over bearing calabashes full of water. They expertly laved our faces, hands and feet. So purified, we eased down onto the mats next to Ilesha's other guests.

The Mistress of the Bright Season was a broad, powerful woman, somewhere past middle age. An intricate pattern of scars covered her arms and as much of her breasts as I could see. Though she studied me keenly, when she spoke it was to my companion.

"Well, Firin? What have you got to say for yourself?" Her words were abrupt; her voice was full of humor. I found the combination irresistible.

"It's a great pleasure to visit your realm again, Mistress Ilesha. But I found my reception in New Venery . . . a bit strained. That's why I've come to seek your counsel."

"Strained? I hope so. Show me your present now and let's get that over with."

Chwefro produced a delicate ivory box and placed it in Ilesha's hands. She opened it: the sound of violins playing a poignant melody filled the air. Her courtiers murmured approval.

"Another music box. Very pretty. Now tell me why your fishbelly kindred has suddenly begun meddling in politics."

Chwefro, for once, seemed at a loss. "I think we're speaking at cross purposes, Mistress Ilesha. Please state your allegations more precisely."

The lady rolled her eyes heavenward and muttered an imprecation. "Very well then, Master Clean-Nose. You must certainly have heard of this beastly new war. Traore invaded her neighbor Lozi, on some pretext or other, before the dawn mists had decently lifted. Ever since then the proud capital of Veii's most ancient dynasty—by which I mean Tolun, of course—had been under siege."

Chwefro confessed to some familiarity with the news.

"You may also have heard that the Traoro have confiscated the property of several Woro merchants resident in Gawi, and that three Woro vessels have been fired upon in the Straits of Ye."

Again Chwefro nodded.

"Then perhaps this tale holds no surprises either. At the beginning of Dark Season a stranger rode into Trokomari carrying a Firin safe-conduct. He gave his name as Pororo, and spoke the Sofo tongue with some awkwardness; for that matter he seemed no more fluent in Ladan or Toso. He immediately went before the reigning Lord of Night and begged to be accepted into Woro's army. Hima took him, and then the trouble started. In short order our friend Pororo had challenged three different ranking officers to contests of honor, and slain all three. Meanwhile he advised everyone who would listen, including on occasion Lord Hima himself, that Woro should declare war on Anago of Traore for the latter's numerous crimes and heresies. Eventually he became such a nuisance that Hima was compelled to dismiss him from the ranks—whereupon he scuttled off to Anago's court and once more offered his sword arm and trigger hand. The same qualities which made him obnoxious to Hima have endeared him to Anago, to the point where he now holds a command in the Traoro army. This man is the very avatar of the Trickster, and woe betide us, for he is in the service of Guje himself."

As Ilesha named these deities her courtiers' hands flew to the fetishes dangling from their necks; there was a brief susurrus of prayer. Chwefro surveyed it all with detached amusement.

"This is your evidence?" the Firin asked mildly.

"Do I need to spell out the fact that this man Pororo is an offworlder, and that it is only through your own connivance that he came to work his mischief here in Veii?"

"It's no secret that we allowed the man to land. From time to time other offworlders have received similar permission; as a rule they've pursued their affairs without arousing the slightest notice or causing the least harm. Given this much, does it occur to you that perhaps Pororo is acting of his own free will, that his misdeeds in no way reflect Firin desires?"

Ilesha pursed her lips. "I never supposed the Firin to be capable of such enormous error."

"We don't claim to be human," Chwefro said, "but we certainly are fallible. Your account of Pororo's mischief is news to me. Though it doesn't particularly surprise me, knowing the man."

"Aha!"

"Therefore I am prepared to make amends. I present to you an excellent young woman, whom the deities name Risha."

I touched my heart and lips; Ilesha did the same. By an odd linguistic coincidence my name meant *nightflower* in Sofo, and was consequently a typical woman's name throughout the Garengazi region.

"You are another meddlesome offworlder, I presume?"

I smiled and lowered my lashes.

"Mistress Ilesha," Chwefro said, "the things we must discuss warrant privacy, I think."

Ilesha laughed, a rich infectious sound. "These people here are all my relatives, and are as nosy as good relations should be. If I exclude them now they'll only eavesdrop, but if I let them stay I can force them to swear deadly oaths of secrecy."

This was agreeable; one by one the company promised to dine on their own sexual organs before divulging the things we said. Satisfied, Chwefro continued, "This woman has her own grievance against Pororo. She is skilled and subtle. I recommend her as the instrument of your revenge."

"One frail woman? Against the warriors of Traore?"

"You are a woman, Ilesha. Are you so frail?"

"I'm an extremely rare woman, dear Chwefro. And my strength is in the higher realms, not this world of blood and iron." Her face grew serious as she regarded me out of enormous eyes. "Have you ever killed a man, Risha-come-down-from-the-dark?"

"No, Mistress Ilesha."

"An innocent! What foolishness is this, Firin?"

"Trust her."

She studied me again. "I can see strength—that much is as clear as the noonday sky. Also I think you know a little about pain. Perhaps there's something here."

Bulky as she was, Ilesha rose in one smooth motion and approached a thick-limbed eucalyptus tree rooted near the center of the peristyle. She reached her hand into its branches, and waited quietly; after a moment a python's head poked out of the drooping leaves. Its body followed in a fluidly seductive descent. Meter after meter it came, gleaming like a rainbow in filtered sunlight, enfolding Ilesha's uplifted arm and massive shoulders in thick, undulant coils. Its polychrome scales bore black markings, more like hieroglyphics than any work of nature, closely resembling the designs on Ilesha's own body.

As its head swayed back and forth the shaman spoke softly to her familiar, and they exchanged quick kisses; the courtiers looked on in admiration. Woman and snake basked in this embrace for several minutes; then Ilesha returned the python to its resting place, and settled down once more on the papyrus mats.

"The house snake is satisfied; therefore so am I. Now please tell me how you will execute this vengeance."

As we outlined our vague plans I suppressed my curiosity and disquiet. The apparition of the snake had disturbed me; did Ilesha really imagine that she could communicate with a mere reptile? At least her superstitions furthered my purpose. She offered no serious objections to our schemes and conjectures—though she did make one odd request. "Show me your belly, skyborn," she said.

I loosened my robe and exposed smooth skin. She nodded. "I suppose the rest of you is equally unscarred?" I said as much. "And you've never borne a child?"

"Never."

"Then it's time to make a woman out of you, Risha. I'll be your sponsor. From this interval until your departure you'll stay with me here in the House of Day."

• • •

I lived very comfortably under Ilesha's roof for the equivalent of a starcycle. An adolescent girl named Soko was my servant and companion, and Lady Day herself frequently summoned me to dine at her own table. Slowly I acquired the manners of Veii—or rather, I discarded the manners of the Hypaethra, for after Gheo's ceremonies and strictures, the informality of the place was perplexing, to say the least. Whatever I considered rude or vulgar was in Ilesha's household the tenderest and most natural of gestures. Servants regularly addressed their superiors by name; young women went around bare-breasted; young men constantly offered each other deadly insults, and laughed rather than taking offense; and everyone teased Ilesha about her girth. It was a topsy-turvy world.

But the strangest part of living there had nothing to do with Veiian mores: it was Veii itself, with its sluggish rotation and endless daylight. The sun never seemed to move, shadows never seemed to shorten or shift, and the heavens remained a clear changeless blue. Twice I saw brief thunderstorms—hardly enough to darken the sky or moisten the dust—but Soko told me that the weather would most likely stay dry till the long rains of late afternoon. Meanwhile the world was stuck in a bright sameness.

The only reference points in the long Veiian day were the gongs sounding from the Horologer's Towers. Elaborate clepsydrae set them off, approximately once every three and a half watches. Three of these so-called "intervals" equalled a spell; and though most people slept at least one interval out of every three, there was no consensus on when the new spell began or which was the proper interval for sleep. For a while my metabolism revolted, and I endured insomnia's curse; then at last I adjusted, and waked or slept as I pleased. Dark windowless chambers underground were the special province of sleep. They held the only night I knew, and the only dreams.

One interval not long after my arrival Soko shook me awake "Risha!" she hissed. "The white demon is abandoning you." She held aloft a burning taper; shadows writhed across the walls, lending her face a look of desperation. I was as confused as I could possibly be.

"What demon? What desertion? Talk sense."

"Chwefro, I mean." Her voice was hoarse and urgent. "That fish-face has just said a formal farewell in the Court of the Snake, and Ilesha has just finished singing prayers for a favorable wind. Your friend plans to take ship across the sea. Without you."

I threw on a gown and hurried out, my skull a cauldron of rage. Threading the bone-white maze of streets, I tried to find reasons for this uncharitable defection, straining my eyes all the while for a glimpse of golden hair and long pale limbs. Just above the harbor I caught sight of my quarry; I let out a throat-splitting cry.

"Chwefro! What is the meaning of this? Where are you going, and why?"

The Firin paused beneath an arbor with a show of patience. I drew closer, and was assaulted yet again by the creature's frightening beauty. My anger cooled a little in the depth of those ice-blue eyes. I was panting and sweaty; Chwefro was glacially calm.

"Northward across the Garengazi, past the broad plains of Golo's island, rocks rise from the mist." The Firin's voice took on a sing-song cadence. "Ira-Ireru, men call them, the Holy Isle: for my kindred maintain another home than Venery. Here we dwell, as it pleases us, and keep alive the memory of the one who made us, and receive all men and women who come in good heart to learn from us. For the Firin this Ira-Ireru is the sweetest place in all creation."

"What a fraud you are," I said, already mollified but loath to show it. "So there's poetry in your vat-born soul after all, just waiting for an occasion to bubble out. Are you taking a holiday, then? Sneaking away from the tedious company of humans, to relax with your own exquisite kindred?"

"No, Risha." Bright curls flew in salt air. "Few places in this round world are as difficult to attain as Ira-Ireru. Its currents defy all but the best navigators; its treacherous shoals have claimed a thousand lives. But I've received an urgent call, echoing and re-echoing in the sea chamber of my ears. Willingly or not, all Firin of my station must convene there, to discuss certain new developments in the matter of Veii."

"Human developments?"

"I won't know the particulars till I arrive."

This was confusing, unsettling. "When will you be back?"

"Soon enough. When the sun is at its zenith comes the season known on Veii as White Shadows. This is the worst time in the whole year, as you will see, and I'm afraid you must endure it without me. But I promise to return before those White Shadows lengthen, before the sun begins to fall toward the east, and when I do I'll take you away again.

I'll guide you as close to Anago's city as I dare—for naturally it won't do if anyone in Traore sees you in my company. Keep your dreams of Seren till then. Hold him in your heart till I come again to give you new visions of power."

"New visions?" My mood rekindled. "What are you saying?"

Chwefro glanced toward the waiting caravel, plainly anxious to be off. "Only something every child in Veii knows. We are the Firin—bringers of dreams. Shaping human fantasies we heal ailing spirits."

I was close to fury now. "You mean you've toyed with my mind? On the lightsail, flying to Veii? You shaped those dreams?" My voice shrilled and broke.

"I only brought out what was already inside, tangled up in shame. A subtle hypnosis. An art I plan to teach you, in fact."

"So that I can do the same to you?"

"Alas, no. We Firin never dream."

I turned away, hugging myself. "I hate you."

Chwefro took hold of me; there was steel hiding in that silken touch. "Don't. And don't try to love me either—I know how impossible that would be. But do trust me. I may feel like the worst deceiver in the whole Matterfield, you may despair of understanding anything I say or do, but simply trust me, Risha. I won't betray you."

The Firin turned and hurried down to the quay with no more fare-well than that. I stood alone; my anger smoldered.

CHAPTER SIX

Even on a formal progress, Ilesha traveled with less ceremony than one of Woro's wealthier merchants, though for a season at least she was the island's head of state. Settled comfortably in her silken palanquin, she nibbled toasted almonds and fresh berries, joking with the six bearers about how much harder this made their job. I rode alongside her on a sorrel gelding in the company of two or three other ladies, all lavishly decorated; a few parasol bearers shaded us, and a handful of armed outriders ensured our safety. We were a cheerful, lighthearted group; our mood was a perfect match to the springtime air of midmorning.

The road we followed took us through the fields east of Trokomari, over water meadows and irrigation ditches, around dikes and cisterns and windmill-driven pumps. Everywhere we saw evidence of the farmers' constant struggle against drought, of their ceaseless efforts to hoard water and turn it to optimum advantage. The land itself gave testimony to success. We rode in the shade of sycamore and acacia, admiring date palms swaying in the distance and barley ripening close at hand. We studied the dangling vines, speculating on this season's vintage. We inhaled the fragrance of orange and lemon trees blossoming alongside whitewashed barns; rose and oleander, Ilesha said, soon would follow.

It struck me then how easily I took this surfeit of worldliness in stride. Gheo and Skhorb already seemed remote and unreal. It amazed me to think that people could bury themselves in stone tombs falling through the void, when places like this existed. My years in High Vrazil felt closer now than those brief intervals in the Hypaethra; apparently the dirtgrubbers' life suited me better than I cared to admit.

Our destination was a manor house nine or ten kilometers outside of town. A canopy had been raised in the garden against our arrival, and refreshments set out underneath. But this would be no mere social call. Ilesha had come to give justice.

It was a routine enough case, especially dull for an outsider like me who knew neither of its principals. These were two prominent landowners who disputed the boundary between their estates. At Lady Day's bidding they argued their claims in the white-hot sun, vehemently and at length, while Ilesha listened quietly from her shady seat. After the presentation we all strolled out to the field in question; it looked like any other. But the Mistress of Trokomari insisted on taking her time. In fact she was so maddeningly thorough, so punctilious and formal, that she exhausted the patience even of the two litigants. Finally they threw up their arms and begged for a decision, no matter which way it went. Only then did Ilesha judge.

Afterwards she murmured, "Maybe this will teach them to bother me with trivialities."

I had amused myself, meanwhile, studying the adornments and conceits of the local people. In typical Woro fashion the unmarried women and girls went around dressed only in loose skirts, showing off the scar patterns etched into belly and breast. In the Sofo language such designs were called *luruka*. By now I was used to all sorts of curiosities, but the unusual fineness of these women's scars fascinated me. Many of the patterns were abstract; others imitated the shapes of trees and flowers, of insects and birds, of a hundred other creatures of the Garengazi coast. Apparently there was some local genius at work with *luruka*'s traditional hook and dagger.

Ilesha noticed my attention and gave a knowing smile. Within minutes a slender youth stood before us, solemn and reserved. "So you are the artist," my mistress said. "They told me your name was Olaro. I think I've seen you around the wrestling grounds and gambling dens of Trokomari." Olaro shot her a glance but said nothing; Ilesha hastened to placate him. "I mean to offer you no blame, but only praise, my young friend. Even at this early age your hands speak truly. Your *luruka* is as fine as any I've seen."

Olaro mumbled a reply while staring fixedly at his toes. But others were not so shy. Catching wind of Lady Day's interest, several of his clients gathered round to display their keloids—more than making up for the young artist's diffidence.

"Yes, yes, this is excellent work," Ilesha said, running a finger along ridges of scar tissue. "How much did he hurt you, girl?" The girl rolled her eyes eloquently. Ilesha chuckled. "The best *luruka* always hurts the worst."

Slowly it dawned on me what the lady had in mind. "I would like to commission some work from you, Olaro," she continued. "There is a girl in my household whose belly is as smooth as a plum. Only the gods know why she's waited so long, but it's high time she assumed the status of womanhood. Will you come to my house on the fourth interval after this—or later if it suits you—and take charge of her patterning? I'll give you six gold pieces for your trouble."

This was a handsome offer indeed, but Olaro gave no sign that it surprised him. "Whatever you say, Mistress Ilesha," he murmured.

"Then be off with you, and return to me at the fourth interval!" Olaro bobbed his head and made tracks; Ilesha's mellow laughter followed after him.

"You're very generous," I said when he was gone.

"No need to thank me," she said blithely. "It's all Chwefro's gold anyway."

I digested this. "Then the Firin intended me for *luruka* all along?"

"How otherwise? No woman of Woro, Golo, Traore, or Lozi is without her scars. By Dalashon, child! *Luruka* is what sets humanity apart from the beasts!"

"Is it? Then what about speech, and clothing, and houses and gardens?"

"Animals speak, and men don't always live in houses or wear clothing. But *luruka* endures forever."

Yes, I thought, remembering the wicked-looking scars I'd seen. Forever. I had changed the color of my skin, and learned a few new languages. Now it was time for more serious measures. I swallowed hard as Ilesha convulsed with laughter.

At the appointed moment Olaro appeared in the peristyle, accompanied by a young boy carrying his woven sack of paraphernalia. I was there waiting—rather nervously, I confess—with Soko and an old woman in Ilesha's service, by name Ezaba. Olaro glanced at me sidewise and muttered, "I thought it would be you."

Ignoring this breach of etiquette, Ezaba began reciting prayers and sprinkling me with powdered haematite. Since I was wrapped in long white draperies I took on a rosy glow. When she finished all five of us set out, with two pack animals, to wend our way down the tiers of Trokomari toward the southern highway. The road yawned before us, parching us in its hot dusty breath; the sun glowered down like Guje in fury.

Woro girls typically underwent *luruka* soon after their first menses, proving by this ordeal that they were ready to bear the lesser pain of childbirth. Boys also took some scarring, but theirs was less extensive and less fraught with meaning. Whether male or female, however, the blood shed during the ritual was considered so polluting that *luruka* had to be performed well away from the ordinary zones of residence. Therefore Ilesha had set aside a little cottage on one of the hills just south of town, to house us for the next eleven spells. Attaining it consumed perhaps a quarter-watch.

Needless to say I was a bit old for scarring. Most Woro women my age were married and bearing children, so upon my arrival in Veii Chwefro had advised me to dress in matronly robes. But once Olaro had finished me I could bare my torso with the best of the maidens of Trokomari.

On that first spell there was no slicing. We simply made ourselves comfortable in the little house, deciding who would sleep where and what we'd have for dinner. Soko would do the cooking; Ezaba would police the sleeping arrangements. Meanwhile Olaro and I climbed to the bowered roof to determine how he would adorn me.

"Ilesha wants me to have the most beautiful *luruka* of any woman in Woro," I said.

"You'll suffer for it, then," Olaro promised me. "Here are some of my designs." He spread out several papyrus scraps, carefully inked in his florid hand. "Tell me which ones you like."

But when I indicated my preferences he scoffed. "Those are farmgirl pictures, milkmaid *luruka*. You need something grand enough for a priestess."

"Then why show me those pictures at all?"

For the first time he grinned. "To see if you were foolish enough to admire them." He produced a few more designs now, far more elegantly conceived. "This is more what I had in mind. Here is the mark of Ijeji. Here is the axis-tree of the universe. Here is the flower of Lanka, which blossomed in the first rains of creation. Here is the spiral of rebirth." We discussed his visions at length.

Slowly—almost as slowly, I'm afraid, as the sun edged across Woro's empty sky—Olaro's hostility abated, and we spoke more freely. With some prodding he waxed eloquent on his favorite subject. "My art is dedicated to the serpent god," he explained. "In your body, in everyone's body, there is a fiery serpent coiled. It maintains us in life and carries our souls to the next incarnation when we die. In women that serpent is stronger, brighter, because women must create new life. My task is to find the *luruka* that will harmonize with the flaming snake inside you."

I was impressed. "So Ilesha and her python in the eucalyptus tree—"

"That snake is Dalashon himself. He's lived two hundred years and ridden a score of holy mistresses before Ilesha. All the shamans pattern their *luruka* after him."

I nodded, trying not to let on that it was news to me—but Olaro lost no time in demonstrating how poor an actress I was.

"You're a strange one," he said slowly. "Though you live in Ilesha's house you know nothing about what goes on there. And now that we've been talking awhile I have the feeling you've misunderstood half my words. As for *your* words—" He mimicked some of my more blatant mispronunciations. "Who ever taught you to speak that way? Certainly no citizen of Trokomari. Even your face—somehow it's not a Woro face, though I don't know what else it could be. Are you enchanted? Or were you perhaps born on the opposite side of the world, where everything is the reverse of here?"

If my skin were paler he would have seen me blush. "It's true that I'm a stranger to Woro," I admitted, "but more than that I can't say."

"Then we won't speak of it," he said brusquely. "Since we've settled on a design I'll be off." In silence he gathered up his papers and hurried downstairs.

"And he calls *me* strange," I said aloud. Though of course Olaro must feel out of his depth. It was rare for a cicatrizer to adorn any woman outside his own kin group, and rarer still to be paid so handsomely. Add that to my advanced age, and Olaro must imagine himself in the midst of some clandestine plot—which of course he was. He was little more than a boy, really, though he tried hard to play a man's part. I couldn't expect him to be a paragon of tact.

Soko interrupted my musings with a call to dinner. We three females ate apart from the menfolk, so I saw no more of Olaro till after we slept.

On the next spell Ezaba commenced praying at the top of her considerable voice as she prepared a smoky charcoal fire in the back garden. Olaro and his brother Tuve sprinkled incense over the embers and purified their instruments in the fumes. I knelt in silence, naked to the waist, fascinated by the flash of sunlight on Olaro's tiny daggers. He stood straight and tall in the blaze of day, his face a bony mask. The muscles of his arms and belly stood out like eels.

Tuve coaxed an aimless melody out of his flute. Olaro approached me, his gaze fixed somewhere between my breasts, and the ordeal began.

Veii has turned twice on her axis since that interval, but in my memory Olaro is still busy with those wicked knives. His speed was a revelation. Commencing well below my navel he would catch a tiny fold of skin in his hook, pull it up, and slice it open, all in the blink of an eye. The pain of each individual cut was small, but on that first spell he must have made over six hundred incisions. They felt like as many bee stings, throbbing along with the pulse in my ears. I bled profusely; the blood gathered in a neat hole in the sand, a steaming puddle of gore. Olaro's sweat flowed just as heavily. I watched the rivulets run off his head as he bent to the task, and smelled the sharp odor of his flesh. Ezaba and Soko supported me on either side, murmuring encouragement all the while.

When he was done Olaro simply collected his tools and left without a word. I had a harder time standing, light-headed as I was from pain and loss of blood. Ezaba had to help me indoors. After rubbing some ashes into my lacerations she urged me to rest, so I did, eating lightly and staying horizontal for the better part of the next two intervals. It was an oddly blank and empty period.

But once I slept and woke I was ready for more. This time the pain was even greater, for Olaro was extending his pattern onto my breasts. In spite of myself I cried out as his tiny knives bit into me, imagining that all my skin was being flayed off, that the flesh underneath was melting in flames. Still I was determined not to faint. Before my inner eye I replayed the most tedious of Gheo's state ceremonies; when I ran out of memories I reviewed the classic stances of Shallowcut, and from there moved on to the dynastic tables of Vaur and Ubain. Such discipline served me well. In a halfwatch my torso's ventral surface was complete, and my dignity relatively intact. As before, Olaro disappeared and I passed the intervals resting.

For the next three spells I did nothing but heal. Olaro came by regularly to check on my progress. His concern took me completely by surprise—though I suspected that he was more interested in the developing texture of my keloids than in my personal well-being. On the third spell he invited me to go walking; I gladly accepted. I caught Soko trying to hide a smirk as we set out.

We ventured no further than the nearest hilltop, but it was enough to relieve my claustrophobia. We trudged up a stony slope, sweating like pigs, and paused at the summit to admire the view. Across a tawny vale Trokomari writhed and shimmered, looking more like a mirage than a real city, with its dreamlike jumble of white cubes, blue domes, and purple bougainvillea. I longed to be cleansed of my pollution and walk those crooked streets again.

"Will Ilesha be pleased?" Olaro asked shyly. His attention was on my belly; I smiled.

"I think so. Every cut is true, every stroke harmonizes. My looking-glass shows me the beginnings of great beauty." An abstract tree now climbed my torso, rooted in my loins and flowering in my breasts. Twin snakes twined around the trunk like Dalashon and Adu in the old legend. Through the upper branches peered the sun itself, Guje of the burning eye. My *luruka* was a blueprint of power.

It was also a labyrinth of tiny scabs, crowning wormlike ridges of keloid. That realization carried with it a moment of panic; try as I might to keep my thoughts in a Veiian frame of reference, my Revenant self still slipped through. Barring extensive cell regeneration I was scarred for life; if Lachis ever saw me again she'd be horrified.

"Look there." Olaro's voice brought me back to Veii. "I found a fine shady spot three spells past." He was pointing toward a copse nestled between two hills, lush with tamarisk and cane and three or four different species of palm. "Let's rest there a while."

Could this be the same man who sneered every time I flinched away from his blade? Suspending disbelief, I followed him into that green worldlet, the only oasis in an otherwise barren landscape. The source of its fertility was a cool spring bubbling at its heart. Reaching in, Olaro pulled out a calfskin flask and brandished it overhead. "Last year's vintage," he said proudly. "I stashed it here two spells ago, so it should be good and cold."

It was. The flask proved clumsy, but with Olaro's help I managed to aim a jet of chilled wine down my throat—the perfect antidote to Veiian heat. We drank our fill and then sprawled in a bed of rushes, listening to the spring's steady music.

The moments lengthened; Olaro watched me lazily without speaking. "You baffle me," he said at last. "At first I thought you were an overgrown child, perhaps even an idiot. There's so much you don't know! Then I began to see that your ignorance was only of the ordinary, obvious things. The hard things you know very well. Things about people, I mean, and about art. You see through me easily enough. You understand that my anger is only fear. And you know what makes one *luruka* pattern better than another, though I'm willing to bet that a halfyear past you'd never even heard of *luruka*."

I smiled fondly. "You're a clever young man, but you know I can't discuss these things."

Still he pressed me. "Did I guess right before? Were you enchanted?"

"Not precisely. But my secret involves the Firin."

His mouth shaped an "O". "Then I *will* have to kill my curiosity. There's no understanding those devils."

I chuckled. "Devils?"

"They're white. That makes them devils to me."

"But white is the color of purity. All the priestesses wear white robes."

"White cloth is fine, but white skin makes me think of illness, of lepers and albinos, of corpses and death. White can also be the color of evil, you know."

I didn't, so I was thankful for my disguise. Olaro would never guess that he's wasted good wine on a she-devil.

"It still bothers me," he went on, "not knowing what you are. I'm giving you the finest *luruka* I've ever done, and you're not even kin to me, you're not even Woro."

"I'm a woman, Olaro. That's enough for you to know."

His eyes brightened. "I suppose you're right."

All the tension that had been building between us fell away in that moment. Our eyes met and neither of us flinched. We moved closer and he touched me, very carefully, on an unbroken patch of skin. I reached back and stroked the smooth ripples of his torso.

"No scars," I whispered.

"Just here," he said, offering me an arm full of stars and zigzags. "Man style." I ran my tongue along the ridges.

"That's what I want to do to you," he said softly. "When you're healed. Will you let me?"

"Yes . . . yes. But we'll wait, won't we?"

"We'll wait."

For the next phase of the *luruka* my upper back became Olaro's field. He inscribed it with whorls, spirals, and wavy lines, all symbols of Ijeji, the river goddess—a perfect balance to the iconography of Dalashon and Guje. Since this was the end of my ordeal he abandoned whatever restraint he had used earlier, working so fiercely that his breath came hot against my neck, and his sweat mingled with my blood in long coursing channels. Likewise I made no attempt at stifling my voice, but cried out with equal fervor. I could see how gentle he had been before. Even though backs are no more sensitive than stomachs or breasts, the pain he gave me now was far more excruciating. "These lines will never fade," he whispered. "I've marked you for all time."

Then he was finished, and Tuve's flute stilled. Ezaba guided me indoors and the two brothers gathered up their belongings. Olaro's role in my initiation was over.

But just before he left he came to the door of the dim chamber where I lay, facedown, struggling with my latest distress. "I have a cousin named Jukun in Lesser Trokomari," he said. "His house is on Fan Street, near the market. I'll wait there for you. Come quickly."

"If I can, Olaro, if I can." I didn't want him to be too sure of me; I wanted him to persuade me, to court me. But he had no more to say. His teeth gleamed briefly in the shadows and disappeared.

Soko turned up immediately afterwards. "I brought you some chilled wine," she said.

"Set it down. And tell me what you're thinking."

"Thinking?"

I propped myself up on an elbow. "Don't play innocent—I know you overheard. Do you approve?"

She stifled a laugh. "Yes, and I'm jealous."

"Is Olaro such a catch, then?"

"Yes!"

"Will he be kind to me?"

That required thought. "Maybe, maybe not—but you won't care. Kindness isn't the secret of his charm, is it."

"No." I let out a long sigh. "It's not."

When four more spells had passed the scars on my chest and stomach were completely healed. My back still had a way to go, but Ezaba decreed that it was time to resume worldly life anyhow. We left the cottage behind and crossed Lady Day's threshold just as the gongs were sounding in the Horologer's Tower.

"Daughter!" Ilesha's eyes danced as she sprang up from her papyrus mat. "Now you are truly beautiful."

Her courtiers crowded round and exclaimed over my *luruka*. Old ladies bared wrinkled breasts to compare their markings with mine; all agreed that Olaro had surpassed himself. I was frankly embarrassed. This was the first time my torso had ever been publicly displayed, and it took some getting used to. Nevertheless I felt a nascent pride after all their attention.

At the feasting later on, Ilesha fed me choice tidbits with her own hand, and the harper sang verses of praise to my breasts. I was caught up in sheer sensory delight. I reveled in the musky smell of women's sweat, in the spicy fragrance of curry, in the sweet explosion of fresh strawberries, in the bite of Golo whiskey, in the dapple of sunlight across a man's naked back, in the riotous colors of Ilesha's garden. It was a heady mixture, a fitting climax to my austerities on that barren hill.

When the celebration finally died down I was in no mood for sleep. Instead I returned to the day-room Soko and I shared and began repairing my coiffure. I had long since bleached my coal-black hair to the reddish-brown favored in Woro, and plaited it with all manner of ornaments. Now I added a fresh gardenia and a silk scarf printed in crimson and violet arabesques. My skirt was saffron; on impulse I tied a short violet apron around my hips and admired the throbbing contrast. I was learning. Slipping on two or three nephrite bangles, I picked up a red parasol and stole into the plaza.

Soko had already told me where to find Jukun's house. It was a long walk in the brilliant sun, downhill and over the canal and uphill again to Beggars' Market. Not many were abroad now; by some statistical fluke most of the city's denizens had chosen this interval for sleep. I stood in a narrow street before a narrow white house, tall and tightly shuttered against the heat, debating what to do. Finally I simply took a deep breath and cried, "Olaro!"

A shutter banged open; a tousled head peered out. "Ssh! My cousin's sleeping!"

Not much of a welcome, but at least he was smiling.

He let me in, very quietly, and drew me into the cool darkness of the house. I smelled old grime and rancid oil and a hundred different spices; Olaro's cousin was far from wealthy, and his residence was typical of Trokomari's working class. We climbed a steep staircase to a tiny chamber overlooking an airshaft.

"You're a fine lady this spell," said Olaro, his eyes twinkling. "And I feel a fine gentleman with all the gold Ilesha's given me." We sat on a bedstead carved of acaciawood and held hands; his were sweaty. Could this cocky blade perhaps be nervous?

"You may have more gold coming your way," I said. "All the Bright Season court is raving over your skill; maybe a few of them will commission work."

"If Yeva wills it."

"And Ijeji."

This brought an even wider grin to his lips, and his eyes traveled from my face down to the splendors of my torso. He cupped my breasts in gentle fingers; I let out a deeply held breath. We didn't speak again for a long, long time.

Olaro was everything I wanted him to be, lusty and passionate and tirelessly physical. Our bodies meshed together like Dalashon and Adu coiling round the Tree of Life, black on black, scarred flesh against smooth muscle, slick with sweat's pungent lubrication. There were no tender caresses, no protestations of love; we knew better than to spoil this moment. One of the few thoughts I had was that he was the youngest man I'd ever pillowed, and the first I'd ever chosen purely out of lust. That made me laugh: what a conniver I'd been! Hearing me, Olaro laughed too, and that was even better.

Afterwards I cradled his tufted head and studied the angular sprawl of his limbs. Seren would be as black by now, though of course he was a much heavier man. Seren—yes, the memory caught me by surprise;

abruptly my indolence gave way to a vague disquiet, and my flesh cooled down a little from its lather. Noticing the change, Olaro reached up and guided my lips to his. A few moments later he was stoking my fires again, and Seren's shadow vanished in the blaze.

"You're my woman now," he said in the afterglow.

"Oh? What does that mean?"

"That you have eyes for me alone, that no other man touches you, that you come when I call, and stay till I say go."

I was in no mood for an argument. I simply muttered something meaningless and continued nuzzling his chest. By now I knew men well enough to realize that they speak a great deal of nonsense while lying in bed with women; little is gained by rebuttal. Before long our sweat dried, our limbs cooled, and Koyo, Lord of Dreams, saved us from any further disagreement, guiding our souls from the white dazzle of the Bright Season to the welcome darkness of sleep.

I half-woke from sweet repose to find Olaro at it again. His tongue flicked here and there, prodding me into response; once again I matched his ardor. When, at long last, we were done, we washed off in water from a tall ewer, and reassembled our costumes for an excursion into the street.

Ijeji only knew how many intervals we had spent together in the coils of passion. Trokomari seemed a different place to me now; the sun was higher and brighter, flowers were more vivid and more fragrant, and people smiled at us wherever we went. For breakfast Olaro cadged an enormous melon off an old fruit vendor; this was followed by fat brown noodles simmered in sesame paste, skewers of pickled radish, and bowls of pepper tea. The latter delicacy was new to me: Olaro had a good laugh watching the faces I made as it burned a path to my intestines.

"You must act like a grown woman," he said, scolding me playfully. "Squeamishness is for children. Don't disgrace the *luruka* you bear, or I'll be ashamed in front of my friends."

But he had no need to worry about that, even in jest. Although Olaro usually lived in a country hamlet, he came to town often enough to be a fixture in the byways of Lesser Trokomari. In one halfwatch he must have introduced me to thirty of his acquaintances, beaming over me all the while like a proud young husband. Had we been in Gheo I would have resented such blatant display, but here my old standards lost their meaning. I accepted his possessiveness as easily as I accepted the admiration of his friends—though to tell the truth, they seemed more impressed by my scars than by any quality that was intrinsically mine.

Nevertheless it was pleasant to stroll about in the company of a dashing young man, with the whole world rendering homage.

Once our breakfast had settled we retired to a pillared court off the Farmers' Market. There beneath the shade of a dozen palm trees was a wrestling school, and for some reason I never properly understood, Olaro's set had made it their headquarters. Few of them actually wrestled, and fewer still were in serious training, but apparently it was as convenient a spot as any to pass the time, gossiping, dicing, sipping pepper tea, or guzzling sour wine. In short order I was shunted off to a circle of women while Olaro joined in a dice game. Several young boys, naked except for a coating of oil and ashes, practiced earnestly in the center of the courtyard; nobody paid them any attention.

I endured the banalities of my companions for as long as I comfortably could. They were as charming and stylish as any other barebreasted maidens of Woro, but I took no particular interest in their company just then; if I couldn't be with Olaro I'd prefer returning to Ilesha's house, or wandering the streets on my own. Thoroughly bored, I ventured to assert myself. I crossed a clear sexual boundary and joined the group of gamblers, squatting down next to my lover, who bent eagerly over the dice.

"What's wrong?" Olaro hissed.

"Nothing."

"Then go back with the other women. You'll queer the game."

"That's ridiculous. I want to be with you, not your friends' mistresses."

"I'm busy."

"Then I'll leave."

I would have risen, but he grabbed my arm and glared at me. The man next to us noticed the exchange and said, "What's this, Olaro? Female trouble already?"

Olaro's nostrils flared; the others laughed. "Your woman needs attending to," said the taunter. "Better show her who's boss."

"Fuck off," Olaro muttered. "This is a well-bred woman with a mind of her own."

"Oho!" cried several voices. Olaro's neighbor was drunk, and didn't take kindly to the obscenity. Standing to his full height, he growled, "You have more than woman trouble on your hands now, my friend."

Olaro sprang up and clinched with him as the rest of the party cleared away dice and coins. The two men worried each other to a chorus of raucous encouragement; neither was much of a wrestler, but

Eshmun, the challenger, did have the advantage in height and bulk. Olaro managed to trip him, only to see both men fall together and roll about in the dust like a pair of scrapping dogs. In a moment Olaro was up again, but Eshmun was on him with a vicious headlock; Olaro went to one knee before breaking loose and butting him in the stomach. Eshmun grasped him around the waist and lifted him bodily. Olaro responded with a twist in mid-air that brought his knee crashing into the other man's head; this was a foul, and fortunately delivered only a glancing blow—otherwise Eshmun might have been seriously injured. Both men went down again. When the dust had cleared Eshmun had his knee in Olaro's chest, and my beloved was stretched full-length with a mouthful of ashes.

There were cheers, applause, and laughter. Eshmun helped Olaro up and the two men embraced. Someone emptied a skin of wine over Olaro's head; he gasped and slapped his conqueror on the back, beaming at him like a brother. I was in a state of total bewilderment.

When the fight had begun I'd been mortified; such overemotional, under-regulated contests invariably result in a loss of prestige for everyone involved. Seeing the wrestlers' lack of finesse had only worsened matters—and when my champion had gone down, my first impulse had been to turn my back on the whole affair and flee to Ilesha's inner court. I found myself estimating how seriously Olaro's status-count would drop, how much my own might be affected. Then with a start I remembered where I was: empty skies above, red dust below, white sun burning. By the time Olaro sought me out I was laughing too.

It was a shameless world I'd come to, a place with neither fixed hierarchies nor orgulous vanities, where men could fight without bearing grudges, and lose without humiliation. For the moment I preferred it to the ones I'd known before.

Olaro put his arm around my waist and suggested leaving. I could think of nothing better. "Come with me to Ilesha's house," I urged him. "We'll get you cleaned up." Scraped, bruised, dusty, reeking of sweat and bad wine, he offered no objection at all.

We walked awhile without speaking, in no hurry but not dawdling either. My hand rested lightly in his. My thoughts strayed to our separate characters; I marveled at how unlikely a couple we made. A Gheo Radiant and a dirt-grubbing peasant, a sophisticated woman and a naive young boy. The cheek of Olaro, thinking he could order me around, imagining he possessed me! It was more amusing than anything else.

"What are you thinking?" Olaro demanded.

"Nothing."

"Are you annoyed with me?"

"No, I don't think so. But I expected you to be furious with me."

"So did I." We stopped in the middle of the street and faced off. "But I've been thinking," he said, "how silly a lot of my ideas are. You're older than me, and probably wiser; you've seen more of life than I have, wherever you've done the seeing. It was wrong of me to think you'd fall into my friends' habits. I've paid the price—thank Yeva it was a small one."

I touched one of my fetishes. "And thank Ijeji." We both grinned.

"So then neither of us is angry?" he asked, very hopefully and very much like a child.

A wave of heat kindled somewhere between my navel and my knees, surging upward through my various organs to crest in my eyes. A little moisture seeped out. "Neither of us is angry," I said. And I embraced him, rubbing my breasts and belly in all that sweaty grime. Enough of men and women; all that mattered was this man and this woman.

We crossed Oro Canal via Old North Bridge, pausing to study our reflections in the still water below. Two black faces stared back. Yes, that really was me, next to the finest lover I'd ever known. I was glad Chwefro had deserted me. I hoped the Firin would leave me here in Trokomari and never return.

We entered the House of Day through a side door and headed straight for the baths. In a public bathhouse we would have been separated; here I could scrub Olaro to my heart's content. Afterwards we massaged each other with nut oils. Then, since one time was as good as any other in this season of endless light, we retired to my dark subterranean bedroom, and after a while even slept.

CHAPTER SEVEN

A striped awning already stretched the length of Pearl Street, and Taffeta Lane had become a forest of parasols. The sun was nearing its zenith; fortunately, at this latitude, it never rode directly overhead. But it was still close enough to shrink all shadows to misshapen dwarves, and light the world with such a radiance that whenever I closed my eyes I saw glowing afterimages. I understood now where the name White Shadows came from.

We turned off Silk Street—a riot of self-luminous colors and seductive threads—and descended the twisting stairs of Armigers' Close. Olaro wanted to buy a dagger, preferably of Traoro manufacture; I was along to make sure he didn't pay too much for it. So we wandered hand in hand from one tiny shop to the next, bantering with the proprietors, inhaling the smells of dusty leather and oiled steel, eyeing blades of all sizes and shapes. We held them, we studied them; on occasion we sent them spinning through the air in bright parabolas. We found a wider selection than even Olaro hoped to see. There were daggers straight and curved, slender and broad, from stilettos to skinning knives to shortswords. Some had blades damascened with golden arabesques, or chased with mythological scenes; others had hilts in the shape of fruits or animals or human hands. I was stunned to see one that was a perfect mate to a piece in Lord Tref's armory. He used to describe it as a priceless heirloom, but when I asked the shopkeeper about its twin she told me it was a Golo piece of the previous century, when barbarian weaponry was in vogue; its quality was no more than middling.

Olaro settled on a fine steel blade costing eight-tenths of a weight. Its hilt was its chief selling point—the silversmithing rivalled his own work in *luruka*. Then he picked out a light, wavy-bladed dagger and presented it to me, saying, "You never know when you might need one of these." I was delighted at his generosity, and ashamed to realize that I hadn't practiced Shallowcut even once since leaving Gheo.

For the fun of it we continued down the close to a broad courtyard specializing in arquebuses. Again there was an enormous variety in style and quality, and again the best work always came from Traore.

"Weapons and fighting are their passion," Olaro said. "If it comes to war between us we'll be hard pressed; we'll have to rely on our ships, and the sea itself, for protection."

He showed me a long pistol with a wheel-lock mechanism, one of the latest products of the Traoro smithies. "A man could fire this from horseback with only one hand. Imagine a whole cavalry unit armed with such weapons."

I said I'd rather not, and suggested a return to the upper streets. Olaro humored me; we examined the brocade shops, and afterwards had a look at linens. Selecting a coarse weave of mixed mauve and canary threads, I said, "What a fine surcoat this would make for you, to wear during the long rains. Soko could do the sewing." Without much effort I bargained the retailer down to a tenth-weight and had him wrap it in blue tissue paper. Olaro beamed.

Trokomari's shops and markets hardly exhausted the list of its diversions, but on that spell, at least, they gave me the most food for thought. Wherever I looked I was confronted with an eerie sense of the already-seen. First there was that Golo dagger; then, at a silk merchant's, I saw the same magnificent print that Lachis had worn to the Masquerade. At a potter's I found the delicate vases favored by Nan Solize for her cut flowers, and at a perfumer's I smelled the very scent that Trithi used to drench her gowns with. Veii, it seemed, was the workshop of the Hypaethra: any object of beauty or craft that found its way to the Revenant cities was inevitably manufactured here.

Olaro and I dined on flat bread and spicy shrimp in a wine shop's back garden; Woro cuisine easily rivalled its craftsmanship. For dessert there were berries soaked in mint liqueur—and while this tasted better than it sounds, it was still a potent concoction. After a few mouthfuls I was drunk. Olaro smirked as I began slurring my words and dropping fruit all over my skirt.

"Save your head for the Carnival, woman. There'll be plenty of wine and whiskey then, and it's only nine spells away."

"If it happens at all," cautioned a woman from a nearby table. "The Syndics may decide to cancel it this Brightyear."

"Why in the name of Dalashon would they do that?" demanded Olaro.

"On account of Nemuri's mischief."

The woman looked pleased with herself; she immediately attracted an eager audience, as everyone within earshot gathered round. "My sister works at scribing for the Syndicate," she continued. "A few spells past she caught wind of an unhappy tale that the Syndics have chosen to suppress. You all know of the war between Lozi and Traore, and the long siege of Tolun? Well, Nemuri is ever following in Guje's footsteps —plague is war's boon companion. The fever has broken out amongst Tolun's besiegers. It's done more to fend them off than all the arrows and shot that Lozi has rained down on them since the sun first peeked over the horizon. As usual in this miserable season, the contagion has spread like wildfire along the Garengazi's northern shore, as far as Gawi, and thence into the argosies that set sail every spell from that suppurating hole. The first cases reached Trokomari not fifteen intervals ago, on a ship bearing highland timber. Ten are already dead; twenty or thirty more households are closed up by now."

Everyone began cursing and babbling. A man in a printer's smock confirmed that one of the sequestered houses was on the same street as his own, whereupon the rest of the company edged nervously away. Many diners rose from half-digested meals, saying they had to put their affairs in order in case flight from town was advised; others broke into rapid incantations to avert the plague deity's curse. Olaro, however, stayed as calm as before.

"There was an outbreak of Yellow Plague when I was a child," he said. "My sister caught it and recovered. I wasn't even touched. My father has survived three or four different epidemics, my mother two. Our family is too healthy for Nemuri's clutches."

The gossipy woman shook her head. "I wouldn't say such things if I were you, my friend. The god might hear and single you out."

Olaro tapped a tiny silk pouch dangling among the rest of his talismans and fetishes. "This is full of powdered floatweed, and a priestess blesses it for me every dawning. I do what I can to stay on Nemuri's good side."

The woman pursed her lips. "That's well and good, but it's nothing compared to what I do." And she began enumerating all the charms she herself wore, including several she'd acquired since her sister's warning. "You can't take too many precautions," she said. "Though I have heard of families endowed with immunity. Yours may be among them, Guje willing."

I listened without comment. They might have been discussing monotonic ions, for all I understood. Disease had been excluded from the

Hypaethra at their foundation; Revenants died only from accidents, suicides, murders, extreme old age, or the Games. As a child I had been immunized against the standard Ethrin diseases, in preparation for my descent to High Vrazil, and then during the long voyage to Veii Chwefro had repeated the process to protect me from the second planet's maladies. Illness, therefore, was something I never thought about. It couldn't touch me, and I had no experience of its effects on other people.

"Have you ever seen Yellow Plague?" asked Olaro, when the woman had gone.

"No."

"Somehow I thought not. The land that bore you must be fortunate indeed."

I was afraid he'd reopen the subject of my origins and start pestering me again, but that was all he said. He seemed to have accepted the fact that I'd always keep a few secrets—and for the time being, speculation about the plague's progress seemed more interesting anyway. We paid our reckoning and left the wine shop, parcels in hand, resuming our climb to the House of Day.

Within two spells Trokomari was bustling with preparations for the Carnival. One of the chief holidays in the year, on a par with the dawn and sunset revelries, it was a gaudy farewell to the flesh before the austerities of White Shadows. Country people converged on the city to witness the masques and processions; their custom swelled local profits. Who could blame the Syndicate for its reluctance to cancel everything, even as plague tolls mounted spell by spell?

Ilesha could. "Three hundred have died in eleven spells," she said, grim-faced. "Granted, that's nothing like the death toll of the last outbreak, when as many fell in a single interval, but the contagion is still in its first stages. We have a long way to go before the rains of twilight."

"But you're Lady Day," I reasoned. "Can't you demand a cancellation?"

"No, child. I can withdraw the House of Day from participation, which will certainly dim the pageantry, but I have no formal power over the Merchants' Syndicate. I can only recommend." Frustration creased her brow. "Ten years I've been Mistress of Day, more terms than any other living shaman, and still the Syndicate ignores my good advice. Though you can bet your weight in pearls that they'll turn to me

when the outbreak reaches the proportions of a crisis. Then, of course,
I'll give them all the help I can."

"Should I tell my friends to leave town and hide themselves in the
country?"

"Who knows? Perhaps they're already infected, perhaps by doing
that they would only spread the contagion further. Nemuri guards his
secrets well; there's little rhyme or reason to his dance. The plague
seems to fall on us from thin air. Certainly large gatherings hasten its
progress, but beyond that we know nothing. I've already sent messengers to the manorial lands, warning farmers to stay away from
Trokomari till the pestilence has run its course. But the Syndicate has
sent its own men to advise the contrary."

"What would the Firin have to say?"

"That we should place our trust in the gods' mercy."

A Firin kind of answer, I thought. Accepting the lady's blessing I
skipped out to keep an assignation with Olaro.

As yet the city streets showed little sign of Nemuri's haunting. Here
and there a gatepost bore the yellow strips of quarantine, and fresh
sprigs of floatweed decorated several upper windows, but the average
citizen moved about as freely and cheerfully as ever. In spite of Ilesha's
gloom my heart was just as light. Olaro scoffed at all doomsayers; since
he refused to worry, so did I. Nothing could intrude on the happiness
we shared, no forebodings of the future, no nightmares from the past,
not even a stray recollection.

Carnival's spell found us in the best of spirits. Olaro came to meet Soko
and me at the House of Day, wearing a short kilt with green and orange
stripes, and a wreath of yellow flowers in his hair. His new dagger jutted
from a tooled leather belt and his chest shone with scented oil. I was
very proud of him then, very pleased that such a stylish young gallant
had offered me his love.

Soko and I, of course, were equally splendid. All three of us exchanged hyperboles and set out for the revels with laughter on our lips.

From the Horologer's Tower came an even brighter pealing and car-
oling. Those cascading melodies announced the halfway mark of the
Bright Season, the moment of temporal balance, the last blessed interval
before the cruel spells of White Shadows. Olaro said that the holiday
crowds were smaller than he had ever seen them, but they still made an
impressive show in their rainbow finery, their jeweled bangles and mirrored vests and polka-dotted turbans, massed before the Kokuzere

Tower in the Plaza of the Sun. Spangled parasols waved over every head, green spectacles with smoked glass lenses rested on every nose; these were Carnival traditions as old as Trokomari itself.

The main event of the spell was the Syndics' Parade. Standing back to belly in the throng, we had to angle our necks around tall farmers' sunhats just to catch a glimpse of the ox-drawn wagons as they lumbered by. First came hoary images of the gods; they gleamed with offerings of clarified butter, and white-robed priestesses fanned them constantly to keep off flies. Next was a cartload of fat children, frizzy heads all garlanded with ivy, chubby fingers scattering candy through the crowd. Flower-decked maidens marched after, singing a paean to Guje in close harmony. Men and women alike shouted praises to their beauty. Then came Lord Hima at the head of a cavalry division, with every horse caparisoned in cloth-of-gold, every lance entwined with roses, every breastplate burnished to rival the sun, and every soldier's face as handsome as a young god's. Bringing up the rear were the standard-bearers of the Syndicate, whose gaudy banners enumerated each of the city's thirty-odd guilds. Firecrackers snapped and rattled; gunpowder mingled with scents of jasmine and whiskey; boys hurled firecrackers in glittering arcs above the parade; and an implacable sun rained down arrows of fire.

Thousands had heeded Ilesha's warning and shut themselves in their own courtyards for quieter celebrations, but thousands more had turned out to do what they had always done at this season. Friends greeted each other with bone-crushing embraces; enemies forgot their quarrels and lifted winecups in neighborly salutes. No one above the age of puberty remained sober.

As we forced our way through the sea of knees and elbows Soko, Olaro, and I kept our arms linked so that the crush wouldn't tear us apart. Although several different processions had been scheduled we were content to witness only one, and thereafter embarked on a voyage through the numberless wineshops and pleasure-gardens of Trokomari. Every square had its orchestra of tuned drums and wooden xylophones; between cooling draughts of wine we shook our hips and snaked our shoulders to the dictates of the beat. Brief memories of Gheo flickered through my mind, scenes from palace levees and masquerades. How tame they seemed next to these visceral delights.

Olaro grew steadily drunker and more amorous as the interval wore on. His hands teased my nipples and stole beneath the crimson folds of my skirt. I couldn't very well scold him, since people all around us were doing the same, but I still hadn't acquired the taste for public sexplay.

"You're too shy, my love," he whispered, wet lips grazing my ear. "I know just the place to cure you of that."

"I'm not ready to go home yet," I whispered back.

But we didn't go home. A stone's throw from the Plaza of the Sun we found a wine garden called the Pearly Grotto, an ordinary-looking establishment that was as noisy and crowded as everywhere else. Wooden stools and tables huddled in the shade of eucalyptus and bougainvillea; drunken parties sang and danced. Nestled between the tables, however, were small curtained pavilions, specially erected for the holiday and redolent of cheap incense. Tossing a coin to the hag on duty, Olaro dragged me into one, laughing merrily at my confusion.

"This is another Carnival tradition," he said, tracing the curves of my *luruka* with sticky fingers. "Ijeji inspires many riders this spell." And as the old woman hummed a lewd melody outside we made quick urgent love; he didn't even give me time to undress.

We climaxed together, still standing, and then collapsed in a close embrace. Olaro's body smelled of sex and whiskey. I licked beads of sweat from his upper lip, savoring the taste. When I would have risen he held me down.

"Not yet, not yet," he said.

I kissed him again, deep and lingering. "But we've left Soko alone too long already. She'll be impatient."

"Soko will be fine. Just lie here with me a moment more."

"What's this?" His mood intrigued me. "You're clinging, Olaro. That's not like you."

"I know. But all of a sudden I'm afraid of losing you." He took a breath and held me tighter. "Just now, when we were dancing, a thought came to me through all the drums and laughter. You told me once that a Firin brought you to Woro. Now, from what I know, the Firin aren't really of this world at all; and in a flash I realized that you aren't either. It would explain everything—yes, I know you're not allowed to admit it, so don't waste your breath in denial. I recognize the truth when I see it. You've come down into Veii from one of those worlds in the sky, for some purpose I can't fathom, and one interval you'll return the way you came. And when you do I'm not sure how I'll go on without you."

I felt a kind of relief then, for my imposture could at last be discarded; but the feeling gave way to a sense of dread. Olaro was as brave as he was clever: much braver than I. He dared face what I had consistently avoided. For Chwefro would return, whether I willed it or not, and then I would have to choose between Olaro and Volshev. Right now my heart inclined toward the man in my arms—but when it came down to the line, could I possibly forget the honor of House Skhorb, the judgment of Lachis Gloy, and the authority of the Despot? Could I make a lifelong commitment to this man and this world? My heart said yes; my mind said maybe; my tongue said, "Somehow we'll find a way to be together, no matter what."

"Will you swear to that, by all the scars in your flesh?"

"Anything, my love, anything."

The hag's scolding voice intruded just then on our vows and deceptions; she shook the curtain, saying, "Time's up for you two! You owe me another coin if you want to stay longer!" Unwillingly we rose and rejoined Soko at a bottle-strewn table, our earlier lightness transformed by the gravity of what had passed between us. We left the Pearly Grotto in a more subdued manner than when we had entered.

Without such cues as sunsets, dawns, or watch-changes, I wondered how the citizens of Trokomari would know when to call enough enough and quit celebrating. Back out on the street the crowds seemed as dense as ever, and far wilder. We descended the Ninety Steps to South Gate and watched a group of fire-dancers performing in the market place. Onlookers shrieked inarticulate challenges and threw small change; a few tried to imitate the dancers' dangerous steps, but were held back by clearer-headed friends.

The combination of yellow flames, oily smoke, massed bodies, and burning sun had become too much for me. I urged a retreat to some shadier corner; my companions agreed, and we started elbowing through the crowd, heading toward Oro Canal and home. The press became denser and denser as we neared the gate. All at once a young girl came hurtling toward me, fists clenched, mouth screaming. I almost fell. Olaro caught me in time, only to be struck by another flailing body. Anxiety and confusion curdled in the heat. Why should anyone attack us? What had we done wrong? Then we realized that a riot was in progress—we'd merely blundered into a general outbreak of mayhem.

Men and women scuffled in the dust; fists struck out wildly, almost at random; voices shouted in terror; thrashing bodies stopped us wherever we turned. Olaro's knife was out as quickly as mine. Backs braced against each other for support, we formed a defensive huddle, trying to make sense of the tumult.

Soko caught on first. People were fleeing, not fighting. They had left a wide circle around the writhing body of a woman, who was wailing in bloodcurdling tones. "It burns, it burns," she cried. "It burns, give me water, it burns my eyes out, help me, help me, it burns."

Yellow pustules decorated her face and upper torso; her lips twitched in violent spasms. Between shrieks she coughed, and bloody sputum flew from her mouth. She was a textbook illustration of the symptoms of Yellow Plague.

At this stage, popular wisdom held, the plague was at its most contagious. My friends and I were therefore as eager to flee as anyone else, but instead we were being driven closer and closer to the unfortunate woman. We hesitated to use our blades offensively; that might precipitate even worse violence, and cause more deaths than the plague itself. For the moment we let the crowd carry us wherever it would.

Since South Gate's market place had only a handful of exits, all of them narrow, the mob was effectively trapped. People milled about in fear and frustration, incongruous in their peacock finery. Hysteria mounted; more scuffles broke out, more voices soared in panic. Inevitably another victim began complaining of the light and the heat, and whether it was plague or hypochondria, the multitude reacted with still greater ferocity. We had no choice but to respond in kind. Knives darting like little birds, we fought our way toward Saffron Street.

Few offered us any resistance once they saw our grim determination; none hindered us after a slash or two. We were within sight of Saffron Archway's geometric reliefs when a body of pikemen came charging through, shouting, "Disperse! In the name of the Syndicate, disperse to your homes!"

Nothing could have been as ill-timed as this exercise of civic authority. Lord Hima's soldiers succeeded only in blocking our escape route and adding to the confusion. I saw children trampled underfoot, despite screams and entreaties; the uproar became so irresistible that even I was thrown down. Soko helped me stand again, but when I turned to take Olaro's hand he was nowhere in sight.

For a few minutes I lost my head. I screamed his name, turning this way and that, straining in every direction for a glimpse of him. But he was gone.

"Take hold of yourself," Soko insisted. "Olaro will be all right; he's a good street fighter, and he knows the city better than a native. We made plans for just this outcome."

True, we had foreseen a possible separation, even under the best of circumstances, and agreed to reunite at Jukun's house on Fan Street. Since Lord Hima's men were finally having a positive effect on the disturbance—people had begun queuing up for an orderly exit—I calmed down and shuffled along with Soko toward the archway. We passed through and found ourselves in the shadowy maze of the dyers' district.

The farther we walked from South Gate the thinner the crowds became, until at last we were alone on the winding street. I sighed with relief and exhaustion. I'd been awake now for three intervals, and drunk far too much in the meantime. Soko and I debated which route to follow into Lesser Trokomari; we were as distant from Fan Street as we could possibly be, and we wanted to avoid another mob scene at all costs. We decided on a circuitous route that skirted the upper levels of the city and bypassed most of its plazas. By now, we reasoned, the plague scare would be spreading through both halves of Trokomari, making any large gathering a potential nightmare.

Saffron Street turned into Mandragora, and we were in the apothecaries' neighborhood. Somewhere a woman sang to the accompaniment of a viol, invisible behind whitewashed walls. We left her behind and trudged onward to the district of the perfume-sellers, where cloying scents of musk and patchouli drifted up from open stills. I was reminded, briefly, of that tent in the Pearly Grotto, and I shared a smile with myself.

As we walked I became aware that a party of men was overtaking us. Their voices and footfalls grew louder and more boisterous with every step we took. A strategic withdrawal seemed wise; we ducked into an appenticed doorway and held our breath. But we were seen. "Don't hide, friends," a man called out. "We're on our way to an intimate party, with fine music. Come join us."

We politely declined, but our would-be swains were persistent. There were six of them—all young farmhands, by their looks—and most were in the latter stages of drunkenness. They surrounded us and paid us bantering compliments. Our lack of interest only spurred them on. One thing led to another, until two of them took hold of Soko, urging her to come away. She begged them to let go; I did the same. When one tried to force a kiss on her I struck him across the ear with a bangled arm.

They were shocked. Some laughed, others swore. Three closed in on me, including the one I had struck, and their intentions no longer seemed friendly. I pulled out my dagger and stood on guard.

With my back against the wall I was in a secure position, but Soko, unarmed, was all too vulnerable—and a knife isn't much of a weapon for offense. Half of them worried me while the rest surrounded her, pinioning her arms and tearing at her skirt. I shouted lustily for help.

More quickly than I dared hope, the door behind me opened. I would have stumbled, but a hand steadied me. Two elderly women stood in the doorway; one held a long pistol whose lit match dangled meaningfully. "Get going," she ordered our assailants. They did.

Satisfied, the old woman doused the match and muttered under her breath. "It gets worse and worse every Bright Season—such riffraff."

Her companion smiled indulgently and turned to us. "You look like you've been through the wars. Why don't you come inside and have a nice cup of pepper tea?"

We accepted gratefully. Though we had roused this pair from a well-earned rest they were the picture of hospitality, and when Soko calmed down enough to realize that she'd been wounded, they positively erupted in grandmotherly concern.

"Lelo!" cried the gunner. "Go boil some more water—I'll fetch the chickweed salve."

One of Soko's admirers had left a deep gash running down her thigh, where a metal brooch had snagged her in the scuffle. By the time her wound was bathed and dressed the two of us were almost unconscious with fatigue, in spite of the fortifying tea. Seeing this, the ladies offered to put us up in their garden; we could sleep in the pergola, and let ourselves out whenever we woke. That suited us fine; we thanked them and staggered out.

I awoke to a silence filled with the fragrance of roses. Though my joints were stiff I felt deliciously rested. Soko and I lay atop a thick soft quilt; she still slept, her face puckered like a child's with some passing dream. I didn't disturb her. Instead I savored my indolence, thinking of Olaro. How often had we wakened together in Veii's changeless light, sniffed the air, and made long lazy love? Mmm . . . not often enough! I desired him then, but there was no urgency in the feeling. Oddly, contrarily, I appreciated him better in his absence. We had known each other only a few dozen spells, but in that time a yawning chasm had been spanned. My mind came alive with memories. I pictured him as the sullen boy who had sliced me with his tiny knives, then watched the image metamorphose into the earnest young man whose reflection wavered in the Oro Canal. Finally I remembered the ardent lover who had confronted me just a few intervals past, unmasking all my ploys, challenging the strength of my vaunted passion. It was good, very good. Reflection was the perfect stimulus to desire. I had to be near him again. I stood up and started smoothing my costume into some semblance of decency.

Soko roused then and yawned ferociously. I told her my intentions; she seconded them. "Go. I'll rest here a while longer and then head back to the Court of Day. You don't need my company at Jukun's house."

"Indeed I don't," I said, stifling a laugh. I kissed her and departed.

Silence followed me down the streets of the city. The whole world was asleep. Crushed flowers, broken pottery, discarded jewelry, decomposing food—these were the only evidence that Carnival had come and gone. Here and there I glimpsed revelers stretched senseless beneath archways and awnings; otherwise I was the only human being in sight.

In spite of the infernal heat and dazzle, my step was light; my lips quietly shaped the words to a popular tune: *Soon I will be in my lover's arms.* I found what shade I could—my parasol had disappeared eons ago—and went along Copperwire Lane toward Old North Bridge.

Crossing Pearl Street I first heard the rumble of laden carts. I paused, staring. This was a plush neighborhood, favored by Syndics, full of tall palaces and stately gardens. It was clear what was happening. Several rich merchants were in the process of fleeing the city, with their choicest possessions piled into wheelbarrows. Now that the Carnival was over they could take Ilesha's advice without appearing ridiculous. I refused to pay them any mind.

In Lesser Trokomari I found still more traces of Nemuri's dance. Here the carts were stacked with corpses, not ebony stools or gilt sconces. I averted my eyes, clinging to my vision of Olaro, and turned onto Fan Street with quickening heartbeat.

The house was quiet, the way it had been on my first visit. As I entered the side garden old Jukun met me with anything but welcome in his eyes. He was carrying a pot of yellow paint.

"Go away," he said tonelessly.

"Is someone ill?" I asked, not wanting an answer.

"We're all dead meat here."

I brushed past him and ran inside. Olaro lay on a cot in the front parlor, naked and still. His skin was grayish and his limbs seemed shrunken. His stomach rose and fell with rhythmic breathing. My mouth gaped, but no sound came out; I felt as though Guje were strangling me with steel wire.

Jukun's wife stood in the doorway and regarded me dispassionately. "He came stumbling in an interval past, saying he'd lost you in the South Gate riots. He stretched out here—I suppose he was too tired to go up to his own chamber. It wasn't long before he was raving with the fever. That's passed; he's been quiet for almost a quarter-interval now. His sister survived it, you know, and his father as well. Jukun and I have never caught it. It's too late for us to leave, now. Too late for you too." She left me kneeling by his side, chewing on my knuckles.

Jukun painted the gatepost and boarded the windows while his wife fretted in the kitchen. I stayed with Olaro, stirring only to fetch him fresh water. There was little I could do except watch, nevertheless I craved activity. I bathed him with wet rags, I cradled his head in my arms, I even lay next to him in a gruesome mockery of love. All the while I prayed to Woro's own gods for mercy—just this once, just for him. There was hope, I was sure of it; even the slatternly housewife allowed that. Olaro was so young and strong. Immunity seemed to run in his family. He had to live.

But what I saw that spell was a shockingly rapid decline. Sometimes he shivered, sometimes he burned; after a few watches the pustules came up and he coughed blood. At no time did he recognize me or acknowledge me in any way. I nursed a stranger, a monstrous changeling; Nemuri's curse had altered him into a demon, moaning in a voice I had never heard before. Hearing it I wept, and prayed.

As my vigil wore on Olaro withered before my eyes, shrinking horribly, aging, failing, his substance consumed by the fire inside. Still I embraced him with all my strength and tenderness, as if that could somehow hold his spirit in the world of life. I could hardly believe that only one spell earlier I had contemplated leaving him. It seemed all too obvious now that we were meant for each other, that his love was the best I would ever find, though I search the Matterfield from Mekkri's orbit out to the frigid kingdom of Tuni and Aida. An existence without him was unthinkable. My own passion gave me comfort: how could such ardor be denied? How could two lovers like us be parted? Ijeji would never allow it.

So I reasoned, in madness and agony, following the suffering of his body with the fevered turnings of my mind. Fleetingly I recalled the *luruka* ordeal. I'd learned a few things about pain during those spells on the mountain, but they seemed piddling and insignificant next to this.

After two intervals he became calmer. I changed the compresses and put my ear to his chest; its beating was slow and steady. His forehead felt cooler also, and his breathing came easier. Could the curse be lifting? I offered thanks to Koyo and rested my head against his wasted flesh. Sleep, Olaro, sleep and heal: I sang the words like a lullaby. Before long they had lulled me too; I dozed without realizing it. When I woke he was even cooler than before, and very, very calm.

He was gone.

I was so drained of vital force that I shed no tears, not at first. I just squatted on the rush-strewn floor for a long while, staring at my lover's corpse. With death's relaxation every vestige of pain and suffering had departed from his face, leaving only an expression of ineffable sorrow. Yes, I thought, I agree with you, but I'll let you mourn for both of us. I still have work to do.

I called Jukun; his wife wouldn't come near the sickroom. We shrouded Olaro in an old curtain and loaded him on a wheelbarrow; it was like hefting a sack of swords. When the curfew lifted—for the Court of Day had already issued edicts, and the dead and the contaminated were allowed out only during specific watches—we ventured onto Fan Street. Side by side we guided our rude bier down to High Gate and took the southern highway toward the hills. A burning ground had been set up there in the barrens, within sight of my *luruka* house.

It was a nightmare made real. Smoke hung in the air; cinders drifted down, searing our uncovered flesh. The heat and stench were suffocating, and the whole scene trembled in a blistering haze. There was nothing that was not tainted with the ashes of death. Teams of criminals tended three brick ovens under the hollow eyes of whip-toting overseers, themselves as miserable-looking as the wretches they guarded. I shuffled along like one of the condemned, my back aching from its unaccustomed labor, my eyes smarting from the fumes.

Jukun handed a few coins to the overseer and entrusted him with our burden. I would have left then, but Jukun asked me to wait with him for the cart. A stout convict was already wheeling it out to the crematorium, ankle-deep in cinders. From a distance I watched the oven door swing open and the yellow flames leap high. Two gnarled men seized the corpse and tossed it in; its black silhouette hovered for an instant against the wall of flames, and the door slammed shut again. A moment later the wheelbarrow came trundling back at a dogtrot.

"Well, that's done," said Jukun, stretching his back with a calcified crackle. "We'll have to hurry to beat the gongs."

"I'm not coming back with you," I replied. "I'll help you guide the barrow as far as High Gate, but from there I'm returning to the Court of Day."

Jukun grunted, mumbling, "Arrogant bitch," or something similar. Aloud he said, "But you're tainted now. If the Syndicate's patrols find out that you've evaded quarantine, they'll pop you in the ovens, symptoms or no symptoms."

"Will you inform on me, Jukun?"

He shrugged. "There's money in it."

I fished a piece of silver out of my kirtle and dropped it in the wheelbarrow. "Accept that for your silence," I said dryly. "I promise not to infect anyone."

He grunted again and held his peace till we reached the walls of Lesser Trokomari, where we parted with as few words as possible.

From there my feet carried me back to Ilesha's house without direction from my conscious mind. I was lost in an inner vacancy. Only when I stood before the carven cedarwood gates did I become aware of the cacophony of drums and voices pouring out of the Python Court. I paused, and wondered if I should go around to the side door—but with my next breath I decided I was too exhausted to make the effort. So I stepped inside, gingerly enough, removing my sandals and adding them to the two score pairs already accumulated. A girl sprinkled me with holy water; an old lady passed me a ladleful of whiskey. One burning swallow sharpened my senses to the chaos around me.

Ilesha was performing a rite. Obviously I had missed the opening ceremonies—the presentation of the water vessels, the invocations, the parade of the sacred flags. By this time the mysteries had already begun their descent, lured earthward by the mad swirl of dance and music. Ilesha herself knelt among the drummers, adding her rich voice to the wailing chorus, her eyes closed in deep meditation, her body dripping with sweat. A dozen dancers in white loincloths and ochre paint leaped and trembled in the semaphoric gestures of the cult.

This was not at all what I needed or anticipated. I should have gone directly to the baths, and from there to my bed. Instead I lingered a moment, and then a few moments more, my burnt-out sensorium overwhelmed by this flood of new stimuli. My head nodded in time with the drums; though I could hardly stand up, my feet itched to dance.

One of the older priestesses entered the circle of dancers, waving sprigs of floatweed overhead. Now I understood the ritual's point. Ilesha and her acolytes were trying to appease the plague-deity's wrath. How timely, I thought. Already they've prepared a requiem for Olaro.

My lips trembled, my throat ached. Grief struggled for expression but found no outlet. I kept beating time with my feet, shuffling my toes in the sand, reminding myself how inappropriate it would be to join in. Then a dancer approached me. He was a tall skinny man, all knees and ribs and elbows, with crude yellow stripes daubed across his torso. From ears to ankles his body shook violently, shuddering like a victim of electroconvulsive discipline. Only the whites of his eyes showed. Clearly he was possessed. He sang the holy words in a squeaky rasp that toyed with my sanity. Whenever he edged toward me, thrusting his sightless face into mine, I shuffled back, dreading his touch. Then he reached out and grabbed my hand.

Blue fire flickered along his arm and exploded in my eyes. I let out a long thin cry and staggered sideways. Veii's brilliant sky went dark; my senses cowered; and I forgot, I forgot, I forgot.

CHAPTER EIGHT

I came back to my senses with a shiver and a start. The room where I lay—blank shadowy walls and a vaulted ceiling, glowing softly in blue phosphorescence—was completely unfamiliar. Two black women sat by my bedside; one was old, the other quite young. The old one studied me expectantly and held out a porcelain cup. "Drink this, dear," she said gently. Without thinking I sipped the tepid beverage, only to gag at its bitterness. Fear mounted my gullet.

"Can you speak yet?" the old lady asked.

My tongue caught behind my teeth; my throat felt raw and mangled. I stammered helplessly and trembled in every nerve.

At last I managed a word: "Ilesha!" With this utterance my memory came rushing back. I was in my own bedroom—these women were my friends. Soko laughed and clapped her hands; Ilesha thanked five or six of her deities.

"What happened to me?" I croaked.

"You found favor in the gods' eyes," said Ilesha.

"Which god?"

"Nemuri took you first, of course, for he was the one we summoned. But once Ijeji saw what a fine mount you made, she pushed him aside and claimed you for her own. Your *luruka* is true."

"Possessed? I was possessed?"

Ilesha nodded. "It is often this way. The steed forgets the rider."

"I—danced? I sang the holy words?"

"Your body did these things, yes, under Ijeji's guidance."

Up till that moment I had suspended judgment on the vast gray area of Veiian religion; it was something I didn't understand, so I had vowed neither to believe nor to doubt. It seemed I could do so no longer. Theistic possession was a fact. My own body offered proof. I had been handmaiden to the goddess of love.

I suppose my confusion and discomfort showed, because Ilesha hurried to reassure me. "Be easy, Risha," she said. "It's difficult at first, especially when it comes so unexpectedly, and so late in life. Most of the susceptible are taken as children, so they have years of training to help them develop their gift." She squinted thoughtfully. "Even I would have doubted that an offworlder could be vessel to the mysteries. But so it is—your lover's hands have shaped you into a true woman of Veii. The mark he left on you is pleasing to the gods; they've accepted the offering with zeal."

"Olaro's dead, you know." Saying it, somehow, detached me from my loss.

"Yes, Soko told me. She visited his cousin's house and saw the signs of quarantine." Ilesha glanced over at the girl and gave a short nod.

"Jukun and his wife are also dead," Soko said bluntly. "You may as well know."

Even that news failed to disturb my composure. "So I was unconscious a long time."

"Four intervals," Soko confirmed.

"But I had no fever, no symptoms of . . . ?"

"None at all," said Ilesha. "Obviously you're immune to the Yellow Plague, just as I am. But grief is another matter. Few children of Dalashon and Adu can withstand that malady. First one must give voice to sorrow; Ijeji helped you there, as the gods often do. Then one must heal. You've made a good start."

Her voice fell on me in soothing cadences. Here at the foundation of the Court of Day I was safe and whole; misery, for a while at least, was excluded.

"Can I go back to sleep now?" I asked.

"Oh yes. But—Risha? What will you do next? You can't ignore the power of Ijeji's disclosure."

"Why—what can I do, but wait for Chwefro?"

Ilesha frowned. "Chwefro. It's true—each one of us has made certain vows. But if you were my own subject I'd send you straight to the priestesses' school. Power like yours must be channeled." She paused and shook her head. "But you're bound to Chwefro; there's no gainsaying that. The Firin must train you as they see fit. Until one of them comes to claim you again you're safe with me. I'll see to it that no malevolent force disturbs you."

I believed her. She bent down to kiss me, with a tenderness even my own mother never displayed. Then she left. Soko stayed on alone to keep watch over me till I slept again.

Through the empty intervals that followed, White Shadows haunted Trokomari, driving all but the corpse-carriers from the city's streets and stairways. Though I chafed against my confinement there was no alternative. At least I had Soko for companionship: she never lost her sensible good cheer. When the gods had fashioned me, alas, I think they left out that essential ingredient.

In spite of Ilesha's promises I fell prey to nightmares, which wounded and tormented me far more than simple grief or sorrow ever could. The species of dream I had experienced on the Firin's lightsail returned to me in full force. These were visions as clear and cogent as reality, gripping me in cruel narratives that seemed more vivid and credible than the routines of daily life. Over and over Seren appeared before my inner eye, handsome, full of vitality, taunting me viciously. "You called me murderer," he would say, "but are you any better, Risha? Why did Olaro have to die? Can you still plead your innocence?" Spell after spell I woke in tears, cursing history, challenging destiny, questioning my reason and fate.

Dreams of Olaro himself were still more harrowing; even Soko's compassion availed me nothing against the pain they brought. All were garbled versions of the deathbed scene, and in every one a third party was present: Chwefro. While Olaro raved the Firin merely sat and watched, smiling contentedly, impervious to his suffering, deaf to my prayers and entreaties. A new, irrational hatred for my former guide and teacher welled up in me with each awakening.

I had enough presence of mind left to wonder why my visions followed the pattern they did. Why should they attack me in free space, leave me untroubled for my first forty-odd spells in Veii, and then return precisely when I was recovering from a serious emotional shock? Chwefro had confessed to an involvement with the first unpleasant series, but how could the Firin exercise any power over me from the distant shores of Ira-Ireru?

There was no unravelling it, so I refused to try. Instead I spent my waking hours in the Python Court, attending Ilesha beneath her silken canopy, listening to the rustle of eucalyptus leaves, watching the old snake slither from branch to branch.

On a spell when the very air seemed to burn like hammered iron, a commotion in the Plaza of the Sun shook me out of my reverie. Children's voices echoed gaily, defying the menace of Nemuri's fevers and White Shadows' curse. Ilesha raised an eyebrow; almost in unison, her entire retinue looked toward the cedarwood gates, which swung open to reveal three pale figures. They were tall and golden-haired, clad in loose white trousers and carefully draped cotton shawls. I was halfway to my feet before Ilesha's hand restrained me.

The foremost among them bowed and spoke a ritual greeting. Ilesha replied hospitably.

"We have traveled far over quiet seas," the Firin said. "We have just now arrived from the Holy Isle, on our way to Liriparo and New Venery. In Golo we heard news of Woro's misfortunes. We condole with you, Mistress Ilesha, but we carry comforting words from the First Circle of Ira-Ireru. Your realm will soon prosper as never before."

"Indeed?" said Ilesha, a bit skeptically. "And how soon will that be?"

"Our savants have just completed a deep reading of the world-line's course." To my ears, at least, the Firin sounded smug. "All indications are of peace, good health, and growing profits for the citizens of Woro."

My fellow attendants whispered happily; Ilesha was less sanguine. "We might enjoy peace as a conquered province of Anago's empire, and health as a tiny tribe of survivors, once all those susceptible to the Yellow Plague have fallen. Can't your inmost philosophers offer us a more specific oracle?"

The Firin bowed. "Alas, no. But I myself will venture one: Woro will flourish as long as it has a leader as clever and hard-headed as Mistress Ilesha."

General laughter greeted this sally, and even Ilesha acknowledged the point. I, however, was still in a fine state of suspense, wondering when the talk would turn toward me. I had only now determined—much to my dismay—that Chwefro was not among these legates.

After some discussion of travel arrangements and right-of-way my moment arrived. "Is there a young woman here named Risha?" the Firin asked. I stepped forward, two parts hope and one part dread. "A colleague in the station of Chwefro has a message for you. Chwefro apologizes for the delay, and promises to send you definite instructions within twenty intervals."

"Is that all?"

"That is all." With a courtly nod the Firin turned away from me, and all three began the ceremonial gestures of leave-taking. I was wrong, I thought to myself. Chwefro *could* affect me, even across the long leagues separating Trokomari from the Holy Isle. Because I was furious. That message was almost no message at all; it was just another example of Chwefro's cavalier indifference to my peace of mind, perhaps to my very existence. I watched the three Firin's retreating backs with the utmost contempt.

Following Ilesha's audience was the usual dinner, complete with music and witty conversation, even during this season of contagion. In my disappointment and general funk I took no part in the discourse; I excused myself early and descended to bed. Sprawling on the cushioned platform I was quickly asleep . . . and dreaming.

I toiled across a nightmare landscape of white sand and brazen sky, stumbling beneath the weight of a huge bundle wrapped in musty cloth. I had no idea where I was or what I was carrying. Still I wept constantly, so that all I could see was a smeary glare. As I trudged onward my face grew hotter and hotter, and the ambient light took on a reddish cast. At last I found myself on the lip of a deep pit filled with flames. There I stooped, and dropped my bundle over the edge, watching the cloth unfurl around its contents. It was a man. He was the very image of Seren. He tumbled into the abyss, limbs wildly askew, falling with more than lunar slowness. He was naked and his flesh was pale as ivory, smooth and superbly muscled. His face was a white knot of anguish. Flames licked around him and charred him a sooty black; only then did he call my name, and when he did it was with Olaro's voice. Squinting against the heat I saw that he had Olaro's face as well—in fact he *was* Olaro, not Seren at all. My tears redoubled. Wailing and grieving I watched the fire consume my dead lover, transforming his substance into a fine white ash that hovered on the updraft. Hanging there it slowly reformed, taking the shape of a huge and flawless face. A white face, to be precise, sexless and untroubled by passion's exigencies: Chwefro.

"Risha," the Firin said. "Come to me now. I cannot stir from this place where I sojourn, so you must set out by yourself and find me. Ilesha will advise you; the people of Golo will direct you to my home. Come at once. Come at once." And Chwefro's command was so powerful that I lost my footing and fell headlong into the flames.

I woke in terror. Soko lay beside me, sleeping soundly. I stifled the impulse that would have wakened her and strove against my fears alone. It was just a dream, just a dream, I told myself, none of it was real. I am alive, Olaro is dead; that was the turning time took and nothing can change it. Just a dream. In a few minutes I had calmed down enough to start analyzing the vision. It was unlike any of my other nightmares, by the simple fact of Chwefro's command. The more I considered it the more I was convinced that the Firin had somehow communicated with me, mind to mind. That legate from Ira-Ireru had just told me to expect a message. Here it was, a little earlier than I would have foreseen, and a great deal vaguer than it should have been, but a definite message nonetheless. I'd been summoned to the Holy Isle.

"Chwefro," I whispered, "you're cruel. I hope you can hear me. How dare you couch your sending in such painful terms? How dare you use my grief as a beacon? You're merciless and vile, an odious lump of protoplasm, and though you picture yourself as humanity's caretaker you haven't a clue what it means to be human. No matter how long you live and observe you'll remain the haughty wretch you are now."

Uttering those words made me feel better. In a while I drifted off to sleep again, and was untroubled by nightmare visions for several spells.

The very next interval I told Ilesha about my dream. She agreed with me on its interpretation, and was almost as irritated as I was by Chwefro's lack of compassion.

"But you face one serious problem right off," she said. "As you must know, there's been no shipping out of Trokomari since Carnival, on account of the plague. And even if quarantine lifts that won't change the weather. During White Shadows the wind is simply too light for sailing. It'll be ten spells or more before our trade winds blow again. Perhaps by then the death tolls will have fallen low enough to allow free travel."

I grimaced. "How did those Firin legates voyage, then?"

"The Firin have their ways," she said, shrugging. "It's no good trying to imitate them."

"It's no good trying to obey them, either," I decided. "Chwefro said to leave at once. But I can't sail to Golo, and I certainly can't fly. So here I stay."

Ilesha patted my arm. "Be easy, girl. If it's important enough, Chwefro will find a way to fetch you."

I pictured an aircraft dropping out of the sky and addressing me in synthetic tones. "Please be so kind as to climb aboard." It didn't seem likely.

"Ilesha," I said, near the point of exasperation. "You must know as much about the Firin as anyone in Veii. Do they strike you as human?"

"They're mortal beings," she said. "I know they don't mate as ordinary men and women do, but when you reach my age you realize that carnal passion is hardly the sum of human existence. Pride and greed and will to power are equally strong motivations—so yes, I'd say they're human enough."

I nodded. "I tend toward a more optimistic view of the species, but I won't argue with you. Very well then—how do you interpret their intentions toward this world?"

"I think they love Veii in the abstract, but have trouble with the particular."

"Do you ever wonder if they could help more than they do?"

"Benevolence comes from the gods, child, and we've already decided that the pale folk are far from divine. To be honest, it's your sort that worries me more. I know something about the regions beyond Veii's strip of blue sky—more than most, for Chwefro and the rest often confide in me—and what I hear of your kingdom makes me grateful for the Firin's presence. I know that in the earliest times all Veii was a sulfurous pit of death. People lived only in the sky worlds, and were as numberless as a young girl's sighs, and as clever as an adulterous wife. Having no gods of their own they made a god, a great fetish of ice and fire. Once it was full grown this god looked back on its creators, and judged them, and found them lacking. So the new god turned toward Veii and said, 'Here I will create paradise.' The Firin assisted it, carrying the least tainted among the clever worldlings into Veii, so that they might be its first inhabitants.

"But the others found out, and there was war, and the new god was slain while the world was still half constructed. The clever folk would have destroyed the innocents too, but the Firin struck a bargain with them first. They said, 'Why kill these people? What use are corpses? Why not let them live, and work as your servants, and pay you a rich tribute?' The clever worldlings agreed, and we have offered our first fruits to the Firin ever since, to pay off your kindred in the sky."

"That's a pretty story," I said. "But do I seem any more clever—or wicked—than the Veiians you know?"

"I suppose not. But there must still be good souls born in heaven, since our ancestors came from there in the beginning."

"Thank you." I was enjoying this skewed picture of the Matterfield. "You realize, of course, that the Firin are the cleverest of all."

"Indeed they are, which is why I stay wary of them. But surely you won't deny that your own people would do us harm if it suited them."

I thought of Volshev's wrath and Seren's mischief and couldn't disagree: but I still hadn't learned what I wanted to know. "I bow to your wisdom, Ilesha," I said. "But do you have any idea what our life is like, up there in the airless void?"

"Not really," she confessed.

"Well, in many ways it's a poor one, though no one ever dies of hunger."

"And no one has in Woro either, at least not in all the seasons I've been Lady Day." Her pride was vehement.

"That's more commendable than you know. But what I mean is—our lives are carefully circumscribed, we follow a million rules, we marry only with the permission of our superiors, and bear children only if granted dispensation. In exchange for this obedience we rest easy in the knowledge that no woman will ever die in childbirth, that no child will ever succumb to the diseases of infancy, that we will all, in fine, live out our natural lifespans in perfect health, unless boredom or daring should make us choose otherwise."

Ilesha's mouth gaped. "There's no canker in your world, then, no lung rot, no cholera, no blackwater, no bleeding stools, no contorting paralysis, no falling sickness, no Gawian pox, no strokes or seizures, no ulcer, no jaundice, no dropsy, no griping in the guts, no spotted fever, no rupture, no palsy, no Yellow Plague?"

"None."

She frowned, shifting in her seat. "Then this old mare has yet to feel a few strokes of the whip. Natural wisdom tells me that illness is humankind's inalienable legacy. What spells have your shamans found to ward off Guje's anger and Nemuri's dance?"

The very phrasing of her question told me I couldn't convey more than a hint of modern biological theory; laziness kept me even from trying. "I'm ignorant of their precise methods," I said, "but believe me, they work."

"Are the Firin also schooled in these practices?"

"Far better than the healers of my own kingdom."

Ilesha looked toward the awning that shaded her peristyle from the sun's heat, but her gaze seemed to penetrate much further. "I myself have never made the pilgrimage to Ira-Ireru," she said slowly, "but I've heard rumors that those who do enjoy phenomenally good health afterwards. Could it be that the Firin possess the means to make us free of illness, and choose to withhold it? Or do they bestow such immunity only sparingly, on those few who serve their ends?"

"So it seems, Ilesha."

"Now I'm a healer myself. I realize that death is sometimes preferable to life. But I see only evil in such a miserly course." She shook her head. "This is something I'll have to think over in the coming intervals."

"As I have, in these sad spells since Olaro's death."

She stroked my braids with her old hand, hard and strong as a tree. "Don't brook, Risha. It'll make you sour, and the gods intended you to be as sweet as morning's berries. You'll learn to laugh again."

But for once I think even Ilesha was wrong.

I did make an effort, though. Despite the heat I took short walks in the open, cowering in the shade of a wide parasol with Soko by my side. We would climb the city wall and gaze out over the fields, where even the crops had to be protected by canopies and tents, and creaking waterwheels delivered their bounty drop by drop to the soil. Every spell we noticed the same few farmers. The only work they had now was some light weeding and pruning, or an occasional fine adjustment to the irrigation tubules; once that was done they squatted in their lean-tos and played dice, humming the sad songs of noon.

Such was our prospect to the east. To the south lay the yellow hills, with their lazy pillars of smoke rising into the sky; that scene I took care to avoid. Instead I looked northward, always northward, to the harbor, where idle ships rested on water as still as wine in a cup. No sea-birds rode the updrafts now, no stevedores toiled at the empty docks, but I daydreamed anyhow. I dreamed of rainclouds, of thunder and lightning, of steady gales that would fatten all that inert canvas and carry me on to my fate. I longed for movement in a paralyzed world. In spite of me the weather stayed calm; plague tolls hovered at eight mortalities per interval.

On our way back from these walks Soko and I usually met a group of slender, saffron-robed girls balancing tall amphorae on their heads. Like us they were hurrying home at the tolling of the curfew bells, bringing fountain water for the spell's main meal. They carried life; they turned their backs on death, on the flap of shrouds and the rumble of carts and the stench of putrescence. Their brave grace always lent me a measure of hope, enough, I suppose, to guide me through the nadir of the year.

When the change came it was abrupt and disorienting. I stepped into Ilesha's back garden one interval and saw a line of clouds blackening the eastern horizon, flowing like ink across a turquoise scroll. I noticed a hint of dampness in the air, a cool moisture that owed nothing to the sea. In the next moment I almost jumped out of my skin. A crack of thunder shook the sky, sounding for all the world like a cannon exploding on the field of battle—or at least the way I imagined such a thing would sound.

My heart lifted. I said a prayer to the god of roads, and almost felt pleased. A few women of the household joined me then and we all streamed into the plaza, where hundreds of other townsfolk had already gathered, despite curfews and quarantines. For the first time since setting foot on Veii's red earth I saw a shadow fall across the land, and the first raindrops followed, somewhat tentatively, wetting the outstretched hands and protruding tongues of Trokomari's ragged children. Cheers rose from a thousand throats into the gray turmoil of heaven.

It rained steadily for seven intervals after that. The House of Day rocked to the sound of prayers, music, and dances of thanksgiving—which, however, I avoided, out of fear that I would be possessed again. Instead I sought news of the plague marshals and the seafarer's guild, and had favorable reports from both sources. Whatever bacterium caused the Yellow Plague was intolerant of cool, moist weather; the plague's course appeared to be checked, and the guild was ready to lift the ban on overseas travel. I combed the docks in search of a ship bound for Golo.

What I found was a smelly old galleon whose master had loaded his cargo at the first sign of rain. The ship was called *Avayu wen Icheko,* the Sea-god's Favorite Girl—though her condition cast some doubt on poor Avayu's taste. Her master was a scrawny little man named Bofan; he sported the emerald nose ornament and peacock-feather fan typical of Woro's merchant class. He couldn't guarantee passage at any particular interval, but promised to set sail as soon as the wind allowed, and gladly accepted advance payment in the form of a hefty weight of metal. I returned to the House of Day under lowering skies and began putting my things in order.

Soko would accompany me, of course, at least as far as Ira-Ireru. It was inconceivable that a young woman would travel alone, and she made the perfect traveling companion, being a native of Golo herself. On the forty-second interval after Olaro's cremation we stood together in the Python Court to receive Ilesha's blessing.

She sang to Yeva, to Avayu, and to Tawataru, Lord of Thunder, her voice as deep and resonant as the wind. Hearing the stark poetry of her invocations, I felt my consciousness shift, catching glimpses of impossible things out of the corner of my eye. I sought Soko's hand for reassurance. Soon enough the chant concluded and Ilesha spoke in her own voice again, folding us in a comforting embrace.

"You're both daughters to me," she said, "yes, even you Risha, though you've only been under my roof half a season. My house is home to you both as long as I live. Now Soko—I expect you back in time for the Feast of Lights. I want you to be first in the procession of torchbearers. Once you've visited the Firin's island you'll be the equal of any young loremistress in Woro. And Risha, my nightblossom—you go onward to grim deeds, but I trust your heart will stay pure, and your liver stout enough to prevail even against the fiercest adversity. Go with my love and my favor."

At this Soko burst into tears; for once I provided comfort, guiding her out of the peristyle into the drizzly plaza. Ilesha waved after us with a wan smile on her beautiful old face.

We descended to the harbor and boarded ship, retiring to our cabin at once to avoid the rain. Our luggage had preceded us; to pass time we rearranged a few of the most essential things. It would be at least an interval before we were under way.

Soko moped. Seeing her anything but cheerful was such a surprise that I didn't know how to react. "What's bothering you?" I asked bluntly.

"I'm returning to Golo for the first time in eight years," she replied. She meant the brief years of Veii. "It's not easy for me."

I waited for her to say more, but she wouldn't. After an uncomfortable silence we began some kind of word game; it quickly bored me out of countenance.

"Do you hear news of your homeland?" I asked, still too curious for my own good.

"Woro is my home."

"I'm sorry. I meant Golo."

She shrugged one shoulder. "No more news than any other woman of Trokomari might have. I've heard only that the weather is bad this season; so far no rain has come."

I stared at her with narrowed eyes; she sighed and let the tale pour out.

"I remember how it was in such times," she said. "The grass withers and dies, and the herders are forced to buy grain in the port towns to feed their cattle. All of Golo is pasture land, you see, except for a few plantations on the north coast—the soil is so poor and rocky everywhere else that it supports only scrub and razorgrass. And even in the best years it's a dry country, drier than Woro, if you can imagine such a thing. So cattle herding is the only livelihood for most families."

"Was it for yours as well?"

"Of course. My father and his two brothers once kept one hundred cows, twenty oxen, eight bulls, and sixty goats. When I was twelve I had two kids of my very own, and a heifer whose horns curved like the branches of the rockflower tree. Every spell I rubbed ashes into her hide and fed her the choicest buds and leaves, and when I drove the cows up into the hills she followed after me, answering my herding song with her own soft calls. Her nose was like velvet and her eyes brimmed over with more affection than I ever hope to see in the eyes of a man. Her hide was reddish-brown with white triangular blotches, a perfect example of the *odungapu* coloration, as we say in west-coast dialect."

As she spoke Soko's eyes glistened; her throat caught on the words *velvet* and *odungapu*. I had never known her to express nostalgia. She had always been quiet and agreeable, never revealing her hopes or regrets.

"This heifer," I said carefully. "Did she have a name?"

"Lagomufana was her given name, but I called her Fana, or sometimes Afafa, especially when I sang. When I was thirteen the rains failed, just the way they're failing now. My father had to sell a quarter of his animals to buy fodder to feed the rest. But then the next year it was worse, and most of the herd caught the wasting sickness. My Lagomufana died then; we made a pyre for her just like a real person, and I hung her horns over the entrance to my sleeping hut. I would have taken a new heifer, but our herds were so depleted that there was none suitable. It didn't matter anyway; by the next Bright Season my family had grown so poor that my father . . . my father . . ." She stopped and couldn't go on. I knew enough of Veii by now to guess what had happened.

Taking her in my arms, I stroked her beaded plaits and nuzzled the nape of her neck. "Your father had to do something he later regretted?" I said quietly.

"Yes, he—he—I was the youngest of four daughters, and they all said I was the prettiest but one. I was fifteen, which is just the right age. They took me into Naith in a bullock cart and brought me in front of a fat man who smelled of whiskey and pomade." She trembled in my arms and her voice trailed away. I kept silent. In a moment she had controlled herself; she stood and faced the wall, her voice clear and measured.

"I was sold into slavery then. I think my price was twenty of the square coins of Traore. I never saw my family after that, never milked another cow, never tied my bells around a nanny-goat's neck. My master intended to sell me into a brothel at the port; I suppose my virginity would have fetched a small fortune. Instead one of Ilesha's daughters saw me in the market place and bought me for service in Trokomari. Woro doesn't recognize the institution of slavery, you see. I was put under contract to work for a specified period of time, until I earned back my purchase price. Ilesha is generous. I'm only twenty-four and already I've worked off my indenture. It's never occurred to me to seek my family again. For all I know they could be dead. The House of Day is my home."

She looked toward me again, and again her eyes filled with tears. "But now we're on this ship bound for Golo, and all my lost years are coming back to me like a palm-leaf carried in on the tide. If Ilesha hadn't asked me to, I never would have come, as much as I care for you, Risha."

Her sorrow took hold of me and put me firmly in my place. Twenty-four Veiian years equal no more than sixteen revolutions of Gheo; Soko was still a child. Though my troubles seemed enormous, hers were hardly less, and they had come much earlier in life.

"This master Bofan," she said, "the shipowner; in an odd way he reminds me of my first master in Naith. That gentleman was fat and this one is thin, but they share the same unwholesomeness. Bofan is also a slaver, you see. That's why he's setting out so early. He wants to reach Golo in the midst of this drought while prices are low."

Unwelcome news: I thought of disembarking at once, while we were still in the harbor, but it was Soko herself who dissuaded me. "You need to reach Ira-Ireru," she said. "This is the fastest means available to you. Bofan will deal in flesh and tears whether you sail with him or not." That was true, and I accepted her argument, however uneasy my conscience. Given the circumstances her judgment counted more than my own.

By a stroke of luck our crossing went quickly. A wind rose during the next interval and blew steadily for three more, carrying us halfway across the Bay of Cho. Soko's equanimity returned, mine maintained, and we had a reasonably comfortable time, staying below deck to avoid both crew and sun. The fact that we were in motion did everything for our spirits.

But by the fourth interval the wind had scanted. With Golo almost within reach this was more than frustrating. As our cabin became narrower and stuffier Soko and I dispensed with our scruples, and went up on deck for air.

All around us was the bright silent sea. The water was as clear as glass, and still as a bathtub: it gave me an eerie feeling. For a moment I wondered if we were sailing a toy through a garden pool. At the end of the world the ocean curved up and merged with the sky; there was no clear horizon line, all detail blurring in the declining sun. Anything might lie beyond. Once more Veii had become a waking dream.

Then the wind blew again and a sense of reality drifted down to reanimate the seascape. In two more intervals we were docking in Naith.

We disembarked as quickly as possible, for we had no farewells to say. As we trudged off, carrying our own gear, the crew of the *Avayu wen Icheko* was unloading a cargo of stockpiled Woro grain. "This is the way of it," Soko said. "Master Bofan will sell his wheat and barley at an exorbitant price to the people here, and use the money to buy twenty or so slaves. Then he'll ferry them over to the market in Gawi and trade them for Traoro guns and gunpowder. With all this talk of war, the armaments can be resold in Trokomari at a handsome profit."

What a perfect circle of cruelty and greed, I thought, and kept my eyes on the dusty ground.

Having seen Liriparo I didn't need to look at this sleepy harbor town. It was as dull and dun-colored as Woro's coast, and much sadder. We went directly to the house of Ilesha's factor and made ourselves known, using a jade seal for identification. A bare-breasted woman wearing an indigo headcloth ushered us in; we sat in her courtyard and sipped well water spiked with whiskey.

The woman was anxious enough to help us. Her name was Ala; she even remembered Soko, though in her present mood my companion didn't feel like sharing reminiscences. We merely stated our requirements and retired to a darkened chamber, to rest till our instructions could be carried out.

Ala worked efficiently. We woke to find a miniature expedition waiting for us in the alleyway: two palfreys, a guide mounted on a donkey, and a sturdy mule to carry our equipment. There was no reason to linger in Naith, and several good ones to leave. We mounted the animals and rode off into the barren plains west of town, leaving Ala shaking her head over our haste.

Golo is a small island, despite poetic references to the contrary. Naith is situated on the south coast of a long peninsula snaking westward from its central plateau, and Ira-Ireru lies off the opposite shore. We had only to cross a narrow isthmus to reach the islet's port of embarkation, a journey of perhaps six intervals. Our guide was tireless, our mounts were strong, and we ourselves were eager and impatient; the leagues disappeared beneath the horses' roughshod hooves.

I had ignored Naith's dreariness, but I couldn't close my eyes to the blasted countryside we rode through. The only grass we saw was brown and close-cropped; most wells we passed were dry or polluted. Occasionally we saw parties of nomads herding a few dozen scrawny cows; they looked with dead eyes on our well-fed mounts, and my heart shrank inside me. I had seen poverty on Ethri, real hunger and privation, but it couldn't compare with the misery of these wretched souls. Most resembled animated skeletons. None wore any ornaments, for by now anything of value must have been sold for fodder. Some vestige of dignity still lingered around them but soon even those straight backs would bend beneath the strain.

"Has the Yellow Plague visited Golo yet?" I asked our guide.

"Oh, for some time now. It's hardly a welcome guest, but at least it spares the cattle."

We slept beneath a felt canopy; my dreams were dim and confused. Soko cried out in her sleep and woke in tears. Both of us were past comfort, either to give or to receive. With a minimum of talk we rose, ate some bread and pickled fruit, and resumed the trail.

On this spell the landscape turned hilly. We saw neither man nor beast for watches at a time. Cacti sprouted amongst the rocks, twisted into bizarre shapes by the wind; umbrella trees made gaunt silhouettes on the horizon. Our horses had to pick their way through rock and gravel, so we made slower progress than during the previous intervals. Still, before a pot of chick-peas could have cooked through, we mounted a hilltop and beheld the Straits of Ireru glinting in the long rays of the late-season sun. A village huddled in a grove of date-palms some distance from the sea.

One part of me felt relief, but the rest was all business. "Are there frequent ferries across to the island?" I asked.

Our guide scowled. "No ferries leave from this village. No boatman would risk the crossing."

"I don't think I understand you. As Mistress Ala said, we must reach Ira-Ireru. You led me to believe we could find passage here in Olpu."

"Perhaps you can, but I doubt it. What you must do is find a man called Jom. He's the blacksmith hereabouts, he lives some way out of town. He'll help you on your journey. You can't miss his homestead—it's out along the sea road. But my job ends here. You'll go the rest of the way on your own."

The guide—a crusty old fellow, native to Olpu—annoyed me more than a little, but I said nothing. There was no doubting his complete unwillingness to accompany us further. We rode into town, disgusted, and left our mounts at the stable. There the guide relented enough to let us take the mule; since she carried our belongings this was a helpful concession. "She's a smart old thing," he explained. "She'll find her way back on her own."

Unfortunately the blacksmith's road was much longer than we expected. As we toiled along in the dusty heat, tugging on the mule's tether when she would have stopped, the sky subtly darkened. Soko sniffed the air and frowned. "There's a storm coming," she said slowly. "It may stay out at sea, but most likely it'll come inland. By Dalashon, by Tawataru, by Ijeji, this could be the rain my people are dying for!"

For her sake I hoped she was right; in fact I would have welcomed a drenching myself. As it happened, the clouds blew in much faster than a mule could plod, and before we so much as caught a glimpse of any cottage the northern sky was alive with serpentine flashes of lightning.

The world turned gray. My skin prickled; my heart boomed like a drum. Soko turned to stare at me in confusion.

Inside my head came a rushing sound, as of many voices carried on a torrent of water. Vast spaces were opening up there within my skull, and my field of vision, my window on the external world, began to darken and narrow. My arms had grown a kilometer long—Soko was holding one, but she was so far away that I could barely feel her hand. When I looked down at my feet, still walking along one in front of the other, they seemed tiny and toylike—clever mechanisms with no connection to the enormous sea-cave behind my eyes. The chorus of voices rose and rose like a tide.

"Risha! Risha!" Soko was calling my name. Dimly I perceived her hands playing with the amulets Ilesha had given me. My head cleared a little; the caverns seemed to shrink, my ocular windows seemed to widen. With those outer senses only I realized that we had come within sight of a thatched dwelling. Two trees flanked it. Each one had forking branches and narrow leaves, and both stretched high into the lightning-rent sky. From the right-hand tree hung twenty or thirty bottles, blown in translucent glass, tinted green and violet. From the left-hand tree dangled scores of whitened bones. As the wind freshened it made strange music among all those tibiae and femora and ribs, a clicking and clocking that sounded like gongs and drums.

A wickerwork screen flapped away from the dwelling's entrance. A man stepped out, peering into the gloom through close-set eyes. He was broad and corrugated with muscle, heavily bearded and dressed only in iron bracelets and a leather apron. With bowlegged grace he scuttled toward me, mumbling words that sounded like, "Keep steady, keep steady."

Rain had started falling. Huge drops blackened the dust and coursed down the ridges of my *luruka*. The sky was completely dark, a counterfeit of night, shattered more and more frequently by the blue-white glare of lightning. Once more the tides were rising inside my head; if there was any thunder its roar was lost in the cellular flood.

The blacksmith was next to me now. His lips moved ponderously, his head and shoulders blazed with actinic flame. Softly, deliberately, his hands traced the figures on my breasts. At his touch a crackling line of fire split my vision. Through the gap crawled a heavy serpent clothed in hieroglyphics, to coil round my heart.

So it happened again. This time I never completely lost consciousness —I could hear that impossible voice calling through my lips, and feel the caress of scaled muscle stroking my breasts and hips. Dalashon was no myth, no superstition: he was real and he was riding me. I shrieked his prophecies in the psychotic tones of a day-priestess, my words a stuttering babble that even I could scarcely follow. Against the roar of thunder my voice squeaked like chalk on slate. There in the mud, as rain drenched down, I screamed and danced, leaping with a ferocity I never dreamed I possessed. My arms undulated like snakes in the god's choreography, my legs kicked and stamped like a wild-stallion's, my tongue flicked in and out with reptilian speed.

Next to me the blacksmith danced with the energy of a demon, his eyes flashing sparks into mine. From time to time he reached out to steady me, stroking my *luruka* like a blind man reading raised characters on a page. At his touch Olaro's figures burned before my eyes: I saw the serpent, the tree, the waves, and the sun, all written in bolts of lightning, trembling in the murky air as if on the brink of manifestation. "Dalashon!" I cried. "Dalashon!"

And the god answered me, hissing in a voice of flame. He took me, he rode me, he used me, he filled my veins with electricity and my skull with a foaming brew, the distillation of the gods' own nectar. I hopped and twitched and shimmied, my hair snaking in witchlocks, my breasts shaking in a syncopated fugue, till at last the storm abated; and then, with a shout to rival the fading thunder, I collapsed in steaming mud.

When I woke it was an easy wakening. I was resting on my side, looking out an open casement. A garden lay beyond; it was walled round and full of fleshy cacti bearing plump yellow fruit. "Golo," I thought. "The blacksmith's cottage. That's where I must be."

Sitting up, I saw Soko assisting a large-boned woman in some kind of kitchen task. Both turned toward me with cheerful greetings. Seeing that I was well and rested, they advised me to seek Jom, who was at work over his forge in back of the house. "Just follow the music of his hammer," his wife advised.

I stepped out into a new world. A whitish fog had settled in while I slept, the first fog I'd seen in Veii. The universe seemed to doze in damp heavy silence. It drew back only reluctantly as I traced the path winding through cacti and thorn-trees, seeking the muffled clang of metal on metal.

"Ijeji's daughter!" Jom's voice cut through the mist. The blacksmith left off hammering and abandoned his forge, which glowed beneath a palm-leaf canopy. We sat together on a long bench nearby.

"You danced some dance, woman," he said. "It's plain you're bound for the Holy Isle."

I smiled. "Thank you for—grounding me. It was so painless this time. Not like before. How did you manage?"

"We all do what we can, Risha. I have one gift, you have another. I turn my sword against enemies, but I open my hands to someone like you. I was glad to dance you through the storm."

"Surely you serve Guje."

"I know something of that mystery. But none of the gods are strangers to me. I just try to stay on the cool side of things—even Guje has a cool side, you know."

I couldn't doubt anything this man said. Looking in his eyes, listening to the melody of his voice, I could well believe that fire was water, and that the iron god dandled babies on his knee.

"You're the man I must see about passage to Ira-Ireru," I said. "Can you find us a boat?"

"You don't have to say a word. It's already arranged."

Even as he spoke his wife came down the trail with Soko in tow, carrying our gear and various other packages. We rose and Jom led us all into the fog, following a pebbled footpath through densely overgrown cacti.

Before long I sensed the nearness of the sea. It was a faint smell in the heavy air, a sighing of waves against the shore. We came down to a rocky strand where mist boiled off the water in great billowing gusts. A bonfire blazed untended; candles burned all around, half-buried in sand.

Over the soft sound of the waves I could hear oars dipping in and out of the water. A boat emerged from the fog, as if manifested that very instant out of vapor and driftwood. It carried two oarsmen, and a third individual who stood quietly at the prow, wrapped in a colorless robe. Just offshore the crewmen shipped oars and ran the vessel onto the beach. Greetings were exchanged; Jom stepped forward and clasped hands with the central personage.

Recognition was quick and bitter. My tongue curled like Dalashon's, ready to spew venom. But the words faded before I could hurl them into the haze. No; I felt too much at peace, too unexpectedly refreshed to vent those old passions. "Chwefro," I said. "I'm here at last."

The Firin smiled; the inhuman beauty of that pale face transfixed me as before. "Well done, Risha. I see you've found a brave companion. Come along and we'll be on Ira-Ireru before another interval is wasted."

Jom kindled a lamp amidships while his wife stowed our belongings and various gifts of fruit and bread. Then they withdrew onto the strand so Soko and I could board. In a few more moments we were gliding off into the fog, our farewells quickly swallowed in the white silence.

Chwefro's estimate was fair enough. We rowed through still water for perhaps a watch, and then contrary currents took hold of us, challenging our oarsmen's best efforts to maintain course. Meanwhile the fog lifted; as it dissipated I saw that we were surrounded by frothy water, churning whirlpools, and white explosions of spray. Still I never doubted our safety, for Chwefro sat as calmly as a wax figure, admiring the view, oblivious to any threat.

"I've been having trouble sleeping," I said conversationally. "Strange dreams, nightmares in fact—visions of torment and death. You know, I had a lover in Trokomari, but the plague got him. Since then my sanity's been a bit shaky. On two occasions I was even possessed by the mysteries. The second time was only an interval ago."

"That's encouraging," said Chwefro. "It could have been worse—you might simply have experienced a nervous collapse. You're even tougher than I thought, Risha."

"I beg your pardon?"

"You remember the injections I gave you on the *Burden of Truth,* those peptide hormones? And the oral dosage I presume you've been taking since then to maintain your pigmentation?"

One flat wafer every twenty-one intervals: the sun's cruelty never let me forget *that* detail. "I'm not sure I understand," I said through a tightening larynx. "Those nightmares, those bouts of holy madness—are you suggesting they were side effects of the drug?"

"In a word, yes. The particular compound we used has a few undesirable properties—it usually stimulates a tumorous growth somewhere in the limbic system. This tumor will be functional; it interferes with the storage and release of neurotransmitters, especially during periods of emotional stress. Your lover's death would have been such an occasion. Sit still, Risha—you don't want us to capsize, do you? There's really nothing to worry about. Your brain has simply been overloaded with certain complex proteins—we'll fix it up in Ira-Ireru. You won't even need surgery. We can break up the malignancy with a proton beam, quickly and without any pain."

"You knew this would happen when you gave me the injections."

"I knew it would happen eventually, but I hoped to have you on the island before then. There were unexpected complications." Chwefro shrugged and maintained a benevolent smile.

The strength and relaxation that Jom had lent me threatened to crumble; I forced myself not to shout or make wild gestures. I caught Soko's eye on me, her disgust for Chwefro's attitude implicit in the set of her face. "Chwefro," I said. "Does that mean that my experiences of the deities were simply hallucinations, manufactured by a disordered brain?"

"Oh, no, no, no. That is, you may believe so if you choose, but I have another interpretation. Without those doses of peptides you would never have become receptive to the mysteries' presence; with them you are able to share in an experience highly valued among the Garengazi cultures."

"So you see no need for an apology, no need for compassion or sympathy."

"I'll offer you whatever comfort you require, my dear lady."

"How about truthful answers to every question I ask from this moment on?"

"I'm not sure how comforting that would be."

I grimaced and desisted. We were passing through a tunnel cut through rock by natural erosion; at its further end I saw clear water and blue sky. We emerged into a bay ringed around with fancifully weathered boulders. Before us lay Ira-Ireru, all rolling hills and lush vegetation, green-gold in the late day sun. I drew a breath and resigned myself to ambiguity.

CHAPTER NINE

The Firin's island is actually the crater of an extinct volcano. An outer ring of land surrounds an inner lake of sparkling salt water, and at the center of this lake lies another island, crowned with a complex of marmoreal domes and colonnades. Part temple, part dormitory, part sanatorium, this rambling structure houses a hundred beds, each one a perfect antidote to insomnia, and no two of them alike. There are hammocks, featherbeds, canopied four-posters, plain pallets of crisp cotton batting, cradles rocking in manicured trees, water-filled divans, sensual heaps of furry cushions, even piles of clean straw mixed with fragrant herbs. Here the pilgrims come to take their rest, sinking into sleep during the droning lectures of somnipathic guides. And they dream.

Over millennia the Firin have gained a formidable reputation in the downlands of Veii. They are shapers of dreams, architects of visions that can cure the ills of troubled human beings. In a world where psyche and soma are so closely intermingled they have assumed the dual role of physician and psychiatrist, and in this covert manner, with extreme care and caution, they dispense knowledge of the Matterfield into Veii's archaic civilizations.

But while pilgrims pursued visions I worked to rid myself of dreams. During my second spell on the island a bland Firin, who might have been Chwefro's twin, passed a wand over my head and told me my tumor had dissolved. Thereafter Chwefro and I spent at least one interval out of three in close company, while I studied the means of controlling the god-state, the mysteries' holy madness.

"But the deities ride men," I objected, during my first lesson. "Not the reverse. How can a mortal have power over a god?"

Chwefro was patient. "Your insight into native ethos is commendable, Risha, but there is such a thing as carrying this participant-observation thing too far. The metabolism of your brain has been subtly altered; this endows you with certain talents and certain liabilities."

"You mean I've become a fit steed for Ijeji, but something of a whipping post for Guje and Nemuri?"

"My references to local religion are metaphorical only. I'm merely giving you a tool that will help you in your mission."

My mission. I tended to get caught up in day-to-day existence, but Volshev's ultimatum loomed over me. To reach Seren I had to infiltrate the court of Anago of Traore. Chwefro was trying to show me how.

We had decided that I would seek the Nightlord's patronage as a dancer. I practiced every spell; a Traoro woman coached me in her country's typical modes, from the most vigorous war-dances to the languorous coils of seduction. Chwefro stood by, and at the peak of my concentration uttered an hypnotic command to put me in trance. I had already seen how contagious the god-state could be, spell after spell in Ilesha's peristyle. Now I was learning how to weave dream-cues into my own choreography, engendering visions in all who watched.

It might happen with the flick of a wrist, the roll of a hip, the flash of light off a gilt bracelet, the winking of a kohl-rimmed eye. What counted in a particular gesture was that it be subtle, compelling, evocative; Chwefro often used the word *unforgettable*. I had to communicate my god-intoxicated state through the postures of my body, so that on-lookers would depart with those gestures etched into their brains, to haunt them and obsess them in dreams. Such performances would at-tract universal attention, and make me worthy of Anago's hall.

I have a phenomenal memory—I'd qualify that remark with dry laughter if I could—but those intervals on Ira-Ireru all blur together. When I wasn't sleeping I was dancing through an inner landscape of crossroads and rivers, sea-caves and sun-blasted mountaintops, snakepits and sighing trees, moving in the company of prophets and demons and gods. I was rarely in my right mind at all. When I had finished working for the spell the world around me seemed as unreal as my visions. Waving branches left trails behind them in the air, tiny gnomelets lurked in the corners of my eyes. Reality itself trembled like a soap-bubble that might burst at any second. Chwefro's potions were my chief consolation: they guaranteed me a sleep that was cool and bland and empty of dreams.

We were resting one spell on a grassy bank overlooking the outer sea; the sun was mellow and golden, the sky half-filled with flocculent clouds, grazing in the blue meadows of heaven. With White Shadows past I'd begun to enjoy the outdoors. My spirits were recovering, slowly but steadily, from the grief that had pressed them down.

"Does the world *love* have any meaning for you, Chwefro?" I asked out of a companionable silence. "I already know about your connection with *lust.*"

"My nonexistent connection, you mean?" Chwefro glanced at me fondly. "In ancient Ethri love was a god, a spiritual force that rained down from heaven. It wasn't limited to the human sphere, like fleshly passion. That higher love is no stranger to me—though you may find its source and object a bit unlikely."

I waited. Memories of Lord Mudriye swam before me in the gauzy air.

"I've spoken of Meqmat before," Chwefro continued. "Among your people he—for convenience let me personify something that transcends any notion of personality—he represents the very pinnacle of evil. I think you've seen how mistaken that idea is. But can you imagine him as the most advanced organism that evolution has yet produced, as the highest expression of good? When that enormous array of processors and auxiliary storage units and input terminals and expressive organs was in place and functioning, the whole Matterfield became a single intelligent organism—a creature fifteen billion kilometers in diameter, possessed not of one but of thirty billion souls. The sun was his heart and belly, the planets were his limbs, the comets his food and drink. Pure photons alone conveyed the information that sustained his consciousness. The whole system became a cat's cradle woven of lasers, a mighty harp of light tuned to resonate in an endlessly modulating chord.

"Do you begin to understand the object of my ardor? It is in the essential nature of humanity to manufacture gods; the creation of Meqmat has been paralleled many times, albeit on a smaller scale. But Meqmat was unique: for, once created, he turned creator himself. Veii was one product of his will, we Firin another. As child loves parent, as dog loves master, as iron loves the magnet's pull, so we turn toward Meqmat with the deepest devotion we can offer. And in loving him we necessarily love the fruit of his industry, this world of Veii itself. We will never forsake his most beloved creation, just as we can never forsake his blessed memory."

Chwefro raised me with one arm and bade me follow along a fern-bordered path. "In fact we do more than remember, Risha. It's time for you to learn a few of those secrets you're so curious about."

We entered the dream-house through a side door. A lift carried us down; my ears popped twice. We emerged in a circular chamber centered around a broad translucent pillar. "The crater lake is above us," Chwefro murmured. We approached the pillar and my companion vocalized a series of clear tones.

"Welcome, scion of Paun and Skhorb." A sexless voice addressed me in perfect Revenant dialect. "It seems that Chwefro wants to impress you with Firin craft."

It is illegal for computers to speak in the Hypaethra, but I was familiar enough with the notion. My suspicions multiplied. "If you don't mind my asking," I said, "just who are you?"

"A shard, a splinter, a fragment of infinity. A small memento of something very grand. You realize, of course, that eternity dwells in a single instant? That time may be subdivided into infinitesimal units, without ever exhausting the powers of division? You yourself represent a whole universe of possibility and limitation, a womb of chance, a sepulcher of will and desire. You're not so different from the mind behind this voice."

"Are you Meqmat?"

"Meqmat was a manifold entity, and this poor scrap is no more than a whim and a chatter. Greater scope is needed than a two-meter box of light.

> *"Long fall, wrong call*   *Facts in immersion*
> *no bottom to break*   *eaters of ends*
> *circling seeker*   *drowning, earth-mad*
> *screams in reverse.*   *nodding, mute:*
> *no call, no vow, no rendering."*

This last was delivered in two-part harmony. The melody was familiar but the sense eluded my best efforts.

"Meqmat," I said. "Do you act, or are you acted upon?"

"The universe was born, and it will die. The gravitational constant hasn't changed since the first instant of creation. Galaxies continue to flee from the primordial void. In the face of such evidence, who can go on asserting the doctrine of free will? All life forms are subject to the strictures of matter."

"But time—time is a river, not a block of ice. It moves and changes. Its course is unknowable, except through hindsight. Certainly we can choose our own futures."

My own voice came back in reply—laughing merrily, as if from five or six different throats, ebbing and surging in a chorus of mirth. Meqmat gave me no other answer. Then Chwefro caught my eye, and we started back the way we came.

"So you salvaged something of your murdered lord," I said, when we walked in the light again.

"A fragment only, which we've tended carefully for more than a thousand revolutions. There are other bits and pieces stashed around the Matterfield just waiting for reunion. Given the Revenant presence, and in particular Lord Volshev's stance, we're content to bide our time."

"You foresee a resurrection?"

"That day will dawn, I promise you."

"But whatever I know, Volshev may discover, whether I consent or not. Won't that inconvenience you?"

"Perhaps we intend Lord Volshev to find out."

"Chwefro! You're spinning schemes within schemes. Please don't trap me in the web. Tell me frankly what you do intend."

For once my teacher made no attempt at evasion. "We hope to rehabilitate Meqmat, to the point where he can recreate himself. Obviously this is a massive undertaking that can never be accomplished in the face of Hypaethral opposition. Therefore we've worked in secret, tinkering about in remote corners of the Matterfield; our next step will be to centralize the operation here on Veii. Before ten more years brighten the western horizon we will have reassembled all existing fragments; then we must raise the system again, and eventually run an abbreviated Meqmat program. I doubt I'll live to see that phase come to fruition. We have so much to reconstruct, and our resources are limited."

"But what is your goal?"

"A restoration of pre-conquest civilization, on Veii rather than Ethri, guided and regulated and enriched by a new version of Meqmat."

I nodded. "And where do my people fit into this design?"

"As valued subordinates."

I walked along and tried this vision on for size. "So you see the present era as a time of waning and decadence, and would revive the glories of the past? I suppose I have no objections. I'll also be dead and forgotten long before your dreams come true, but I hope no present strife arises on account of what you've just told me."

"I'm confident of the wisdom of the Inner Circle," said Chwefro, and we spoke no more of it.

Thirty-nine intervals languidly pursued one another across the green meadows and flowering arbors of Ira-Ireru. I learned what I had to learn: the proper dances, the correct oneiric cues, the peculiar accents of the Toso language, even the personal habits of Lord Anago himself. A spell or two before my departure I was subjected to the final test. In a broad courtyard inside the dream-house, to the music of a Traoro-style orchestra, I danced for an audience of newly arrived pilgrims.

The drums resounded in my blood. My heartbeat quickened to the trilling of a bone flute. My eyes glazed, and that familiar *inhabited* feeling overtook my body, so that my limbs seemed to move of themselves. Call it holy possession, call it the triumph of the unconscious mind: to any Veiian I was treading the gods' own measures.

Chwefro had assigned me a sequence of cues, which my muscles executed automatically. The onlookers watched in fascination as I whirled and gestured, writhed and perspired. When I was finished I fell on my face—for even a guided trance exhausts body and mind. Soko and another woman carried me off to my chambers, while the pilgrims retired to hammocks, pallets, and divans, for a consultation of their own dreaming oracles. The tales they told on waking would determine how well I'd done my work.

My teacher delivered the verdict along with a breakfast of melons and cream. "The dreams ran true," Chwefro announced. "One woman saw a casket full of light, which opened and showered her with golden coins. A child imagined an egg hatching, and when a gorgeous bird crawled out he climbed on its back and flew up to the sky. An old man dreamed he was waiting before a glowing door; it swung aside to reveal his father, who handed him a plate of sweet oranges. You've learned quickly, Risha. You're ready for the challenge of Traore."

In my mind I rejoiced, but my stomach was somewhat less optimistic. Whether my own or another's, death waited for me across the broad Garengazi.

I wept when we parted. Chwefro held me in an embrace so powerful and warm that I was amazed to think we'd ever quarreled, astonished to recall that this being had once toyed with my health and sanity. "Go, and be sure that my thoughts follow after you," Chwefro said. "We'll meet again at Anago's court." We kissed and my tongue tasted salt.

On the north side of Ira-Ireru is a small harbor. There Soko and I boarded a caravel specially chartered by the Firin to carry us and a dozen other pilgrims across the sea to Gawi, chief port of entry into Anago's realm. Our sails stretched taut in a following wind; the figures on the shore dwindled; I turned my face to the open sea. Three spells later we stood off the teeming delta of the Shibu River.

"Even from here this land of Traore has a foul smell," Soko said, curling her lip in the breeze that reached us from shore. The water was mud-brown, and odors of fish and decaying seaweed mingled in a fecal bouquet.

"We shouldn't judge the whole country by one port," I said reasonably. "I'm sure Imari has its charms."

Gawi, however, did not. Sprawling untidily along the east bank of the Shibu, it was a crowded, dirty town, overbuilt and overpopulated, echoing at all intervals with the noises of vehicles and voices, factories and forges. The only thing to be said in its favor was that it led the cities of Veii in trade. Anything could be obtained here, with enough money: rare jewels, fair virgins, learned volumes, fine wines—not to mention the high-quality armaments that were its chief export.

Soko and I had some difficulty at the customs house. All disembarking passengers were questioned about their recent travels and future plans, and asked point blank to declare their sympathies in the war between Lozi and Traore. Of course there was only one permissible answer. We posed as young women of Golo; we claimed to be on our way to visit some kinsmen living in a suburb of Imari. After a thorough search they let us pass.

Needless to say, we tarried very briefly in Gawi. Within two intervals we found space on a riverboat sailing to the capital; we paid dearly for our cabin, but at least it was clean, and the boat loaded only to its legal capacity.

The journey upriver was pleasant. Fertile countryside unfolded to either side of us; Traore is a moister region than Woro, with a more varied landscape. We saw villages with thatched and gabled houses, wooded areas where pine and cedar grew, big plantations of wheat and cotton, compact groves of fruit trees, rolling hills topped with white-washed shrines, and finally the distant mountains of Azen. When the wind allowed we unfurled our sails, making good progress against the current; otherwise the boatmen poled us along, singing basso chanties as they worked.

We disembarked a few intervals' journey outside Imari, after a passage lasting five spells. Our landing was a farming town straddling one of the Shibu's tributaries. Its houses were tall and half-timbered, its people placid, hardworking, and incurious. We purchased provisions in the central market—Chwefro had supplied us liberally with the iron counters of Traore—and hired both a moveable pavilion and a donkey to carry it. A visit to the local bathhouse refreshed us enough to continue on foot.

"It won't be long now," I promised Soko. We walked on either side of the donkey's head, moving slowly and deliberately. "The Firin know the ways of these Traoro folk as well as they understand the currents in the Strait of Ireru. I have faith in their advice."

"So do I," she conceded, "but it makes me feel like a puppet on the stage in Beggars' Market."

I thought of Meqmat, and suppressed a shiver.

The town was ringed around with hedged fields and scattered islands of forest. We made for one of the latter, following a well-worn trail into the gloomy ranks of juniper, cedar, and oak. After a while we saw signs of human meddling: white ribbons fluttering from low branches, bags of herbs and soil swinging from higher ones, clay dolls propped in the treetops. In the green-tinged light everything assumed an air of sinister watchfulness and mystery. We could hear the sound of a wind harp thrumming somewhere down the trail; our donkey's pace quickened, and we emerged in a wide clearing. A stream bisected it noisily. Numerous chimes and harps swung from the surrounding shrubbery, adding their music to the song of swift water running over rocks and fallen branches.

"Exactly as Chwefro described it," I said. "There should be a waterfall further upstream."

We had only to follow our ears. A narrow cascade plunged about five meters into a rock-strewn pool, raising a curtain of spray. Its ceaseless pounding and splashing had a mesmerizing effect on me; here was a perfect haunt for hydromancers. We chose a spot some distance away, beyond the range of ribbons and cult-images, and raised our pavilion. Murmuring a prayer to Dalashon for patience and fortitude I settled down to wait.

Over the next few spells the waterfall had many visitors, arriving in groups of two or three, occasionally in larger parties. Many came from Imari; we were very near the city now. Most wore white garments and seemed well educated in the cult's gestures. I watched them swimming in the pool, bathing in the waterfall, praying to Yeva and Ijeji, tying intricately knotted ribbons, and assembling little heaps of stones, feathers, and shells. As promised, this modest clearing was a gathering place for Imari's spiritual elite.

They regarded me with polite interest, there where I sat bare-chested with my beautiful *luruka* on display. With Soko's tambourine in plain sight it wasn't difficult to guess our specialty. When enough of the curious had gathered, when enough of my energy was tuned, I rose, made obeisance to the six directions and the four waters, and began my dance.

The first time I nearly lost control and abandoned myself to the rushing voices inside. It was one thing to practice in a supporting circle of friends and quite another to perform before a group of specialists. But I held on, I held steady, thanks in large measure to Soko's presence. I invoked Ijeji without being utterly possessed by her, and her own queenly guise projected a series of potent dream-cues. By any strict definition I falsified the mysteries; I freely confess to charlatanism, and plead only that my end justified my means.

I spun and coiled, stretched long and bent deep. My audience watched closely and returned home to dream. Within six spells the crowds around the waterfall had grown much larger.

They waited patiently in a buzz of gossip. "She has the mark of Izezi on her," one old lady whispered, in the accents of Traore.

"She threads the maze of dreams, no question about it," said her younger companion.

"My son is with the army besieging Tolun," a stout burgher confided, "and last round I dreamed I saw him standing before the Lord of Night, as hale as the spell he went off to war. Lord Anago was handing him the gold dagger of captaincy. I swear it, she must gave given me the dream, for I saw her at Anago's side, looking like his favorite wife. It's a sure sign of induction when the dancer shows up in the dream. I only pray to Guza that I see my vision come true."

They weighed and wondered, unaware that I listened behind the calico panels of my tent. My reputation was improving with each new vigil.

After my dancing that round I was assailed by a crowd of city folk asking me idle questions about the future. "I have nothing to say," I told them. "It's all in the dance. Dream and let that be your answer."

They were reluctant to leave me, but then a tall fat man appeared in their midst with two armed bodyguards. I had marked him in the audience earlier; he moved with cheerful nonchalance, but his eyes watched shrewdly.

"Let the woman be!" he commanded. "If you exhaust her powers now, she'll have no energy to dance for you next time." To my surprise the idlers immediately dispersed into the surrounding forest.

"You can thank me by sparing me a little of your time," he said genially, sitting next to me on the mat. His companions remained some distance away, so we spoke in private, screened from view inside my pavilion. "My name is Falabon. If you haven't heard of me, you're either an imbecile or a corpse."

"Or a foreigner newly arrived from Golo," I countered, with my heavy accent as proof.

"Aha! Then more fool you, for not discovering the way of things here in Imari, for not learning who counts and who doesn't, and what's done and what's best avoided."

"Is there a darker meaning in those words?"

He laughed easily; despite his girth he was a well-favored man, and his face was mobile and handsome. "Soon there will be a darker meaning in all creation, as the sun sinks and the night's influence steals forth. But no, I intend no threat. I'm a praise-poet at Anago's court; my verse as well as my feet carry considerable weight around Imari. I advise the Lord of Night on sundry issues, tempering his passions, cooling him down from the hot moods that seize him now and again."

"Surely those moods have nothing to do with me?"

"Ah!" Falabon winked, with a show of amiable slyness. "Who can tell? Your fame has traveled quickly, even to Anago's ears. All of us at court find it curious that a foreign woman should suddenly appear, performing the dream-dance at the very gates of Imari. Perhaps you don't realize that the old religion has been out of favor for some years now. I speak candidly. Forty seasons ago there was a civil war in Traore; Anago, then a stripling, led the army that drove Mistress Uzuwa from the House of Day. She had abused her powers and enfeebled the state; Anago restored order and reformed the practice of the rituals. Since then the old mystery cults have lost ground. The Warlord still honors the Twelve Fetishes with public sacrifices, but does little else according to the old custom. In particular he has no use for shamans such as you; since the office of Lady Day was abolished, such women have plotted ceaselessly against him, causing him no end of trouble. They all seek revenge for what they see as a sacrilegious murder—namely, the Warlord's legal execution of a witch."

"Mistress Uzuwa, you mean?"

"Of course. Now this has all died down in recent years. Few priests or priestesses invoke the mysteries any more, fewer still perform this dream-dance you do so well. In Anago's mind such practices smack of sedition. So when news drifted up to the citadel concerning a young prophetess spinning dreams in the forest, the Warlord was naturally annoyed."

"And he sent you here to question me."

"Have I asked a single question? No, dear lady, I came of my own accord, out of curiosity and compassion. They told me you were beautiful, and I was unwilling to see a beautiful woman run afoul of my master."

"Does he plan to cause me any trouble?"

"He may. There was some talk of sending a few magistrates by, next round, to see if you're breaking the law."

His eyes twinkled with amusement; I had a harder time finding the humor. "You're very kind—I think. But why have you gone out of your way to warn me?"

"Because I owe you a debt of gratitude. You see, this isn't my first visit to your forest clearing; I was here last round also, though I took pains that you wouldn't notice me. Since then I've slept and dreamed: and what a sweet vision it was. I dreamed of a woman, tender as a ripe fig, and she was handing me a newborn son. In spite of my master's leanings I'm a superstitious man. I have a wife who's neither beautiful nor sweet, and she's borne me nothing but daughters. Your vision gave me hope. It's decided me to take a second wife and try my fortune again."

What power men have to delude themselves, I thought, taking care to keep sarcasm from my voice. "I'm honored that I helped you toward that decision, Lord Falabon. Now you see how harmless my dances are. I care nothing about your master's dynastic struggles. I came here in ignorance of his intrigues, seeking only to practice the art I know best."

"Why exactly *did* you travel here from Golo?" Finally he questioned me, and though his tone was offhand I knew I was still being judged.

"What future did I have there? You must know about the drought and the misery in my country; any who can afford to are emigrating."

"But why Traore rather than Woro? Surely you'd find a warmer welcome in Mistress Ilesha's realm."

I shrugged. "I'm young and curious. I want to see the world. Traore offers wider scope than any island."

Falabon appeared to accept that at face value. I omitted reference to another factor—the greater popularity I would enjoy in a place with so little competition. Already my admirers had begun bringing me gifts, which Falabon couldn't fail to notice. Let him think there was a mercenary side to my character.

"I have an offer to make you," he said. "It may be wise for you to suspend your performances for a little while. I could find you some secluded place to stay until Anago's mind turns in another direction."

I smiled as sweetly as I could, avoiding anything of the tease or the harlot. "You *are* kind. But I have an inner prompting in this matter. I have nothing to hide from your lord; I plot no intrigues and I intend no mischief. In fact I would welcome the opportunity to appear before him, whether as a subject of interrogation or as a dancer performing her art. I'm confident that he could find no fault whatsoever with my behavior."

"Woman!" Falabon bellowed in mock horror. "Do you realize what you're saying?" I stared him down and his features softened into a grin. "It seems you do. You're a bold one, perhaps a trifle too ambitious for your own good. But if you want rumor of this 'inner prompting' to reach my master, I'll see that it does. Are you game?"

"I am."

We brushed palms together and Falabon rose to leave. "We'll meet again," was all he said.

As he and his men departed Soko came walking back from the stream with a jug of water on her head. Falabon cast her an appraising glance, looked back in my direction, and nodded sagely. It was clear to me then what a perfect ally I'd found.

Only Koyo's infinite grace allowed me any sleep during the next interval. My mind whirled with the manifold perils I risked. Naturally nothing Falabon had said was news to me; Chwefro had briefed me thoroughly in Ira-Ireru, so I knew what a thin wire I walked. Anago would suspect me of anything and everything: my life was in his hands.

A far smaller crowd gathered to see me dance that round. I guessed that Falabon's official presence at my last performance had engendered paranoia, keeping prudent folk away. Nevertheless, the old drummer who played for me was on hand and ready, and Soko sat waiting with her tambourine.

We had just begun the invocation when a commotion in the audience stopped us short. A party of men appeared on horseback, all armed to the teeth and most wearing face paint in bold geometric patterns. They dismounted and took up a position at the very front of the crowd; a folding chair was produced for one of their number. This individual sat down with exaggerated casualness, and a warrior came to stand by his side, holding aloft an elaborate fan. There was no mistaking that insignia. The Lord of Night had arrived.

Many in the audience slipped away in the next few minutes. When the rest had settled down we resumed our ceremonial—drums throbbing, tambourine jangling. I recited the rhyme Chwefro had taught me and counted my breaths till the trance came on; then it was as if a veil were drawn over the world, and a new universe uncovered inside my mind. I danced until the drums told me to stop.

Afterwards I retired to my tent as I always did, limp with sweet exhaustion. Just as on the previous spell my rest was disturbed by the good Master Falabon. "Risha," he said. "The Warlord wants to see you."

I followed him to the seated gentleman. He was a tall, gaunt man with a five-pointed star painted on his forehead. He regarded me dispassionately for several breaths—trying to intimidate me, I suppose—before he finally spoke.

"I heard you were eager to dance before the Lord of Night." His voice was deep and measured, a more thoughtful tone than I would have expected. "Your artistry moved me, and I'm inclined to reward you. What would you consider a suitable bounty?"

Here was a test worthy of a leader of men. My reply came without hesitation. "Simply the freedom to dance before the gentlefolk of Imari, as often as they wish to see me."

"You don't want gold, or perhaps an hereditary title for one of your kinsfolk?"

"The will of the gods brings us all what we deserve. I'm confident of my own worthiness."

"What if I offered to make you my wife?" He regarded me intently, with no trace of affection in his gaze; I betrayed my shock.

"Why, to be—to be the wife of the Warlord of Traore would honor any woman," I said slowly. My gaze strayed to the fanbearer, who was watching me with a broad grin. "But I understand that you already have four wives, so how would there be room for me in your household? A woman like me could never flourish with superiors looking over her shoulder, chiding her and inhibiting her, subjecting her to jealous slights and spiteful whims—which I would deserve, of course, being a foreigner of common birth, completely unsuited to a noble harem."

"Shouldn't I be the judge of that?" he said testily. "Don't you think the Warlord's mansion is roomy enough to house a hundred wives? Don't you think I can keep order in my own family? Don't I hold the whole land of Traore in the palm of my hand?"

"Why no, I don't think you do."

Jaws gaped; my interrogator frowned. "What are you suggesting, young woman? Do you realize whom you're addressing?"

"As a matter of fact I have no idea who you are—but I do know that *this* man is Lord Anago of Traore." And I knelt before the sturdy fanbearer, paying him the respect I had never shown the impostor.

Laughter rewarded me, booming out of every belly. "Stand and face me, Risha," said the Warlord of Traore. "I don't know how you managed to unmask me, but I'll allow you your secrets." He handed the insignia to another of his attendants and sank into the ivory chair.

Anago was a large man with a broad, sensual face. His hair was brushed back to reveal a five-pointed star scarred into his forehead—the same symbol the impostor had mimicked in paint. "So you're not interested in marrying my cousin Felo," he said. "What would you say to me?"

"Why, the same thing. You're toying with a poor girl's heart. If you crave my company there are easier ways to arrange it."

"So there are, so there are." He smiled roguishly. "We tried to have a joke at your expense, but since you've turned it back on us we may as well get down to business. It's true that I value your talent. For too long such arts have been used against me, so I'm glad to find an initiate like yourself who brings auspicious dreams. My subjects are full of the visions you brought—and the oneirologists of Imari interpret them in the most favorable terms. Therefore I would like you to come and live in the capital for a-while. I want you to dance for all the leading citizens of the land. That way you'll have the reward you claimed, and material comfort besides. If, after a season, you decide to leave, you may go with my blessing; but for now I hope you'll grant my wish and come along to Imari."

Blood warmed my face, and my flesh tingled, reminding me that I was a human being and not a puppet. But I couldn't shake the feeling that we were all reading from a script, acting out a play. It seemed that everything had happened before. "Your desire is mine," I replied, inclining my head as graciously as a Radiant of Gheo. "I'll follow wherever you lead."

"Well spoken!" Anago sprang up and barked a few quick commands to his followers; then, mounting, he led the party off into the woods, without another glance at me.

Falabon stayed behind as my escort. While we waited for more horses to be fetched he regarded me narrowly, and finally asked, "How did you see through our deception?"

"You forget, Falabon, that I dream too. I saw Lord Anago in a vision not two intervals past, so I knew very well what he looked like." Falabon nodded, visibly impressed; I practiced my most mysterious smile. Actually Chwefro had shown me his picture while I stayed in Ira-Ireru.

By the time Falabon, Soko, and I set out for Imari the Warlord's party was nowhere in sight; even the dust of their passage had settled. We rode down the highway at an easy pace, through fields of golden wheat—tall enough for a harvester's sickle and fair enough for an artist's brush. The sun slanted down at a shallow angle. As it neared the horizon its disk turned yellow, and its radiance softened, so tame and beneficent where once it had been cruel. The whole countryside glowed.

Green ramparts loomed before us, enclosing an area of perhaps twenty-five square kilometers. These were the outermost of Imari's defenses: enormous earthworks overgrown with grass, far more effective against siege cannon than any pile of stone. Cast iron gates allowed entrance at several points, each one guarded by a pair of towers and a whole squadron of soldiers. The area before the walls was crowded with tents and pavilions; many were patched and tattered, but a few gleamed with satin insets and metallic stitchery.

"Is it a fair?" I wondered.

"Sort of a permanent fair," said Falabon. "We call it Ragtown." He reached into his saddlebag and pulled out a scroll tied with green cords. "See this? It's an entry permit, granting two Golo females, answering to the names of Soko and Risha, the privilege of walking into Imari. If you read it carefully, you'll notice that entrance is permitted only at the West Gate, the Gate of Blue Masks, and the Gate of Skulls, strictly between the first and fifth vigils of the round. You're very, very fortunate to have one. None of the poor wretches in Ragtown do, though many would kill to get their hands on one."

We had reached the outskirts of the shantytown. Our horses picked their way nervously through the mass of unwashed bodies that pressed in from every side. Dozens of grubby hands thrust cheap wares into our faces, importuning us to buy; others begged outright. "If we'd come with soldiers we wouldn't be bothered by all this," Falabon shouted over the din. "A great pity."

I looked on in a daze; here was poverty such as we'd seen in Golo, multiplied a hundredfold. Children ran about naked, showing off the sores that covered their twiglike limbs; scrawny women nursed scrawnier babies. Young boys idled against tent poles, a bit of rag their only garment; withered crones shivered with palsy. Most of the tents I saw made some pretense to commerce, with a collection of cast-off goods spread out for sale, but I saw no one buying.

"Peasants who've lost their lands—younger sons—fallen women—runaway slaves—thieves and murderers—all come to Imari like flies to the dungheap, looking for work, for money, for new life." Falabon gestured expansively. "This is what they find. Because Anago, like his father Ugendi before him, has made Imari a closed city. No one enters without the magistrates' permission, set down in writing. No one engages in business without rendering his accounts to Anago's actuaries. No one changes residence without notifying the captain of the watch. No one marries without a license from the civil court. Rigorous as they may seem, these laws have made a prosperous city, unblemished by crime or poverty. All those who cannot contribute to the common good are excluded."

I nodded, thinking how Anago had taken the first small step toward the society I knew in the Hypaethra. These unfortunates huddled at the gate would be analogues of Ethri's savages, squatting on their frozen dirtball, cut off from the higher realms of the Matterfield.

The tangle of tents and bodies ended twenty meters from the ramparts. "Another of Anago's laws," said Falabon. "His men enforce it with zeal. Sometimes they set fire to a few tents or chop off a few heads just for the sport of it, whether the town encroaches on his boundary or not."

The poet had chosen the Gate of Skulls as our introduction to Imari. Past the imposing outer portals, past the functionaries who examined our documents and scratched syllabics in fat ledgers, we found ourselves in an echoing tunnel of stone, as long as the rampart was thick. Pots of luminescent fungus gave bluish light; set in niches from floor to ceiling were hundreds of skulls. Some were rotten with age, overgrown with mold and cobwebs; others looked freshly polished.

"Were these trespassers from Ragtown?" I asked.

"No, no. These were soldiers in the Warlord's army, guardsmen at the city gates; they keep watch even in death." Falabon laughed. "Anago is no easy master."

After the squalor of the tent city Imari itself seemed an urban jewel. We rode down avenues lined with palm trees, past tall houses fronted with glazed tiles and painted a range of delicate hues: pink, lavender, pale green, saffron, ivory, cornflower blue. Most buildings had gently sloping tiled roofs, giving the city an overall coherence quite at odds with the discordant geometry I remembered from Trokomari. But there was no comparing the two cities: each one had its charms, each one seduced the traveler's senses.

Then we entered a public square and I had to gag. From a broad whitewashed platform rose twelve images of polished hardwood, abstract figures that approached the simplicity of plain pillars. Evidently they represented the Traoro pantheon, from Guza on down to Adu. Each image was liberally smeared with dried blood and bits of flesh; on spikes set around them were severed heads, dismembered torsoes, mutilated hands, mangled feet. Dalashon even boasted a shriveled garland of male genitalia.

"These are the Fetishes," said Falabon. "It pleases Anago to offer them the blood of criminals and war-captives. Quite a sight, eh?"

I kept silent, thinking suddenly of Seren. This paradoxical city was his home now. He must be very near—my heart quickened at the thought. Soon, very soon, we'd meet again.

Overlooking the center of town was a broad hillside walled about with cyclopean blocks; we headed toward it, but turned aside at the gate. "That's the Citadel," said our guide. "Anago lives there with his wives, his servants, and two thousand men at arms. He's assigned you a house nearby." We circled around to the back of the fortress, where the defenses looked much older. A scattering of houses had been built into the wall; they faced what must have been the original city center, a close-packed quarter of narrow streets and balconied dwellings. We climbed to a modest villa set halfway up the hillside, enclosed in an untended garden. It fell somewhere between picturesque and shabby and I took to it at once.

Falabon left us at the threshold with a song.

> *Blessed is this house*
> *that holds two beauties.*
> *O that my arms were as fortunate*
> *as these enclosing walls.*
> *Let them echo with my voice.*
> *Let a part of me remain.*

"The best part," he said slyly, and departed with his eyes aglow.

The house was comfortable, and for several intervals Anago left us alone. Two female servants named Vata and Merulo were on hand to see to our needs. Unfortunately they seemed a cross between chaperones and spies; their constant presence made it impossible for me to make independent forays into the city. In the end it was they who let drop the name Pororo—Seren's alias in Traore.

My ears pricked up. "Is he one of the Warlord's men?" I asked blandly.

"Of course he is. He's commander of the army laying siege to Tolun. Two seasons ago he was nothing—now he's next to Nezumi and Falabon in the Warlord's favor." Merulo clucked her tongue. "Such quick climbs can bring quicker falls, I'm afraid."

Vata caught her arm warningly; she could just as easily be describing me, and that would be tactless. "The old man who lives in the stair below me has a nephew under Pororo's command," Vata said. "By all accounts he's a fair and clever man, not undeserving of his place."

Merulo bridled. "If that's so, then why has the siege dragged on so long? All the gold of Imari's being turned into powder and shot, and look at the price of bread! You talk of neighbors and nephews—my husband's own brother is in the field, as you ought to know, so we get news from the front around my stairwell, too. Do you remember those monstrous cannons that rolled out of West Gate in the first light of day? Well, not twelve rounds past, the biggest one of all exploded before the walls of Tolun, and killed twenty of Traore's best. And it was Master Pororo's own toy, cast according to his express design—slaughtering more Traoro than Lozi!"

"Yes, I marked that, but—"

"But nothing! I've been waiting for his recall ever since. Lord Anago won't tolerate the service of fools." And she gave a pointed look in Vata's direction before stalking down to the laundry room.

Vata lingered, her hands busy with a needle and thread. My own fists clenched in frustration. "Merulo seems upset this round," I said.

"Her husband missed a promotion, nothing more."

"Have you ever seen this man Pororo?"

She gave me a glance that told me my curiosity had registered. "Only from a distance. He's rather short; nothing else sticks in my memory."

"And he's been in Lozi all during this Bright Season?"

"Yes, and according to Merulo he'll stay there till either Tolun falls or Anago demands his head."

"The Warlord's favorites must tread carefully," I concluded. Vata grunted and went back to her stitching.

So Seren was out of reach. Lozi lay on the southeast border of Traore, and Tolun was some 1700 kilometers distant from the city where I stood. How could the Firin, with all their sources of information, not know of my quarry's absence? Again my faith in Chwefro wavered. I felt thwarted, boxed in; after all this traveling I was still so far from my goal. What finagling could win me a trip to the front? Nothing I could think of; the very idea seemed absurd, now that I was ensconced in Imari.

On the other hand, perhaps Anago would do my job for me; perhaps Seren would disappoint him and pay with his life. But that thought did nothing to comfort me. No. What I entertained was an obsession, a haunting, a compulsion, an attraction strong enough to draw me across the void to a new world, all in quest of one man. There had been distractions along the way but my purpose was clear. I had to see Seren with my own eyes; and if he was to die, my hands must do the deed.

•   •   •

One of the many differences between Woro and Traore was the manner
in which the two nations told time. In place of the island's vague *spells*
and self-defined *intervals,* in which waking and sleeping followed one
another all haphazardly, the mainland fixed time's flight in *vigils.*
Twelve vigils made one *round,* equal to a single spell in Woro usage.
Within this round the intervals of work and leisure were strictly demar-
cated. Business could be transacted only from the second to the sixth
vigils, and a curfew was enforced between the ninth and the twelfth.
During the latter period no one could venture forth without official
clearance, so virtually everyone chose to sleep.

I spent my vigils wondering how I would find Seren, and when
Anago would finally summon me to dance. As the rounds passed I
began to suspect he'd set me up in town merely to deactivate me, as if
he feared my influence over the mob. A groundless fear, that: for the
time being I wished him only success.

Curfew had begun. Soko and I were drinking tea in an upstairs parlor, looking out over the weatherbeaten panorama of Imari's rooftops.
Another round had passed in idleness and unease. A scratching at the
doorjamb caught my attention; it was Merulo, announcing visitors—
clandestine visitors at that.

Two large men in plain headcloths barged into the room without
waiting for invitations. I rose and bowed clumsily. "Lord Anago! What,
another disguise? How you challenge my powers of detection."

"But I still haven't fooled you." The Warlord grinned wolfishly. "Tell
your servant to draw the drapes and leave us. Your kinswoman may
stay."

It was done. We all settled onto the floor, Soko a bit nervously.
Anago's companion was none other than Falabon, who produced a flask
of brandy and enjoined us to drink.

"I never told you about my dream," said Anago as the alcohol
warmed our throats. "The very next round after you danced I dreamed
I was in my banqueting hall, and a woman came in carrying a platter of
meat. In the midst of it was the head of the Prince of Lozi, gaping and
apple-stuffed like any common swine's. I ate, and the flavor was sub-
lime."

"What did the oneirologists say?"

"Oh, that Tolun would fall before the harvest feast—a simple enough
reading. But the serving woman had your face, Risha. Will you be the
one to hand me victory?"

"No, no—that was just my signature; it happens like that with the dream-dance."

"I wondered." He moved closer. "You've given me a great deal to wonder about. Can you control the visions your audience sees?"

His eyes were amorous but his words breathed suspicion. "Not at all," I replied. "I only stimulate each person's clairvoyant gift. Anything else would be beyond my talent, not to mention a falsification of the mysteries."

"Of course." His hand touched mine. "These are strange times; even the Nightlord must stay on guard. Especially around a woman as disarmingly beautiful as you."

I caught his drift. I'd never doubted this situation might arise, and accepted the consequences. We bantered a bit longer before I suggested a tour of my bedroom. As we left the parlor Falabon was doing his best to entertain Soko, though from a more respectful distance than Anago had done. I glimpsed the beginnings of a smile blooming on her close-set lips.

In my chambers Anago behaved as any other drunken soldier might. I watched at a certain remove; once more it was puppets on a portable stage, and I played my part as directed. His hands on my body recalled Mudriye's, recalled Tref's, recalled the other men I'd pleasured for worldly favors. Not that Anago was uncomely or insensitive. Though middle-aged he was a fine figure of a man, and though I didn't dare resist him he was considerate and slow, even making an attempt at satisfying my own needs. I relaxed and gave way to him; I let go of my thoughts, let go of my distance, tried to live only in the moment, in the heat of the flesh. Clearly this man was proud of his skill. He was heady and bold, grinning fiercely in his passion, pleased to quicken my heartbeat and hear my breath come fast and hot. As he felt my ardor rise he fanned the flames still higher. Now there was blue fire crackling over our skin, tingling and electric, an inflammation of cellular lust. I watched it burning and saw visions in the blaze. Something collapsed behind my eyes, like wooden rafters splintering in a conflagration; the props of my self-control gave way and my imagination raged upward in a pyrotechnic discharge, a bonfire of will.

I heard Yeva's laughter and the cruel ringing of Guje's hammer. The iron-god's forge was white-hot now. Its draft was a burning wind, carrying charred images of a well-remembered face—Olaro, the last living being to bring me to this stage of desire. My mind was full of fire and death, full of the holy madness, and Anago gazed into it through the two windows of my eyes.

He recoiled in horror. "What are you?" he whispered. "Can't you take pleasure as ordinary women do?"

Even through the haze of delirium his confusion frightened me. In this town they offered up witches on gibbets and spikes. I forced my mind to cool and quiet; I had to reassure him fast.

"It comes on me like this with a man sometimes," I confessed raggedly, slumped over the edge of the bed. "Your passion overwhelmed me—it carried me into the god-state. Only one other man could ever do that."

"Who?" he demanded; then sense got the better of his vanity. "No, I don't care. But you should have warned me." He rubbed his unsatisfied groin. "Maybe you ought to take vows of celibacy."

I crouched with my head down. "If you think so, my lord, I will. I beg your forgiveness. I'm ashamed that my mind and body are too frail to contain your energies." I touched his thigh. "If there's anything I can do . . ."

"No." He drew back. "But—you *are* beautiful, so beautiful to look at. Those scars in your skin—I've never seen anything half as fine. I suppose they should have made me wary."

I rose up slowly, arching my back, rippling my muscles as sinuously as the old snake in Ilesha's peristyle. Anago looked at me with renewed interest. I played with my breasts, ran my tongue across parted lips, watched him take firm hold of himself. Without rising from my knees I did a dance, writhing with viscous sensuality; without touching him I helped him find the release he craved, letting his own hands respond to the mood I created.

He sank back and sighed deeply. I kept watch, not daring to disturb him, hoping I'd allayed his suspicions, praying his heart hadn't closed me out. After a few minutes his breathing told me he was asleep. I lay down next to him, quietly, carefully, hooding the blue lamp. My mind was in an uproar. Chwefro had promised me that these states of visionary transport were under control; it wasn't so. I was all too vulnerable. I didn't dare meet another man's passion. And Anago—what would he do? Had I disgusted him, unnerved him, would he banish me from the city, throw me in prison, murder me slowly? Any disaster seemed possible. It was a miracle that I slept at all.

We woke together toward the middle of the twelfth vigil. Anago gave me a searching look; I met his eyes. "Well," he said, "I won't try this again. You're not what I expected." My lip trembled. "No. You're much more. You have a power I'd be foolish to trifle with."

"I could say the same of you, my lord."

"And wisely. You're correct to fear me. But I still have uses for you, never doubt it. You'll dance for my guests at the fifth vigil of this round. Falabon will see to the particulars. Just keep doing what comes naturally."

A half-smile played on my lips. He mimicked it, and the air cleared again. "You move on the hot side of things, don't you, Risha."

"No more than you, Lord Anago." I bowed, stifling a laugh, and he gathered up his clothes to go.

So at last I was presented at the Warlord's court. I had no trouble repeating the success I'd achieved in the forest clearing; I rode on top of the energies, channeled the psychic currents, and flashed indelible images out of my eyes and fingers into the hearts and minds of Anago's guests. Having mingled with the best society in Skhorb, Gheo, Trokomari, and High Vrazil, it was no problem to impress these grandees of Imari. I retained an air of mystery, preserving that necessary distance behind my outlandish accent and exotic dress. At Anago's command I danced every fifth watch for six rounds running. By the seventh I was the toast of the Citadel, and my fame was creeping even into Ragtown. Meanwhile the sun burned low in the east; lightning flickered in the west; and Seren was never far from my thoughts or daydreams. The only obstacle left was time.

CHAPTER TEN

At every performance the semaphore of my dream-dance predicted victory for Anago. All of Imari came to believe in it, from the lowliest beggar to the Nightlord himself. All accepted those visions as an oracle emanating directly from the gods. Only I knew otherwise. As a consequence, I found it hard to credit my own prophecies; they offered too pat a solution to my dilemma.

But when the first runners reached the capital I could doubt no longer. Commander Pororo sent electrifying news. Tolun's walls had been breached; the city was taken; the whole kingdom of Lozi lay in Lord Anago's hand. The army was even now en route to Imari bringing wagonloads of booty and thousands of captives.

A few rounds later the crowds gathered outside the Gate of Righteousness to cheer Pororo home. It was the twilight of the year; half the sun's disk had already sunk below the horizon. The eastern sky was a riot of luminous colors, from scarlet through mauve to gold; grotesque shadows stretched away from every angle into the remote distance. We waited on makeshift stages and grandstands, clad in cotton togas and printed scarves, straining our eyes into the western darkness, speculating on Pororo's success.

A muted cacophony was our first clue to his approach. Out of the dust and gloom appeared a military orchestra in massed ranks; we heard the thunder of kettledrums, the rattle of snares, the deep-throated belling of pipes, and the monstrous groan of brazen horns, so huge they needed two men to carry them and two more to blow. Long before we could pick out individual musicians we had to shout over the din.

After the orchestra came ten score soldiers carrying ten score severed heads on poles. A select few were identified with placards, and cheers arose as this or that champion of Lozi went sailing by. Suits of captured armor followed: steel helmets and quilted breastplates, burnished greaves and battered armguards, most of them liberally stained with blood. Next came a display of weaponry: notched broadswords and blackened arquebuses, brandished overhead in the hands that had won them. Then a team of mules toiled along pulling Pororo's premier siege weapon, a bronze culverin of enormous bore, the titan that represented Veii's first foray into the industrial age.

The fruits of victory shuffled afterwards in golden chains: a whole phalanx of smooth-limbed children, graceful scions of Tolun's leading families, heading for the slaver's block and decades of misery. I happened to be standing near Falabon in the viewing-mansion just then; he turned to me and sang softly in my ear.

> *To say the word war*
> *is nobler than to wage war.*
> *The mob says war*

and thinks only of pride.
The hero says war
and thinks only of glory.
War turns children into orphans
wives into widows
cities into dust.
What good is war?

We exchanged a long, sad look; few others shared our compassion, I'm afraid.

Certainly not the man who rode in the high-wheeled chariot with his face gilded by the sun's last rays. All my senses focused in on him like iron drawn to a magnet. Surrounded by an elite guard of lancers, standing tensely in a carriage pulled by eight vanquished nobles of Tolun, Seren of Khryasha, alias Pororo of Imari, gazed out on the cheering masses with the light of victory in his eyes. It was a miracle that I recognized him at all. Darker pigmentation and unfamiliar garments were the least of his metamorphoses. No. Here was a new man, a man at the peak of his pride and strength, a man who had found his ideal station in life and reveled in it. His posture, his expression, his whole body had been transformed.

He was leaner than I remembered him from those brief spells in Gheo. I saw a taut mechanism of muscle and bone, a stripped-down physique that breathed speed and deadly efficiency. His helmet was in the shape of a horse's skull; parallel scars, the distinctive badge of Traore's military, lent an austere elegance to his face. A padded corselet of black leather clung to his torso; its dorsal surface was embossed with a screaming death's head. The same savage motif was repeated in his warriors' accoutrements. Skulls, crossbones, rotting corpses, and bloody swords decorated their shields and breastplates, while red and white paint transformed their faces into gruesome masks. Surrounded by these symbols of cruelty and death, surrounded by the spoils of a brutal war, Seren thrived as never before.

He drove his chariot up to the central grandstand, dismounted, and knelt before Lord Anago. As he raised his head the Warlord struck him sharply; this was the traditional greeting for conquering heroes, a reminder not to let victory engender ambition. Ten thousand voices cried out in delight.

The two men exchanged the standard phrases of welcome and fealty. Then Seren addressed his master in a more personal vein. "Lord

Anago," he began, his voice a rich and measured baritone, "I present to you the costliest prize my sword has won. Here is the former prince of Lozi and both his heirs."

Anago's face froze. An uncomfortable silence settled over his courtiers as the prisoners were led forth. First was Prince Iru, a white-haired man with a seamed, ascetic face; then came his two sons, handsome young men in the prime of life. None of the trio were in chains, and all were reasonably well dressed—though the sons at least bore ugly battle scars. They knelt before the Warlord exactly as Seren/Pororo had done. Anago made no sign of acknowledgement; he merely stared over their bent heads into his commander's eyes, with the kind of look that a stern but indulgent father might give a wayward son.

"Our friend Pororo is on dangerous ground," Falabon informed me in a rapid whisper. "This is not the way war captives are displayed to their conqueror, especially not the Prince of Lozi. Anago once vowed to offer that man's heart to the Fetishes—but Pororo has introduced him and his sons almost as if they were guests."

Falabon edged forward, to be closer to the drama; I followed in the wake of his passage. The prisoners from Lozi had been removed and Anago was speaking softly to Pororo.

"You've brought vast new territories under Traoro rule, so I shrink from any accusation of meanness." The Warlord's mailed hand rested heavily on Pororo's shoulder; he towered over the outlander. "But you must tell me at once why you have done this thing."

"It was a difficult siege, my lord, and the plague had taken its toll among attackers and defenders alike." Pororo spoke with forthright confidence; he was stating facts, not making excuses. "At the close of an especially miserable round a Tolunthite warrior came to my tent, alone and without guarantees of safe conduct. He introduced himself as the eldest son of Prince Iru, a brave warrior, one of the men who lately knelt here before you. He offered me terms: immediate surrender, on the condition that I took only two thousand slaves, left the rest of Tolun's people their freedom, and spared his aged father's life. He offered himself as hostage till peace could be made, and begged that any punishment envisioned for his father be visited on his own head instead.

"You gave me permission to conduct negotiations on your behalf, Lord Anago. I weighed the alternatives and found this young duke's proposal the most sensible path to victory. We came to terms; Tolun's gates were opened to us, and Traore took rich booty. Now all the gold and silver, all the fertile plantations, all the workshops and factories of

Lozi are yours. Moreover, you have your army intact; there were no further losses in battle, and once we retired from that fever-ridden shore the plague abated as well."

"But what about my honor? What about the promises I made to Guza and Dalashon? Prince Iru flouted my authority; he denied that I was the legal ruler of Traore. The Fetishes are thirsty for his blood."

"By your leave, my lord. Iru is an old man with little time left to him in this world. Yebba, Taker of Souls, will visit him soon, whether through the carnificial knife or by the simple agency of illness. What satisfaction will the mysteries derive from such meager fare?"

"A point to consider," Anago conceded. "Perhaps the Fetishes *would* be more pleased with the heart of his brave and compassionate heir. Or do you have a contrary opinion on that subject also?" Pororo said nothing. "We'll talk of this later," his master decided. He gestured and horses were brought round for himself and the other members of his circle. All mounted, including Falabon. Soko and I watched them ride away through clouds of propitiatory incense and masses of shouting bodies.

We followed on foot, making slow progress in the crush. I took no notice of the sweaty flesh jostling me on all sides, ignored the racket of drums and voices, disregarded the glittering prizes and fly-infested corpses that still swayed overhead. No, my mind was still full of this changeling I had just seen. Whether Seren or Pororo, pale or dark, sleek Radiant or savage conqueror, the fascination lingered, mixed now with a healthy measure of revulsion. By my own choosing I had made my life dependent on his. The time of waiting was over.

Certain unknowns remained, however, nagging at my confidence. All the while Pororo had argued his case before the Warlord I'd studied him closely; never once had his eyes strayed toward mine. Was I as invisible to him now as I'd been in Gheo? Could he possibly recognize me as a fellow Radiant, as the court lady who declared her timid affection so long ago? It seemed unlikely. Seren/Pororo had mostly seen me from a distance, or wearing a mask; there were only those few brief minutes of face-to-face confrontation. My mirror showed me how drastically I'd changed since then.

Nevertheless, the thrill of danger lurked at the edge of my mind, lending a darker cast to the world around me, a vivid gloom like that descending over all Veii.

• • •

I danced that round in Anago's hall, where Pororo was being feted as his achievements merited. For the first time torches burned—a great luxury on such a fuel-poor world—and their yellow blaze and oily smoke added new textures to the deceptions I wove. Though I wasn't the only entertainment that vigil, not by a long shot. There were jugglers and acrobats, pipers and clowns; Falabon himself sang the requisite anthem of praise. As a result my performance was shorter than usual, and attracted less than undivided attention. The banqueters seemed more intent on their whiskey and roast pork than on the fading novelty of a Golo dream-dancer. But for those who watched my signals were unmistakable.

As the drums stilled and the veils lifted from my senses Anago summoned me before the seat of honor. "Pororo," he said, in his loose whiskey-voice, "here's a clever woman who holds converse with the gods. Look at the *luruka* carved into her flesh."

Pororo took a good look at me then, through red-rimmed eyes. "A serpent woman, are you? How does it feel to carry the gods' mark?"

"It's a constant challenge, Master Pororo." I regarded him boldly. "I have to live up to the gifts I've been granted or they'll be withdrawn."

He nodded. "Spoken truly. I'm eager to see what visions your dancing brings."

"Sleep and dream, brave lord. They'll steal into your brain on soft, sly feet." I withdrew bowing as Falabon struck up a song.

Over the next seven rounds I danced three more times. Pororo was always present, but we never spoke. As much as I stared at him he never seemed to notice. After my third performance Soko and I walked home by our usual route—made strange and new by night's arrival—to find two visitors waiting in the shadows by our front door.

There was no doubting who they were: Falabon and Anago, the same pair who had come that other time. Falabon, at least, was no surprise. Since his first visit he had found favor in Soko's eyes, and vice versa; he was no stranger to the house behind the hill. But Anago's presence was a complete shock. After our erotic misadventures I never thought to see him in private again.

"The very Lord of Night!" I called out, with false heartiness. "How have you beat me to my own door?"

"Can't you guess?" Anago's tone was mellow and jovial. "There's a shortcut between my house and yours; that's why you were given these lodgings in the first place. You're not the first young woman who's ever tarried here."

"I should say not! You never tire of mischief, do you."

"Never."

We went in laughing and withdrew to our respective chambers. I envied Soko the easy pleasure she was about to enjoy; my interview with the Warlord could only mean business. Still, I kept my light-hearted pose, trimming the moss-lamp, pouring the brandy, making him comfortable on the couch. After a few swallows he was ready to talk.

"You're acquainted with the nature of my office, aren't you, Risha? I'm sure Golo has something similar. It works like this: In the light of day men's hearts rest easy; then crops are tended, commerce is conducted, chivalry paraded on the field of battle. Of course there's the threat of plague, and the unpleasantness of White Shadows, but in general the Bright Season is a comfortable time. Even warfare is little more than a game—or at least it was until my father's time." He smiled ironically. "So by tradition the people of the Garengazi have taken female rulers during the long day, creatures as mild and nurturing as the season itself.

"Night, on the other hand, is a time of peril. The unrelenting darkness oppresses men's souls. How many murders, how many suicides have you seen during this season, how many adulteries and bitter quarrels? A man's authority is needed to keep the peace. Thus my office—the Lordship of Night. Now since my infancy, history has conspired to make the entire year a time of difficulties, so the Nightlord's jurisdiction has been extended. But the principle remains the same. I am here to keep order in society, to prevent humankind's baser qualities from taking over.

"So far your presence has served me well. There had been some muttering against the Lozi war, but once you began dancing in Imari the omens turned favorable, and the opposition died. Now Lozi is mine; no longer can Iru claim that I rule without the deities' consent. Still you dance—at my invitation, of course—but something odd has been happening. My courtiers' dreams have taken a turn for the worse. They have nightmares. Not every one of them; only a few are susceptible, after all. But we're only seven rounds into the Dark Season and the soothsayers are already making dire predictions. Normally I scoff at such blather; except for you I've steered clear of the mystic arts. But too many people listen. It's not good."

"You know I have no control over this," I said quietly. "If the signs are evil it's no fault of mine."

"I never suggested otherwise. In fact those grim visions are already coming true. A highborn woman gave birth to a two-headed baby two rounds past; five of my warriors have been murdered in heated quarrels since the setting of the sun. And then there's this business of Master Pororo and the Prince of Lozi. My most valuable subordinate is flirting with outright disobedience. Things are not as they should be."

"Are you telling me to stop dancing?"

He rubbed his chin. "I don't know. In fact I'm not sure what to do about you."

"What sort of dreams has Pororo had?" I asked.

Anago chuckled. "That's the strange part. He doesn't dream at all. He's even less superstitious than I am—he's hinted more than once that you're a fraud."

"But—when we spoke he seemed so friendly and open to me."

"I suppose he was, in that moment, but then the englightenment you promised never occurred. Now he thinks all our true believers are simply deluding themselves."

"Quite frankly," I said, "I have no defense, because I myself don't understand how this dream induction occurs. I just dance and it happens. But if you think my performances are doing more harm than good I'll certainly stop. I'll even leave Imari if you wish; you've been so kind that there's no room for any resentment between us."

He said nothing and the silence lengthened. Finally he asked, in an offhand tone, "What do you think of Pororo?"

"He's a man of dangerous passions," I replied, without hesitation. "A strong man, an effective man, but one who needs close watching from his superiors. He'll serve you well if you treat him with just severity."

"You speak as if you've known him for years."

"I'm not a bad judge of character, and his is plain to read."

"What do you think of his protection of the Prince of Lozi and his sons?"

Careful, I told myself. A wrong answer might kill me. "Spare the old man, but one of the sons must die. Even the young duke agreed to that."

"But Pororo doesn't. He keeps the whole family under his own roof, and sits at table with the eldest son at his right hand."

I inclined my head. "If I say more I'll fear the consequences. Pororo is more important to you than I am. You're wise enough to decide for yourself, Anago."

"Ah, but you also possess a certain wisdom. A certain knowledge of hidden things. Listen. Pororo is a foreigner. His origins are a mystery even to me. His thoughts run completely contrary to those of my other ministers. Unlike them he stimulates my ambitions, he encourages my wildest fancies. He urges me to pursue wars of conquest and add new territories to my realm, and he's provided me with a detailed agenda for achieving these ends. He's taught my smiths how to temper finer steel, he's taught my engineers how to cast better cannon, he's introduced new field strategies, he's devised new methods of colonial administration. His energy and ability are exemplary. Some speak against him, saying he's an evil influence, but look at what he's accomplished.

"Now I have a suspicion about him. When I was a young man a priestess told me that the world didn't grow like a plant from a seed, as many poets claimed, but rather was constructed, in much the same way as a man constructs a house. She said that there were people living in the sky who could work such miracles, and that they could descend into Veii when it suited them."

"Had this priestess ever visited Ira-Ireru?"

"So you do know something of this. Yes, she had. Anyhow I think that perhaps Pororo is a visitor from the higher worlds. I think he's been sent to tempt me. And I wonder sometimes if listening to him is a great folly."

"Anago, I don't know. I've been to Ira-Ireru, I've heard the Firin weave their tales, but I can't tell you whether Pororo's ambitions will bring you good or evil. They'll bring you endless wars: that much is certain. Is that what you want for Veii?"

"As long as I keep winning!"

"Then there's your answer."

He grunted. "I should know better than to ask a woman." Tossing off another cup of brandy, he fell silent again, sprawled across the couch. It was obvious that he planned to stay. I kept my hands as busy as my mind, putting the room in order, helping him undress, and hooding the lamp. In a few minutes we lay side by side; he fell asleep immediately.

It was like sharing a bed with a hungry lion. I was amazed that he could feel so comfortable with me, astonished that he could ask my advice, profoundly disturbed by the things he said. At the moment I was on his good side, but that could change quickly. It was too easy for the people of Veii to see through us outworld impostors. Olaro had penetrated my disguise, and Anago had all but unmasked Pororo. What if he began suspecting me? What if he told Pororo his suspicions?

And what was Pororo's game? For the first time I wondered if his presence in Veii was not the consequence of personal whim, but the result of careful scheming on the part of House Khryasha. If so, then my mission involved much more than simple revenge.

When the first vigil bells rang I was still awake and thinking.

I left off dancing for an indefinite period. Anago thought it best; I didn't disagree. I'd already helped establish a certain mood around Imari. It could sustain itself without me.

The Warlord let me and Soko stay on in the little villa. Our stipend continued as before, and we were even allowed to dismiss Vata and Merulo, and replace them with quieter, less inquisitive servants. Our time was our own, though I had to be available in case I was needed at court.

I spent the watches wandering Imari, sometimes with Soko, sometimes alone. There were markets to visit, people to see, and, when Falabon thought to invite us, parties to attend. Always, always I watched and listened for Pororo, but he kept to himself. The Prince of Lozi lived on as his guest and Anago bided his time.

Now that the war was over the city was full of soldiers. That made for some lively times but it also occasioned endless quarrels. Military discipline was not enough to keep our conquering heroes in line. As Falabon put it, "Maybe we *should* launch another invasion—at least we'd be rid of them." Meanwhile they contributed to the tide of violence and bloodshed, as Dark Season fulfilled its somber portents.

Returning home at the close of the eighth vigil, or venturing out, despite curfew, in the middle of the tenth, I saw the city as a vast shadowy stage on which some drama was about to unfold. Fitful moss-lamps glowed on random corners, casting pools of bluish light: ideal settings for clandestine meetings or sad farewells. Candles flickered in high towers, beacons for paid assassins or errant lovers. People hurried down alleys in twos and threes, muffled in cloaks, speaking little, their faces closed around secrets, grayish in the gloom.

It was in the blank plaza before the Citadel that I caught my first glimpse of Pororo since Anago's disclosures. I slipped into the angle of a bastion and watched him go by; never once did he glance my way. He was too intent in conversation with another man, a young warrior I recognized as Lokota, Prince Iru's heir; their voices stayed low, but it was plain that they were arguing. Pororo's face held a pleading expression—something I never thought to see on those haughty lineaments. Lokota simply looked unhappy, shaking his head over and over. Only one sentence came through clearly: "Your life is worth more than any of that." It was Pororo's line, and I would have given a great deal to hear more. But they passed out of range and I didn't dare follow, even through the shadows of night.

As I skirted the Haymarket, on my way back home, I met Soko hurrying in the opposite direction. "Risha!" she cried, almost out of breath. "I've been looking for you everywhere." Her volume dropped and we put our heads together. "Falabon just told me. One of Anago's wives, Kokoro, has had a miscarriage. There's a great uproar in his house, and Kokoro is making wild accusations of witchcraft. Your name is among those mentioned."

"I? But Anago is my best friend."

"That's exactly it. Many think you're his mistress, that you're jealous of his wives' position."

"What did Falabon advise?"

"He has horses waiting outside the Azen Gate. He thinks you should leave town at once."

We'd already begun walking in an easterly direction. "Falabon is always counseling flight," I protested. "I ignored him the last time, and everything turned out fine."

"It can't hurt to take precautions."

"But I'm not ready—I'm so far from doing what I have to do."

Soko knew my business very well, and she shook her head darkly. "Perhaps you should abandon all that. Let's leave Traore, find passage back to Trokomari."

"I can't, Soko. It's not conceivable."

"Falabon says you'll be taken in for questioning before the round is through."

I shrugged. "I'll trust to Anago's favor."

Soko was on the verge of calling me a fool—the word hovered on her lips, I could see it. It gave me an obscure satisfaction to see how much spirit she'd developed since we left Woro.

"You go, Soko," I said gently. "That way at least you'll be safe if anything happens. I don't want to cause you any harm."

"No. I'm not leaving you." And that settled things. We returned to our house, sending word to Falabon that we didn't feel like riding just then. Soko stayed on edge, but no soldiers appeared, no threatening agents of the Warlord's justice.

Instead Anago himself arrived without a single attendant, sometime during the middle of the tenth vigil. For once there was no sign of his accustomed joviality. He entered, spoke a few monosyllables, and directed me to the upstairs sitting room.

"I suppose you've heard the news." His words and face were completely without expression.

"Some of it."

"It's a lot of foolishness, in my opinion. Yes, it's unfortunate that my dear wife lost the baby, but it's not as if she doesn't have others, and won't have more. But she's quite hysterical, and there are those ready to listen to her. I myself have played no small part in making all this possible. After ignoring the old religion for so long I brought you to court, and then when Pororo started acting headstrong I used promises I'd made to the Fetishes as my reprimand. Superstition is superstition— I was an idiot to set the chain of events in motion. Now Kokoro, Nezumi, and several other powerful officials are dead set on a witch hunt."

"And I'm to be the quarry?"

"Not necessarily. There are many possibilities." He looked ashamed for a moment. "Could you have done such a thing? I mean, is it within your capacity? You do have unusual talents."

"If Kokoro had watched me dance recently, and then had a hideous nightmare that resulted in this abortion, there might be grounds for suspicion. But we both know that isn't true. I'm quite innocent."

He sighed. "I believe you. But others may not. Even Pororo . . ."

"Pororo, who scoffs at everything supernatural?" My throat tightened. "Has he spoken against me too?"

"He says you've been lurking around the Citadel, spying and eavesdropping. He says you're up to no good."

I felt dizzy. I'd been detected after all. Did Pororo think I harbored sinister intentions toward him too? "I'm a curious and inquisitive person," I said evenly, "but not a witch, not a blighter of fecund wombs."

"You've convinced me, but you'll have to convince someone else as well. As long ago as the Bright Season I sent messengers to the Firin's isle, asking that an embassy come to me. I need to confer with them over my unprecedented military activity—I want to see where they stand, and if possible secure a pledge of noninterference. Finally an envoy is on his way—her way?—and ought to arrive within a few rounds. I'll ask that person, whoever it is, to be the judge of our differences. No one can argue with a Firin."

That was an enormous relief; I could relax and breathe easier. Anago, of course, had no idea what he was getting into, but in Firin hands I at least would be safe.

"I submit to Firin justice," I declared. "But I'm curious about one thing. Has anyone suggested that perhaps the cause of these unpleasant events is the wrath of Guza? Could it be that the Fetishes are eager for the sacrifice you promised, in that vow you've lived to regret?"

Anago shook his head. "I'm afraid I'm the only one who thought of that angle, and I absolutely refuse to be part of this paranoid folly."

"Of course. But the idea has its attractions, don't you think?"

"I prefer not to complicate the issue any further. I'll find other ways of handling Pororo and his protégés." His voice dropped. "That man—he baffles me and tempts me all at once. Whenever I make remarks about offworlders he blandly ignores me. Then, just a few vigils ago, he told me that the universe was a larger place than I suspected, that I might win allies I never dreamed of, who could help me attain anything I desired." He fixed me with his eyes. "It's plain that our presumptions are fact. He has access to things we can't imagine."

"I'll agree to that. Accepting his unparalleled ability and usefulness, just what do you hope to accomplish?"

For the first time a smile lit his face. "Whatever no man has done before. It's true, I'm not as young as I used to be, but there's still a lot of life in me." He flexed a beefy arm as proof. "I've already changed my own country beyond recognition. At last we have sensible government, decent laws, and spiraling wealth. I want Traore's progress to continue, and I want to spread my reforms to other lands. Already I've set up a university here in Imari to advance the state of human knowledge—my learned doctors make new discoveries every season, and everyone benefits." Not the folk in Ragtown, I thought, but I kept listening. "Once the reign of ignorance is overthrown," he went on, "who knows what humanity is capable of?"

"Then what is the end of all this, Anago? Wealth? Power? Pleasure?"

"They're just different words for the same thing, aren't they?" he countered. "Yes, I want all that, for everyone." His eyes danced. "I want to rule the world."

"You do, don't you," I murmured. Anago had risen in the course of this harangue, and stood in majestic stillness, underlit by the lamp's glow. In that instant he defined the word magnificent. "You do," I repeated, "and you could."

He reached down and touched my face, very carefully, still wary of my proclivities. "It's good that we're not lovers," he said. "I can talk with you as with no other woman, Risha. You have such a way of listening—you help me know my own mind."

I bowed.

"I'll send for you as soon as the Firin tribunal arrives," he said in more formal tones, making for the door. "Be prepared."

"I will be."

Soko appeared to usher him out; when he was gone she came in and sat beside me.

"We have nothing to worry about," I told her confidently, taking her hand. "Anago is on our side." But to myself I thought, who is really on the other side? What kind of tangle are we in? Chwefro hadn't told me nearly enough.

Hobnailed boots sounded on the villa's threshold. Soko struggled to look brave as she opened the door. A grim-faced captain, his helmet shaped like a snarling monster, handed me a document signed by Lord Anago and three of his ministers, summoning me to the Hall of Justice. A subordinate came forward with light shackles, but the captain waved him away. I managed to smile. The soldiers made a tight square around me and we marched off, Soko gazing sadly after.

We walked in flickering torchlight to the upper Citadel. The sky was full of stars, the same stars I had seen all my life, whether from Skhorb's observation windows, Ethri's frozen steppes, or the rooftops of this shadowy town. Their constancy offered me little comfort.

The Hall of Justice had been screened off, so I saw my examiners at close range, in an intimately proportioned space. They knelt in a line on a low dais, before an arras depicting two swords crossed before a flame. Anago's absence was conspicuous and surprising. I faced Chancellor Nezumi—an unassuming man in a black and purple toga—and not one but three envoys from Ira-Ireru. All resembled Firin I'd met before, but none gave any sign of recognition.

Nezumi began the proceedings. "You have been named by three witnesses as a putative witch. By the statutes of this city, a witch is a man or woman, trained in the mysteries, who uses his or her power to cause mental anguish, physical illness, or death. First of all, do you deny your reputation as a practitioner of the natural arts?"

"No."

"Then we may proceed to the accusations. During the First Vigil of Darkyear 42, Round Thirteen, you were seen lingering in an arcade across from the House of Red Sunset, staring fixedly at the lighted window of a chamber in which a certain noble lady lay in childbed. Two out of three witnesses testify that you muttered continually, reciting some charm or incantation. When you departed you left behind this figurine." He held up a crude stick figure decorated with a lock of hair. "During the Second Vigil of the round that same noble lady was delivered of a stillborn infant. It was a girl, bearing odd markings on her belly." He produced an ink sketch of some geometric figures. "These markings are said to be identical with those on your own body."

Nezumi motioned me closer. I wore only a long skirt and a bit of drapery; my naked torso was plainly visible, and the sketch he held was an accurate copy of my *luruka.*

"You stand accused then of causing the death of this lady's child." According to court etiquette Kokoro's name was never mentioned, but everyone knew whom Nezumi meant. "Do you deny your presence on the Street of Sunset during that particular vigil?"

"I can't say." In spite of the flimsy evidence against me I was starting to feel nervous. "I often walk the streets of Imari, whether in the Citadel or in the Lower Town. I may have been there; I don't recall."

Nezumi gestured to his secretary. "Mistress Risha does not deny the witnesses' testimony on this point." Turning back to me, he asked, "Do you deny working magic so as to cause the stillbirth in question?"

"I do."

There was silence. One of the Firin eventually spoke, with exaggeratedly careful diction. "As we understand your laws, Chancellor Nezumi, the accused must now be subjected to various ordeals, in order to determine her honesty. We would like to know if the accusers must endure the same trials."

"No, they do not."

The Firin nodded. "In that case, may we at least question these three witnesses?"

"As you wish."

My accusers appeared one at a time. The first was one of Kokoro's serving women; she gave a detailed account of the stillbirth, as well as of my alleged activities in that cloister outside Kokoro's mansion. Careful questioning from the Firin failed to weaken her testimony. Next came a woman I knew well: Merulo. Apparently she had been transferred to Kokoro's residence after leaving mine, to assist with the extra work occasioned by the delivery. She gave me a cool glance and repeated the same tale almost verbatim.

At that, one of the Firin drew Nezumi's attention to the unlikelihood of two different witnesses describing an event with identical words; the Chancellor merely said, "Since there is only one truth, why shouldn't it be told in one manner?"

His smug prejudice made me ill. It was obvious that a conspiracy was afoot; how many more were involved? I consoled myself with the knowledge that the Firin would judge me—surely they would never let this vicious travesty prevail.

But the sight of my third accuser shook my faith to its foundations. Pororo sauntered in wearing full military regalia; he looked as though he'd been summoned from the training field.

"Yes, I saw this woman on the Street of Sunset," he declared. "She's often there, lurking in shadows, veiling her face when anyone chances to notice her. I can't say I saw her performing any witchery, but I have witnessed her dancing, and it's given me nothing but nightmares. In the hollow of Round Twelve I had this dream. Mistress Risha stood over a naked woman's heaving belly, next to a man who seemed to be the pregnant woman's husband. As he watched, apparently ensorcelled, she reached in and pulled forth a witch-child, a wizened creature with the mark of the serpent. This she cast into a steaming cauldron. After a moment it rose up out of the brew in the form of a ghost, its head aflame, and taking a ghostly dagger it slew both its father and its mother. Meanwhile this Risha looked on with glee. When I woke I hurried to warn my master, for the portent was clear, but by then the child was dead. I was the one who urged her imprisonment; it's evident she means to strike at the Nightlord himself."

The leading envoy raised a hand. "Chancellor Nezumi—can this man's testimony be allowed? He speaks sheer fancy."

"In cases involving the supernatural," said Nezumi, "supernatural evidence is quite in order."

Tears stung my eyes. I wanted to run over to that handsome warrior and beat him with my fists. I wanted to shout, "Seren! Will you murder me too?" But I held my peace.

Nezumi turned to the trio of Firin. "Are you finished examining the witnesses?"

"We are," said the envoy, "but we will let our superior speak for us."

The arras behind them parted, and Chwefro stepped forth. None of the others showed the least surprise; clearly my preceptor's attendance had been concealed only from me.

For an instant I felt like I would burst with anger and outrage. My vision dimmed, my ears roared; a tide of wrath rose up in my veins. My lips drew back in a snarl—but with a quick, covert gesture Chwefro silenced me. There was something in progress that I mustn't upset; it seemed we were to behave as strangers.

"I question the reliability of all three witnesses," said the tall Firin. "Still I bow to your laws, and will continue with due process as your statutes define it. All that remains is to put this woman to the test. This will be done one round from now. In the meantime I ask her to examine her heart and decide whether she has anything to add to her testimony. I enjoin the witnesses to do the same: for they must realize that false accusation is also a crime."

The black-coated soldiers surrounded me and guided me firmly to the door. I couldn't help looking back. Chwefro was conferring solemnly with the three subordinates, Nezumi was already on his way out another exit, and Seren/Pororo was standing still, gazing after me. If I've ever seen guilt and shame on a human face I know I saw it then. Our eyes locked; his lips shaped words I couldn't decipher. Then one of the guards caught my elbow and propelled me out into the night.

My cell was well lit, well furnished, and poorly guarded. Escape, however, was the furthest thought from my mind. There was no doubting that I'd been caught in some bizarre scheme, in which I had as many allies as enemies. It seemed wisest to play along. In spite of such confidence I was completely unable to sleep.

At the beginning of the twelfth vigil my tossing and turning were interrupted by a visitor. Chwefro glided in, uncovered the lamps, and sat by my bedside.

"What in the name of all the gods are you doing in Imari?" I demanded.

"I told you I'd be on hand to rescue you whenever you needed it."

"But we agreed you'd come at midseason."

"Last time I was late; this time I'm early. You have no cause for complaint."

"No, no, I'm thankful you're here. Do they plan to burn me alive?"

"They plan to drown you, grill you, and feed the leftovers to the pigs. At least Lady Kokoro does, and she's found some influential conspirators."

"Why?"

"For some reason—simple jealousy, I suppose—Kokoro hates you. Anago is bored with her and she blames you rather than herself. This pregnancy was her chance to give him a son, and she failed yet again. She wants to save her prestige by accusing you of sorcery. You *are* an obvious scapegoat, after all."

"How does Seren—I mean Pororo—fit in?"

"That took some sleuthing to discover. But Chancellor Nezumi is Kokoro's uncle, and the Chancellor has been given the last word in deciding the fate of Prince Iru's family. Pororo wants to save them, especially Duke Lokota—you may have noticed that they've become inseparable companions. So Pororo agreed to support Kokoro in exchange for her influence with the Chancellor. Thus you die, Lokota lives, Kokoro stays on as Anago's principal wife, and Nezumi stays on as Chancellor. All very neat."

"Do they think Anago will stand by and do nothing?"

"Anago needs Pororo too much to thwart him in this. You'll be the gods' offering, in place of Iru or Lokota."

I buried my face in my hands. "This is a wicked place. Night does poison men's souls."

Chwefro touched my head affectionately. "I'm doing what I can. You have a chance of coming through alive."

"A chance?"

"Just listen and do exactly what I say."

Men wearing skull masks ushered me into a flagstone courtyard as sad gongs tolled the third vigil of the round. In the torchlight I saw a line of dark, solemn faces: Anago, Nezumi, Pororo, Falabon, and various other gentlemen of the court. The four Firin stood opposite them like white shadows. I was relaxed and alert, a delicious combination; though my senses were a bit scrambled from the Firin drug, my mood was optimum. I looked no further than the present moment.

I was standing at the head of a steep stairway leading down into a pit, flanked by my masked guards. I wore an ankle-length white robe and absolutely nothing else. Even my hair hung loose and unbraided. With grave mien and ponderous step Nezumi approached me, to inquire formally if I still maintained my innocence. I did. He nodded and said a prayer to the mysteries. The guards removed my garment and I descended the steps.

Accused witches were tried by a succession of elemental forces: earth, water, and fire. Depending on how each element received the suspect, her guilt or innocence was decided.

For the trial of earth I stepped naked into a pit full of snakes. I did it almost cheerfully. It would be the least of the ordeals I faced that round.

The pit smelled the way I imagined a freshly opened grave might: foul and acrid, moist and slimy, gripping my guts with the stench of putrefaction. Every square centimeter of the floor writhed with scaly coils, and scores of serpentine heads reared up around me in slow curiosity, swaying back and forth, flicking slender tongues like whips. I took shallow breaths and concentrated on the memory of Chwefro's face. Among my companions I recognized the common viper, the yellow cobra, the copperhead, and the asp, any one of which could kill me with a single bite.

The rationale behind this trial was that witches were fond of snakes, and vice versa; the reptiles would fawn over a witch and ignore an innocent woman. Witches were furthermore supposed to be immune to snakebite, so that if by chance a snake did attack an ordinary person her death would be the ultimate exoneration. In reality the accused stood little chance of survival.

I advanced gingerly into the center of the pit, prodding the serpents out of my way with a bare foot. After that first moment of interest they avoided me; shortly I stood with a half-meter of bare earth surrounding me on every side, as unthreatened as if I wore steel armor. Extending bowls of moss-light, my four judges peered down into the excavation with professional detachment, studying the scene for several seconds before turning back to Nezumi.

"In our opinion," stated Chwefro, "the defendant has demonstrated no witchy attachment to the element of earth. Risha of Golo, you may ascend."

I climbed back up, shivering a little in the night breeze. Anago gazed at me with narrowed eyes. He suspected trickery, and he was right. Two vigils earlier Chwefro had coated me from toes to armpits with an extract of the *agbala*-plant, whose odor is repugnant to serpents and undetectable by human beings. I stared the Nightlord straight in the face and volunteered nothing.

On Chwefro's arm I moved onward to my next ordeal, a well full of water. By tradition the watery element rejected witches and accepted blameless women; witches floated and innocents sank. Here we had no subterfuge prepared. I simply took long deep breaths as two men attached leaden weights to my ankles. Then, stepping to the brink, I lowered myself in.

The water was icy and uliginous. I plummeted through numbing darkness to the well's bottom, a distance of perhaps three meters: no great depth, but sufficient for drowning. Without the tranquilizing influence of Chwefro's potion I would have been nervous and short of wind. As it was I stood calmly, holding my breath, counting the passing seconds. The very fact that I had sunk should have proved my benevolence, but I knew it was customary to wait a certain interval—to see whether the accused would demonstrate supernatural power at the last instant and shoot upward into the air.

The question was, how long would my judges wait? If Nezumi had his way it would be long indeed, but Chwefro and Anago were up there too.

The tightness in my chest and throat became oppressive. My lungs were begging to exhale, my body to reassert its natural function of breath. But survival depended on resisting instincts; even in my extremity I noted the irony. I could only wait and hope, living from instant to instant in death's cold embrace.

A cable struck my head in the last second before surrender. I grabbed hold of it and sailed up to the surface, gasping and gulping. Two or three guards assisted me onto the pavement again and removed the weights; another handed me my robe. I was chilled to the marrow.

Chwefro spoke the second judgment in a quiet voice. "The defendant has demonstrated no unnatural aversion to the element of water. She is two-thirds innocent, but by the laws of Traore we must pursue justice to the limit. The fires may now be lit."

Beyond the well was a square structure measuring about eight meters to the side, a flimsy box of light wood, smeared liberally with pitch. At a signal from their captain several of the masked guards threw in lit torches, and the whole contrivance burst into a pillar of fire.

Here was the final winnowing of the witchcraft ordeal. The accused had to walk through that house of flame. A witch would burn; an innocent would be protected by the mercy of Yebba, and emerge without even a singed eyelash. It was very simple.

In the heat of the blaze my flesh warmed rapidly; my goosebumps smoothed down and my face erupted in gouts of sweat. I stood poised at the edge of the conflagration, watching for Chwefro's signal, but the Firin waited with a distracted air, as if lost in some inner monologue. Nezumi fidgeted, Anago frowned. Finally the Firin looked up.

"My task is to dispense justice according to the statutes of this realm. In my research through past cases, however, I've discovered a peculiar asymmetry. No accused witch ever survives the ordeal by fire; all persons suspected of witchcraft are burned. In the context of Traoro justice these statements are tautologies. But common sense tells us that a naked human being placed in such a fire will die quickly and horribly, witch or no witch. In good faith, therefore, I cannot allow this trial to proceed."

"But you must," Nezumi shouted. "You were consulted not to evaluate our laws but to execute them. So get on with the test. The fire is already dwindling."

"Tarry a little. If you believe an innocent woman, or man, can cross those flames unscathed, why don't you demonstrate how it's done, Chancellor Nezumi?"

"I'm not an accused witch."

"Should that make a difference? Innocence is innocence; guilt is guilt; fire is fire. But I see that your kidney is not inclined toward bold gestures. What then of you, Master Pororo, sacker of cities, enslaver of heroes? Will you show us how blameless flesh survives a furnace blast?"

Pororo looked at his feet. "I'm not on trial either."

"Ah, but you could be. Those who bear false witness are subject to the same punishment as those they accuse. What if I could prove to you that the evidence against this woman is nothing but lies and slander? Listen, then. In the course of my investigation I interviewed several of Lady Kokoro's servants, not just the ones who testified in the Hall of Justice." Chwefro produced a small sheaf of documents. "Here are their statements. Not one mentions anything about serpentine markings on the dead child's body. That part of the official testimony is surely false."

"I made no such claim," Pororo said, raising his head in the first flush of anger. "I told no lies. I only described seeing this dancer lingering in the street. And I related a dream I had. No one can say they know my dreams better than I do."

"But you were the first to suggest that she was a witch, that she meant to threaten the Warlord himself."

"And so I believed. Other witnesses upheld my suspicions."

"Witnesses who are now exposed as perjuring schemers. No, Master Pororo, you have made false accusations. I call you to justice—"

"—and I," said each of the remaining Firin.

"Four accusers, then," Chwefro said. "One more than the law requires. Here is the challenge; there is the fire. Prove yourself."

The flames turned Pororo's face to molten bronze. Sweat beaded his lips; his fists clenched spasmodically. "Show us your courage," Chwefro taunted again.

"Peace, gentle Firin." At last Anago spoke. "You've been found out, Pororo. Submit with dignity."

A look of desperation had stolen across Pororo's features. It fell away now, and his arms hung limply at his sides, fists unclenched, fingers dangling. "What do you want of me, my lord?" he asked.

"Just tell me why you've done this thing. What made you conspire?"

Pororo gazed into the fire as if it were consuming his past, yielding up memories like smoke. "I was told that if I cooperated in a certain plan, I would gain support in my efforts to preserve the life of the young Duke of Tolun. So I embroidered a little on the truth, I was creative with my recollections. Nothing I said threatened you in any way, my lord."

"Commendable. But why this attachment to Duke Lokota?"

"He's a brave and noble man. He's been a faithful friend to me. I've offered him nothing more than a warrior's loyalty."

"Don't undervalue the stirrings of your heart, my friend. Admit it. You love Lokota the way a man loves a woman, the way a woman loves a man. He shares your bed and your dreams. In your passion you were moved to conspiracy and deception; you were ready to do anything to prolong his life. Admit your folly."

"Folly?" Pororo repeated bitterly. "No, you had it right the first time. Love moved me. When he came to my tent at the siege of Tolun he put his life in my hands. He was so brave and beautiful, so young and fine, that he captured my heart, far more easily than my sword could take his high-towered city. From that moment I vowed to keep him by my side, whether I crossed your will or not."

"Those are dangerous words," Anago warned. "There is no shame in the love of one warrior for another. Recall the passion of Ban and Mogu, as sung in the *Deeds of the Fallen Kings,* or the undying love of Jala and Bakarija, as recounted in the *Sack of Ten Cities.* But such love should move a man to deeds of valor, to courage and heroism, not to skulking behind the back of his rightful lord. No, Pororo, you may love where you choose, but you may not hatch conspiracies at the Nightlord's court. You may not set so little store by my judgment that you descend to these contemptible depths. Your first loyalty is not to some fresh-faced youth, but to me."

Pororo dropped to his knees. "So be it, Lord Anago. You are the master of my soul. But I beg you—spare Lokota's life."

"Mercy, is it? What mercy did you have on Risha here?" He gestured to me; I stood wrapped in my robe again, tears streaming down my face.

Pororo gave me a level look. "I'm sorry, my lady, but when the choice fell between your life and that of my lover, there was only one possible decision."

"My dilemma is all too similar," Anago said. "I can't allow you to go unpunished, but your crime hardly merits the extreme penalty. Lokota, however, has already offered his life to the gods. You once asked me to spare Prince Iru. I will; but Lokota must die. Balance will be restored, and you will learn the error of flouting my authority. I go to these lengths because I value you both as a man and as a leader of men. I want you to continue in your present rank. Tell me now if you submit to my justice, for I'll have no service from dissidents."

"I submit," Pororo whispered.

"Louder! Let everyone hear."

"I submit," he repeated, at full volume.

"That's better. Let's quit this miserable place." Anago nodded to the captain of the guard, who ordered his men into a neat phalanx. They led the exodus from the courtyard; lesser gentlemen came after, then the four Firin, and finally Lord Anago, with his handful of intimates. I leaned on Falabon's arm, feeling sick and thoroughly exhausted. The Firin drug was wearing off and leaving me in bleak depression.

All during the exchange between Anago and Pororo, Chancellor Nezumi had scarcely breathed. Now he walked along with heavy-footed steps, ignored by the other gentlemen of rank. Anago likewise paid him no heed, reserving his attention for Pororo. He rested his hand on the smaller man's shoulder, speaking quietly into his ear, never letting him lapse into maudlin silence. How the Warlord relished these games of power.

I had no stomach for any of it. My life had been spared; Chwefro's wit and loyalty had been amply demonstrated; Anago had resolved the dilemma exactly as I advised; yet I felt no satisfaction, and precious little relief. Pororo's disclosure and humiliation had touched me too deeply. Of course my old obsession had been completely vain. He had no taste for me, or any other woman; his desires had quite another slant. I understood him now; and though he would have sent me to my death, I could still pardon him, for he would endure a pain surpassing even my own. Love fell away in ashes, both his love and mine. My mission seemed pointless; my passion seemed false.

Night winds scoured the Citadel's blank stones. Behind us the fire died down to red-glowing coals, and stars writhed in the ascending heat.

CHAPTER ELEVEN

One small carriage was enough to convey us out of Imari. We'd come with few belongings and we left with scarcely more. Our driver followed a zig-zagging detour, sticking to side streets and bypassing open squares, doing his best to avoid the massive crowds abroad in the city this round. For the moment the Plaza of the Fetishes was Imari's center of gravity; upward of seventy thousand people had gathered there to watch Duke Lokota ascend to the gods. Tangling with that multitude was unthinkable.

The driver halted within sight of the Gate of Blue Masks. Though my journey had hardly begun, I took the opportunity to step down and stretch my legs. We waited in silence till a dim lantern approached from the Avenue of Progress. Its circle of light wobbled and expanded; at fifteen paces I recognized Soko, and shook the carriage man from his doze. We climbed back in and headed for the gate.

"It was all you thought it would be," said Soko, settling on the cushions next to me and wiping soot from her forehead. "Drums, firelight, bloodlust. At least Lokota had been dosed with extract of thornapple. He felt no pain. The fleshmen cut him in very small pieces, dainty little morsels for the mysteries' pleasure. It must have taken them a whole vigil. I'm not sure, though. I didn't stay till the end."

"And Pororo?"

"He wasn't there. Anago has some small concept of mercy, I suppose."

"And Anago himself?"

"He sat on his ebony stool like an image of Guje. No emotion crossed his face."

"What did Falabon say?"

"That he loved me. Oh, and he sang some little song. I didn't listen."

I nodded. The drama was played out. Anago's majesty had been reaffirmed and Pororo had been put in his place. The forces of night were in check.

It was a time of many leave-takings, many more than just our own. The Firin had departed after promising not to intrigue against Anago's militarism. In return Ira-Ireru would receive a seasonal allotment of pearls and diamonds, adding Traore to the list of its client states. I wondered how Chwefro would explain that bit of diplomacy to Mistress Ilesha. And Chancellor Nezumi had stepped down from his office, pleading illness; he was going into retirement on an estate outside Gawi. Lady Kokoro, moreover, had been formally dismissed from Anago's household. She had already returned to her father's mansion in the northern marshes, taking with her sundry maidservants who had likewise exhausted their welcome in the capital. And after this round's ceremonial, the aged Prince of Lozi would be sent to a lonely outpost in the Azen, with his remaining son; both would live out their lives in exile.

Next to all these luminaries Soko and I made our exit unnoticed. Both Chwefro and Anago had agreed that I should lie low for a-while, and I was eager to leave Imari anyhow. Falabon offered us the use of a cottage only eight vigils' journey east of the capital, the same refuge he had suggested on our first meeting. Within three rounds everything was ready for our move.

The Gate of Blue Masks fell behind us. Imari's imposing silhouette straddled the Shibu River, twinkling with mosslight and candleflame, a mirror to the star-scattered darkness overhead. Of the open coutryside to the north nothing was visible outside a few isolated lights, feeble in the distance.

"What now, Risha?" Soko's curiosity was blunted and drowsy; the carriage rocked us with soporific regularity.

"Chwefro says wait. The right moment will come. I just hope I recognize it when it does." Soko mumbled something more; I turned my face to the night and tried to sleep.

Falabon's retreat was a rustic affair of thatch and unmortared stone, set among wooded hills overlooking a stream. We lived there quite modestly. At our request there were no servants; with so little to occupy our time we found housework a relief. I grew fond of those long walks I took to fetch water from the stream, and cooking dinner became my favorite pastime. How scandalized Lachis would have been to see me chopping and measuring and stirring!

Our nearest neighbors were some goatherds whom we never saw. Falabon was our only visitor; he ventured out approximately once every ten rounds to retail court gossip and refresh his memory of Soko's charms. It touched me to see her flattered and courted by such a lively suitor. She grew in confidence and self-esteem, ripening into womanhood as the season lengthened.

I did no ripening, however. Left to myself, away from the homeyness of the kitchen and the two lovers' temperate pleasures, I brooded. I felt aimless, unmotivated, lost; an unspeakable sorrow welled up inside me whenever I wasn't busy with mindless chores. I tried putting a name to it: Olaro? Seren? Pororo? But none of them quite fit. It was a larger feeling than unfulfilled desire or personal loss. It encompassed my whole being—all my past, all my present—and it negated any possible future.

"You feel the night," Soko said. "Nothing more. You're not accustomed to this never-ending darkness."

But what of the darkness of interplanetary space, the void in which I'd spent most my life? Wasn't that as lonely and empty as the Veiian night? Perhaps not; perhaps each time and place had its requisite humor, and Veii's Dark Season was the unique province of melancholy.

Once again dreams haunted me—not the vivid nightmares I had known on the Firin lightsail, or during the toils of White Shadows—but merely long and convoluted fantasies that filled my mind from the moment my eyes closed until the moment they opened again, vigils later, on a quieter and less compelling reality. Most of the time I wasn't even a character in these narratives; I simply watched them unfold. Nor did I tend to remember any specific content; but the prevailing mood lingered with me, and it was always sad.

Soko and Falabon had been cavorting on the cottage's single bed for a vigil or more. I was wandering along the rocky trails just above our homestead, listening to night sounds, watching stars move through the figures of their ancient dance. Occasionally a meteor would flash into quick brilliance, and I would think of wishes, and realize I had none. Then a light appeared out of nowhere and refused to die. It moved laterally, growing steadily brighter, until I made out the streamlined shape of a Firin aircar. It settled on the heath a few meters from my feet and Chwefro stepped out, smiling.

"My calendar said you'd be needing company around now," the Firin said. "How does the simple life suit you?"

"Well enough," I replied.

"Aren't you surprised to see me?"

"I don't surprise very easily these rounds."

"I see." Chwefro came closer and shined a penlight in my eyes, irritating me quite a bit. "Your pupils are slow to dilate, Risha. Did you realize that? No, probably not. Well. You look depressed, my dear. Your affect seems flat. Have you been suffering from headaches?"

"No."

"Then it still isn't too serious."

"What isn't?"

"Why, your neural dysfunction."

"I thought that was taken care of in Ira-Ireru. I've stopped taking those tablets."

"Yes, you do look pale. But as for those ion treatments—they were only a temporary measure. Your cerebral metabolism is still upset. Didn't you mention having a seizure shortly before I arrived in Imari?"

"Chwefro! Are you telling me I'm going mad?"

"It's a reversible process; you needn't worry."

I fought the tears forming in my eyes, held back the sobs that caught at my throat, and concentrated on my rage. Unfortunately there wasn't much there; it made more sense to cry. Chwefro held me till I finished.

"That's better," the Firin said, in a passable imitation of concern. "You should be away from this planet within a starcycle."

I sniffed and wiped damp hairs out of my eyes. "I'm not sure I want to go back."

"But you must."

"Why? Why can't I stay here? You must have more effective melanin therapies than the one you've been using on me. Pororo doesn't seem to suffer any brain dysfunction, and he's been living here longer than I have. For that matter, as far as I'm concerned, he can go right *on* living here. I don't want to kill him. I've been on Veii long enough to achieve a new outlook on things. All those issues of status and vengeance that once seemed so crucial have lost their meaning for me. Rhamant is dead; another death won't resurrect him. So I won't be Pororo's assassin, and I won't go back to Gheo. I've decided I can live just as well on Veii as in any of those claustrophobic canisters of the Hypaethra. I'll stay with Ilesha in Trokomari, just as I did before. Why—you could take me there now, and Soko too, and this long dreary nightmare can end."

Chwefro regarded me with folded arms. "Your mental state is not the best, Risha. Can you accept for a moment that perhaps this new outlook is merely a delusion? Can you entertain the possibility that this is not a good time to change your mind about something as fundamental as your entire future?"

"Am I supposed to say yes?"

"If you do," the Firin said, smiling, "it will suggest that you're still amenable to reason. Because I can and will descend to threats."

My chin went up. "Threaten away."

"There's another tumor forming just behind your hypothalamus. As time passes it will interfere more and more with your brain functions. You will be increasingly prone to depressions, to nightmares, to god-intoxicated fugue. Eventually it will impair your gross motor functions, and within a revolution you will be dead. That is, unless Firin medical science intervenes. And for that I require your cooperation."

"So you've taken pains all along to ensure that I will remain a puppet."

"No. We merely subjected you to a course of therapy with some undesirable side effects, thinking that before those side effects had time to appear we could reverse the process and restore you to health. That scenario, of course, depended on your carrying out your mission as Volshev conceived it. If you go along with the original plan there's no problem."

"It sounds like you've ceased being a disinterested third party. It sounds like you want Pororo dead too—and for some reason you won't do the deed yourself. So I'm back to the same dilemma I faced in that miserable courtyard outside the Hall of Justice. Either I die, or someone else does."

"That's right, Risha. And I think you do value your own life a bit higher than that of some murdering pederast."

"That may be—because I certainly value it a lot higher than yours!" And I struck the Firin across the face as hard as I could, three or four times. Though the pale skin reddened, Chwefro showed no other sign of discomfort.

For a moment I thought I'd start crying again: but no, I'd found my anger at last. "Chwefro!" I shouted. "What does all this mean? Why must you keep lying and manipulating? Why can't you just tell me what's going on?"

"Because the rules prevent me." Chwefro watched me with that habitual half-smile. "Meqmat is reinventing history as a game with fixed rules and strategies. Veii is the field of action; we Firin are among the players; and you, frankly, are one of the key pieces. Cooperate and you'll be rewarded beyond your wildest dreams. Obstruct me and you will die. Decide, Risha."

"Why do you want Pororo out of the way?"

"I'll tell you when the time comes."

I thought back to Rhamant's glorious entry into the Court of Victory, to Lachis weeping in the Despot's Presence Chamber, to Pororo telling me how coolly he'd plotted my death. "You win," I said. "I don't want to die yet, and I certainly don't want to go insane."

"That's better. Now I can show you the gifts I brought." Chwefro handed me a slender crystalline vial and a jeweled finger-ring. "The first is poison; the second is a signaling device. Press down on the opal to call me from wherever you are. From now until midseason I'll be staying in a Firin outpost very close to Imari. If you should need to leave in a hurry just let me know; I'll be on hand with this aircraft. You know the rest."

I nodded.

"I'll be going now. A short visit, but I hope a crucial one. Don't fail yourself, Risha."

I said nothing. Chwefro climbed back into the vehicle and took off again. I headed back toward the cottage's glow.

On Falabon's next visit he formally requested Soko's hand in marriage. "She has no kin here," he explained, "so you're the next best thing."

"I can only say yes," I replied. "But what about the wife you have already?"

"Soko will be given exactly the same status. She won't be a secondary wife, and she certainly won't be a concubine. I'm wealthy enough to maintain two households in Imari now; they won't even have to live under the same roof. And as soon as Soko gives me a son she'll be set for life, a true matron of Traore."

"When is the ceremony, then?"

"Ah!" Falabon's eyes danced. "Normally marriages wait till the dawning of Brightyear, as you know well. But Anago is overturning yet another precedent. He's found a young bride to take the place of

Kokoro, and their wedding is set for the fifty-fourth round of this very season. As part of the nuptial celebrations every citizen of Trokomari will be feted for ten rounds, entirely at the Warlord's expense, and during that time the Darkyear restrictions on matrimony will be suspended. It's the perfect opportunity for us. We'll be wed as soon as the festivities begin."

"Then Soko and I will have to start packing this same round!"

"That's right. I'll be glad to help."

Much earlier than I expected, then, Soko and I took the long road back into the capital. She was as pleased and excited as a young bride should be, and I was genuinely relieved. This marriage ensured her security, no matter what became of me; Falabon was well placed enough to take care of her. Once we arrived in town he put us up in a mansion off the public gardens, and sent round a succession of seamstresses, jewelers, hairdressers, cooks, vintners, decorators, and singing girls, to make sure we were perfectly content in these new lodgings. No expense was spared on our comfort.

Like the rest of the city, our new household devoured any gossip concerning the Warlord's marriage. Along with this lightweight fare came rumors of something more substantial: Anago was about to launch an invasion of Trokomari. His wedding, apparently, was just a cover, a mere farewell celebration. Even during the conflict in Lozi an armada had been under construction in Gawi's extensive shipyards. Now the work was done. A fleet of warships big enough to hold all his battle-scarred legions stood waiting in the Straits of Ye. Anago's new bride would have little opportunity to enjoy her husband, for this time he planned to lead his armies in person, across the Garengazi to Ilesha's island realm.

I'd suspected that such a move would come eventually, but the Warlord's present haste amazed me. He must be counting both on Woro's unpreparedness and on the simple shock value of a nighttime invasion. Otherwise his strategy made no sense. Certainly his legions were neither as numerous nor as well supplied now as they had been at the outset of the Lozi war—and Trokomari would put up a resistance at least as stubborn, if I knew anything about Lord Hima.

Only Pororo's influence could be making Anago act so recklessly. His impetuosity, along with the Nightlord's monumental ambition, made a deadly combination. I began to understand Chwefro's design a little better.

My thoughts were never far from Ilesha and the threat she faced, even in the midst of Soko's wedding feast. Garlanded well-wishers filled our courtyard, members of Falabon's extended family rubbing elbows with various middle-ranking courtiers. On account of Soko's foreign birth none of the higher aristocracy attended, which actually made for a more pleasant time. Easy good humor prevailed; music played, gifts of money poured in, wine and whiskey flowed, and a pair of hogs roasted over an open fire.

The central moment came when Soko and Falabon were served a trayful of tiny millet cakes. Gourmandizer though he was, the poet took only three, as his guests laughed and cheered. Soko ate five or six in quick succession, amid more laughter. So the requirements of matrimony were satisfied; by the laws of Trokomari they were man and wife.

From that round on the city was neither dark nor quiet. Torches flooded every square with dancing red light, rivaling even daylight's splendor. Revelers filled the streets with raucous merriment, during all twelve vigils of the round; curfew was suspended till after the holiday. With Falabon to inspire her Soko abandoned herself to frivolity. She was as aware as I was of the sword hanging over her adopted country, but she was also young and in love, and Falabon was showering her with such favors as she had never dared dream of. So she refused to burden her mind with ugly facts. I didn't blame her—nor did I share in her cheer.

I spent my waking hours in the mansion's pillared garden, inhaling the scent of blooming nightflowers, ignoring my confusion, biding my time till the awaited summons should arrive. When it did it came on two feet, wearing a face I knew too well.

A servant ran ahead to warn me. I was surprised at Anago's choice of messenger, but I had already steeled myself for what had to be. In deference to form I draped a shawl over my head, leaving my breasts as bare as ever, and waited for him on a terrace overgrown with phosphorescent mold.

Pororo mounted the shallow staircase with stiff, formal steps. His two attendants waited beneath a wilted magnolia, well out of earshot. Though he approached to within a meter of where I stood he kept his eyes fixed on the ground.

"Anago sent me," he began, without any greeting, as if to announce that he would never be here of his own will. "He apologizes for not sending word sooner, but he only just learned of your presence in Imari." That was a polite lie; I let it go. "You know he'll be married in the hollow of this same round. He earnestly desires your attendance at the festivities. He wants you to dance."

I laughed quietly and Pororo flicked me a wary glance. "I'd be delighted to come," I said. "Now that wasn't difficult, was it?"

"No, it wasn't. And since you've given me a reply I'll be on my way." He stepped back and half-turned toward the stairs before I caught his arm.

"Please, Master Pororo. Don't feel uncomfortable. You honor this house. Won't you stay long enough for a drink? It is a holiday, after all."

He looked back at his companions and then at me, meeting my gaze for the first time since the ordeal. "I have no use for false hospitality, Mistress Risha. Don't make this silly whim of Anago's any more trying than it has to be."

"I'm not attempting to. I just wanted to let you know that I bear you no ill will. Can we forget the past?"

"I wish we could." His face was bleak. "I'm thoroughly ashamed of what I did. It's brought me nothing but misery. Is your spirit large enough to forgive such a wrong?"

"I understand what prompted you. No one can blame you for wanting to save someone you loved."

"I hope you mean that. It has a comforting sound, coming from the same person I wronged. But I really must go. The Warlord has other uses for my time."

"All right. But I hope we can meet again soon. We have more in common than you realize, my friend." I made a solemn bow; he did the same. Then he was gone.

In the plaza outside Anago's house the drums of war were throbbing. There were four of them, four enormous sections of a single ancient tree, their heads covered with taut human skin. Two drummers pounded each one. They were the Nightlord's albinos, pale misfits with pink eyes and ashen hair who lived out their lives in darkness. They alone were allowed to touch those ill-omened drums.

I pushed my way through the throng, past drunken warriors firing rifles into the air, past wild children setting off long strings of firecrackers. The captain of the guard recognized me at once. He detailed a pair of pikemen to escort me as far as the banqueting hall. At the great bronze doors I let them go, and stood there watching the gaudy crowd within.

Many striking women graced Anago's table. In my first quick glance I saw beauties plump and slender, quiet and bold, painted and unadorned. But when I walked in on Falabon's arm, and took my place at the lower end of the long table, every eye was on me. I was already a legend; the scandal of my trial and exile had only enhanced my notoriety. Now I returned in glory.

What woman there could rival the elegance of my costume, the dignity of my bearing? Who could outmatch the chiseled harmony of my face? My looks, which in Gheo were little better than average, dazzled these notables of Imari—where eugenics was as unknown as quantum theory. I'd never before chosen to flaunt my physical beauty before Anago's court; I'd always carried myself as a sorceress, a wise woman, a figure of mystery. That pose was abandoned once and for all.

The flurry inspired by my entrance subsided, little by little, and the wedding guests returned to their boasting and wisecracking. But I felt Anago's eyes on me, and Pororo's. My knack for making indelible gestures hadn't failed me yet.

The celebration reached new heights of idiocy and abandon. The ceremonial millet cakes were served; kegs of whiskey were broached. Jugglers juggled, fiddlers fiddled, singers sang. My fellow diners began speculating on when the Warlord would retire with his toothsome bride. I sipped wine and toyed with bits of food, chatting disjointedly with Soko and Falabon. I felt as calm as a mountain or a star.

When the note came from Anago's table I laughed. I needed Falabon's help to compose my reply, for I still wasn't proficient in any of Veii's written languages. "My belly is full," I wrote, "and my limbs are heavy. How can I dance the dream-summons? I'll need strong temptation, my lord."

Anago was in a jolly enough mood to play my game. After a few more notes we came to terms.

Draping a spangled purple veil over my head and torso I approached the Warlord's seat, bowing down to the ground. "What is your will, Lord Anago?" I asked in my throatiest voice.

"This is a momentous time for the fortunes of Traore," he replied. "Speak with the gods; give us an omen."

"Since this is your wedding-feast, lord, may I claim a boon before I dance?"

"Ask what you desire, up to half of all I possess." Our exchange brought laughter from the whole room; we were reciting stilted dialogue from an old romance, and everyone caught on to the joke.

"Izezi has stolen into my heart," I said. I let my veil slip to show off the scars on my back, the whorls and ripples denoting the goddess of desire. "You've set an amorous example for your subjects, Lord Anago. Whose thoughts wouldn't turn to romance, now that even you have fallen under the spell of a new love? But my bed has been half-empty during these chilly hollows of Darkyear; I've been in need of company for the long sad vigils. Lend me one of your warriors, just for a round. Give me a fine young hero to fight off the ravages of loneliness."

Anago laughed. "You claim such ephemeral pleasures, when the Lord of Night can grant you so much more?"

"So it is. This one favor is all I ask."

"Then you've let me off easily. Name the warrior of your choice, and he'll be yours till the hollow gives way to a new round."

I raised my arms in triumph. "Only one man will satisfy me—the bravest hero of Traore, barring the Warlord himself. Give me Pororo, conqueror of Lozi, commander of the Company of Night."

I'd expected more laughter, but there was none. It seemed I'd gone beyond the limits of taste. I heard only a babble of confused asides, saw a comic panorama of craning necks. Pororo looked me dead in the eye with an unreadable expression. I stood my ground and stared back.

"Well, Pororo?" Anago turned and regarded him benignly. "Will you rise to the challenge?"

"I haven't failed you yet, my lord, and I won't now." Pororo bowed in my direction, with exactly the same flourish a Radiant gallant would use to lead his lady into a pavane. I made the appropriate countermove —did his eyes flicker in surprise?—and signaled the drums to begin.

At first I moved in contorted, crouching steps, imitating the antic style of Yebba's priests. I let the god-fugue come up slowly, very slowly, playing out the feeling one breath at a time. For once I had no specific dream-cues to weave into my improvisations; my dance would be as suggestive as ever, but this time I played the mirror rather than the lens. My audience's own private fantasies would take over when eventually they relaxed into Koyo's embrace.

The drummers followed me with an attentiveness I'd never known before. As my gestures became larger and more fluid they put more space into the beat, building a structure of voluptuous syncopation within which I moved like a nymph through summer rain. I took on the attributes of Ijeji, the Traoro Izezi, sinuous and seductive and maddeningly cool. My bones turned to water, my muscles to foam, I shook and rippled like an image in a wind-tossed pool. The space behind my eyes opened wider and wider, carrying me ever higher on the vascular tide, till I soared like a fountain, surging, cresting, showering all those eager minds with the essence of sensuality. They ached beneath my teasing ministrations, but it was a delicious ache, a glad sorrow, an emptiness more sweet than fulfillment itself. In the midst of my undulations I focused in on Pororo, imagining his hands on my body, imagining him dancing in the same spell that held me, and when I looked at him through the blood-haze I saw his senses fixed on me with a fascination equal to that of any other man in the hall. My exultation knew no bounds. I'd won him, I'd entranced him, I'd broken through the wall of his reserve, I'd caught him in the dream-web he had eluded for so long. For this moment he was mine.

My motion stilled somewhat, drew in; I began a complex finger-play, which one of the percussionists supported with popping strokes on a woodblock. My long sweeping curves became tighter, more jagged; I hopped and waggled, hunching my back, jabbing my elbows; my face screwed up and my tongue flicked in and out like a snake-tongue or a flame. Water metamorphosed into fire. I was performing the most dangerous invocation I knew, calling down Guje himself, the war-god, the angry eye of heaven, the iron jaw of death. He deigned to answer me. His cruel heat inflamed me, briefly, in passing, for I couldn't hold him long. From tiny kindling flamelets my dance ascended to a raging blaze, and I leaped about like a madwoman, kicking out my legs and flying into the air with blatant disregard for gravity, just like a fire coursing upward to the sky. My audience had been seduced before, but now they were amazed. Rarely had they seen a mere woman embody such ravening force. I whirled around in one last series of jumps and then stopped, as abruptly and finally as a swordstroke, balanced with outstretched arms before Anago's seat.

Some of the revelers started to applaud, but they were quickly hushed by the rest; the dream-dance is no idle entertainment. I saluted Anago and his bride, did the same for the other guests at the high table, and made my last bow to Pororo, who watched me with amused respect. Then with my veil modestly draped again I walked out of the hall, my brain still echoing with the footsteps of the mysteries, my blood still rushing in divine intoxication.

A page overtook me in the south portico. He was one of Pororo's retinue, an elfin-eyed lad with sinewy thighs. Murmuring formal greetings he escorted me to a carriage waiting in the avenue, which drove us the short distance to his master's house.

A few smoky torches lit our way to Pororo's lavish bathinghall. There I was bathed, massaged, and rubbed with scented oil, by a whole team of good-looking slaves. I'm afraid I presented the masseur with a difficult challenge. Knead me though he would, the tension singing through my limbs refused to dissipate.

At last—taut nerves or no—I was judged fit for the master's bed-chamber. They freshened up my hair and dressed me in a robe of lus-trous Woro silk; I was careful to transfer the pouch I'd concealed in my other gown to its wide sash. Taking me by the hand the page led me to an upstairs room, painted mauve, with faded frescoes decorating its high ceiling. Three or four nephrite vessels held the rare golden strain of night-moss; its light was softer even than a candle.

Seren awaited me, sprawled languidly in a heap of quilts. I could smell a musky aroma rising off his skin; it was the same scent his slaves had used on me. He watched me through half-closed eyes and signaled the page to leave.

I went to him at once. Without a word I lay down beside him, lightly resting my hand on his chest. His response was to catch my arm in a vise-grip and squeeze it till I felt the blood vessels break. I started back; his lips curved in a slow mocking grin.

"What were you expecting?" he asked, his mouth close to mine, his breath a warm whisper against my flesh. "Did you think I'd be a sweet and gentle lover? With you?" He took me in both arms and pinioned me against the hard ridges of his torso, forcing my lips apart with quick jabs of his tongue. Though his strength was overpowering I resisted as lustily as I could, wrestling him off my body even as I responded to his kiss. He eased up, matching his force to mine, and we rolled among the coverlets with our legs entwined, our loins knocking together with more violence than heat.

I was absolutely terrified. The god-fever roared inside me, threatening to inundate my self-control; a slender thread of consciousness sus-pended me over the flood. This is it, I thought, my dream of passion fulfilled, my dream of vengeance on the brink of reality. But can I survive it? I kept remembering who it was I tangled with. This man could kill with his bare hands and laugh about it afterwards. He could break me into pieces at any moment. Already our loose garments were slipping off; what if my pouch slipped out of reach, what if our game took a more serious turn, and he restrained me in earnest? My blood raced on in an ecstasy of fear.

Suddenly he let go of me and fell back on the bed. I sat up, incredulous. Seren lay there stark naked, his arms thrown wide, his belly heaving with silent humor. I leaned over him, frowning, squinting at him in the dim light. He took one look at my face and broke out in wild laughter.

"I can't, I can't," he gasped, wiping tears from his eyes. He grasped my fingers and guided me into the curve of his arm. "Whatever possessed you to do this, woman? Why should you seek the bed of a boy-lover?"

Crosscurrents swirled in my mind. I was dizzy, vertiginous. "Because you obsess me. It's as simple and as crazy as that. Since I first saw you I've wanted to touch you, to hold you, to have you, to make a dent in you, to make you feel something for me. There's no love or reason in any of it."

He sighed, a tiny murmur of sympathy. "And now?"

"Now it's all a joke, isn't it. You were just playing. You're no amorous brute at all."

"Oh, don't be too sure of that! But I have little experience with women."

"You could have some before this hollow rounds out."

He put his hand beside my face. He was very beautiful there in the golden light. "I could," he agreed. "But I don't think I want to. Why don't we just go to sleep, and afterwards you can tell the world any story you want? I won't contradict you."

I slumped back. Voices chittered and chattered in my head. One of them belonged to my everyday self, playing out this scene, speaking coherently and convincingly. Others issued from various sub-personalities, from lesser bundles of will and desire. Some urged me to come clean: reveal myself to Seren, tell him frankly what I was up to, divest myself of the whole business. Others said: Do it now! What better moment? Listen to him making light of your terrible needs.

The consensus was a silence stretched as tightly as a bowstring. I said nothing; he said nothing. We lay within a few centimeters of each other, but there was no bridging the chasm between our hearts. The lamps glowed on. Antique figures postured on the fading ceiling. Distant voices carried up through half-shuttered windows. Seren's chest rose and fell in steady rhythm. His mouth sagged open, his eyelids fluttered. I'd confessed my passion; he'd fallen asleep.

I whispered a prayer to Ijeji—strange how easily I'd come to accept her existence. Goddess, I thought, I've never seen a man more enticing. You created him just to tantalize my soul. Look at those soft eyelashes, that fine nose, those lips parted as sweetly as a child's. Look at the glorious sculpting of those arms, that torso, those thighs. Forgive this betrayal of desire.

I pressed the fire-opal on my ring. I felt in my sash for the crystal vial, drew it forth, and extracted a long slender syringe from the milky solution inside. It gleamed briefly in the light, dripping a few drops onto the quilt. I took a breath and drove it deep in Seren's throat.

His body twitched once. His eyes opened and looked at me, curiously, questioningly. I counted to five and they glazed over, losing all their animation and light. He was finished.

I hugged my knees and started trembling. Quiet down, I told my brain. Let me be now. Cut the strings. Slowly the inner voices subsided and left me alone with this perfect corpse.

His body was relaxing; I smelled a foul odor and realized that his bowels had emptied. Not as pleasant a companion as I'd expected. But I stayed in my place alongside him, waiting. Gongs rang in the eleventh vigil; my legs stiffened and my skin chilled. Where was Chwefro?

Before the watch rang out a voice called me softly from the furthest window. I leaped up and ran over, rejoicing as never before at the sight of the Firin's ghost-pale face. I fiddled with the shutter and helped my preceptor in.

"Good job," Chwefro said, leaning over the corpse with a laser in one hand and a hexagonal box in the other. A wire-fine beam sprang out of the apparatus and cut through Seren's neck. "We'll take this much as a trophy," the Firin said. "It's tricky keeping all the neurons in order, but I think we'll manage." Chwefro lifted the severed head and popped it into the container, which was brimming with some colorless gel. I averted my eyes from the cadaver. That was one vision I didn't need cluttering up my memory.

"Don't dawdle, girl." Chwefro was already climbing out the window again. "Help me with these boxes."

I realized that there were two of the peculiar hexagonal containers, not one. I picked up the second and followed Chwefro over the sill. A narrow ledge ran the whole length of the building at this level; we flattened ourselves against the wall and shuffled along until we came to a convenient pine tree. Dropping the boxes ahead of us, we climbed down to the ground on sticky branches. Now we were in Seren's garden. Chwefro led us to the back gate and on into the street.

"Where is your airship?" I whispered.

"In Ragtown," my companion whispered back. "I couldn't land within the city limits."

It was a long and tiresome walk to the Gate of Skulls. Since curfew was in effect there was no chance of hiring a carriage; we trudged onwards, avoiding the night watch, both of us muffled in black cloaks that disguised sex as well as skin color. Chwefro refused to say a word. My questions banged against each other inside a hollow cranium. I felt squeezed out, pressed flat, like a husk or an empty rind, a bit of discarded trash.

We reached the gate shortly after the new round began. We passed through without difficulty, and traversed the tunnel of skulls. Every single one stared after me. Finally we emerged onto the barrens just outside the wall, and Chwefro let me speak at last.

I dropped my burden and expelled a long breath. "I don't know where to begin," I confessed. "But how about explaining these two boxes? You have Seren's head in that one. Is there another gruesome prize in mine?"

"Yes."

"Somebody's head?"

"Yes."

"Oh Chwefro—what are we doing?" I let my sobs break loose, I let my tears run free. "Who else have we murdered?"

"The only other obvious choice: Anago. Our surgery is complete, dear Risha. We've saved the world."

I howled with rage. As if in echo, another cry came down from the nearest tower, a challenge of some sort, official-sounding but indecipherable at this range.

"No time to explain now," Chwefro shouted. "Word is out. They must have found the bodies already. Run. We've got to get into the air."

And we pelted into the maze of tents, still clutching our miserable baggage. I knew nothing more till I collided with Chwefro's back. We'd reached the canvas-covered aircar, we piled in without even pausing to remove the camouflage. It flew off as we rose into the air, and I looked down to see Imari transformed into a child's toy, a little jumble of blocks lit here and there with matchsticks. It was all too cruel, too vicious, too absurd.

CHAPTER TWELVE

Chwefro made noises about historical necessity. I countered with compassion. Chwefro discoursed on ideological balance. I suggested humanity. Chwefro alluded to the chances of the game. I recommended mercy. We talked past each other, around each other, neither one of us conceding the least validity to the other's arguments. Our discussions lasted from one spell to the next, from the floodplain of the Shibu to the Afarotian desert, from the Firin aircar to the port of New Venery, from the sky-piercing Lift to the spinning Hypaethron, and on into the void. At last I gave up; I could talk as long as I wanted, but I'd never change Chwefro's mind, and I'd never undo the past.

Seren was dead. I hadn't even begun to sort out what that meant to me. But for Anago my grief was sharp and unequivocal. True, he had been a stern dictator, a greedy imperialist who would have sacked Trokomari and tortured my beloved Ilesha without a qualm. But he could also be a warm and generous man—and, however briefly, he'd been my friend.

Slowly and with great difficulty I pieced together a picture of the Firin's schemes. "We may all look alike," Chwefro said, "but we don't think alike."

Their pivotal dissension had begun much earlier than I dreamed. There had been many among the Fair Kindred who had disapproved of Anago from the start, who had wanted him assassinated or otherwise removed from office long seasons before his recent campaigns. But they had been overruled by a powerful isolationist faction. Chwefro had remained aloof from this debate, choosing merely to wait and see.

Then came Seren's request for landing privileges on Veii—"a transparent Khryashan ploy," as Chwefro described it, during the long ride up the Lift. "It was inconceivable that the Heir of Khryasha could be acting as an individual. His request had to reflect his own House's interest in establishing a toehold in Veii."

"To what purpose?" I demanded.

"Child! Did you live in Gheo so long without observing Khryasha's towering pride and contentiousness?" Chwefro rolled enormous eyes. "For generations Volshev has furthered Gloy's interests at the expense of Khryasha's, and Lady Sorich, old harridan that she is, has vowed to set things right. She shrinks at nothing—it's plain she meant to defy the Despot himself. And what a delectable scheme she devised! Seren had just been passed over for the office of Spear of Gheo, so for the time being he was at loose ends. The idea was for him to go down into Veii, live there for revolutions on end, if necessary, and attain some high rank in one of the native polities. You see how quickly he attained that goal."

"Like a blue star," I whispered.

"Then, when his position was unassailable, he would introduce bits and pieces of more advanced technologies, taking his chosen people step by step into an industrial revolution. Just as Veii in general is the workshop for the Revenant Hypaethra, Traore, the wealthiest nation in the Garengazi, would become Khryasha's own preserve. Sorich and family intended to bypass the Firin Lift and establish direct trade with Traore, using the new generation of thrusters for takeoff and landing. Khryasha would become independent of Gheo and eventually make a bid for hegemony over the entire Matterfield."

"But Traore would make a pitifully weak ally against Gloy and Gheo," I objected.

"At first, yes, but ultimately Traoro warriors could be trained in freespace combat, and Traoro factories could turn out modern weapons. It wouldn't happen in one lifetime—Sorich was content to set the process in motion. There's more, you see. Even before Seren went to Veii, Khryasha had reopened the old mines in Shadan's rings, untouched since the Wars of Reconquest. It's been a well-kept secret; Seren's jaunts out to Shadan were passed off as sheer bravado, as one more move in his status-rivalry with Rhamant of Gloy. Raw material from Shadan is waiting even now to be hurled into Veiian orbit; all that is needed is a downworld industrial base sufficient to exploit those riches."

I shook my head, marveling over the enormity of old Sorich's daring. As clouds whirled around our carriage I studied their patterns, imagining human destiny as so many streams of vapor—fleeting, evanescent, possessing more form than substance.

"How could Seren and Sorich expect the rest of the Matterfield to sit by and do nothing?" I asked.

"Volshev isn't as clever as you think. He moves in predictable old grooves. His attention is confined in large measure to the ten Hypaethra, and in a lesser degree to Ethri, to Lin, and to the Rocks. Sorich wisely chose to work outside his sphere of interest. It was the Firin she underestimated." Chwefro smiled. "We misled her very carefully. As I was saying before, we tend to group ourselves in factions. Only one faction ever negotiated with her. My own."

"And what do you stand for?"

"For the resurrection of Meqmat, naturally. But I saw in Sorich's proposal an effective smokescreen for our collective project, as well as a source of useful dissension among the Revenant Houses. It's always best to keep one's adversary confused and ignorant."

"Then why have you worked so assiduously to undo everything Seren accomplished? Why help me kill him—why kill Anago?"

Chwefro's face took on a look that might or might not signify regret. "Seren, as Pororo the mighty warrior, was moving too fast, and in the wrong direction. He talked his way into Anago's good graces by appealing to the Nightlord's territorial ambitions, by stroking his desire to be remembered as the greatest conqueror in Traoro history. That's the sort of thing Anago could understand, not industrial revolutions or interplanetary alliances. Seren had to work with what was there. As a result Anago sidetracked him, and their partnership was turning Veii into one huge battlefield. Surely you wouldn't want to see Woro laid waste, and Ilesha sacrificed to the Fetishes."

"Of course not."

"Well, then." Chwefro smiled again. "That's why I had to kill Anago. I had been instrumental in unleashing the menace, so it was my responsibility to negate it. And I did so in such a way that Firin hands will never be suspected. No, Risha. Anago will be remembered as a great lord, a mighty warrior. You will be remembered as a traitress, a sorceress, and an assassin."

"I??"

"Yes, you. You were never actually subjected to the final ordeal of the witchcraft trial—that won't be forgotten. And there's no doubt in any Traoro mind that you killed—and decapitated—Pororo. That style of killing, incidentally, is favored by evil sorceresses in all the old tales; they throw the heads into a soup-pot and make goblets of the skulls. Therefore, since Pororo and Anago were killed during the same hollow, in precisely the same manner, and you subsequently vanished from Imari, all suspicion devolves on you—on Risha, the dream-dancer, the nightflower, the witch."

I covered my face in horror. "I'm past hating you, Chwefro. You're beyond any emotion of mine. It's plain I can never go back to Traore— but what about Soko?" The realization filled me with unease. "Won't she be implicated through her association with me?"

"Not with Falabon to shield her," Chwefro replied. "Civil war will tear Traore apart for seasons to come; Anago completely dismantled the old system of government, and left no heir to carry on his dynastic ambitions. I'm sure the praise-singer fled Imari at the first sign of danger, taking his beloved wife with him. Soko will be safe; so will Woro, and the rest of Veii."

And that accounted for historical necessity, with a touch of social conscience thrown in for good measure.

I underwent brain surgery in the spinning terminus of Old Venery, a quick, painless process that restored my gray matter to its former health. Afterwards I was put on a program of drugs to counteract the effects of the hormones I'd taken; Chwefro insisted that they had no side effects, so I can only blame my ensuing depression on myself.

For the free-space voyage back to Gheo was tedium made manifest. During its sixty-odd spells there was absolutely nothing I had to do, and less than nothing I wanted to do. I tried anticipating my new life in the imperial city, but any thought of Volshev or Lachis or Mudriye brought on an ill-defined anxiety. And reminiscence quickly reduced me to tears. So I confined myself to the flat, unvarying present. I exercised a little, to prevent my muscles from turning to jelly; I ate a little, to keep flesh on my bones; and I played and replayed the same stale collection of dataspools. Also I slept, sometimes five watches out of every ten. Never once did I dream.

Somewhere near the halfway mark of the journey Chwefro came to visit me while I was busy staring at the wall. "At the risk of darkening your spirits further," the Firin said, "I have something special to show you. It may shock you out of this gloom."

"It sounds unpleasant already," I replied. But I still hadn't lost my curiosity, so I followed my preceptor into the common room.

Conspicuously displayed on a wall-bracket was the hexagonal container we had brought away from Veii—the trophy-box holding Seren's head. Next to it was an ordinary monitor screen, which Chwefro must have rigged up while I slept. The Firin rippled fingers over the touchpanel and moved back with a flourish.

On the screen a blur of colors coalesced into a face. I knew those heavy-lidded eyes; I was well acquainted with the line of that delicate cheekbone, restored now to its original unscarred pallor. "Seren," I said. My voice grated like chalk on slate. "Are you aware of me?"

"I'm not aware of anything," the face replied. "I'm just a program. But I can imitate Seren's responses—so if you like, we can pretend that he's actually present, carrying on a conversation with you."

"Chwefro—why?"

The pseudo-Seren answered. "Firin don't like to waste things. I'm an unusual subject, with a unique mind. Just as Revenant Houses routinely keep samples of superior genetic material, Firin keep records of living personalities. That poison you injected into my bloodstream kept my brain in suspended animation, until Chwefro could pop it into a miniature life-support system—the box you see next to me. The same thing was done to Anago. In the Firin Hypaethron, biotechnicians were able to restimulate a degree of neural activity in both our brains, and then make records of our psychic matrices. Both of us will eventually be incorporated into the larger Meqmat program. For now, only this limited simulation has been processed. They beamed me out of Old Venery just last watch."

"So that we can talk over old times? Patch up our differences?"

"If you like. I did care for you, Risha. But no woman could ever dominate my emotions, not the way a man could. If it's any consolation, I might even have married you, if this Veiian affair hadn't intervened and called me away from Khryasha. You would have made a good wife for me. In spite of your status-count."

"But I would never have been your lover."

"Probably not."

I shivered. "This is mad. I'm talking to a ghost! Don't you hate me? I'm your assassin."

"You were misled. You thought you had good reasons."

Time snagged like silk on a fingernail. I turned to Chwefro and screamed. "DID YOU LIE TO ME ABOUT THIS TOO?"

"No," Chwefro said quietly. "Seren's tale was news even to me."

I turned back to the screen, slightly calmer. "Let's hear it, then."

"That dataspool Volshev played for you," said the simulation, "that spool which allegedly documented Rhamant's death, and which you all saw in Gheo—that was a complete forgery. Oh, don't mistake me; I did kill Rhamant. But it didn't happen the way you assumed. No. After you spoke to me at the Masquerade—and so touchingly revealed your emotions—Rhamant came over and accused me of insulting you. I denied it, and begged him to abandon our quarrel. Just as you hoped I would.

You see, I was about to depart for Veii, and I thought that perhaps I could resolve our differences after all. Though our inter-House rivalry would remain, at least Rhamant might think of me with something besides contempt. Even at that late stage of the game his opinion still mattered.

"I invited Rhamant aboard the *Blue Star*. He was suspicious, but he realized I was showing him a new side of my character, revealing a frankness I'd previously hidden. In the end he trusted me enough to come along. We went to the bridge; I showed him how to take the ship out, just as the tape described. Then, when we were beyond the range of Volshev's sensors, I opened my heart to him. It was very much like your declaration to me.

"This shouldn't surprise you, now that you know me as well as you do. Since childhood Rhamant had been my idol, my hero, my ideal. But he'd always rejected my friendship. It was absolutely impossible for me to be close to him, in any way. So he became an obsession. At first I wanted to be exactly like him; then I wanted to be better than him, I wanted to outdo him, I wanted to leave him in the dust. I loved and hated him, my whole life became a response to—"

"Seren," I interrupted, completely under the program's spell. "You don't have to explain obsessions to me."

"No." The face grimaced. "And what similar outcomes we both attained. I told Rhamant the way I'd always felt, in fact I told him, yes, I even told him that I loved him. And he denied me. He told me I disgusted him. He told me I wasn't a man."

"Could Rhamant really be that inhuman?"

"He was, in the shock of the moment. You know what the Canon says about homoerotic passion. Rhamant practically quoted scripture to me."

With one part of my mind I knew I was only seeing scan-lines on a screen, but with another, more essential area, I was deeply involved with another human being's pain. The false Seren's face contorted with a real man's anguish.

"You've heard of my temper, I'm sure," said the construct. "Rhamant broke my heart, and I couldn't face the pain. I went into a rage. I struck him, I challenged him to a duel there and then, I dared him to prove I wasn't every bit as good and worthy as he. And we fought. We struggled with our bare hands there in the cabin of the *Blue Star*." The image paused and fixed me with wide brown eyes. "And I killed him. I had no choice. It was him or me, and I won.

"I jettisoned the corpse in an emergency pod, including a spool to document the deed. Apparently Volshev preferred to falsify my record."

I nodded. My throat was very dry. "Chwefro," I said, "please turn it off now."

The Firin complied. Seren's face stretched sideways and disappeared.

"You were right," I said. "It does make a difference. He was wrong, and I was wrong. We were both haunted by the same passion. We were both guilty of the same crime. It makes a crazy kind of sense." I pivoted in mid-air, preparing to launch myself back toward my own cabin, thoroughly fed up with the past. Before I could move, the ship's alarm went off.

"The Revenant craft that has been following us," said the ship's voice, "has now matched orbits at close range. A boarding tube has been ejected; shall I allow it to couple?"

"Yes, of course," said Chwefro.

"Are we having visitors?" I asked uneasily.

"We are indeed."

The farscan tank showed me the clean lines of a Khryashan thruster lying not a hundred meters to starboard. Figures jetted along the transparent umbilical, heading our way.

I clutched a bulkhead, calming myself, so boggled with Chwefro's machinations that I was past questions or accusations. I simply waited.

The ship's voice kept us informed of our visitors' movements. They were at the airlock, they were in the airlock, they were skimming along the central shaft. Then five or six armed men appeared in the portal of the common room and offered grave salutes. Their captain bowed to Chwefro.

"Is this the woman, Your Excellency?" he asked.

"The very same," Chwefro replied with a smile.

"Take her," said the captain.

Five warriors surrounded me with drawn swords. I saw no point in resistance. They fitted manacles to my wrists and attached a short lead; then, with a gentle tug, the captain pulled me along behind them. Chwefro followed with the six-sided box.

Aboard the Khryashan ship I was conducted to a comfortable salon and locked in. It occurred to me that this was the third time I'd been imprisoned since meeting Chwefro. Twice before, the Firin had managed to spring me, but this time I had my doubts.

Spells passed; I was held completely incommunicado. Chwefro's initial intimacy with the Khryashans hadn't escaped my notice. I came to wonder whether I'd been betrayed at last. But I let it go no further than wondering; I suspended judgment and kept my spirits up, using my time as constructively as possible.

There were exercise machines in my room, so I worked out at least two watches every spell, determined not to succumb to gravity prostration once I regained my weight. The rest of my waking moments I spent at the terminal, studying history, reading poetry, composing music, and watching my skin tone fade. That one confrontation with Seren's ghost had been the perfect therapy for me.

On the 163rd watch of the voyage I was released from confinement. Since I'd been fastidious with my attire, and kept my hair in impeccable shape, I emerged from that cell with all the elegance and style of a Gheo Radiant. A security detail led me through the airlock and on into a crowded docking zone. Broad windows set into the walls offered views of an Hypaethron's baroque exterior; obviously we had arrived in Khryasha. I was whisked through the crowd, guided along a series of corridors and lifts, ushered through a sequence of ever larger and more richly furnished rooms, and deposited at last before the agate desk of Lady Sorich herself.

She squinted over an illuminated viewer, her face underlit and faintly purplish. Her hair was pure silver; it stood out stiffly, like a mane or a sunburst. Her gown was dead black, completely free of ornament. It matched the look she leveled at me.

"They say you killed my grandson."

"I did." I met her eye to eye.

"Why in the name of Radiance did you do a stupid thing like that?"

"Volshev wanted him dead, and he promised me a tempting reward. It wasn't stupid at all."

"Are you telling the truth? Or did that Firin really put you up to it?"

"Chwefro helped me, but I was executing the Despot's will."

She threw up her hands in disgust. "All that work! All that planning! Now we're set back fifty revolutions. I don't understand those Firin at all. They play both ends against the middle, and then play the middle against itself."

I smiled. "You're catching on."

She snorted. "You have a smart mouth for such a low-born thing."

"Low-born, yes, but high-status."

She muttered under her breath, something about trash and impertinence. Then she continued in more audible tones. "You're a big problem now, you realize, for just about everyone. I have half a mind to put you out the nearest airlock. Volshev would probably thank me. Hah—I suppose that's a good reason not to." She regarded me over clenched knuckles. "Chwefro kept in touch with me all during your passage to Khryasha. I even got to talk with that ghost the Firin spooked up. A neat trick; maybe I'll have them do it to me when I go. Meanwhile it's helped me find one possible solution."

She fiddled with things on her desk and produced a bright cylinder hovering in mid-air. "The Firin sent me a copy of the software," she said. "Damned inconvenient to run on the system we've got here."

The cylinder metamorphosed into an image of Seren, clothed in Khryasha's traditional colors. He almost looked real.

"Well, Seren," his grandmother said. "Apparently you've already tried to kill this girl once. What would you say if I gave you a second chance?"

The image's response was slow. "Be a little more specific," it finally managed.

"I'm making you the judge," she persisted. "Risha Skhorb has done murder. What should her sentence be?"

"Life," said the ghost, carefully and without heat. "Let her live. This corpse, at least, has no interest in revenge. I played and lost. My turn is over; let her keep trying. You'll doubtless find some use for her, won't you? You found enough use for me."

Sorich twitched her shoulders and shut off the projection. Once more I watched Seren fade into oblivion. "Recriminations from beyond the grave!" she cried. "That's all I need, at my age. But I'm not sure how accurate that thing's responses are. Would Seren really be capable of mercy?"

She wasn't asking me, but I answered anyway. "Maybe death has given him a new outlook on life."

"I could learn to hate you very quickly," the old lady snapped. "But the ghost was right. You're more useful to me alive than dead. Welcome to House Khryasha, Radiant Skhorb."

I bowed formally, showing her deference now that she'd remembered her own manners. She acknowledged me and summoned a pair of retainers, who showed me to lodgings not far from the office. Before I had time to wonder what the lady really wanted of me a printout scrolled down from the nearest console, silver letters on black vellum, listing a schedule of upcoming social functions and my precise role in each one.

Apparently I was an honored guest. As I scanned the list more servants arrived with gowns, trouser skirts, unlined dresses, footwear, and jewelry. Everything was dyed mourning's deep purple. My eyes found the bottom of the document:

R.Y. 2089, spell 318.	Cortege and obsequies for the defunct heir, Seren of Khryasha, Radiant 29 of the Community of Hypaethra.

Sorich had cast me in the role of chief mourner.

The next five spells produced an eerie sense of estrangement and alienation. Here I was among Revenants again, speaking my own language, performing all the courtesies which I had so painstakingly acquired, yet I felt more dazed and displaced than if I were wandering through Golo's wasteland or spying in the shadows of Imari. These were Khryashans, true enough—people outside my former acquaintance—but they weren't so unlike the worthies of Skhorb or Paun or Gloy among whom I'd lived for decades. No, it was I who was the oddball. Veii and all I'd done there had changed me more profoundly than I knew. I felt whole, I felt completely myself, I felt cleansed and purified by the anguish I'd suffered: while this Hypaethron, this fragile structure of ego and vanity, seemed the acme of the absurd—an unreal halfworld where shadow-figures strutted and prattled nonsense.

It didn't help that I had to keep playing a part. My life wobbled in the balance; Sorich plainly had designs on me, and Guje only knew what waited me in Gheo. News of my return, and Seren's untimely death, had certainly reached Volshev by now. In the face of all that I had to hold my feelings inside and stay alert to the shifting shadowplay around me, volunteering no information, keeping secret the details of my sojourn on Veii. I wasn't a puppet anymore, but I still hadn't escaped the theatre.

Chwefro avoided me. We had one brief conversation at a levee, wedged between a silver teapot and a statue of Sorich's great-grandfather.

"So you're keeping up your ties with Khryasha after all," I said amicably.

"The game isn't over," Chwefro replied.

"No; it's just a matter of timing, isn't it. You're content to move much more slowly than Sorich, but the same plan is in effect."

Chwefro regarded me benignly and said nothing.

I tried again. "You seem to want me kept alive. That means you have more in store for me. Can I still trust you, Chwefro? Will all this have a happy ending?"

"There are those who will be happy, yes, and you could be among them."

"That *could* sounds risky."

"Even I am at risk, Risha."

I nodded, calm and proud of it. "Volshev is going to pick my brains once I'm in his power. Does that worry you? Don't I know too much?"

"You know everything you're supposed to know," said Chwefro. "I'm not the least bit worried."

And that was all my onetime friend would say.

Seren's funeral was as lavish as his grandmother's fortune could make it, outdoing even the Presentation of the Heir in pomp and pageantry. His remains rested on a diamond-flashing catafalque; a 200-piece orchestra played the requiem on priceless antique instruments. One by one the Radiants and Immaculates of Khryasha came up to pay their last respects, moving in precisely choreographed steps, costumed as if for a somber masque. Each one deposited some gift or token on the bier until it was heaped high with treasure. When everyone had done so a narrow white beam kindled the pile into flame, and all those silks and pearls and fruitwood harps and painted scrolls went up in a great crackling blaze, taking Seren's severed head long with them. He would have appreciated the effect, I'm sure.

I occupied the place of honor. After making my presentation, near the beginning of the rite, I waited with Lady Sorich and a few others on an electrum-plated balcony overlooking the hall. Once the flames had died down, and the ventilation units had removed the last wisps of smoke, we paraded off to the music of a majestic recessional. I followed the Khryashan notables down a long corridor leading back to Sorich's residence, my face composed in suitably melancholic lines.

As we turned into the first of the official anterooms I found myself lagging behind the others. Had they quickened their footsteps, or was I dawdling? Their purple-draped backs were already passing through the half-moon portal when a sudden noise made me glance over my shoulder. Three veiled figures were coming up on me, extending gloved fingers toward my throat.

My skin prickled; time slowed down. I pivoted and aimed a blow at my left-hand assailant's face, recovering in time to kick the middle one in the groin. But they were much better fighters than I. In two seconds they were swarming all over me, pinning my arms and stifling my cries. I saw a hand pass before my eyes; it held a compact white canister. Fingers squeezed. Blue vapor poured out. Vision thinned into blindness.

I woke alone and in silence. I was drifting in free fall within the loose restraints of a sleepnet. Around me were hexagonal bulkheads, three farscan tanks, and an array of meters and telltales. I didn't have to check the readouts to realize I was in free space again.

I felt undamaged, in spite of the assault I vaguely recalled. I wondered how long I'd been out. Looking over the controls, I found a calendar: it was eight spells later than Seren's funeral. "So," I murmured. "It's back to puppethood again."

But I seemed to be in excellent condition, without a trace of chemical hangover. Only the Firin had drugs that clean. In that case—where was I going? My heart quickened with the hope that it might be Veii.

A rapid reading of the long dashed any such fantasies. Beyond doubt I was heading for Gheo. My heartbeat came still faster. I was within a hundred kilometers of the Despot's Hypaethron, and my homing pattern had already been registered. Tanks one and three offered views of the sky-city's bulbous integument.

Here it comes, I thought coolly. My punishment or my reward. Am I ready?

I decided I was. Less than a watch later I was being greeted by two Confessors, three port officials, and a whole security detachment. "Better keep your distance," I warned them. "I've been a prisoner in Khryasha. For all I know they might have turned me into a human bomb." Both Confessors made abrupt exits and the captain of security called for emergency backup.

In a blastproof compartment I was scanned by at least ten different methods, all very delicate and nondisruptive. The sabotage specialists found nothing unusual. They were replaced by a team of medics, who performed intensive analyses of my blood, urine, mucous membranes, and DNA. The verdict came quickly.

"You're in excellent health," the senior medic told me. "No inimical germs or viruses, not even a stray fungus. Though you might consider getting rid of those scars. And by the way—why didn't you mention you were pregnant?"

"I'm still shy about it," I replied. I stayed in shock all the way to Volshev's chambers.

A laser-generated will-o'-the-wisp guided me down empty passages to a court I'd never seen before. Though it was Fourth Watch in the rest of Gheo the setting here was full night. Walls and ceiling had been transformed into a facsimile of pitch-black sky, dusted with stars and dominated by the Milky Way's luminous river. The floor was covered with grayish sand; half-buried in miniature rills and dunes stood a dozen or more boulders—upright bluestones, to be precise—lichen-covered and weathered in a way that suggested Ethrin origin. It was a wild, haunting place, an exquisitely realized piece of stagecraft; my backbone chilled.

"Are those goosebumps, Risha?" Volshev's baritone hailed from somewhere in back of me. I turned and saw his Sending perched on a skewed stone; his robe glowed whitely, his hair streamed in an imaginary wind.

"I was just admiring your antiquarianism," I said lightly. "These rocks must have been shaped in the Neolithic."

"A team of archeologists rescued them from Ethri's largest landmass, right after the Reconquest. They're among my prize possessions."

"Then I'm honored to be given the chance to admire them." I bowed very low.

"Honored, yes. You've done very well, Risha Skhorb, and you deserve high honor indeed. Even my friend Sorich of Khryasha agrees."

"Oh? Has she perhaps been in touch with you?" I strove for nonchalance but fell well short of the mark.

"Just after your thruster docked she radioed to register an officially sanctioned conception. Why don't you sit down?"

I did. "I suppose I deserve repose," I said, "in my condition."

"Exactly. Did you consent to this bizarre setup?"

"No. I'm afraid I've been more victim than agent all along."

He made tut-tutting noises. "First things first. You've fulfilled your obligation to me, and your reward will be personal wealth and brilliant status. But since you've become involved in a far-reaching scheme to upset the balance of the Matterfield—whether wittingly or not—there are severe constraints on the requital I can offer you. For example, are you aware whose sperm fertilized your ovum?"

"I've been waiting for you to tell me."

"Waiting, or dreading?" The Sending chuckled dryly. "It was Seren's; his house preserved quantities of seed against just such an occasion."

It didn't surprise me. "But what they did can't be legal," I objected. "Can't I get rid of it?"

"Risha! I'm shocked. In the First Book of the Canon, chapter three, verse twelve, it is written, *All human beings have a right to life, which none may deny.* That precept is fundamental to our society."

"But this embryo is only eight spells old. And you're the Despot! It would be too horrible to make me go through with this."

"Not at all. Your pregnancy is a neat solution to several dilemmas. Khryasha is an open wound. Lady Sorich has been quietly threatening mutiny on account of my alleged disregard for her honor—"

"Those aren't such quiet threats, my lord," I said. "There's a lot I have to tell you."

Silvery eyebrows lifted. "You must do so, at length. In the meantime this is a perfect sop to her arrogance. You'll bear that child with distinction, for I have just rescinded Seren's exile and declared him an Heroic Ancestor."

I fell to my knees. "No, Volshev, please, no. Anything but that."

The Sending blithely ignored me. "I'll say he died a hero's death while fulfilling some crucial mission for me—and you won't contradict the lie. Because you, my dear Risha, my little scion of Skhorb, you are about to succeed Lady Solize as Virgin Mother of Gheo."

I cried out as if I'd been scalded with hot oil. Like an idiot I tried to grasp the hem of Volshev's robe, in a pathetic gesture of entreaty. My fingers clutched thin air; my supplication was still less effective. Volshev had doomed me to glory.

"Stand, Risha," intoned his Sending. "Rise to the greatest honor a woman can attain. Your name will be remembered ten thousand years. Your life will be an exercise in perfection. Your womb will be as fruitful as the primal particle. This is my will."

If lightning had crashed down then I might have burst into hysterics, but even Volshev had more taste than that. I stood slowly, clumsily, facing the mock stars, glimpsing scenes from a future as gaudy and false.

My first discovery was that I hated pregnancy. Starting with the early watches of my thirteenth spell I became ill, and the illness returned at every spell's outset for the next starcycle. Besides nausea, I experienced sensations of bloat and heaviness; also my breasts ached, food disgusted me, and I was exhausted all the time. Tradition prevented me from taking any symptomatic medication. To bear the perfect child I must follow nature's path, even after artificial insemination, even while sealed in a spinning Hypaethron.

My second discovery, almost coincident with the first, was that I had no friends left in Gheo. Lachis had long since removed to Gloy, in anticipation of her own parturition; her condition prevented her even from attending my investiture. Lord Tref of Paun had received a posting to Marithi, whose miserable frostbitten deserts made Ethri seem a paradise by contrast. He would be tied to this assignment for the next five revolutions.

And Mudriye, my old paramour, whose wit had given me more solace than any other man's passion, had committed *samuvize* shortly after I left for Veii. "It was an exquisite death," Volshev assured me. "He invited twelve select companions and dined with them on mouthwatering delicacies, while singers changed Interglacial poetry and pipers struck up a dirge. For dessert Mudriye drank poisoned wine. He passed away rhapsodizing on the bliss of approaching union with the divine."

"How like him," I muttered, and thought, *four.* It seemed that the most perilous thing a man could do was share my bed.

My third discovery was that Volshev watched me every second of every spell. Though I had the freedom of Gheo, it was a meaningless kind of freedom, for my new rank severely restricted my social contacts as well as my actions. The Virgin Mother can't simply take a stroll through Victory Court, or sip warm brandy in Grishanka Park. I limited myself to the Palace and the mansions of the highest Radiants, and every word I spoke conformed to Volshev's code of censorship.

Somehow I retained a sense of optimism. I'd weathered many tempests since that long-gone Masquerade, and I had an implicit confidence that I'd ride out this one too. My central problem was my failure to act. Once I recognized that, I was on my way to clear skies. I simply had to find the right course.

Unfortunately Volshev monitored even the turnings of my mind. Every spell he examined me, repeating the same questions in a thousand different phrasings, asking me about my association with Mudriye, with Chwefro the Firin, with Lady Sorich, with Seren himself. I held nothing back. I saw no reason to evade him, especially since Chwefro had encouraged me to speak out. But Volshev was manifestly dissatisfied. He stopped short of chemical interrogation only because I was carrying a future Child Emperor. Once I gave birth there was no telling what he might do.

I watched my belly grow, therefore, with a certain foreboding. When the first stirrings of life came my preoccupation only deepened. There's a child inside me, I mused, kicking me, punching me, jostling my kidneys and spleen. He's half Seren and he's half me—at best an uneasy union, made possible only through treachery and murder. Will his life be as unquiet as his origin? I imagined him newborn, I imagined him growing into boyhood, I envisioned him more beautiful than any Child Emperor had ever been, more carefully schooled, more elegant, more adorable. But I never pictured myself along with him. What could that mean? Had my unconscious visions achieved clairvoyance?

In spite of such misgivings the latter stages of my pregnancy went well. The sickness abated; I adjusted to obesity and sloth. On the fifth spell of the cycle of the Scales, as morning mists were doubtless lifting over Veii's turquoise gardens, my contractions began. A team of midwives crowded round that vast bed in the Chamber of Auspicious Origins. Holocameras on remote control taped my exertions for the delectation of the entire Matterfield. I breathed; I pushed; I screamed. A red, wizened infant emerged from the birth canal; a gentlewoman held him aloft, and I smiled, faintly, just as a long syringe entered my throat.

The cameras clicked off. My consciousness passed on into realms of bliss.

And now I hang suspended in Violshev's web. That initial euphoria has given way to a whole range of mental states, from terror through contempt to boredom. The Despot has questioned me to his putrid heart's content, applying every resource of Revenant pharmacology, and I have answered him again and again, narrating uncounted versions of my pursuit and conquest of Khryasha's heir. But it seems I've done my last retelling. My audience is finally content.

His voice resounds in this dim chamber near the midpoint of Gheo's axis. "Chewfro has doomed you, my poor Risha. You've learned secrets even a Virgin Mother has no business knowing." I see his pale face hovering before me, ageless and infinitely kind. "I won't take your life, but I must confiscate those damnable memories. I won't have my majesty reduced to the posturings of a fool."

I would protest, but I've done that too often already. Nothing I can say will change his mind. "At least keep this record," I ask. "Don't let my visions be lost."

"All knowledge has its uses," he replies. "Everything will be preserved."

The last drug begins its journey down the canals of my cerebrum. I glimpse Seren in his moment of triumph, waving to Imari's mob from the high-wheeled chariot. I see Olaro's face lighting up in a smile, dark eyes shining into mine as we dance at the Carnival of White Shadows. I see Ilesha and her snake, coiled together in a long embrace, basking in the peristyle's green shade. I hear the gods' voices welling up inside me, calling my name from the deep caverns of my unconscious, exhorting me not to let go of the power I once channeled. But it all slips away, it all trickles out, it all runs off, like water through a sieve.

FILENAME: White Shadows 13
CLASSIFICATION: A.   Miscellaneous historical document, recent period
                            B.   Autobiographical narrative
                            C.   Voluntary confession, subject Risha [4763] Skhorb [9918]
SOURCE: Shiplog *Burden of Truth* [6363]
AGENT: Ionawr [9999] Phi Iota Rho [2341]

CHAPTER THIRTEEN

I first met the Radiant Seren of Khryasha during Archer Cycle's festivities, in R.Y. 2088. I can still remember the effect he had on me from the very start, a kindling, quickening sensation that brought his likeness before my mind's eye at every unguarded moment. Unfortunately I can remember nothing whatsoever of our meeting's aftermath. There is a yawning chasm in my memory from that date until the middle of R.Y. 2092, the revolution in which Seren's only child—my firstborn son—was proclaimed Heir Apparent. I *can* retrieve misplaced shards and splinters from oblivion's abyss; I *can* piece of together odd fragments of broken visions and interrupted speeches; I can even draw logical inferences from such wreckage as remains, and reconstruct a rough outline of my history in that long-gone period; but I cannot truly relive the past, I cannot follow the thread of my life's unwinding in one continuous strand, from my childhood until the present moment.

If I try hard, I can still see the high-gabled house where I lived at twelve. I can still feel the silken texture of my third son's skin, the son I bore when I was thirty-four. But I can't summon up the least flavor or fragrance of those lost revolutions, and my frustration has been bitter indeed, holding all the pain of violation.

The official story is that I quietly went mad. Unrequited passion, they say, ate away at my reason, slowly, insidiously, from my first glimpse of Seren until the nadir of my misfortune. Somehow I managed to disguise my ailment from the world, wearing a cheerful mask of courtesy and affability. In fact I did such a good job of it that I was elevated to the office of Virgin Mother. Only then did Volshev discover my imbalance, and his therapy, while alleviating my obsession, resulted in partial amnesia.

I spent long revolutions in seclusion. No one in Gheo thought it odd; they expected Nans to be eccentric, and Nan Risha was no different from the rest. Like Solize before me I grew a garden and wore antique clothes. I also bore four sons, and took five lovers, and grew older and more beautiful, and learned to hate Volshev.

Like Mudriye before me I became a careful student of the Despot's secrets. How cautiously I moved, how coolly I endured his unceasing scrutiny; for the revolutions had taken all the fire from my blood. In time I became even cannier and cagier than Volshev himself.

That wasn't as difficult a feat as it once had been. My tenure as Virgin Mother saw a steady decline in Volshev's public persona, an increasingly hieratic quality in everything he said and did. His decisions became less intuitive and more ineffective; his speeches became mere variations on a set of stock phrases. Clearly the man was failing and the machine was taking over. Meanwhile, the dissension between Gloy and Khryasha continued to escalate, till the threat of actual war hung over the proud cities of the Matterfield. Gheo was turning into a museum; perhaps one spell it would become a tomb.

During that period the Firin kept their distance from all ten Hypaethra. Now I realize how the Despot himself had taken steps to exclude them, but at the time I had no idea. I only knew that for fourteen revolutions I never found myself in a private conversation with any of the Fair Kindred.

Then one spell shortly after the Red Games an embassy appeared in the Court of Victory. I took note of the news as it appeared on my farscan, but paid little attention; what interest could the Firin possibly hold for me? Awhile later, the chief envoy requested a private audience in my chambers, for no reason I could fathom. That annoyed me. I called Volshev to see which protocols governed Nan-Firin meetings, and wasn't surprised when he failed to respond. Such lapses had become more and more frequent in the past few revolutions. In the end I decided to be gracious. I sighed and resigned myself to a halfwatch of idle pleasantries.

The envoy's name was Ionawr—a tall, pale Firin with eyes like blue ice. I was arrested (and slightly repelled) by this creature's untouchable perfection. We sat in a drawing room off the Opal Court and sipped spiced liqueur, discussing music, fashion, and doublehand strategies.

"I understand you were a great traveler in your youth," Ionawr said after a while. "Planetary excursions are one of my passions; perhaps we could discuss our experiences among the dirtgrubbers."

"Certainly," I replied, on the verge of yawning. "Though I'm afraid you've been misled. My downworld experience is limited to one childhood sojourn in Ethri's tropics. I haven't breathed real air in almost twenty revolutions."

Ionawr half-smiled and nodded twice. "I was mistaken, then. A colleague of mine claims to have known you in Veii."

My throat tightened; I had no idea why. "Who was this colleague?" I asked, in a voice I hardly recognized.

"We Firin have no personal names," the envoy said. "We are known simply by our station, that is, by the particular rank and position we occupy, at any given moment, in the overall hierarchy. But the individual who mentioned you was then in the station of Chwefro."

"Chwefro?" I whispered. "No, I've never met anyone of that title."

Ionawr smiled broadly and nodded three times. "Nan Risha. Do you realize that Volshev's operating systems are at this moment in a state of partial failure?"

My heartbeat skipped and danced. "How do you know any of that?"

"Firin designed most of his hardware, and a great deal of his software. We're privy to his most intimate secrets. That's why he never allows us access to White Wing, and limits our contact with ordinary citizens."

"What about me, then? Why should he let you speak with me?"

"He wouldn't; but at the moment he's in no position to object."

I was feeling less and less comfortable. "It's dangerous even to discuss these things," I said softly. "Our conversation is being recorded, and the old man will undoubtedly replay it when his systems recover. He'll find ways to punish us both."

The Firin seemed amused. "Why so timid, Risha? You don't sound like the same woman Chwefro described. That Risha was bold and daring."

"But I'm *not* the woman this Chwefro knew!" Exasperation broke through my restraint. "You're talking sheer nonsense."

Instead of replying Ionawr began humming a peculiar melody. Its phrases rose and fell monotonously, varying within a narrow tonal range. After a minute or two I realized that it was an actual song, with discernible words: liquid rolling syllables in a language I'd never heard before.

"What song is that?" I demanded.

"Hush. Just listen."

I did. The words penetrated deeply into my consciousness, well past the level of analysis, beyond my stubborn skepticism and doubt. I had the sensation that I was waking from a profound sleep, grasping at shreds of a dream that glided away from me like papers blowing in the wind. I reached, I stretched, I strained to catch those scraps and tatters, to hold them in my hands, to reassemble them. I reached and it was as if a wire behind my eyes were pulling tighter and tighter, whining with tension. I reached further. My fingertips brushed what I sought. The wire screamed and snapped.

Into my mind came the memory of a face, bony and boyish, dripping with pungent sweat. It melted into a vision of lithe black dancers in red silk gowns, into the sound of massed drums throbbing in midday swelter, into a pillar of fire that paled the stars. My reason cringed; such people and places had no business in my brain. I looked pleadingly at Ionawr but found nothing to comfort me there.

Then one more picture insinuated itself into my sensorium: a mathematical formula, a sequence of symbols glowing amber on a farscan screen. For a moment it was completely without meaning; then in a surge of intuition I saw what it was. I was looking at the series of commands that would deactivate Volshev's support system. I was looking at the old tyrant's death warrant.

Ionawr smiled and nodded, three times, four times. "Yes, Risha, yes. You see it, don't you."

"How—how did you put it there?"

"Long ago, far away, in a place you've forgotten, an island at the edge of a pale quiet sea. We buried it deep, so deeply even Volshev's drugs never found it."

"But what—what can I do with this knowledge?"

"Whatever you want, Risha."

"Why me? Can't you do it for yourself?"

"Even in his present distress Volshev has crucial fail-safe devices working. No Firin could ever get near that chamber at Gheo's axis. But you can. You've been there. The door will recognize your pattern and let you pass. You know the way, don't you?"

Of course I did. I'd spent long revolutions seeking the one pathway that led to the heart of the maze. But I had no idea that I'd ever followed it.

"Apparently you know me better than I know myself, Ionawr. When did I enter Volshev's lair?"

"On the same spell that you lost your memories of Seren and Veii."

Eyes, throat, heart, mind: everything froze and shivered at once. I stood suddenly and smoothed out my robes, calling for a carriage to meet me in the Tourmaline Cloister. Ionawr gazed after me as I swept through the door.

The tubes carried me as high as White Landing. I stepped off in an antiseptic foyer and felt around on the wall for the manual override switch. My hands brushed moist, spongy fabric; I thought of flayed muscles, exposed entrails. A circular valve dilated, and before me stretched a dim passage dripping with germicidal foam. To the best of my recollection I'd never been there—but I remembered the way as well as I knew my own children's pedigrees.

The tunnel was ruddy and warm. I moved feverishly now, all too aware that Volshev might recover at any moment and blast me to cinders. I was so close to the axis that I weighed no more than a kilo or two; I could leap and bound like a demon. After two hundred meters I reached a second control point and entered the requisite string of codes. A cloud of antiviral mist was my reward; it occurred to me that those nozzles could just as easily have sprayed acid or poison, had I made the least mistake. I passed into another, shorter corridor, blazing in ultraviolet light. I shielded my eyes and hurried onward.

The third control was an airlock, which I attained after three or four minutes. I entered more passwords and went inside, donning the pressurized breathing helmet that hung waiting for me. Sterile water poured in. Within moments I was completely submerged. Then as the water drained away it was replaced by fresh, untainted air. Blowers dried me and the farther panel slid aside. I was absolutely pure now. Pushing off from the wall, I floated into Volshev's inner sanctum.

It took my eyes several seconds to adjust to the gloom. This chamber was still dimmer than the first passageway, with little more than a firefly's glow to dispel the overpowering darkness. It was a huge sphere crammed with tubes, cables, jointed arms, banks of sensors, tanks of chemicals, vats of tissue, strung together on a gossamer web of finespun keratin. At its center hovered a pinkish lump of flesh, the focal point of all these heroic props. I could make out vestigial limbs—the merest nubs of cartilage—attached to a squat, flabby torso, so thin-skinned that every vein and artery was visible as it throbbed. There was no sign of a skeleton; even the head, a misshapen bulb trailing feebly off the body, seemed free of confining skullbones. Through the parchment-like tissue of the scalp I saw the brain. It had a diseased look; perhaps this was pure fancy on my part, but it resembled a massive bruise, a dull patch of mutilation. From their resting place beneath it two gray eyes regarded me.

I stared back, balancing horror with contempt. This pathetic leftover had once been a man. Three hundred revolutions earlier Volshev had walked and breathed and hoped and wondered just as I did, but he had since chosen to trade his humanity for immortality. Or so he thought. For who could look on this quivering blob and call it alive? How long since this moribund creature had truly controlled the persona we knew as Volshev? What remained of consciousness and volition within that wasted sack of fluids? His programs and projections had taken over long ago; I was in the presence of a breathing corpse.

The chamber was blood-warm. Its still air was a tangible presence, threatening to stifle me. But all my reflection had occurred in the space of a second or two, and I hesitated no longer. Before sweat could bead my skin I moved to the emergency panel and coded the final terms of Ionawr's formula.

Since my entrance I'd been aware of a deep, slow pulse, a bass note repeating at mechanically precise intervals. As I completed the sequence it stopped. I saw no other evidence of transition, no flashing signals, no wailing alarms. The gray eyes watched me as before, but I knew with unshakable certainty that they were dead. Volshev's reign had ended.

I turned to leave, unsure now which direction to take or what to do. It seemed I had a future to face.

For want of a better idea I sailed back down the passageway. Nothing impeded me; all doors stood open, all sterilization measures suspended. I came to White Landing and found Ionawr waiting for me with a long narrow box.

"Well done," said the envoy. "I haven't the words or the time to explain how great a deed you've accomplished, for many things still need doing. I believe there's a terminal hidden somewhere in this room, an interface with Gheo's data-net. Can you help me find it?"

I did so, and Ionawr inserted a cable into the outlet, connecting it with the long box. The Firin grinned. "I don't want the city's orbit to decay, or see its life-support systems run down. They were all part of Volshev's web, you know."

"But what will happen to the social fabric now that he's gone? Do you have backup programs for that, too?" I spoke sarcastically, but Ionawr's reply was matter-of-fact.

"Certainly. We've been planning this for decades. We've written our own version of the Volshev program. No one will ever notice the change."

I wasn't so sure of that. "What are your plans for me, then?"

"Why, Risha, you can continue as Nan of Gheo, or return to Skhorb, or Ethri, or any other place you care to go. Or I can suggest another destination, one that's bound to delight you."

"Please do."

"It's a planet, a poor dry place where people starve and armies devastate whole continents. A place where superstition thrives and half the year is spent in darkness. It will please you enormously, I guarantee."

"It sounds like Veii. I think you're talking nonsense again."

Ionawr bent down and reached into a compartment in the long narrow box. Straightening, the envoy handed me a single spool. "Replay this at your leisure, Lady Risha. It's a brief text I just retrieved from Volshev's archives. It will explain a great deal."

I took the spool; as soon as I was in my own chambers again I popped it into a viewer. Ionawr stayed long enough to watch me thread it and then retired to the next room. "By the way," the Firin said in parting. "I misled you earlier. I myself was once called Chwefro."

Within a watch I knew what a difficult confession that had to be.

Now I float lazily in a transparent nacelle, a personal observation blister in the sleek outer skin of the *Burden of Truth*. Veii hangs before me like a rosy pearl. This approach is actually a return, but for my damaged memory it holds all the excitement of the first time. How strange it is to know my past at second hand, through the words of a self I've lost. It's strange, and sad, and marvelous. For I go to relearn the places I loved most, and meet my best friends over again—and what pleasure can compare with that? Chwefro—I insist on using the more familiar name —has told me that Ilesha is still alive and healthy, enjoying her old age on an estate near Trokomari. And Soko and her husband Falabon sit high in the councils of the Syndicate, having fled to Woro during the civil wars.

Much else has changed, I'm sure, from the time when I danced the dream-dance before Veii's wondering throngs; but I won't feel the loss. Seren, Anago, Olaro: These names have shed their envelope of pain. Oblivion does have a few advantages.

Gheo I utterly renounce. I've played that game and held all its prizes. I'm for a new contest now, a Firin game; and though they used me cynically the first time, I've learned a few things about winning since then.

I'm neither young nor old, neither innocent nor bitter. My trials have only made me stronger. Veii will be my stage, though I act for no one but myself. Let the drums begin.